THE COLLECTED WORKS OF WILLIAM FAULKNER

*

THE MANSION

The Mansion concludes the *Snopes* trilogy of which
the first two volumes are *The Hamlet* and *The Town.*

By the Same Author

*

SOLDIERS' PAY

MOSQUITOES

SARTORIS

THE SOUND AND THE FURY

AS I LAY DYING

SANCTUARY

LIGHT IN AUGUST

PYLON

ABSALOM, ABSALOM!

THE UNVANQUISHED

THE WILD PALMS

THE HAMLET

GO DOWN, MOSES

INTRUDER IN THE DUST

KNIGHT'S GAMBIT

REQUIEM FOR A NUN

A FABLE

THE TOWN

THE MANSION

THE REIVERS

Short Stories

THESE THIRTEEN

UNCLE WILLY AND OTHER STORIES

DOCTOR MARTINO AND OTHER STORIES

COLLECTED STORIES

FAULKNER'S COUNTY

ESSAYS, SPEECHES AND PUBLIC LETTERS

NEW ORLEANS SKETCHES

Poetry

THE MARBLE FAUN

A GREEN BOUGH

For Children

THE WISHING TREE

THE MANSION

William Faulkner

1969

CHATTO & WINDUS

LONDON

PUBLISHED BY

Chatto and Windus Ltd
42 William IV Street
London W.C.2

0701106778
~~X000080764~~

First published in Great Britain 1961
This edition first published 1965
Reprinted 1969

SK Ke/NL

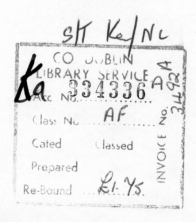

CO DUBLIN
LIBRARY SERVICE
Ka 334336 A
Acc No.
Class No.   AF
Cated   Classed
Prepared
Re-Bound   £1. 7s.
INVOICE No. 3492A

© COPYRIGHT, 1955, 1959, BY WILLIAM FAULKNER

LEABHARLANNA ATHA CLIATH
BALLYROAN LIBRARY
ACC. NO.   0701 106778
COPY NO.   TF 2004
INV. NO.   BACKSTOCK
PRICE IRL
CLASS   F

TO PHIL STONE

TO PHIL STONE

VOLUME THREE

SNOPES

CONTENTS

THE MANSION

THIS BOOK is the final chapter of, and the summation of, a work conceived and begun in 1925. Since the author likes to believe, hopes that his entire life's work is a part of a living literature, and since "living" is motion, and "motion" is change and alteration and therefore the only alternative to motion is un-motion, stasis, death, there will be found discrepancies and contradictions in the thirty-four-year progress of this particular chronicle; the purpose of this note is simply to notify the reader that the author has already found more discrepancies and contradictions than he hopes the reader will—contradictions and discrepancies due to the fact that the author has learned, he believes, more about the human heart and its dilemma than he knew thirty-four years ago; and is sure that, having lived with them that long time, he knows the characters in this chronicle better than he did then.

W. F.

MINK

Leabharlanna Atha Club

ONE

THE jury said "Guilty" and the Judge said "Life", but he didn't hear them. He wasn't listening. In fact, he hadn't been able to listen since that first day when the Judge banged his little wooden hammer on the high desk until he, Mink, dragged his gaze back from the far door of the courtroom to see what in the world the man wanted, and he, the Judge, leaned down across the desk hollering: "You, Snopes! Did you or didn't you kill Jack Houston?" and he, Mink, said, "Don't bother me now. Can't you see I'm busy?" then turned his own head to look again toward the distant door at the back of the room, himself hollering into, against, across the wall of little wan faces hemming him in: "Snopes! Flem Snopes! Anybody here that'll go and bring Flem Snopes! I'll pay you—Flem'll pay you!"

Because he hadn't had time to listen. In fact, that whole first trip, handcuffed to the deputy, from his jail cell to the courtroom, had been a senseless, a really outrageously foolish interference with and interruption, and each subsequent daily manacled trip and transference, of the solution to both their problems—his and the damned law's both—if they had only waited and let him alone: the watching, his dirty hands gripping among the grimed interstices of the barred window above the street, which had been his one, his imperious need during the long months between his incarceration and the opening of the Court.

At first, during the first few days behind the barred window, he had simply been impatient with his own impatience and—yes, he admitted it—his own stupidity. Long before the moment came when he had had to aim the gun and fire the shot, he knew that his cousin Flem, the only member of his clan with the power to and the reason to, or who could at least be expected to, extricate him from its consequences, would not be there to do it. He even knew why Flem would not be there for at least a year; French-man's Bend was too small: everybody in it knew everything about everybody else; they would all have seen through that Texas trip even without the hurrah and hullabaloo that Varner girl had been causing ever since she (or whoever else it was) found the first hair on her bump, not to mention just this last past spring and summer while that durn McCarron boy was snuffing and fighting everybody else off exactly like a gang of rutting dogs.

So that before Flem married her, he, Mink, and everybody else in ten miles of the Bend knew that old Will Varner was going to have to marry her off to somebody, and that quick, if he didn't want a woods colt in his back yard next grass. And when it was Flem that finally married her, he, Mink, anyway was not surprised. It was Flem, with his usual luck. All right, more than just luck then: the only man in Frenchman's Bend that ever stood up to and held his own with old Will Varner; that had done already more or less eliminated Jody, old Will's son, out of the store, and now was fixing to get hold of half of all the rest of it by being old Will's son-in-law. That just by marrying her in time to save her from dropping a bastard, Flem would not only be the rightful husband of that damn girl that had kept every man under eighty years old in Frenchman's Bend in an uproar ever since she was fifteen years old by just watching her walk past, but he had got paid for it to boot: not only the right to fumble his hand every time the notion struck him under that dress that rutted a man just thinking even about somebody else's hand doing it, but was getting a free deed to that whole Old Frenchman place for doing it.

So he knew Flem would not be there when he would need him, since he knew that Flem and his new wife would have to stay away from Frenchman's Bend at least long enough for what they would bring back with them to be able to call itself only one month old without everybody that looked at it dying of laughing. Only, when the moment finally came, when the instant finally happened when he could no longer defer having to aim the gun and pull the trigger, he had forgot that. No, that was a lie. He hadn't forgot it. He simply could wait no longer: Houston himself would not let him wait longer—and that too was one more injury which Jack Houston, in the very act of dying, had done him: compelled him, Mink, to kill him at a time when the only person who had the power to save him and would have had to save him whether he wanted to or not because of the ancient immutable laws of simple blood kinship, was a thousand miles away; and this time it was an irreparable injury because in the very act of committing it, Houston had escaped forever all retribution for it.

He had not forgotten that his cousin would not be there. He simply couldn't wait any longer. He had simply had to trust *them*—the *Them* of whom it was promised that not even a sparrow should fall unmarked. By *them* he didn't mean that whatever-it-was that folks referred to as Old Moster. He didn't believe in any Old Moster. He had seen too much in his time that, if any Old Moster existed, with eyes as sharp and power as strong as was claimed He had, He would have done something about. Besides, he, Mink, wasn't religious. He hadn't been to a church since he was fifteen years old and never aimed to go again—places which a man with a hole in his gut and a rut in his britches that he couldn't satisfy at home, used, by calling himself a preacher of God, to get conveniently together the biggest possible number of women that he could tempt with the reward of the one in return for the job of the other—the job of filling his hole in payment for getting theirs plugged the first time the husband went to the field and she could slip off to the bushes where the preacher was waiting; the wives coming because here was the best market they knowed of to swap a mess of fried chicken or a sweet-potato pie; the husbands coming not to interrupt the trading because the husband knowed he couldn't interrupt it or even keep up with it, but at least to try and find out if his wife's name would come to the head of the waiting list today or if maybe he could still finish scratching that last forty before he would have to tie her to the bedpost and hide behind the door watching; and the young folks not even bothering to enter the church a-tall for already running to be the first couple behind the nearest handy thicket bush.

He meant, simply, that *them*—*they*—*it*, whichever and whatever you wanted to call it, who represented a simple fundamental justice and equity in human affairs, or else a man might just as well quit; the *they*, *them*, *it*, call them what you like, which simply would not, could not harass and harry a man forever without some day, at some moment, letting him get his own just and equal licks back in return. They could harass and worry him, or they could even just sit back and watch everything go against him right along without missing a lick, almost like there was a pattern to it; just sit back and watch and (all right, why not? he—a man—didn't mind, as long as he was a man and there was a justice to it) enjoy it too; maybe in fact They were even testing him, to see if he was a man or not, man enough to take a little harassment and worry and so deserve his own licks back when his turn came. But at least that moment would come when it was his turn, when he had earned the right to have his own just and equal licks back, just as They had earned the right to test him and even to enjoy the testing; the moment when they would have to prove to him that They were as much a man as he had proved to Them that he was; when he not only would have to depend on Them but had won the right to depend on Them and find Them faithful; and They dared not, They would not dare, to let him down, else it would be as hard for Them to live with themselves afterward as it had finally become for him to live with himself and still keep on taking what he had taken from Jack Houston.

So he knew that morning that Flem was not going to be there. It was simply that he could wait no longer; the moment had simply come when he and Jack Houston could, must, no longer breathe the same air. And so, lacking his cousin's presence, he must fall back on that right to depend on *them* which he had earned by never before in his life demanding anything of them.

It began in the spring. No, it began in the fall before. No, it began a long time before that even. It began at the very instant Houston was born already shaped for arrogance and intolerance and pride. Not at the moment when the two of them, he, Mink Snopes also, began to breathe the same north Mississippi air, because he, Mink, was not a contentious man. He had never been. It was simply that his own bad luck had all his life continually harassed and harried him into the constant and unflagging necessity of defending his own simple rights.

Though it was not until the summer before that first fall that Houston's destiny had actually and finally impinged on his, Mink's, own fate—which was another facet of the outrage: that nothing, not even *they*, least of all *they*, had vouchsafed him any warning of what that first encounter would end in. This was after Houston's young wife had gone into the stallion's stall hunting a hen nest and the horse had killed her and any decent man would have thought that any decent husband would never have had another stallion on the place as long as he lived. But not Houston. Houston was not only rich enough to own a blooded stallion capable of killing his wife, but arrogant and intolerant enough to defy all decency, after shooting the horse that killed her, to turn right around and buy another stallion exactly like it, maybe in case he did get married again; to act so grieving over his wife that even the neighbours didn't dare knock on his front door any more, yet two or three times a week ripping up and down the road on that next murderer of a horse, with that big Bluetick hound running like a greyhound or another horse along beside it, right up to Varner's store and not even getting down: the three of them just waiting there in the road—the arrogant intolerant man and the bad-eyed horse and the dog that bared its teeth and raised its hackles any time anybody went near it—while Houston ordered whoever was on the front gallery to step inside and fetch him out whatever it was he had come for like they were Negroes.

Until one morning when he, Mink, was walking to the store (he had no horse to ride when he had to go for a tin of snuff or a bottle of quinine or a piece of meat); he had just come over the brow of a short hill when he heard the horse behind him, coming fast and hard, and he would have given Houston the whole road if he had had time, the horse already on top of him until Houston wrenched it savagely off and past, the damn hound leaping so close it almost brushed his chest, snarling right into his face, Houston whirling the horse and holding it dancing and plunging, shouting down at him: "Why in hell didn't you jump when you heard me coming? Get off the road! Do you still want him to beat your brains out too before I can get him down again?"

Well, maybe that was what they call grieving for the wife that maybe you didn't actually kill her yourself and you even killed the horse that did it. But still arrogant enough or rich enough to afford to buy another one exactly like the one that did kill her. Which was all right with him, Mink, especially since all anybody had to do was just wait until sooner or later the son-of-a-bitching horse would kill Houston too; until the next thing happened which he had not counted on, planned on, not even anticipated.

It was his milk cow, the only one he owned, not being a rich man like Houston but only an independent one, asking no favours of any man, paying his own way. She—the cow—had missed some way, failed to freshen; and there he was, not only having gone a winter without milk and now faced with another whole year without it, he had also missed out on the calf for which he had had to pay a fifty-cents-cash bull fee, since the only bull in reach he could get for less than a dollar was the scrub bull belonging to a Negro who insisted on cash at the gate.

So he fed the cow all that winter, waiting for the calf which wasn't even there. Then he had to lead the cow the three miles back to the Negro's house, not to claim the return of the fifty cents but only to claim a second stand from the bull, which the Negro refused to permit without the payment in advance of another fifty cents, he, Mink, standing in the yard cursing the Negro until the Negro went back into the house and shut the door, Mink standing in the empty yard cursing the Negro and his family inside the blank house until he had exhausted himself enough to lead the still-barren cow the three miles again back home.

Then he had to keep the barren and worthless cow up under fence while she exhausted his own meagre pasture, then he had to feed her out of his meagre crib during the rest of that summer and fall, since the local agreement was that all stock would be kept up until all crops were out of the field. Which meant November before he could turn her out for the winter. And even then he had to divert a little feed to her from his winter's meat hogs, to keep her in the habit of coming more or less back home at night; until she had been missing three or four days and he finally located her in Houston's pasture with his beef herd.

In fact, he was already in the lane leading to Houston's house, the coiled ploughline in his hand, when without even knowing he was going to and without even pausing or breaking stride he had turned about, already walking back toward home, rapidly stuffing the coiled rope inside his shirt where it would be concealed, not to return to the paintless repairless tenant cabin in which he lived, but simply to find privacy in which to think, stopping presently to sit on a log beside the road while he realised the full scope of what had just dawned before him.

By not claiming the worthless cow yet, he would not only

winter her, he would winter her twice—ten times—as well as he himself could afford to. He would not only let Houston winter her (Houston, a man not only rich enough to be able to breed and raise beef cattle, but rich enough to keep a Negro to do nothing else save feed and tend them—a Negro to whom Houston furnished a better house to live in than the one that he, Mink, a white man with a wife and two daughters, lived in) but when he would reclaim the cow in the spring she would have come in season again and, running with Houston's beef herd-bull, would now be carrying a calf which would not only freshen her for milk but would itself be worth money as grade beef where the offspring of the Negro's scrub bull would have been worth almost nothing.

Naturally he would have to be prepared for the resulting inevitable questions; Frenchman's Bend was too little, too damn little for a man to have any privacy about what he did, let alone about what he owned or lacked. It didn't even take four days. It was at Varner's store, where he would walk down to the cross-roads and back every day, giving them a chance to go ahead and get it over with. Until finally one said—he didn't remember who; it didn't matter: "Ain't you located your cow yet?"

"What cow?" he said. The other said,

"Jack Houston says for you to come and get that bone rack of yours out of his feed lot; he's tired of boarding it."

"Oh, that," he said. "That ain't my cow any more. I sold that cow last summer to one of the Gowrie boys up at Caledonia Chapel."

"I'm glad to hear that," the other said. "Because if I was you and my cow was in Jack Houston's feed lot, I would take my rope and go and get it, without even noticing myself doing it, let alone letting Jack Houston notice me. I don't believe I would interrupt him right now even to say Much obliged." Because all Frenchman's Bend knew Houston: sulking and sulling in his house all alone by himself since the stallion killed his wife four years ago. Like nobody before him had ever lost a wife, even when, for whatever incomprehensible reason the husband could have had, he didn't want to get shut of her. Sulking and sulling alone on that big place with two nigger servants, the man and the woman to cook, and the stallion and

the big Bluetick hound that was a high-nosed and intolerant and
surly as Houston himself—a durn surly sullen son of a bitch that
didn't even know he was lucky: rich, not only rich enough to
afford a wife to whine and nag and steal his pockets ragged of
every dollar he made, but rich enough to do without a wife if he
wanted: rich enough to be able to hire a woman to cook his
victuals instead of having to marry her. Rich enough to hire
another nigger to get up in his stead on the cold mornings and
go out in the wet and damp to feed not only the beef cattle which
he sold at the top fat prices because he could afford to hold them
till then, but that blooded stallion too, and even that damn
hound running beside the horse he thundered up and down the
road on, until a fellow that never had anything but his own two
legs to travel on, would have to jump clean off the road into the
bushes or the son-of-a-bitching horse would have killed him too
with its shod feet and left him laying there in the ditch for the
son-of-a-bitching hound to eat before Houston would even have
reported it.

All right, if Houston was in too high and mighty a mood to be
said much obliged to, he, Mink, for one wasn't going to break in
on him uninvited. Not that he didn't owe a much obliged to
something somewhere. This was a week later, then a month later,
then Christmas had passed and the hard wet dreary winter had
set in. Each afternoon, in the slicker held together with baling
wire and automobile tyre patching which was the only winter
outer garment he owned over his worn patched cotton overalls,
he would walk up the muddy road in the dreary and fading
afternoons to watch Houston's pedigreed beef herd, his own sorry
animal among them, move, not even hurrying, toward and into
the barn which was warmer and tighter against the weather than
the cabin he lived in, to be fed by the hired Negro who wore
warmer clothing than any he and his family possessed, cursing
into the steamy vapour of his own breathing, cursing the Negro
for his black skin inside the warmer garments than his, a white
man's, cursing the rich feed devoted to cattle instead of humans
even though his own animal shared it; cursing above all the
unaware white man through or because of whose wealth such a
condition could obtain, cursing the fact that his very revenge
and vengeance—what he himself believed to be simple justice

and inalienable rights—could not be done at one stroke but instead must depend on the slow incrementation of feed converted to weight, plus the uncontrollable, even unpredictable, love mood of the cow and the long subsequent nine months of gestation; cursing his own condition that the only justice available to him must be this prolonged and passive one.

That was it. Prolongation. Not only the anguish of hope deferred, not even the outrage of simple justice deferred, but the knowledge that, even when the blow fell on Houston, it would cost him, Mink, eight dollars in cash—the eight dollars which he would have to affirm that the imaginary purchaser of the cow had paid him for the animal in order to make good the lie that he had sold it, which, when he reclaimed the cow in the spring, he would have to give to Houston as an earnest that until that moment he really believed he had sold the animal—or at least had established eight dollars as its value—when he went to Houston and told him how the purchaser had come to him, Mink, only that morning and told him the cow had escaped from the lot the same night he had bought it and brought it home, and so reclaimed the eight dollars he had paid for it, thus establishing the cow not only in Houston's arrogant comtempt but in the interested curiosity of the rest of Frenchman's Bend too, as having now cost him, Mink, sixteen dollars to reclaim his own property.

That was the outrage: the eight dollars. The fact that he could not even have wintered the cow for eight dollars, let alone put on it the weight of flesh he could see with his own eyes it now carried, didn't count. What mattered was, he would have to give Houston, who didn't need it and wouldn't even miss the feed the cow had eaten, the eight dollars with which he, Mink, could have bought a gallon of whiskey for Christmas, plus a dollar or two of the gewgaw finery his wife and his two daughters were forever whining at him for.

But there was no help for it. And even then, his pride was that he was not reconciled. Not he to be that meagre and niggling and puny as meekly to accept something just because he didn't see yet how he could help it. More, since this too merely bolstered the anger and rage at the injustice: that he would have to go fawning and even cringing a little when he went to recover his cow; would have to waste a lie for the privilege of giving eight dollars which he wanted, must sacrifice to spare, to a man who didn't even need them, would not even miss their lack, did not even know yet that he was going to receive them. The moment, the day at last at the end of winter when by local custom the livestock which had run loose in the skeletoned cornfields since fall, must be taken up by their owners and put inside fences so the land could be ploughed and planted again; one afternoon, evening rather, waiting until his cow had received that final feeding with the rest of Houston's herd before he approached the feed lot, the worn ploughline coiled over his arm and the meagre lump of worn dollar bills and nickels and dimes and quarters wadded into his overall pocket, not needing to fawn and cringe yet because only the Negro with his hayfork would be in the lot now, the rich man himself in the house, the warm kitchen, with in his hand a toddy not of the stinking gagging homemade corn such as he, Mink, would have had to buy with his share of the eight dollars if he could have kept them, but of good red chartered whiskey ordered out of Memphis. Not having to fawn and cringe yet: just saying, level and white-man, to the nigger paused in the door to the feeding shed to look back at him:

"Hidy. I see you got my cow there. Put this rope on her and I'll get her outen your way," the Negro looking back at him a second longer then gone, on through the shed toward the house; not coming back to take the rope, which he, Mink, had not expected anyway, but gone first to tell the white man, to know what to do. Which was exactly what he, Mink, had expected, leaning his cold-raw, cold-reddened wrists which even the frayed slicker sleeves failed to cover, on the top rail of the white-painted fence. Oh yes, Houston with the toddy of good red whiskey in his hand and likely with his boots off and his stocking feet in the oven of the stove, warming for supper, who now, cursing, would have to withdraw his feet and drag on again the cold wet muddy rubber and come back to the lot.

Which Houston did: the very bang of the kitchen door and the squish and slap of the gum boots across the back yard and into the lot sounding startled and outraged. Then he came on through the shed too, the Negro about ten feet behind him. "Hidy, Jack," Mink said. "Too bad to have to roust you out into the cold and wet again. That nigger could have tended to it. I jest learned today you wintered my cow for me. If your nigger'll put this ploughline on her, I'll get her out of your way."

"I thought you sold that cow to Nub Gowrie," Houston said.

"So did I," Mink said. "Until Nub rid up this morning on a mule and said that cow broke out of his lot the same night he got her home and he ain't seen her since, and collected back the eight dollars he paid me for her," already reaching into his pocket, the meagre wad of frayed notes and coins in his hand. "So, since eight dollars seems to be the price of this cow, I reckon I owe you that for wintering her. Which makes her a sixteen-dollar cow now, don't it, whether she knows it or not. So here. Take your money and let your nigger put this ploughline on her and I'll—"

"That cow wasn't worth eight dollars last fall," Houston said. "But she's worth a considerable more now. She's eaten more than sixteen dollars' worth of my feed. Not to mention my young bull topped her last week. It was last week, wasn't it, Henry?" he said to the Negro.

"Yes sir," the Negro said. "Last Tuesday. I put it on the book."

"If you had jest notified me sooner I'd have saved the strain on your bull and that nigger and his pitchfork too," Mink said. He said to the Negro: "Here. Take this rope—"

"Hold it," Houston said; he was reaching into his pocket too. "You yourself established the price of that cow at eight dollars. All right. I'll buy her."

"You yourself jest finished establishing the fact that she has done went up since then," Mink said. "I'm trying right now to give the rest of sixteen for her. So evidently I wouldn't take sixteen, let alone jest eight. So take your money. And if your nigger's too wore out to put this rope on her, I'll come in and do it myself." Now he even began to climb the fence.

"Hold it," Houston said again. He said to the Negro: "What would you say she's worth now?"

"She'd bring thirty,' the Negro said. "Maybe thirty-five"

"You hear that?" Houston said.

"No," Mink said, still climbing the fence. "I don't listen to niggers: I tell them. If he don't want to put this rope on my cow, tell him to get outen my way."

"Don't cross that fence, Snopes," Houston said.

"Well well," Mink said, one leg over the top rail, the coil of rope dangling from one raw-red hand, "don't tell me you bring a pistol along every time you try to buy a cow. Maybe you even tote it to put a cottonseed or a grain of corn in the ground too?" It was tableau: Mink with one leg over the top rail, Houston standing inside the fence, the pistol hanging in one hand against his leg, the Negro not moving either, not looking at anything, the whites of his eyes just showing a little. "If you had sent me word, maybe I could a brought a pistol too."

"All right," Houston said. He laid the pistol carefully on the top of the fence post beside him. "Put that rope down. Get over the fence at your post. I'll back off one post and you can count three and we'll see who uses it to trade with."

"Or maybe your nigger can do the counting," Mink said. "All he's got to do is say Three. Because I ain't got no nigger with me neither. Evidently a man needs a tame nigger and a pistol both to trade livestock with you." He swung his leg back to the ground outside the fence. "So I reckon I'll jest step over to the store and have a word with Uncle Billy and the constable. Maybe I ought to done that at first, saved a walk up here in the cold. I would a suh-jested leaving my ploughline here, to save toting it again, only likely you would be charging me thirty-five dollars to get it back, since that seems to be your bottom price for anything in your lot that don't belong to you." He was leaving now. "So long then. In case you do make any eight-dollar stock deals, be sho you don't take no wooden nickels."

He walked away steadily enough but in such a thin furious rage that for a while he couldn't even see, and with his ears ringing as if someone had fired a shotgun just over his head. In fact he had expected the rage too and now, in solitude and privacy, was the best possible time to let it exhaust itself. Because he knew now he had anticipated something like what had happened and he would need his wits about him. He had known by instinct that his own outrageous luck would invent something like this, so that even the fact that going to Varner, the justice of the peace, for a paper for the constable to serve on Houston to recover the cow would cost him another two dollars and a half, was not really a surprise to him: it was simply *them* again, still testing, trying him to see just how much he could bear and would stand.

So, in a way, he was not really surprised at what happened next either. It was his own fault in a way: he had simply under-estimated *them*: the whole matter of taking the eight dollars to Houston and putting the rope on the cow and leading it back home had seemed too simple, too puny for Them to bother with. But he was wrong; They were not done yet. Varner would not even issue the paper; whereupon two days later there were seven of them, counting the Negro—himself, Houston, Varner and the constable and two professional cattle buyers—standing along the fence of Houston's feed lot while the Negro led his cow out for the two experts to examine her.

"Well?" Varner said at last.

"I'd give thirty-five," the first trader said.

"Bred to a paper bull, I might go to thirty-seven and a half," the second said.

"Would you go to forty?" Varner said.

"No," the second said. "She might not a caught."

"That's why I wouldn't even match thirty-seven and a half," the first said.

"All right," Varner said—a tall, gaunt, narrow-hipped, heavily moustached man who looked like what his father had been: one of Forrest's cavalrymen. "Call it thirty-seven and a half then. So we'll split the difference then." He was looking at Mink now. "When you pay Houston eighteen dollars and seventy-five cents, you can have your cow. Only you haven't got eighteen dollars and seventy-five cents, have you?"

He stood there, his raw-red wrists which the slicker did not cover lying quiet on the top rail of the fence, his eyes quite blind again and his ears ringing again as though somebody had fired a shotgun just over his head, and on his face that expression faint and gentle and almost like smiling. "No," he said.

"Wouldn't his cousin Flem let him have it?" the second trader said. Nobody bothered to answer that at all, not even to remind them that Flem was still in Texas on his honeymoon, where he and his wife had been since the marriage last August.

"Then he'll have to work it out," Varner said. He was talking to Houston now. "What have you got that he can do?"

"I'm going to fence in another pasture," Houston said. "I'll pay him fifty cents a day. He can make thirty-seven days and from light till noon on the next one digging post holes and stringing wire. What about the cow? Do I keep her, or does Quick" (Quick was the constable) "take her?"

"Do you want Quick to?" Varner said.

"No," Houston said. "She's been here so long now she might get homesick. Besides, if she's here Snopes can see her every day and keep his spirits up about what he's really working for."

"All right, all right," Varner said quickly. "It's settled now. I don't want any more of that now."

That was what he had to do. And his pride still was that he would not be, would never be, reconciled to it. Not even if he were to lose the cow, the animal itself to vanish from the entire equation and leave him in what might be called peace. Which— eliminating the cow—he could have done himself. More: he could have got eighteen dollars and seventy-five cents for doing it, which, with the eight dollars Houston had refused to accept, would have made practically twenty-seven dollars, more cash at one time than he had seen in he could not remember when, since even with the fall sale of his bale or two of cotton, the subtraction of Varner's landlord's share, plus his furnish bill at Varner's store, barely left him that same eight or ten dollars in cash with which he had believed in vain that he could redeem the cow.

In fact, Houston himself made that suggestion. It was the second or third day of digging the post holes and setting the heavy locust posts in them; Houston came up on the stallion and sat looking down at him. He didn't even pause, let alone look up.

"Look," Houston said. "Look at me." He looked up then, not pausing. Houston's hand was already extended; he, Mink, could see the actual money in it. "Varner said eighteen seventy-five. All right, here it is. Take it and go on home and forget about that cow." Now he didn't even look up any longer, heaving on to his shoulder the post that anyway looked heavier and more solid than he did and dropping it into the hole, tamping the dirt home with the reversed shovel handle so that he only had to hear the stallion turn and go away. Then it was the fourth day; again he only needed to hear the stallion come up and stop, not even looking up when Houston said,

"Snopes," then again, "Snopes," then he said, "Mink," he —Mink—not even looking up, let alone pausing while he said:

"I hear you."

"Stop this now. You got to break your land for your crop. You got to make your living. Go on home and get your seed in the ground and then come back."

"I ain't got time to make a living," he said, not even pausing, "I got to get my cow back home."

The next morning it was not Houston on the stallion but Varner himself in his buckboard. Though he, Mink, did not know yet that it was Varner himself who was suddenly afraid, afraid for the peace and quiet of the community which he held in his iron usurious hand, buttressed by the mortgages and liens in the vast iron safe in his store. And now he, Mink, did look up and saw money in the closed fist resting on Varner's knee.

"I've put this on your furnish bill for this year," Varner said. "I just come from your place. You ain't broke a furrow yet. Pick up them tools and take this money and give it to Jack and take that damn cow on home and get to ploughing."

Though this was only Varner; he could pause and even lean on the post-hole digger now. "Have you heard any complaint from me about that-ere cow court judgment of yourn?" he said.

"No," Varner said.

"Then get out of my way and tend to your business while I tend to mine," he said. Then Varner was out of the buckboard —a man already old enough to be called Uncle Billy by the debtors who fawned on him, yet agile too: enough so to jump down from the buckboard in one motion, the lines in one hand and the whip in the other.

"God damn you," he said, "pick up them tools and go on home. I'll be back before dark, and if I don't find a furrow run by then, I'm going to dump every sorry stick you've got in that house out in the road and rent it to somebody else tomorrow morning."

And he, Mink, looking at him, with on his face that faint gentle expression almost like smiling. "Likely you would do jest exactly that," he said.

"You're god-damned right I will," Varner said. "Get on. Now. This minute."

"Why, sholy," he said. "Since that's the next court judgment in this case, and a law-abiding feller always listens to a court judgment." He turned.

"Here," Varner said to his back. "Take this money."

"Ain't it?" he said, going on.

By midafternoon he had broken the better part of an acre. When he swung the plough at the turn-row he saw the buckboard coming up the lane. It carried two this time, Varner and the constable, Quick, and it was moving at a snail's pace because, on a lead rope at the rear axle, was his cow. He didn't hurry; he ran out that furrow too, then unhitched the traces and tied the mule to the fence and only then walked on to where the two men still sat in the buckboard, watching him.

"I paid Houston the eighteen dollars and here's your cow," Varner said. "And if ever again I hear of you or anything belonging to you on Jack Houston's land, I'm going to send you to jail."

"And seventy-five cents," he said. "Or maybe them six bits evaporated. That cow's under a court judgment. I can't accept it until that judgment is satisfied."

"Lon," Varner said to the constable in a voice flat and almost gentle, "put that cow in the lot yonder and take that rope off it and get to hell back in this buggy."

"Lon," Mink said in a voice just as gentle and just as flat, "if you put that cow in my lot I'll get my shotgun and kill her."

Nor did he watch them. He went back to the mule and untied the lines from the fence and hooked up the traces and ran another furrow, his back now to the house and the lane, so that not until he swung the mule at the turn-row did he see for a moment the buckboard going back down the lane at that snail's pace matched to the plodding cow. He ploughed steadily on until dark, until his supper of the coarse fatback and cheap molasses and probably weevilly flour which, even after he had eaten it, would still be the property of Will Varner until he, Mink, had ginned and sold the cotton next fall which he had not even planted yet.

An hour later, with a coal-oil lantern to light dimly the slow lift and thrust of the digger, he was back at Houston's fence. He

had not lain down nor even stopped moving, working, since
daylight this morning; when daylight came again he would not
have slept in twenty-four hours; when the sun did rise on him he
was back in his own field with the mule and plough, stopping only
for dinner at noon, then back to the field again, ploughing again—
or so he thought until he waked to find himself lying in the very
furrow he had just run, beneath the canted handles of the still-
bedded plough, the anchored mule still standing in the traces and
the sun just going down.

Then supper again like last night's meal and this morning's
breakfast too, and carrying the lighted lantern he once more
crossed Houston's pasture toward where he had left the post-hole
digger. He didn't even see Houston sitting on the pile of waiting
posts until Houston stood up, the shotgun cradled in his left arm.
"Go back," Houston said. "Don't never come on my land again
after sundown. If you're going to kill yourself, it won't be here.
Go back now. Maybe I can't stop you from working out that
cow by daylight, but I reckon I can after dark."

But he could stand that too. Because he knew the trick of it.
He had learned that the hard way; himself taught that to himself through simple necessity: that a man can bear anything by
simply and calmly refusing to accept it, be reconciled to it, give
up to it. He could even sleep at night now. It was not so much
that he had time to sleep now, as because he now had a kind of
peace, freed of hurry and haste. He broke the rest of his rented
land now, then opened out the middles while the weather held
good, using the bad days on Houston's fence, marking off one
day less which meant fifty cents less toward the recovery of his
cow. But with no haste now, no urgency; when spring finally
came and the ground warmed for the reception of seed and he
saw before him a long hiatus from the fence because of the
compulsion of his own crop, he faced it calmly, getting his corn-
and cotton-seed from Varner's store and planting his ground,
making a better job of sowing than he had ever done before,
since all he had to do now was to fill the time until he could get
back to the fence and with his own sweat dissolve away another
of the half-dollars. Because patience was his pride too: never to
be reconciled since by this means he could beat Them; They
might be stronger for a moment than he but nobody, no man, no

nothing could wait longer than he could wait when nothing else
but waiting would do, would work, would serve him.

Then the sun set at last on the day when he could put down
patience also along with the digger and the stretchers and what
remained of the wire. Houston would know it was the last day
too of course. Likely Houston had spent the whole day expecting
him to come trotting up the lane to get the cow the minute the
sun was below the western trees; likely Houston had spent the
whole day from sunrise on in the kitchen window to see him,
Mink, show up for that last day's work already carrying the
ploughline to lead the cow home with. In fact, throughout that
whole last day while he dug the last holes and tamped into them
the post at all but the last of that outrage which They had used
old Will Varner himself as their tool to try him with, to see how
much he really could stand, he could imagine Houston hunting
vainly up and down the lane, trying every bush and corner to
find where he must have hidden the rope.

Which—the rope—he had not even brought yet, working
steadily on until the sun was completely down and no man could
say the full day was not finished and done, and only then
gathering up the digger and shovel and stretchers, to carry them
back to the feed lot and set them neatly and carefully in the angle
of the fence where the nigger or Houston or anybody else that
wanted to look couldn't help but see them, himself not glancing
even once toward Houston's house, not even glancing once at the
cow which no man could now deny was his, before walking on
back down the lane toward his cabin two miles away.

He ate his supper, peacefully and without haste, not even
listening for the cow and whoever would be leading it this time.
It might even be Houston himself. Though on second thought,
Houston was like him; Houston didn't scare easy either. It
would be old Will Varner's alarm and concern sending the
constable to bring the cow back, now that the judgment was
worked out to the last penny, he, Mink, chewing his fatback and
biscuits and drinking his coffee with that same gentle expression
almost like smiling, imagining Quick cursing and stumbling up
the lane with the lead rope for having to do the job in the dark
when he too would rather be at home with his shoes off eating
supper; Mink was already rehearsing, phrasing what he would tell

him: "I worked out eighteen and a half days. It takes a light and a dark both to make one of them, and this one ain't up until daylight tomorrow morning. Just take that cow back where you and Will Varner put it eighteen and a half days ago, and I'll come in the morning and get it. And remind that nigger to feed early, so I won't have to wait."

But he heard nothing. And only then did he realise that he had actually expected the cow, had counted on its return you might say. He had a sudden quick shock of fear, terror, discovering now how spurious had been that peace he thought was his since his run-in with Houston and the shotgun at the fence line that night two months ago; so light a hold on what he had thought was peace that he must be constantly on guard now, since almost anything apparently could throw him back to that moment when Will Varner had told him he would have to work out eighteen dollars and seventy-five cents at fifty cents a day to gain possession of his own cow. Now he would have to go to the lot and look to make sure Quick hadn't put the cow in it unheard and then run, fled; he would have to light a lantern and go out in the dark to look for what he knew he would not find. And as if that was not enough, he would have to explain to his wife where he was going with the the the lantern. Sure enough, he had to do it, using the quick hard unmannered word when she said, "Where you going? I thought Jack Houston warned you,"—adding, not for the crudeness but because she too would not let him alone:

"Lessen of course you will step outside and do it for me."

"You nasty thing!" she cried. "Using words like that in front of the girls!"

"Sholy," he said. "Or maybe you could send them. Maybe both of them together could make up for one a-dult. Though from the way they eat, ara one of them alone ought to do hit."

He went to the barn. The cow was not there of course, as he had known. He was glad of it. The whole thing—realising that even if one of them brought the cow home, he would still have to go out to the barn to make sure—had been good for him, teaching him, before any actual harm had been done, just exactly what They were up to: to fling, jolt, surprise him off balance and so ruin him: Who couldn't beat him in any other way: couldn't beat him with money or its lack, couldn't outwait him; could beat him only by catching him off balance and so topple him back into that condition of furious blind earless rage where he had no sense.

But he was all right now. He had actually gained; when he took his rope tomorrow morning and went to get his cow, it wouldn't be Quick but Houston himself who would say, "Why didn't you come last night? The eighteenth-and-a-half day was up at dark last night"; it would be Houston himself to whom he would answer:

"It takes a light and a dark both to make a day. That-ere eighteenth-and-a-half day is up this morning—providing that delicate nigger of yourn has done finished feeding her."

He slept. He ate breakfast; sunrise watched him walk without haste up the lane to Houston's feed lot, the ploughline coiled on his arm, to lean his folded arms on the top rail of the fence, the coiled rope loosely dangling, watching the Negro with his pitchfork and Houston also for a minute or two before they saw him. He said:

"Mawnin, Jack. I come by for that-ere court-judgment cow if you'll kindly have your nigger to kindly put this here rope on her if he'll be so kindly obliging," then still leaning there while Houston came across the lot and stopped about ten feet away.

"You're not through yet," Houston said. "You owe two more days."

"Well well," he said, easily and peacefully, almost gently. "I reckon a man with a lot full of paper bulls and heifers, not to mention a half a mile of new pasture fence he got built free for nothing, might get mixed up about a little thing not no more important than jest dollars, especially jest eighteen dollars and seventy-five cents of them. But I jest own one eight-dollar cow, or what I always thought was jest a eight-dollar cow. I ain't rich enough not to be able to count up to eighteen seventy-five."

"I'm not talking about eighteen dollars," Houston said. "I'm—"

"And seventy-five cents," Mink said.

"—talking about nineteen dollars. You owe one dollar more."

He didn't move; his face didn't change; he just said: "What one dollar more?"

"The pound fee," Houston said. "The law says that when

anybody has to take up a stray animal and the owner don't claim it before dark that same day, the man that took it up is entitled to a one-dollar pound fee."

He stood quite still; his hand did not even tighten on the coiled rope. "So that was why you were so quick that day to save Lon the trouble of taking her to his lot," he said. "To get that extra dollar."

"Damn the extra dollar," Houston said. "Damn Quick too. He was welcome to her. I kept her instead to save you having to walk all the way to Quick's house to get her. Not to mention I have fed her every day, which Quick wouldn't have done. The digger and shovel and stretchers are in the corner yonder where you left them last night. Any time you want to—"

But he had already turned, already walking, peacefully and steadily, carrying the coiled rope, back down the lane to the road, not back toward his home but in the opposite direction toward Varner's store four miles away. He walked through the bright sweet young summer morning between the burgeoning woodlands where the dogwood and redbud and wild plum had long since bloomed and gone, beside the planted fields standing strongly with corn and cotton, some of it almost as good as his own small patches (obviously the people who planted these had not had the leisure and peace he had thought he had to sow in); treading peacefully the rife and vernal earth boiling with life—the frantic flash and glint and crying of birds, a rabbit bursting almost beneath his feet, so young and thin as to have but two dimensions, unless the third one could be speed—on to Varner's store.

The gnawed wood gallery above the gnawed wood steps should be vacant now. The overalled men who after laying-by would squat or stand all day against the front wall or inside the store itself, should be in the field too today, ditching or mending fences or running the first harrows and shovels and cultivators among the stalks. The store was too empty, in fact. He thought *If Flem was jest here*—because Flem was not there; he, Mink, knew if anyone did that that honeymoon would have to last until they could come back home and tell Frenchman's Bend that the child they would bring with them hadn't been born sooner than this past May *at* the earliest. But even if it hadn't been that, it would have been something else; his cousin's absence when he was needed was just one more test, harassment, enragement They tried him with, not to see if he would survive it because They had no doubt of that, but simply for the pleasure of watching him have to do something extra there was no reason whatever for him to have to do.

Only Varner was not there either. Mink had not expected that. He had taken it for granted that They certainly would not miss this chance: to have the whole store crammed with people who should have been busy in the field—loose idle ears all strained to hear what he had come to say to Will Varner. But even Varner was gone; there was nobody in the store but Jody Varner and Lump Snopes, the clerk Flem had substituted in when he quit to get married last summer.

"If he went to town, he won't be back before night," Mink said.

"Not to town," Jody said. "He went over to look at a mill on Punkin Creek. He said he'll be back by dinner time."

"He won't be back until night," Mink said.

"All right," Jody said. "Then you can go back home and come back tomorrow."

So he had no choice. He could have walked the five miles back home and then the five more back to the store in just comfortable time before noon, if he had wanted a walk. Or he could stay near the store until noon and wait there until old Varner would finally turn up just about in time for supper, which he would do, since naturally They would not miss that chance to make him lose a whole day. Which would mean he would have to put in half of one night digging Houston's post holes since he would have to complete the two days by noon of day after tomorrow in order to finish what he would need to do since he would have to make one trip into town himself.

Or he could have walked back home just in time to eat his noon meal and then walk back, since he would already have lost a whole day anyway. But They would certainly not miss that chance; as soon as he was out of sight, the buckboard would return from Punkin Creek and Varner would get out of it. So he waited, through noon when, as soon as Jody left to go home to dinner, Lump hacked off a segment of hoop cheese and took a handful of crackers from the barrel.

"Ain't you going to eat no dinner?" Lump said. "Will won't miss it."

"No," Mink said.

"I'll put it on your furnish then, if you're all that tender about one of Will Varner's nickels," Lump said.

"I'm not hungry," he said. But there was one thing he could be doing, one preparation he could be making while he waited, since it was not far. So he went there, to the place he had already chosen, and did what was necessary since he already knew what Varner was going to tell him, and return to the store and yes, at exactly midafternoon, just exactly right to exhaust the balance of the whole working day, the buckboard came up and Varner got out and was tying the lines to the usual gallery post when Mink came up to him.

"All right," Varner said. "Now what?"

"A little information about the Law," he said. "This here pound-fee law."

"What?" Varner said.

"That's right," he said, peaceful and easy, his face quiet and gentle as smiling. "I thought I had finished working out them thirty-seven and a half-bit days at sundown last night. Only when I went this morning to get my cow, it seems like I ain't quite yet, that I owe two more days for the pound fee."

"Hell fire," Varner said. He stood over the smaller man, cursing. "Did Houston tell you that?"

"That's right," he said.

"Hell fire," Varner said again. He dragged a huge worn leather wallet strapped like a suitcase from his hip pocket and took a dollar bill from it. "Here," he said.

"So the Law does say I got to pay another dollar before I can get my cow."

"Yes," Varner said. "If Houston wants to claim it. Take this dollar—"

"I don't need it," he said, already turning. "Me and Houston don't deal in money, we deal in post holes. I jest wanted to know the Law. And if that's the Law, I reckon there ain't nothing for a law-abiding feller like me to do but jest put up with it. Because if folks don't put up with the Law, what's the use of all the trouble and expense of having it?"

"Wait," Varner said. "Don't you go back there. Don't you go near Houston's place. You go on home and wait. I'll bring your cow to you as soon as I get hold of Quick."

"That's all right," he said. "Maybe I ain't got as many post holes in me as Houston has dollars, but I reckon I got enough for just two more days."

"Mink!" Varner said. "Mink! Come back here!" But he was gone. But there was no hurry now; the day was already ruined; until tomorrow morning, when he was in Houston's new pasture until sundown. This time he hid the tools under a bush as he always did when he would return tomorrow, and went home and ate the sowbelly and flour gravy and undercooked biscuits; they had one timepiece, the tin alarm clock which he set for eleven and rose again then; he had left coffee in the pot and some of the meat cold in the congealed skillet and two biscuits so it was almost exactly midnight when the savage baying of the Bluetick hound brought the Negro to his door and he, Mink, said, "Hit's Mister Snopes. Reporting for work. Hit's jest gone exactly midnight for the record." Because he would have to do this in order to quit at noon. And They—Houston—were still watching him because when the sun said noon and he carried the tools back to the fence corner, his cow was already tied there in a halter, which he removed and tied his ploughline around her horns and this time he didn't lead her but, himself at a trot, drove her trotting before him by lashing her across the hocks with the end of the rope.

Because he was short for time, to get her back home and into the lot. Nor would he have time to eat his dinner, again today, with five miles still to do, even straight across country, to catch the mail carrier before he left Varner's store at two o'clock for Jefferson, since Varner did not carry ten-gauge buckshot shells. But his wife and daughters were at the table, which at least saved argument, the necessity to curse them silent or perhaps even to have actually to strike, hit his wife, in order to go to the hearth and dig out the loose brick and take from the snuff tin behind it the single five-dollar bill which through all vicissitudes they kept there as the boat owner will sell or pawn or lose all his gear but will still cling on to one life preserver or ring buoy. Because he had five shells for the ancient ten-gauge gun, ranging

from bird shot to one Number Two for turkey or geese. But he
had had them for years, he did not remember how long; besides,
even if he were guaranteed that they would fire, Houston
deserved better than this.

So he folded the bill carefully into the fob pocket of his overalls
and caught the mail carrier and by four that afternoon Jefferson
was in sight across the last valley and by simple precaution, a
simple instinctive preparatory gesture, he thrust his fingers into
the fob pocket, then suddenly dug frantically, himself outwardly
immobile, into the now vacant pocket where he knew he had
folded and stowed carefully the bill, then sat immobile beside
the mail carrier while the buckboard began to descend the hill.
I got to do it he thought *so I might as well* and then said quietly
aloud, "All right, I reckon I'll take that-ere bill now."

"What?" the carrier said.

"That-ere five-dollar bill that was in my pocket when I got in
this buggy back yonder at Varner's."

"Why, you little son of a bitch," the carrier said. He pulled
the buckboard off to the side of the road and wrapped the lines
around the whip stock and got out and came around to Mink's
side of the vehicle. "Get out," he said.

Now I got to fight him Mink thought *and I ain't got no knife and
likely he will beat me to ere a stick I try to grab. So I might jest as well
get it over with* and got out of the buckboard, the carrier giving
him time to get his puny and vain hands up. Then a shocking
blow which Mink didn't even feel very much, aware instead
rather merely of the hard ungiving proneness of the earth,
ground against his back, lying there, peaceful almost, watching
the carrier get back into the buckboard and drive on.

Then he got up. He thought *I not only could a saved a trip, I
might still had them five dollars*. But for only a moment; he was
already in the road, already walking steadily on toward town
as if he knew what he was doing. Which he did, he had already
remembered: two, three years ago it was when Solon Quick or
Vernon Tull or whoever it was had seen the bear, the last bear
in that part of the country, when it ran across Varner's mill dam
and into the thicket, and how the hunt had been organised and
somebody rode a horse in to Jefferson to get hold of Ike McCaslin
and Walter Ewell, the best hunters in the country, and they came

out with their buckshot big-game shells and the bear and deer hounds and set the standers and drove the bottom where the bear had been seen but it was gone by then. So he knew what to do, or at least where to try, until he crossed the Square and entered the hardware store where McCaslin was junior partner and saw McCaslin's eyes. Mink thought quietly *Hit won't do no good. He has done spent too much time in the woods with deer and bears and panthers that either are or they ain't, right quick and now and not no shades between. He won't know how to believe a lie even if I could tell him one.* But he had to try.

"What do you want with two buckshot shells?" McCaslin said.

"A nigger came in this morning and said he seen that bear's foot in the mud at Blackwater Slough."

"No," McCaslin said. "What do you want with buckshot shells?"

"I can pay you soon as I gin my cotton," Mink said.

"No," McCaslin said. "I ain't going to let you have them. There ain't anything out there at Frenchman's Bend you need to shoot buckshot at."

It was not that he was hungry so much, even though he hadn't eaten since midnight: it was simply that he would have to pass the time some way until tomorrow morning when he would find out whether the mail carrier would take him back to Varner's store or not. He knew a small dingy back-street eating place owned by the sewing-machine agent, Ratliff, who was well known in Frenchman's Bend, where, if he had a half a dollar or even forty cents, he could have had two hamburgers and a nickel's worth of bananas and still had twenty-five cents left.

For that he could have had a bed in the Commercial Hotel (an unpainted two-storey frame building on a back street also; in two years his cousin Flem would own it though of course Mink didn't know that now. In fact, he had not even begun to think about his cousin yet, not once again after that moment when he entered Varner's store yesterday morning, where until his and his wife's departure for Texas last August, the first object he would have seen on entering it would have been Flem), but all he had to do was to pass time until eight o'clock tomorrow morning and if it cost cash money just to pass time he would have been in the poorhouse years ago.

Now it was evening, the lights had come on around the Square, the lights from the drugstore falling outward across the pavement, staining the pavement with dim rose and green from the red- and green-liquid-filled jars in the windows; he could see the soda fountain and the young people, young men and girls in their city clothes eating and drinking the gaudy sweet concoctions, and he could watch them, the couples, young men and girls and old people and children, all moving in one direction. Then he heard music, a piano, loud. He followed also and saw in a vacant lot the big high plank stockade with its entrance beside the lighted ticket window: the Airdome they called it; he had seen it before from the outside by day while in town for Saturdays, and three times at night too, lighted as now. But never the inside because on the three previous times he had been in Jefferson after dark he had ridden a mule in from Frenchman's Bend with com-panions of his age and sex to take the early train to a Memphis brothel with in his pocket the few meagre dollars he had wrenched as though by main strength from his bare livelihood, as he had likewise wrenched the two days he would be gone from earning the replacement of them, and in his blood a need far more urgent and passionate than a moving-picture show.

Though this time he could have spared the dime it would cost. Instead he stood a little aside while the line of patrons crept slowly past the ticket window until the last one passed inside. Then the glare and glow of light from beyond the fence blinked out and into a cold flickering; approaching the fence and laying his eye to a crack he could see through the long vertical interstice a section, a fragment—the dark row of motionless heads above which the whirring cone of light burst, shattered into the passion-ate and evanescent posturings where danced and flickered the ephemeral hopes and dreams, tantalising and inconsequent since he could see only his narrow vertical strip of it, until a voice spoke from the ticket window behind him: 'Pay a dime and go inside. Then you can see."

"No much obliged," he said. He went on. The Square was empty now, until the show would let out and once more the young people, young men and girls, would drink and eat the confections which he had never tasted either, before strolling home. He had hoped maybe to see one of the automobiles; there were two in Jefferson already: the red racer belonging to the mayor, Mr de Spain, and the White Steamer that the president of the old bank, the Bank of Jefferson, owned (Colonel Sartoris, the other rich bank president, president of the new bank, not only wouldn't own an automobile, he even had a law passed three years ago that no motor-driven vehicle could operate on the streets of Jefferson after the home-made automobile a man named Buffaloe had made in his back yard frightened the colonel's matched team into running away). But he didn't see either one; the Square was still empty when he crossed it. Then the hotel, the Holston House, the drummers sitting in leather chairs along the sidewalk in the pleasant night; one of the livery-stable hacks was already there, the Negro porter loading the grips and sample cases in it for the south-bound train.

So he had better walk on, to be in time, even though the four lighted faces of the clock on top of the courthouse said only ten minutes past eight and he knew by his own experience that the New Orleans train from Memphis Junction didn't pass Jefferson until two minutes to nine. Though he knew too that freight trains might pass at almost any time, let alone the other passenger train, the one his experience knew too, going north at half-past four. So just by spending the night, without even moving, he would see certainly two and maybe five or six trains before daylight.

He had left the Square, passing the dark homes where some of the old people who didn't go to the picture show either sat in dim rocking-chairs in the cool dark of the yards, then a section all Negro homes, even with electric lights too, peaceful, with no worries, no need to fight and strive single-handed, not to gain right and justice because they were already lost, but just to defend the principle of them, his rights to them, but instead could talk a little while and then go even into a nigger house and just lay down and sleep in place of walking all the way to the depot just to have something to look at until the durn mail carrier left at eight o'clock tomorrow. Then the depot: the red and green eyes of the signal lamps, the hotel bus and the livery-stable hacks and Lucius Hogganbeck's automobile jitney, the long electric-lighted shed already full of the men and boys come down to see the train pass, that were there the three times he had got off of it, looking at him also like he had come from a heap further than a Memphis whorehouse.

Then the train itself: the four whistle blasts for the north crossing, then the headlight, the roar, the clanging engine, the engineer and the fireman crouched dim and high above the hissing steam, slowing, the baggage and day coaches then the dining-car and the cars in which people slept while they rode. It stopped, a Negro even more uppity than Houston's getting out with his footstool, then the conductor, and the rich men and women getting gaily aboard where the other rich ones were already asleep, followed by the nigger with his footstool and the conductor, the conductor leaning back to wave at the engine, the engine speaking back to the conductor, to all of them, with the first deep short ejaculations of starting.

Then the twin ruby lamps on the last car diminished rapidly together in one last flick! at the curve, the four blasts came fading back from the south crossing and he thought of distance, of New Orleans where he had never been and perhaps never would go, with distance even beyond New Orleans, with Texas somewhere in it; and now for the first time he began really to think about his absent cousin: the one Snopes of them all who had risen, broken free, had either been born with or had learned, taught himself, the knack or the luck to cope with, hold his own, handle the They and Them which he, Mink, apparently did not have the knack or the luck to do. *Maybe I ought to waited till he got back* he thought, turning at last back to the now empty and vacant platform, noticing only then that he had thought, not *should* wait for Flem, but should *have* waited, it already being too late.

The waiting-room was empty too, with its hard wooden benches and the cold iron tobacco-spattered stove. He knew about signs in depots against spitting but he never heard of one against a man without a ticket sitting down. Anyhow, he would find out —a small man anyway, fleshless, sleepless and more or less foodless too for going on twenty-two hours now, looking in the empty barren room beneath the single unshaded bulb as forlorn and defenceless as a child, a boy, in faded patched overalls and shirt, sockless in heavy worn iron-hard brogan shoes and a sweat-and-grease-stained black felt hat. From beyond the ticket window he could hear the intermittent clatter of the telegraph, and two voices where the night operator talked to somebody now and then, until the voices ceased and the telegraph operator in his green eyeshade was looking at him through the window. "You want something?" he said.

"No much obliged," Mink said. "When does the next train pass?"

"Four twenty-two," the operator said. "You waiting for it?"

"That's right," he said.

"That's six hours off yet. You can go home and go to bed and then come back."

"I live out at Frenchman's Bend," he said.

"Oh," the operator said. Then the face was gone from the window and he sat again. It was quiet now and he even began to notice, hear the katydids in the dark trees beyond the tracks buzzing and chirring back and forth, interminable and peaceful, as if they might be the sound of the peaceful minutes and seconds themselves of the dark peaceful summer night clicking to one another. Then the whole room shook and trembled, filled with thunder; the freight train was already passing and even now he couldn't seem to get himself awake enough to get outside in time. He was still sitting on the hard bench, cramped and cold while the ruby lights on the caboose flicked across the windows then across the open door, sucking the thunder behind them; the four crossing blasts came back and died away. This time the operator was in the room with him and the overhead bulb had been switched off. "You were asleep," he said.

"That's right," Mink said, "I nigh missed that un."

"Why don't you lay down on the bench and be comfortable?"

"You ain't got no rule against it?"

"No," the operator said. "I'll call you when they signal Number Eight."

"Much obliged," he said, and lay back. The operator went back into the room where the telegraph was already chattering again. *Yes* he thought peacefully *if Flem had been here he could a stopped all this on that first day before it ever got started. Working for Varner like he done, being in with Houston and Quick and all the rest of them. He could do it now if I could jest a waited. Only it wasn't me that couldn't wait. It was Houston his-self that wouldn't give me time.* Then

immediately he knew that that was wrong too, that no matter
how long he had waited They Themselves would have prevented
Flem from getting back in time. He must drain this cup too:
must face, accept this last ultimate useless and reasonless risk
and jeopardy too just to show how much he could stand before
They would let his cousin come back where he could save him.
This same cup also contained Houston's life, but he wasn't
thinking about Houston. In a way, he had quit thinking about
Houston at the same moment when Varner told him he would
have to pay the pound fee. "All right," he said peacefully, aloud
this time, "if that's what They want, I reckon I can stand that
too."

At half-past seven he was standing in the small lot behind the
post office where R.F.D. carriers' buckboards would stand until
the carriers came out the back door with the bags of mail. He had
already discerned the one for Frenchman's Bend and he stood
quietly, not too near: simply where the carrier could not help
but see him, until the man who had knocked him down yesterday
came out and saw, recognised, him, a quick glance, then came
on and stowed the mail pouch into the buckboard, Mink not
moving yet, just standing there, waiting, to be refused or not
refused, until the carrier got in and released the wrapped lines
from the whip stock and said, "All right. I reckon you got to
get back to your crop. Come on," and Mink approached and
got in.

It was just past eleven when he got down at Varner's store and
said Much obliged and began the five-mile walk home. So he was
home in time for dinner, eating steadily and quietly while his
wife nagged and whined at him (evidently she hadn't noticed the
disturbed brick) about where he was last night and why, until
he finished, drank the last of his coffee and rose from the table
and with vicious and obscene cursing drove the three of them, his
wife and the two girls, with the three hoes out to the patch to
chop out his early cotton, while he lay on the floor in the cool
draft of the dog-trot hall, sleeping away the afternoon.

Then it was tomorrow morning. He took from its corner
behind the door the tremendous ten-gauge double-barrelled
shotgun which had belonged to his grandfather, the twin
hammers standing above the receiver almost as tall as the ears

of a rabbit. "Now what?" his wife said, cried. "Where you fixing to go with that?"

"After a rabbit," he said. "I'm burnt out on sowbelly," and with two of the heaviest loads out of his meagre stock of Number-Two and -Five and -Eight-shot shells, he went not even by back roads and lanes but by hedgerows and patches of woods and ditches and whatever else would keep him private and unseen, back to the ambush he had prepared two days ago while waiting for Varner to return, where the road from Houston's to Varner's store crossed the creek bridge—the thicket beside the road, with a log to sit on and the broken-off switches not yet healed over where he had opened a sort of port to point the gun through, with the wooden planks of the bridge fifty yards up the road to serve as an alert beneath the stallion's hooves in case he dozed off.

Because sometimes a week would pass before Houston would ride in to the store. But sooner or later he would do so. And if all he, Mink, needed to beat Them with was just waiting, They could have given up three months ago and saved Themselves and everybody else trouble. So it was not the first day nor the second either that he would go home with no rabbit, to eat his supper in quiet and inflexible silence while his wife nagged and whined at him about why there was none, until he would push away his empty plate and in a cold level vicious monotone curse her silent.

And it might not have been the third day either. In fact, he couldn't remember how many days it had been, when at last he heard the sudden thunder of the hooves on the bridge and then saw them: the stallion boring, frothing a little, wrenching its arrogant vicious head at the snaffle and curb both with which Houston rode it, the big lean hound bounding along beside it. He cocked the two hammers and pushed the gun through the porthole, and even as he laid the sight on Houston's chest, leading him just a little, his finger already taking up the slack in the front trigger, he thought *And even now. They still ain't satisfied yet* as the first shell clicked dully without exploding, his finger already moving back to the rear trigger, thinking *And even yet* as this one crashed and roared, thinking how if there had only been time, space, between the roar of the gun and the impact of the shot, for him to say to Houston and for Houston to have to hear it:

"I ain't shooting you because of them thirty-seven and a half four-bit days. That's all right; I done long ago forgot and forgive that. Likely Will Varner couldn't do nothing else, being a rich man too and all you rich folks has got to stick together or else maybe some day the ones that ain't rich might take a notion to raise up and take hit away from you. That ain't why I shot you. I killed you because of that-ere extry one-dollar pound fee."

TWO

So the jury said "Guilty" and the Judge said "Life", but he wasn't even listening. Because something had happened to him. Even while the sheriff was bringing him in to town that first day, even though he knew that his cousin was still in Texas, he believed that at every mile post Flem or a messenger from him would overtake them or step into the road and stop them, with the money or the word or whatever it would be that would make the whole thing dissolve, vanish like a dream.

And during all the long weeks while he waited in jail for his trial, he would stand at the little window of his cell, his grimed hands gripped among the bars and his face craned and pressed against them, to watch a slice of the street before the jail and the slice of the Square which his cousin would have to cross to come to the jail and abolish the dream, free him, get him out. "Which is all I want," he would tell himself. "Jest to get out of here and go back home and farm. That don't seem like a heap to ask."

And at night too still standing there, his face invisible but his wan hands looking almost white, almost clean in the grimed interstices against the cell's darkness, watching the free people, men and women and young people who had nothing but peaceful errands or pleasures as they strolled in the evening cool toward the Square, to watch the picture show or eat ice-cream in the drugstore or maybe just stroll peaceful and free because they were free, he beginning at last to call down to them, timidly at first, then louder and louder, more and more urgent as they would pause, almost as though startled, to look up at his window and then seem almost to hurry on, like they were trying to get beyond where he could see them; finally he began to offer, promise them money: "Hey! Mister! Missus! Somebody! anybody that will send word out to Varner's store to Flem Snopes! He will pay you! Ten dollars! Twenty dollars!"

And even when the day finally came and they brought him handcuffed into the room where he would face his jeopardy, he had not even looked once toward the Bench, the dais which could well be his Golgotha too, for looking, staring out over the pale identical anonymous faces of the crowd for that of his cousin or at least the messenger from him; right up to the moment when the Judge himself had to lean down from his high desk and say, "You, Snopes! Look at me. Did you or didn't you kill Jack Houston?" and he answered:

"Don't bother me now. Can't you see I'm busy?"

And the next day too, while the lawyers shouted and wrangled and nagged, he hearing none of it even if he could have understood it, for watching the door at the rear where his cousin or the messenger would have to enter; and on the way back to the cell, still handcuffed, his unflagging glance which at first had been merely fretted and impatient but which now was beginning to be concerned, a little puzzled and quite sober, travelling rapid and quick and searching from face to face as he passed them or they passed him, to stand again at his cell window, his unwashed hands gripping the grimed bars and his face wrenched and pressed against them to see as much as possible of the street and the Square below where his kinsman or the messenger would have to pass.

So when on the third day, handcuffed again to the jailor he realised that he had crossed the Square without once looking at one of the faces which gaped at him, and had entered the courtroom and taken his accustomed place in the dock still without once looking out over the massed faces toward that rear door, he still did not dare admit to himself that he knew why. He just sat there, looking as small and frail and harmless as a dirty child while the lawyers ranted and wrangled, until the end of the day when the jury said Guilty and the Judge said Life and he was returned, handcuffed, to his cell, and the door clanged to and he sitting now, quiet and still and composed on the mattressless steel cot, this time only looking at the small barred window where for months now he had stood sixteen or eighteen hours a day in quenchless expectation and hope.

Only then did he say it, think it, let it take shape in his mind: *He ain't coming. Likely he's been in Frenchman's Bend all the time. Likely he heard about that cow clean out there in Texas and jest waited till the word came back they had me safe in jail, and then come back to make sho they would do ever thing to me they could now that they had me helpless. He might even been hid in the back of that room all the time, to make sho wouldn't nothing slip up before he finally got rid of me for good and all.*

So now he had peace. He had thought he had peace as soon

as he realised what he would have to do about Houston, and that
Houston himself wasn't going to let him wait until Flem got back.
But he had been wrong. That wasn't peace then; it was too full of
too many uncertainties: such as if anybody would send word to
Flem about his trouble at all, let alone in time. Or even if the
word was sent in time, would the message find Flem in time. And
even if Flem got the message in time, there might be a flood or
a wreck on the railroad so he couldn't get back in time.

But all that was finished now. He didn't have to bother and
worry at all now since all he had to do was wait, and he had
already proved to himself that he could do that. Just to wait:
that's all he needed; he didn't even need to ask the jailor to send
a message since the lawyer himself had said he would come back
to see him after supper.

So he ate his supper when they brought it—the same sidemeat
and molasses and undercooked biscuits he would have had at
home; this in fact a little better since the meat had more lean in it
than he could afford to eat. Except that his at home had been
free, eaten in freedom. But then he could stand that too if that
was all *they* demanded of him now. Then he heard the feet on the
stairs, the door clashed, letting the lawyer in, and clashed again
on both of them—the lawyer young and eager, just out of law
school they told him, whom the Judge had appointed for him—
commanded rather, since even he, Mink, busy as he was at the
time, could tell that the man didn't really want any part of him
and his trouble—he never did know why then because then he
still thought that all the Judge or anybody else needed to do to
settle the whole business was just to send out to Frenchman's
Bend and get hold of his cousin.

Too young and eager in fact, which was why he—the lawyer
—had made such a hash of the thing. But that didn't matter
now either; the thing now was to get on to what came next. So he
didn't waste any time. "All right," he said. "How long will I
have to stay there?"

"It's Parchman—the penitentiary," the lawyer said. "Can't
you understand that?"

"All right," he said again. "How long will I have to stay?"

"He gave you life," the lawyer said. "Didn't you even hear
him? For the rest of your life. Until you die."

"All right," he said for the third time, with that peaceful, that almost compassionate patience: "How long will I have to stay?"

By that time even this lawyer understood. "Oh. That depends on you and your friends—if you have any. It may be all your life, like Judge Brummage said. But in twenty or twenty-five years you will be eligible under the Law to apply for pardon or parole—if you have responsible friends to support your petition, and your record down there at Parchman don't hold anything against you."

"Suppose a man ain't got friends," he said.

"Folks that hide in bushes and shoot other folks off their horses without saying Look out first or even whistling, don't have," the lawyer said. "So you won't have anybody left except you to get you out."

"All right," he said, with that unshakable, that infinite patience, "that's what I'm trying to get you to stop talking long enough to tell me. What do I have to do to get out in twenty or twenty-five years?"

"Not to try to escape yourself or engage in any plot to help anybody else escape. Not to get in a fight with another prisoner or a guard. To be on time for whatever they tell you to do, and do it without shirking or complaining or talking back, until they tell you to quit. In other words, to start right now doing all the things that, if you had just been doing them all the time since that day last fall when you decided to let Mr Houston winter your cow for nothing, you wouldn't be sitting in this cell here trying to ask somebody how to get out of it. But mainly, don't try to escape."

"Escape?" he said.

"Break out. Try to get away."

"Try?" he said.

"Because you can't," the lawyer said with a kind of seething yet patient rage. "Because you can't escape. You can't make it. You never can. You can't plan it without some of the others catching on to it and they always try to escape with you and so you all get caught. And even if they don't go with you, they tell the Warden on you and you are caught just the same. And even if you manage to keep everybody else from knowing about it and go alone, one of the guards shoots you before you can climb

D

the fence. So even if you are not in the dead house or the hospital, you are back in the penitentiary with twenty-five more years added on to your sentence. Do you understand now?"

"That's all I got to do to get out in twenty or twenty-five years. Not try to escape. Not get in no fights with nobody. Do whatever they tell me to do, as long as they say to do it. But mainly not try to escape. That's all I got to do to get out in twenty or twenty-five years."

"That's right," the lawyer said.

"All right," he said. "Now go back and ask that judge if that's right, and if he says it is, to send me a wrote-out paper saying so."

"So you don't trust me," the lawyer said.

"I don't trust nobody," he said. "I ain't got time to waste twenty or twenty-five years to find out whether you know what you're talking about or not. I got something I got to attend to when I get back out. I want to know. I want a wrote-out paper from that judge."

"Maybe you never did trust me then," the lawyer said. "Maybe you think I made a complete bust of your whole case. Maybe you think that if it hadn't been for me, you wouldn't even be here now. Is that it?"

And he, Mink, still with that inflexible and patient calm: "You done the best you knowed. You jest wasn't the man for the job. You're young and eager, but that wasn't what I needed. I needed a trader, a smart trader, that knowed how to swap. You wasn't him. Now you go get that paper from that judge."

Now he, the lawyer, even tried to laugh. "Not me," he said. "The Court discharged me from this case right after he sentenced you this afternoon. I just stopped in to say good-bye and to see if there was anything else I could do for you. But evidently folks that don't have friends don't need well-wishers either."

"But I ain't discharged you yet," Mink said, rising now, without haste, the lawyer already on his feet, springing, leaping back against the locked door, looking at the small figure moving toward him as slight and frail and harmless-looking as a child and as deadly as a small viper—a half-grown asp or cobra or krait. Then the lawyer was shouting, bellowing, even while the turnkey's feet galloped on the stairs and the door clashed open and the turnkey stood in it with a drawn pistol.

"What is it?" the turnkey said. "What did he try to do?"

"Nothing," the lawyer said. "It's all right. I'm through here. Let me out." Only he was not through; he only wished he were. He didn't even wait until morning. Instead, not fifteen minutes later he was in the hotel room of the Circuit Judge who had presided on the case and pronounced the sentence, he, the lawyer, still breathing hard, still incredulous at his recent jeopardy and still amazed at his escape from it.

"He's crazy, I tell you!" he said. "He's dangerous! Just to send him to Parchman, where he will be eligible for parole and freedom in only twenty or twenty-five years, let alone if some of his kin—God knows he has enough—or someone with an axe to grind or maybe just some bleeding-heart meddler with access to the Governor's ear, doesn't have him out before that time even! He must go to Jackson, the asylum, for life, where he'll be safe. No: we'll be safe."

And ten minutes after that the District Attorney who had prosecuted the case was in the room too, saying (to the lawyer): "So now you want a suspended sentence, and a motion for a new trial. Why didn't you think of this before?"

"You saw him too," the lawyer said, cried. "You were in that courtroom with him all day long for three days too!"

"That's right," the District Attorney said. "That's why I'm asking you why now."

"Then you haven't seen him since!" the lawyer said. "Come up to that cell and look at him now, like I did thirty minutes ago!"

But the Judge was an old man, he wouldn't go then so it was next morning when the turnkey unlocked the cell and let the three of them in where the frail-looking fleshless small figure in the patched and faded overalls and shirt and the sockless iron-stiff brogans got up from the cot. They had shaved him this morning and his hair was combed too, parted and flattened down with water across his skull.

"Come in, gentle-men," he said. "I ain't got no chair, but likely you ain't fixing to stay long enough to set nohow. Well, Judge, you not only brought me my wrote-out paper, you brought along two witnesses to watch you hand it to me."

"Wait," the lawyer said rapidly to the Judge. "Let me." He

said to Mink: "You won't need that paper. They—the Judge—is going to give you another trial."

Now Mink stopped. He looked at the lawyer. "What for?" he said. "I done already had one that I never got much suption out of."

"Because that one was wrong," the lawyer said. "That's what we've come to tell you about."

"If that un was wrong, what's the use of wasting time and money having another one? Jest tell that feller there to bring me my hat and open that door and I'll go back home and get back to me crop, providing I still got one."

"No, wait," the lawyer said. "That other trial was wrong because it sent you to Parchman. You won't have to go to Parchman now, where you'll have to work out in the hot sun all day long in a crop that isn't even yours." And now, with the pale faded grey eyes watching him as if not only were they incapable of blinking but never since birth had they ever needed to, the lawyer found himself babbling, not even able to stop it: "Not Parchman: Jackson, where you'll have a nice room to yourself—nothing to do all day long but just rest—doctors—" and stopped then; not he that stopped his babbling but the fixed unwinking pale eyes that did it.

"Doctors," Mink said. "Jackson." He stared at the lawyer. "That's where they send crazy folks."

"Hadn't you rather—" the District Attorney began. That was as far as he got too. He had been an athlete in college and still kept himself fit. Though even then he managed to grasp the small frantic creature only after it had hurled itself on the lawyer and both of them had gone to the floor. And even then it took him and the turnkey both to drag Mink up and away and hold him, frantic and frothing and hard to hold as a cat, panting,

"Crazy, am I? Crazy, am I? Ain't no son a bitch going to call me crazy, I don't care how big he is or how many of them."

"You damn right, you little bastard," the District Attorney panted. "You're going to Parchman. That's where they've got the kind of doctors you need."

So he went to Parchman, handcuffed to a deputy sheriff, the two of them transferring from smoking-car to smoking-car of local trains, this one having left the hills which he had known all his life, for the Delta which he had never seen before—the vast flat alluvial swamp of cypress and gum and brake and thicket lurked with bear and deer and panthers and snakes, out of which man was still hewing savagely and violently the rich ragged fields in which cotton stalks grew ranker and taller than a man on a horse, he, Mink, sitting with his face glued to the window like a child.

"This here's all swamp," he said. "It don't look healthy."

"It ain't healthy," the deputy said. "It ain't intended to be. This is the penitentiary. I can't imagine no more unhealth a man can have than to be locked up inside a bobwire pen for twenty or twenty-five years. Besides, a good unhealthy place ought to just suit you; you won't have to stay so long."

So that's how he saw Parchman, the penitentiary, his destination, doom, his life the Judge had said; for the rest of his life as long as he lived. But the lawyer had told him different, even if he couldn't really trust him: only twenty-five, maybe only twenty years, and even a lawyer a man couldn't trust could at least be trusted to know his own business that he had even went to special law school to be trained to know it, where all a judge had to do to get to be a judge was just to win a election vote-race for it. And even if the Judge hadn't signed a paper saying only twenty or twenty-five years, that didn't matter either since the Judge was on the other side and would naturally lie to a man coming up against him, where a lawyer, a man's own lawyer, wouldn't. More: his own lawyer couldn't lie to him, because there was some kind of rule somebody had told him about that if the client didn't lie to his lawyer, the Law itself wouldn't let the lawyer lie to his own client.

And even if none of that was so, that didn't matter either because he couldn't stay at Parchman all his life, he didn't have time, he would have to get out before then. And looking at the tall wire stockade with its single gate guarded day and night by men with shotguns, and inside it the low grim brick buildings with their barred windows, he thought, tried to remember, with a kind of amazement of the time when his only reason for wanting to get out was to go back home and farm, remembering it only for a moment and then no more, because now he had to get out.

He had to get out. His familiar patched faded blue overalls

and shirt were exchanged now for the overalls and jumper of coarse white barred laterally with black which, according to the Judge, would have been his fate and doom until he died, if the lawyer hadn't known better. He worked now—gangs of them—in the rich black cotton land while men on horses with shotguns across the pommels watched them, doing the only work he knew how to do, had done all his life, in a crop which would never be his for the rest of his life if the Judge had his way, thinking *And that's all right too. Hit's even better. If a feller jest wants to do something, he might make it and he might not. But if he's GOT to do something, can't nothing stop him.*

And in the wooden bunk at night too, sheetless, with a cheap coarse blanket and his rolled-up clothing for a pillow, thinking, dinning it into himself since he was now having to change overnight and forever for twenty or twenty-five years his whole nature and character and being: *To do whatever they tell me to do. Not to talk back to nobody. Not to get into no fights. That's all I got to do for jest twenty-five or maybe even jest twenty years. But mainly not to try to escape.*

Nor did he even count off the years as they accomplished. Instead, he simply trod them behind him into oblivion beneath the heavy brogan shoes in the cotton middles behind the mule which drew the plough and then the sweep, then with the chopping and thinning hoe and at last with the long dragging sack into which he picked, gathered the cotton. He didn't need to count them; he was in the hands of the Law now and as long as he obeyed the four rules set down by the Law for his side, the Law would have to obey its single rule of twenty-five years or maybe even just twenty.

He didn't know how many years it had been when the letter came, whether it was two or three as he stood in the Warden's office, turning the stamped pencil-addressed envelope in his hand while the Warden watched him. "You can't read?" the Warden said.

"I can read reading, but I can't read writing good."

"You want me to open it?" the Warden said.

"All right," he said. So the Warden did.

"It's from your wife. She wants to know when you want her to come to see you, and if you want her to bring the girls."

Now he held the letter himself, the page of foolscap out of a school writing-pad, pencilled over, spidery and hieroglyph, not one jot less forever beyond him than Arabic or Sanscrit. "Yettie can't even read reading, let alone write writing," he said. "Miz Tull must a wrote it for her."

"Well?" the Warden said. "What do you want me to tell her?"

"Tell her it ain't no use in her coming all the way here because I'll be home soon."

"Oh," the Warden said. "You're going to get out soon, are you?" He looked at the small frail creature not much larger than a fifteen-year-old boy, who had been one of his charges for three years now without establishing an individial entity in the prison's warp. Not a puzzle, not an enigma: he was not anything at all; no record of run-in or reprimand with or from any guard or trusty or official, never any trouble with any other inmate. A murderer, in for life, who in the Warden's experience fell always into one of two categories: either an irreconcilable, with nothing more to lose, a constant problem and trouble to the guards and the other prisoners; or a sycophant, sucking up to whatever of his overlords could make things easiest for him. But not this one: who assumed his assigned task each morning and worked steady and unflagging in the cotton as if it was his own crop he was bringing to fruit. More: he worked harder for this crop from which he would not derive one cent of profit than, in the Warden's experience, men of his stamp and kind worked in their own. "How?" the Warden said.

Mink told him; it was automatic now after three years; he had only to open his mouth and breathe: "By doing what they tell me to. Not talking back and not fighting. Not to try to escape. Mainly that: not to try to escape."

"So in either seventeen or twenty-two years you'll go home," the Warden said. "You've already been here three."

"Have I?" he said. "I ain't kept count.—No," he said. "Not right away. There's something I got to attend to first."

"What?" the Warden said.

"Something private. When I finish that, then I'll come on home. Write her that." *Yes sir* he thought. *It looks like I done had to come all the way to Parchman jest to turn right around and go back home and kill Flem.*

THREE

V. K. Ratliff

LIKELY what bollixed Montgomery Ward at first, and for the next two or three days too, was exactly why Flem wanted him specifically in Parchman. Why wouldn't no other equally secure retired place do, such as Atlanta or Leavenworth or maybe even Alcatraz two thousand miles away out in California, where old Judge Long would a already had him on the first train leaving Jefferson while he was still looking at the top one of them French postcards; jest exactly why wouldn't no other place do Flem to have Montgomery Ward sent to but Parchman, Missippi.

Because even in the initial excitement, Montgomery Ward never had one moment's confusion about what was actively happening to him. The second moment after Lawyer and Hub walked in the door, he knowed that at last something was happening that he had been expecting ever since whenever that other moment was when Flem found out or suspected that whatever was going on up at that alley had a money profit in it. The only thing that puzzled him was, why Flem was going to all that extra trouble and complication jest to usurp him outen that nekkid-picture business. That was like the story about the coon in the tree that asked the name of the feller aiming the gun at him and when the feller told him, the coon says, "Hell fire, is that who you are? Then you don't need to waste all this time and powder jest on me. Stand to one side and I'll climb down."

Not to mention reckless. Having Flem Snopes take his business away from him was all right. He had been expecting that: that sooner or later his turn would come too, running as he did the same risk with ever body else in Yoknapatawpha County owning a business solvent enough for Flem to decide he wanted it too. But to let the county attorney and the county sheriff get a-holt of them pictures, the two folks of all the folks in Yoknapatawpha County that not even Grover Winbush would a been innocent enough to dream would ever turn them loose again—Lawyer Stevens, so dedicated to civic improvement and the moral advancement of folks that his purest notion of duty was brow-beating twelve-year-old boys into running five-mile foot races

when all they really wanted to do was jest to stay at home and
set fire to the barn; and Hub Hampton, a meat-eating Hard-
Shell-Baptist deacon whose purest notion of pleasure was counting
off the folks he personally knowed was already bound for hell.

Why, in fact, Montgomery Ward had to go anywhere, if all
his uncle or cousin wanted was jest to take his business away
from him, except maybe jest to stay outen sight for a week or
maybe a month or two to give folks time to forget about them
nekkid pictures, or anyway that anybody named Snopes was
connected with them. Flem being a banker now and having to
deal not jest in simple usury but in respectability too.

No, what really should a puzzled Montgomery Ward, filled
him in fact with delighted surprise, was how he had managed to
last even this long. It never needed the Law nor Flem Snopes
neither to close out that studio, pull the blinds down (or rather
up) for good and all on the French-postcard industry in Jefferson,
Missippi. Grover Winbush done that when he let whoever it
was ketch him slipping outen that alley at two o'clock that
morning. No: Grover Winbush had done already wrecked and
ruined that business in Jefferson at the same moment when he
found out there was a side door in a Jefferson alley with what
you might call a dry whorehouse behind it. No, that business was
wrecked in Jefferson the same moment Grover Winbush got
appointed night marshal, Grover having jest exactly enough
sense to be a night policeman providing the two wasn't no bigger
and never stayed awake no later than Jefferson, Missippi, since
that would be the one job in all paid laborious endeavour—
leaning all night against a lamppost looking at the empty
Square—you would a thought he could a held indefinitely,
providing the influence of whoever got it for him or give it to
him lasted that long, without stumbling over anything he could
do any harm with, to his-self or the job or a innocent bystander
or maybe all three; and so naturally he would be caught by
somebody, almost anybody, the second or third time he come
slipping outen that alley.

Which was jest a simple unavoidable occupational hazard of
running a business like that in the same town where Grover
Winbush was night marshal, which Montgomery Ward knowed
as well as anybody else that knowed Grover. So when the

business had been running over a year without no untoward interruption, Montgomery Ward figgered that whoever had been catching Grover slipping in and out of that alley after midnight once a month for the last nine or ten of them, was maybe business acquaintances Grover had made raiding crap games or catching them with a pint of moonshine whiskey in their hind pockets. Or who knows? Maybe even Flem his-self had got a-holt of each one of them in time, protecting not so much his own future interests and proposed investments, because maybe at that time he hadn't even found out he wanted to go into the a-teelyer (that's what Montgomery Ward called it; he had the name painted on the window: Atelier Monty) business, but simply protecting and defending solvency and moderate profit itself, not jest out of family loyalty to another Snopes but from pure and simple principle, even if he was a banker now and naturally would have to compromise, to a extent at least, profit with respectability, since any kind of solvency redounds to the civic interest providing it don't get caught, and even respectability can go hand in hand with civic interest providing the civic interest has got sense enough to take place after dark and not make no loud noise at it.

So when the county attorney and the county sheriff walked in on him that morning, Montgomery Ward naturally believed that pure and simple destiny was simply taking its natural course, and the only puzzling thing was the downright foolhardy, let alone reckless way Flem Snopes was hoping to take advantage of destiny. I mean, getting Lawyer Stevens and Sheriff Hampton into it, letting them get one whiff or flash of them nekkid pictures. Because of what you might call the late night shift his business had developed into, the Square never seen Montgomery Ward before noon. So until Lawyer and Hub told him about it, he hadn't had time yet to hear about them two fellers robbing Uncle Willy Christian's drug cabinet last night, that none of the folks watching the robbers through the front window could find hide nor hair of Grover Winbush to tell him about it until Grover finally come slipping back outen Montgomery Ward's alley, by which time even the robbers, let alone the folks watching them, had done all went home.

I don't mean Montgomery Ward was puzzled that Lawyer

and Hub was the first ones there. Naturally they would a been
when his a-teelyer business finally blowed up, no matter what
was the reason for the explosion. He would a expected them
first even if Yoknapatawpha County hadn't never heard the
word Flem Snopes—a meal-mouthed sanctimonious Harvard-
and Europe-educated lawyer that never even needed the excuse
of his office and salaried job to meddle in anything providing
it wasn't none of his business and wasn't doing him no harm; and
old pussel-gutted Hampton that could be fetched along to look
at anything, even a murder, once somebody remembered he was
Sheriff and told him about it and where it was. No. What
baffled Montgomery Ward was, what in creation kind of a
aberration could Flem Snopes been stricken with to leave him
believing he could use Lawyer Stevens and Hub Hampton to get
them pictures, and ever dream of getting them away from them.

So for a moment his faith and confidence in Flem Snopes
his-self wavered and flickered you might say. For that one horrid
moment he believed that Flem Snopes could be the victim of
pure circumstance compounded by Grover Winbush, jest like
anybody else. But only a moment. If that durn boy that seen
them two robbers in Uncle Willy's drug cabinet had to pick
out to go to the late picture show that same one night in that
whole week that Grover picked out to take jest one more slip
up that alley to Montgomery Ward's back room; if Flem Snopes
was subject to the same outrageous misfortune and coincidence
that the rest of us was, then we all might jest as well pack up
and quit.

So even after Lawyer and Hub told him about them two
robbers in Uncle Willy's store, and that boy that his paw ought
to burned his britches off for not being home in bed two hours
ago, Montgomery Ward still never had one second's doubt that
it had been Flem all the time—Flem his-self, with his pure and
simple nose for money like a preacher's for sin and fried chicken,
finding out fast and quick that profit of some degree was taking
place at night behind that alley door, and enough of it to keep
folks from as far away as three county seats sneaking up and down
that alley at two and three o'clock in the morning.

So all Flem needed now was to find out exactly what was going
on up that alley that was that discreet and that profitable, setting

his spies—not that Grover Winbush would a needed anybody
calling his-self a respectable spy with pride in his profession to
ketch him, since any little child hired with a ice-cream cone
would a done for that—to watch who come and went around
that corner; until sooner or later, and likely sooner than later,
one turned up that Flem could handle. Likely a good deal
sooner than later; even spread over four counties like that
business was, there wasn't many among the set Montgomery
Ward drawed his clientele from that hadn't at least offered to
put his name on to a piece of paper to Flem at forty or fifty
percent of three or four dollars, so that Flem could say to him:
"About that-ere little note of yourn. I'd like to hold the bank
offen you myself, but I ain't only vice-president of it, and I can't
do nothing with Manfred de Spain."

Or maybe it was Grover his-self that Flem caught, catching
Grover his-self in the active flesh on that second or third time
which was the absolute outside for Grover to slip outen that alley
without somebody ketching him, long in fact before them two
fellers robbing Uncle Willy Christian's store exposed him by
rifling that prescription desk in plain sight of half Jefferson
evidently going home from the late picture show except that
couldn't nobody locate Grover to tell him about it. Anyway,
Flem caught somebody he could squeeze enough to find out jest
what Montgomery Ward was selling behind that door. So now
all Flem had to do was move in on that industry too, move
Montgomery Ward outen it or move it out from under Montgomery Ward the same way he had been grazing on up through
Jefferson ever since he eased me and Grover Winbush outen that
café we thought we owned back there when I never had no more
sense neither than to believe I could tangle with Flem.

Only, a banker now, a vice-president, not to mention being
the third man, after the Negro that fired the furnace and the
preacher his-self, inside the Baptist Church ever Sunday morning,
and the rest of his career in Jefferson doomed to respectability
like a feller in his Sunday suit trying to run through a field of
cuckleburs and beggarlice, naturally Flem not only couldn't
show in it, it couldn't even have no connection with the word
Snopes. So as far as Jefferson was concerned the Atelier Monty
would be closed out, cleaned up and struck off the commercial

register forevermore and the business moved into another alley
that hadn't never heard of it before and under a management
that, if possible, couldn't even spell Snopes. Or likely, if Flem
had any sense, clean to another town in Montgomery Ward's
old district, where it would be clean outen Grover Winbush's
reach until at least next summer when he taken his next two
weeks' vacation.

So all Montgomery Ward had to do, all he could do in fact,
was jest to wait until Flem decided the moment was ripe to
usurp him outen his a-teelyer or usurp that a-teelyer out from
under him, whichever Flem seen fittest. Likely Montgomery
Ward had at least one moment or two of regretful musing that
his business wasn't the kind where he could a held some kind of a
quick-fire sale before Flem would have time to hear about it.
But his stock in trade being such a nebulous quantity that it
never had no existence except during the moment when the
customer was actively buying and consuming it, the only thing
he could a sold would be his capital investment itself, which
would not only be contrary to all the economic laws, he wouldn't
even have no nebulous stock in trade to sell to nobody during
whatever time he would have left before Flem foreclosed him,
which might be weeks or even months yet. So all he could do was
to apply whatever methods and means of speed-up and increased
turnover was available while waiting for Flem to move, naturally
speculating on jest what method Flem would finally use—whether
Flem had done found some kind of handle or crowbar in his,
Montgomery Ward's, own past to prize him out, or maybe
would do something as crude and unimaginative as jest offering
him money for it.

So he expected Flem. But he never expected Hub Hampton
and Lawyer Stevens. So for what you might call a flashing
moment or two after Hub and Lawyer busted in that morning,
Montgomery Ward figgered it was this here new respectability
Flem had done got involved with: a respectability that delicate
and tetchous that wouldn't nothing else suit it but it must look
like the Law itself had purified the Snopes a-teelyer industry
outen Jefferson, and so Flem was jest using Lawyer Stevens and
Hub Hampton for a cat's-paw. Of course another moment of
thoughtful deliberation would a suh-jested to him that once a

feller dedicated to civic improvement and the moral advancement of youth like Lawyer Stevens, and a meat-eating Hard-
Shell Baptist deacon like Hub Hampton got a-holt of them
nekkid photographs, there wouldn't be nothing left of that
business for Flem to move nowhere except the good will. Though
them little hard pale-coloured eyes looking down at him across
the top of Hub Hampton's belly wasn't hardly the time for
meditation and deliberation of any kind, thoughtful or not.
In fact, Montgomery Ward was so far from being deliberate or
even thinking a-tall for that matter, that it ain't surprising if in
that same flashing moment he likely cast on his cousin Flem
the horrid aspersion that Flem had let Lawyer Stevens and Hub
Hampton outfigger him; that Flem had merely aimed to close
him, Montgomery Ward, out, and was innocent enough to
believe he could get them nekkid pictures back outen Hub
Hampton's hands once Hub had seen them, and that that
cat's-paw's real name was Flem Snopes.

Though even in his extremity Montgomery Ward had more
simple sense and judgment, let alone family pride and loyalty,
than to actively believe that ten thousand Lawyer Stevenses and
Hub Hamptons, let alone jest one each of them, could a diddled
Flem Snopes. In fact, sooner than that foul aspersion, he would
believe that Flem Snopes was subject to bad luck too, jest like a
human being—not the bad luck of misreading Grover Winbush's
character that Grover could slip up and down that alley two or
three times a week for seven or eight months without ever body
in Yoknapatawpha County ketching him at least once, but the
back luck being unable to anticipate that them two robbers
would pick out the same night to rob Uncle Willy Christian's
drugstore that that Rouncewell boy would to climb down the
drain pipe and go to the late picture show.

So all Montgomery Ward had to do now was set in his jail cell
where Hub taken him and wait with what you might call almost
professional detachment and interest to see how Flem was
going to get them pictures back from Hub. It would take time
of course; even with all his veneration and family pride for
Flem Snopes, he knowed that even for Flem it wouldn't be as
simple as picking up a hat or a umbrella. So when the rest of that
day passed and hadn't nothing more happened, it was exactly

as he had anticipated. Naturally he had toyed with the notion
that, took by surprise too, Flem might call on him, Montgomery
Ward, to pick up whatever loose useful ends of information he
might have without even knowing he had none. But when Flem
never showed up nor sent word, if anything his admiration and
veneration for Flem jest increased that much more since here
was active proof that Flem wasn't going to need even what little
more, even if it wasn't no more than encouragement and moral
support, that Montgomery Ward could a told him.

And he anticipated right on through that night and what
you might call them mutual Yoknapatawpha County bedbugs,
on into the next morning too. So you can imagine his interested
surprise—not alarm yet nor even astonishment: jest interest and
surprise—when whatever thoughtful acquaintance (it was
Euphus Tubbs, the jailor; he was a interested party too, not to
mention having spent most of his life being surprised) come in
that afternoon and told him how Hub Hampton had went back
to the studio that morning jest in case him and Lawyer had
overlooked any further evidence yesterday, and instead captured
five gallons of moonshine whiskey setting in the bottles on the
shelf that Montgomery Ward his-self assumed never held
nothing but photograph developer. "Now you can go to Parchman instead of Atlanta," Euphus says. "Which won't be so fur
away. Not to mention being in Missippi, where a native Missippi
jailor can get the money for your keep instead of these durn
judges sending our Missippi boys clean out of the country where
folks we never even heard of before can collect on them."

Not alarm, not astonishment: jest interest and surprise and
even that mostly jest interest. Because Montgomery Ward
knowed that them bottles never had nothing but developer in
them when him and Hub and Laywer left the a-teelyer yesterday
morning, and he knowed that Hub Hampton and Lawyer
Stevens both knowed that was all there was in them, because for
a feller in the nekkid-photograph business in Jefferson, Missippi,
to complicate it up with peddling whiskey, would be jest pleading
for trouble, like the owner of a roulette wheel or a crap table
dreaming of running a counterfeiting press in the same basement.

Because he never had one moment's doubt it was Flem that
planted that whiskey where Hub Hampton would have to find it;

and this time his admiration and veneration notched right up to
the absolute top because he knowed that Flem, being a banker
now and having to be as tender about respectability as a un-
escorted young gal waking up suddenly in the middle of a
drummers' convention, not only couldn't a afforded to deal
with no local bootlegger and so probably had to go his-self back
out to Frenchman's Bend or maybe even all the way up into
Beat Nine to Nub Gowrie to get it, he even had to pay twenty-
five or thirty dollars of his own cash money to boot. And indeed
for a unguarded fraction of the next moment the thought might
a occurred to him how them twenty-five or thirty dollars revealed
that Flem too in the last analysis wasn't immune neither to the
strong and simple call of blood kinship. Though that was jest a
fraction of a moment, if as much as that even, because even
though Flem too at times might be victim of weakness and
aberration, wouldn't none of them ever been paying even
twenty dollars for a Snopes.

No, them twenty-five or thirty dollars simply meant that it
was going to be a little harder than Flem had expected or figgered.
But the fact that he hadn't hesitated even twenty-four hours to
pay it, showed that Flem anyhow never had no doubts about the
outcome. So naturally Montgomery Ward never had none
neither, not even needing to anticipate no more but jest to wait,
because by that time about half of Jefferson was doing the
anticipating for him and half the waiting too, not to mention
the watching. Until the next day we watched Flem cross the
Square and go up the street to the jail and go into it and half a
hour later come out again. And the next day after that Montgomery Ward was out too with Flem for his bond. And the
next day after that one Clarence Snopes was in town—Senator
Clarence Egglestone Snopes of the state legislature now, that
used to be Constable Snopes of Frenchman's Bend until he made
the mistake of pistol-whipping in the name of the Law some feller
that was spiteful and vindictive enough to object to being pistol-
whipped jest because the one doing the whipping was bigger than
him and wore a badge. So Uncle Billy Varner had to do something with Clarence so he got a-holt of Flem and both of them
got a-holt of Manfred de Spain at the bank and all three of them
got a-holt of enough other folks to get Clarence into the legis-

lature in Jackson, where he wouldn't even know nothing to do until somebody Uncle Billy and Manfred could trust would tell him when to mark his name or hold up his hand.

Except that, as Lawyer Stevens said, he seemed to found his true vocation before that: finally coming in to town from French-man's Bend one day and finding out that the country extended even on past Jefferson, on to the north-west in fact until it taken in Mulberry and Gayoso and Pontotoc streets in Memphis, Tennessee, so that when he got back three days later the very way his hair still stood up and his eyes still bugged out seemed to be saying, "Hell fire, hell fire, why wasn't I told about this sooner? How long has this been going on?" But he was making up fast for whatever time he had missed. You might say in fact he had done already passed it because now ever time he went or come between Frenchman's Bend and Jackson by way of Jefferson he went by way of Memphis too, until now he was what Lawyer Stevens called the apostolic venereal ambassador from Gayoso Avenue to the entire north Mississippi banloo.

So when on the fourth morning Montgomery Ward and Clarence got on Number Six north-bound, we knowed Clarence was jest going by Memphis to Jackson or Frenchman's Bend. But all we thought about Montgomery Ward was, jest what could he a had in that a-teelyer that even Hub never found, that was worth two thousand dollars of bond money to Flem Snopes to get him to Mexico or wherever Montgomery Ward would wind up? So ours wasn't jest interested surprise: ours was interested all right but it was astonishment and some good hard fast thinking too when two days later Clarence and Montgomery Ward both got off of Number Five south-bound and Clarence turned Montgomery Ward back over to Flem and went on to Jackson or Frenchman's Bend or wherever he would have to go to leave from to come back by Gayoso Street, Memphis, next time. And Flem turned Montgomery Ward back over to Euphus Tubbs, back into the cell in the jail, that two-thousand-dollar bond of Flem's rescinded or maybe jest withdrawed for all time like you hang your Sunday hat back on the rack until the next wedding or funeral or whenever you might need it again.

Who—I mean Euphus—apparently in his turn turned Mont-gomery Ward over to Miz Tubbs. We heard how she had even

E

hung a old shade over the cell window to keep the morning sun from waking him up so early. And how any time Lawyer Stevens or Hub Hampton or any other such members of the Law would want a word with Montgomery Ward now, the quickest place to look for him would be in Miz Tubbs's kitchen with one of her aprons on, shelling peas or husking roasting ears. And we—all right, me then—would kind of pass along the alley by the jail and there Montgomery Ward would be, him and Miz Tubbs in the garden while Montgomery Ward hoed out the vegetable rows, not making much of a out at it maybe, but anyhow swinging the hoe as long as Miz Tubbs showed him where to chop next.

"Maybe she's still trying to find out about them pictures," Homer Bookwright says.

"What?" I says. "Miz Tubbs?"

"Of course she wants to know about them," Homer says. "Ain't she human too, even if she is a woman?"

And three weeks later Montgomery Ward stood up in Judge Long's court and Judge Long give him two years in the state penitentiary at Parchman for the possession of one developer jug containing one gallon of moonshine whiskey herewith in evidence.

So ever body was wrong. Flem Snopes hadn't spent no two thousand dollars' worth of bond money to purify Montgomery Ward outen the U.S.A. America, and he hadn't spent no twenty-five or thirty dollars' worth of white-mule whiskey jest to purify the Snopes family name outen Atlanta, Georgia. What he had done was to spend twenty-five or thirty dollars to send Montgomery Ward to Parchman when the government would a sent him to Georgia free. Which was a good deal more curious than jest surprising, and a good deal more interesting than all three. So the next morning I happened to be on the depot platform when Number Eleven south-bound was due and sho enough, there was Montgomery Ward and Hunter Killegrew, the deputy, and I says to Hunter: "Don't you need to step into the washroom before you get on the train for such a long trip? I'll watch Montgomery Ward for you. Besides, a feller that wouldn't run off three weeks ago under a two-thousand-dollar bond ain't likely to try it now with nothing on him but a handcuff."

So Hunter handed me his half of the handcuff and moved a little away and I says to Montgomery Ward:

"So you're going to Parchman instead. That'll be a heap better. Not only you won't be depriving no native-born Missippi grub contractor outen his rightful and natural profit on the native-born Missippi grub they'll be feeding a native-born Missippi convict, you won't be lonesome there neither, having a native-born Missippi cousin or uncle to pass the time with when you ain't otherwise occupied with field work or something. What's his name? Mink Snopes, your uncle or cousin that got in that little trouble a while back for killing Jack Houston and kept trying to wait for Flem to come back from Texas in time to get him outen it, except that Flem was otherwise occupied too and so Mink acted kind to put out about it? Which was he, your uncle or your cousin?"

"Yeah?" Montgomery Ward says.

"Well, which?" I says.

"Which what?" Montgomery Ward says.

"Is he your uncle or is he your cousin?" I says.

"Yeah?" Montgomery Ward says.

FOUR

Montgomery Ward Snopes

"So the son of a bitch fooled you," I said. "You thought they were going to hang him, but all he got was life."

He didn't answer. He just sat there in the kitchen chair—he had toted it up himself from Tubbs's kitchen. For me, there wasn't anything in the cell but the cot—for me and the bedbugs that is. He just sat there with the shadow of the window bars crisscrossing that white shirt and that damn little ten-cent snap-on bow tie; they said the same one he had worn in from Frenchman's Bend sixteen years ago. No: they said not the same one he took out of Varner's stock and put on the day he came in from that tenant farm and went to work as Varner's clerk and married Varner's whore of a daughter in and wore to Texas while the bastard kid was getting born and then wore back again; that was when he wore the cloth cap about the size for a fourteen-year-old child. And the black felt hat somebody told him was the kind of hat bankers wore, that he didn't throw away the cap: he sold it to a nigger boy for a dime that he took out in work and put the hat on for the first time three years ago and they said had never taken it off since, not even in the house, except in church, and still looked new. No, it didn't look like it belonged to anybody, even after day and night for three years, not even sweated, which would include while he was laying his wife too which would be all right with her probably since the sort of laying she was used to they probably didn't even take off their gloves, let alone their hats and shoes and overcoats.

And chewing. They said when he first came in to Frenchman's Bend as Varner's clerk it was tobacco. Then he found out about money. Oh, he had heard about money and had even seen a little of it now and then. But now he found out for the first time that there was more of it each day than you could eat up each day if you ate twice as much fried sowbelly and white gravy. Not only that, but that it was solid, harder than bones and heavy like gravel, and that if you could shut your hands on some of it, there was no power anywhere that could make you let go of more of it than you had to let go of, so he found out that he couldn't afford to chew up ten cents' worth of it every week because he had discovered chewing gum by then that a nickel's worth of would last five weeks, a new stick every Sunday. Then he came to Jefferson and he really saw some money, I mean all at one time, and then he found out that the only limit to the amount of money you could shut your hands on and keep and hold, was just how much money there was, provided you had a good safe place to put that other handful down and fill your fists again. And then was when he found out he couldn't afford to chew even one cent a week. When he had nothing, he could afford to chew tobacco; when he had a little, he could afford to chew gum; when he found out he could be rich provided he just didn't die beforehand, he couldn't afford to chew anything, just sitting there in that kitchen chair with the shadow of the cell bars crisscrossing him, chewing that and not looking at me or not any more anyway.

"Life," I said. "That means twenty years, the way they figure it, unless something happens between now and then. How long has it been now? Nineteen eight, wasn't it, when he hung all day long maybe in this same window here, watching the street for you to come on back from Texas and get him out, being as you were the only Snopes then that had enough money and influence to help him as he figured it, hollering down to anybody that passed to get word out to Varner's store for you to come in and save him, then standing up there in that courtroom on that last day and giving you your last chance, and you never came then either? Nineteen eight to nineteen twenty-three from twenty years, and he'll be out again. Hell fire, you've only got five more years to live, haven't you? All right. What do you want me to do?"

He told me.

"All right," I said. "What do I get for it?"

He told me that. I stood there for a while leaning against the wall, laughing down at him. Then I told him.

He didn't even move. He just quit chewing long enough to say, "Ten thousand dollars."

"So that's too high," I said. "All your life is worth to you is about five hundred, mostly in trade, on the installment plan." He sat there in that cross-barred shadow, chewing his mouthful of nothing, watching me or at least looking toward me. "Even if it works, the best you can do is get his sentence doubled, get twenty more years added on to it. That means that in nineteen forty-three you'll have to start all over again worrying about having only five years more to live. Quit sucking and smouching around for bargains. Buy the best: you can afford it. Take ten grand cash and have him killed. From what I hear, for that jack you could have all Chicago bidding against each other. Or ten grand, hell, and Chicago, hell too; for one you could stay right here in Mississippi and have a dozen trusties right there in Parchman drawing straws for him, for which one would shoot him first in the back."

He didn't even quit chewing this time.

"Well well," I said. "So there's something that even a Snopes won't do. No, that's wrong; Uncle Mink never seemed to have any trouble reconciling Jack Houston up in front of that shotgun when the cheese began to bind. Maybe what I mean is, every Snopes has one thing he won't do to you—provided you can find out what it is before he has ruined and wrecked you. Make it five then," I said. "I won't haggle. What the hell, ain't we cousins or something?"

This time he quit chewing long enough to say, "Five thousand dollars."

"Okay, I know you haven't got five grand cash either now," I said. "You don't even need it now. That lawyer says you got two years to raise it in, hock or sell or steal whatever you'll have to hock or sell or steal."

That got to him—or so I thought then. I'm a pretty slow learner myself sometimes, now and then, mostly now in fact. Because he said something: "You won't have to stay two years. I can get you out."

"When?" I said. "When you're satisfied? When I have wrecked the rest of his life by getting twenty more years hung on to it? Not me, you won't. Because I won't come out. I wouldn't even take the five grand; I was kidding you. This is how we'll do it. I'll go on down there and fix him, get him whatever additional time the traffic will bear. Only I won't come out then. I'll finish out my two years first; give you a little more time of your own, see. Then I'll come out and come on back home. You know: start a new life, live down that old bad past. Of course I won't

have any job, business, but after all there's my own father's
own first cousin every day and every way getting to be bigger and
bigger in the bank and the church and local respectability and
civic reputation and what the hell, ain't blood thicker than
just water even if some of it is just back from Parchman for
bootlegging, not to mention at any minute now his pride might
revolt at charity even from his respectable blood-kin banker
cousin and he might decide to set up that old unrespectable but
fairly damned popular business again. Because I can get plenty
more stock-in-trade and the same old good will will still be here
just waiting for me to tell them where to go and maybe this
time there won't be any developer-fluid jugs sitting carelessly
around. And suppose they are, what the hell? it's just two years
and I'll be back again, already reaching to turn over that old
new leaf—"

He put his hand inside his coat and he didn't say "Yep"
in that tone because he didn't know how yet, but if he had
known he would. So he said, "Yep, that's what I figgered," and
drew out the envelope. Oh sure, I recognised it. It was one of
mine, the *Atelier Monty Jefferson Miss* in the left corner, all
stamped and showing the cancellation clear as an etching and
addressed to *G. C. Winbush, City* so I already knew what was in it
before he even took it out: the photo that Winbush had insisted
on buying for five bucks for his private files as they call it that I
hadn't wanted to let him have it because anybody associating
with him in anything was already in jeopardy. But what the
hell, he was the Law, or what passed for it in that alley at one
or two in the morning anyway. And oh yes, it had been through
the mail all right even though I never mailed it and it hadn't
been any further than through that damn cancelling machine
inside the Jefferson post office. And with the trouble Winbush
was already in from being in my back room instead of getting
what he called his brains beaten out by old dope-eating Will
Christian's burglars, it wouldn't have taken any Simon Legree
to find out he had the picture and then to get it away from him;
nor anything at all to make him swear or perjure to anything
anybody suggested to him regarding it. Because he had a wife
and all you'd heed would be just to intimate to Winbush you
were going to show it to her since she was the sort of wife that

no power on earth would unconvince her that the girl in the photo—she happened to be alone in this one and happened not to be doing anything except just being buck-naked—was not only Winbush's private playmate but that probably only some last desperate leap got Winbush himself out of the picture without his pants on. And it wouldn't take any Sherlock Holmes to discern what that old sanctimonious lantern-jawed son of a bitch up there on that federal bench would do when he saw that cancelled envelope. So I said,

"So it looks like I've been raised. And it looks like I won't call. In fact, it looks like I'm going to pass. After I go down there and get him fixed, you get me out. Then what?"

"A railroad ticket to wherever you want, and a hundred dollars."

"Make it five," I said. Then I said, "All right. I won't haggle. Make it two-fifty." And he didn't haggle either.

"A hundred dollars," he said.

"Only I'm going to cut the pot for the house kitty," I said. "If I've got to spend at least a year locked up in a god-damned cotton farm—" No, he didn't haggle; you could say that for him.

"I figgered that too," he said. "It's all arranged. You'll be out on bond tomorrow. Clarence will pick you up on his way through town to Memphis. You can have two days." And by God he had even thought of that too. "Clarence will have the money. It will be enough."

Whether what he would call enough or what I would call enough. So nobody was laughing at anybody any more now. I just stood there looking down at him where he sat in that kitchen chair, chewing, not looking at anything and not even chewing anything, that everybody that knew him said he never took a drink in his life yet hadn't hesitated to buy thirty or forty dollars' worth of whiskey to get me into Parchman where I could wreck Mink, and evidently was getting ready to spend another hundred (or more likely two if he intended to pay for Clarence too) to reconcile me to staying in Parchman long enough to do the wrecking that would keep Mink from getting out in five years; and all of a sudden I knew what it was that had bothered me about him ever since I got big enough to understand about such and maybe draw a conclusion.

"So you're a virgin," I said. "You never had a lay in your

life, did you? You even waited to get married until you found
a woman who not only was already knocked up, she wouldn't
even have let you run your hand up her dress. Jesus, you do
want to stay alive, don't you? Only, why?" And still he said
nothing: just sitting there chewing nothing. "But why put out
money on Clarence too? Even if he does prefer nigger houses
where the top price is a dollar, it'll cost you something with
Clarence as the operator. Give me all the money and let me go
by myself." But as soon as I said it I knew the answer to that too.
He couldn't risk letting me get one mile out of Jefferson without
somebody along to see I came back, even with that cancelled
envelope in his pocket. He knew better, but he couldn't risk
finding out he was right. He didn't dare. He didn't dare at his
age to find out that all you need to handle nine people out of
ten is just to trust them.

Tubbs knew about the bond so he was all for turning me out
that night so he could put the cost of my supper in his pocket and
hope that in the confusion it wouldn't be noticed but I said Much
obliged. I said: "Don't brag. I was in (on the edge of it anyway)
the U.S. Army; if you think this dump is lousy, you should have
seen some of the places I slept in," with Tubbs standing there
in the open cell door with the key ring in one hand and scratching
his head with the other. "But what you can do, go out and get
me a decent supper; Mr Snopes will pay for it; my rich kinfolks
have forgiven me now. And while you're about it, bring me the
Memphis paper." So he started out until this time I hollered it:
"Come back and lock the door! I don't want all Jefferson in
here; one son of a bitch in this kennel is enough."

So the next morning Clarence showed up and Flem gave him
the money and that night we were in Memphis, at the Teaberry.
That was me. Clarence knew a dump where he was a regular
customer, where we could stay for a dollar a day even when it
wasn't even his money. Flem's money, that you would have
thought anybody else named Snopes would have slept on the
bare ground provided it just cost Flem twice as much as anywhere
else would.

"Now what?" Clarence said. It was what they call rhetorical.
He already knew what, or thought he did. He had it all lined up.
One thing about Clarence: he never let you down. He couldn't;

everybody that knew him knew he would have to be a son of a bitch, being my half-brother.

Last year Virgil (that's right. Snopes. You guessed it: Uncle Wesley's youngest boy—the revival song leader that they caught after church that day with the fourteen-year-old girl in the empty cotton house and tar-and-feathered him to Texas or anyway out of Yoknapatawpha County; Virgil's gift was inherited) and Fonzo Winbush, my patient's nephew I believe it is, came up to Memphis to enter a barbers' college. Somebody —it would be Mrs Winbush; she wasn't a Snopes—evidently told them never to rent a room to live in unless the woman of the house looked mature and Christian, but most of all motherly.

So they were probably still walking concentric circles around the railroad station, still carrying their suitcases, when they passed Reba Rivers's at the time when every afternoon she would come out her front door to exercise those two damn nasty little soiled white dogs that she called Miss Reba and Mr Binford after Lucius Binford who had been her pimp until they both got too old and settled down and all the neighbourhood —the cop, the boy that brought the milk and collected for the paper, and the people on the laundry truck—called him landlord until he finally died.

She looked mature all right in anything, let alone the wrappers she wore around that time in the afternoon, and she would probably sound Christian all right whether religious or not, to anybody near enough to hear what she would say to those dogs at times when she had had a little extra gin; and I suppose anybody weighing two hundred pounds in a wrapper fastened with safety pins would look motherly even while she was throwing out a drunk, let alone to two eighteen-year-old boys from Jefferson, Mississippi.

Maybe she was motherly and Virgil and Fonzo, in the simple innocence of children, saw what us old long-standing mere customers and friends missed. Or maybe they just walked impervious in that simple Yoknapatawpha juvenile rural innocence where even an angel would have left his pocketbook at the depot first. Anyway, they asked if she had an empty room and she rented them one; likely they had already unpacked those paper suitcases before she realised they didn't even know they were in a whorehouse.

Anyhow, there she was, having to pay the rent and pay off the cops and the man that supplied the beer, and pay the laundry and Minnie, the maid, something on Sunday night, not to mention having to keep those big yellow diamonds shined and cleaned until they wouldn't look too much like big chunks of a broken beer bottle; and that Yoknapatawpha innocence right in the middle of the girls running back and forth to the bathroom in nighties and negligees or maybe not even that, and the customers going and coming and Minnie running stacks of towels and slugs of gin up the stairs and the women screaming and fighting and pulling each other's hair over their boys and clients and money, and Reba herself in the hall cursing a drunk while they tried to throw him out before the cops got there; until in less than a week she had that house as quiet and innocent as a girls' school until she could get Virgil and Fonzo upstairs into their room and in bed and, she hoped, asleep.

Naturally it couldn't last. To begin with, there was the barbers' college where they would have to listen to barbers all day long when you have to listen to enough laying just spending thirty minutes getting your hair cut. Then to come back there and get a flash of a leg or a chemise or maybe a whole naked female behind running through a door, would be bound to give them ideas after a time even though Virgil and Fonzo still thought they were all Reba's nieces or wards or something just in town maybe attending female equivalents of barbers' colleges themselves. Not to mention that pure instinct which Virgil and Fonzo (did I say he was Grover Winbush's nephew?) had inherited from the pure fountainheads themselves.

It didn't last past the second month. And since the Memphis red-light district is not all that big, it was only the course of time until they and Clarence turned up at the same time in the same place, especially as Virgil and Fonzo, still forced to devote most of their time to learning yet and not earning, had to hunt for bargains. Where right away Virgil showed himself the owner of a really exceptional talent—a capacity to take care of two girls in succession to their satisfaction or at least until they hollered quit, that was enough for two dollars, in his youthful enthusiasm and innocence not only doing it for pleasure but even paying for the chance until Clarence discovered him and put him into the money.

He—Clarence—would loaf around the poolrooms and the sort of hotel lobbies he patronised himself, until he would find a sucker who refused to believe his bragging about his—what's the word?—protégé's powers, and Clarence would bet him; the first victim would usually give odds. Of course Virgil would fail now and then—

"And pay half the bet," I said.

"What?" Clarence said. "Penalise the boy for doing his best? Besides, it don't happen once in ten times and he's going to get better as time goes on. What a future that little sod's got if the supply of two-dollar whores just holds out."

Anyway, that's what we were going to do tonight. "Much obliged," I said. "You go ahead, I'm going to make a quiet family call on an old friend and then coming back to bed. Let me have twenty-five—make it thirty of the money."

"Flem gave me a hundred."

"Thirty will do," I said.

"Be damned if that's so," he said. "You'll take half of it. I don't aim to take you back to Jefferson and have you tell Flem a god-damn lie about me. Here."

I took the money. "See you at the station tomorrow at train time."

"What?" he said.

"I'm going home tomorrow. You don't have to."

"I promised Flem I'd stay with you and bring you back."

"Break it," I said. "Haven't you got fifty dollars of his money?"

"That's it," he said. "Damn a son of a bitch that'll break his word after he's been paid for it."

Wednesday evenings were nearly always quiet unless there was a convention in town, maybe because so many of the women (clients too) came from little Tennessee and Arkansas and Mississippi country towns and Baptist and Methodist families, that they established among the joints and dives and cathouses themselves some . . . analogous? analogous rhythm to the mid-week prayer-meeting night. Minnie answered the bell. She had her hat on. I mean her whole head was in it like a football helmet.

"Evening, Minnie," I said. "You going out?"

"No sir," she said. "You been away? We ain't seen you in a long time."

"Just busy," I answered. That was what Reba said too. The place was quiet: nobody in the dining-room but Reba and a new girl and one customer, drinking beer, Reba in all her big yellow diamonds but wearing a wrapper instead of the evening-gown she would have had on if it had been Saturday night. It was a new wrapper, but it was already fastened with safety pins. I answered the same thing too. "Just busy," I said.

"I wish I could return the compliment," she said. "I might as well be running a Sunday school. Meet Captain Strutterbuck," she said. He was tall, pretty big, with a kind of roustabout's face; I mean, that tried to look tough but wasn't sure yet how you were going to take it, and hard pale eyes that looked at you hard enough, only he couldn't seem to look at you with both of them at the same time. He was about fifty. "Captain Strutterbuck was in both wars," Reba said. "That Spanish one about twenty-five years ago, and the last one too. He was just telling us about the last one. And this is Thelma. She just came in last week."

"Howdy," Strutterbuck said. "Were you a buddy too?"

"More or less," I said.

"What outfit?"

"Lafayette Escadrille," I said.

"Laughing what?" he said. "Oh, La-Fayette Esker-Drill. Flying boys. Don't know anything about flying, myself. I was cavalry, in Cuba in '98 and on the Border in '16, not commissioned any longer, out of the army in fact: just sort of a private citizen aide to Black Jack because I knew the country. So when they decided to send him to France to run the show over there, he told me if I ever got across to look him up, he would try to find something for me. So when I heard that Rick—Eddie Rickenbacker, the Ace," he told Reba and the new girl, "the General's driver—that Rick had left him for the air corps, I decided that was my chance and I managed to get over all right but he already had another driver, a Sergeant Somebody, I forgot his name. So there I was, with no status. But I still managed to see a little of it, from the back seat you might say

—Argonne, Showmont, Vymy Ridge, Shatter Theory; you probably saw most of the hot places yourself. Where you were stationed?"

"Y.M.C.A.," I said.

"What?" he said. He got up, slow. He was tall, pretty big; this probably wasn't the first time both his eyes had failed to look at the same thing at the same time. Maybe he depended on it. By that time Reba was up too. "You wouldn't be trying to kid me, would you?" he said.

"Why?" I said. "Don't it work?"

"All right, all right," Reba said. "Are you going upstairs with Thelma, or ain't you? If you ain't, and you usually ain't, tell her so."

"I don't know whether I am or not," he said. "What I think right now is—"

"Folks don't come in here to think," Reba said. "They come in here to do business and then get out. Do you aim to do any business or don't you?"

"Okay, okay," he said. "Let's go," he told Thelma. "Maybe I'll see you again," he told me.

"After the next war," I said. He and Thelma went out. "Are you going to let him?" I said.

"He gets a pension from that Spanish war," Reba said. "It came today. I saw it. I watched him sign his name on the back of it so I can cash it."

"How much?" I said.

"I didn't bother with the front of it. I just made damn sure he signed his name where the notice said sign. It was a United States Government post-office money order. You don't fool around with the United States Government."

"A post-office money order can be for one cent provided you can afford the carrying charges," I said. She looked at me. "He wrote his name on the back of a piece of blue paper and put it back in his pocket. I suppose he borrowed the pen from you. Was that it?"

"All right, all right," she said. "What do you want me to do: lean over the foot of the bed and say, Just a second there, Buster?"—Minnie came in with another bottle of beer. It was for me.

"I didn't order it," I said. "Maybe I should have told you right off. I'm not going to spend any money tonight."

"It's on me then. Why did you come here then? Just to try to pick a fight with somebody?"

"Not with him," I said. "He even got his name out a book. I don't remember what book right now, but it was a better book than the one he got his war out of."

"All right, all right," she said. "Why in hell did you tell him where you were staying? Come to think of it, why are you staying there?"

"Staying where?" I said.

"At the Y.M.C.A. I have some little squirts in here now and then that ought to be at the Y.M.C.A. whether they are or not. But I never had one of them bragging about it before."

"I'm at the Teaberry," I said. "I belonged to the Y.M.C.A. in the war."

"The Y.M.C.A.? In the war? They don't fight. Are you trying to kid me too?"

"I know they don't," I said. "That's why I was in it. That's right. That's where I was. Gavin Stevens, a lawyer down in Jefferson, can tell you. The next time he's in here ask him."

Minnie appeared in the door with a tray with two glasses of gin on it. She didn't say anything: she just stood in the door there where Reba could see her. She still wore the hat.

"All right," Reba said. "But no more. He never paid for that beer yet. But Miss Thelma's new in Memphis and we want to make her feel at home." Minnie went away. "So you're not going to unbutton your pocket tonight."

"I came to ask you a favour," I said. But she wasn't even listening.

"You never did spend much. Oh, you were free enough buying beer and drinks around. But you never done any jazzing. Not with any of my girls, anyway." She was looking at me. "Me neither. I've done outgrowed that too. We could get along." She was looking at me. "I heard about that little business of yours down there in the country. A lot of folks in business here don't like it. They figure you are cutting into trade un—un— What's that word? Lawyers and doctors are always throwing it at you."

"Unethical," I said. "It means dry."

"Dry?" she said.

"That's right. You might call my branch of your business the arid or waterproof branch. The desert-outpost branch."

"Yes, sure, I see what you mean. That's it exactly. That's what I would tell them: that just looking at pictures might do all right for a while down there in the country where there wasn't no other available handy outlet but that sooner or later somebody was going to run up enough temperature to where he would have to run to the nearest well for a bucket of real water, and maybe it would be mine." She was looking at me. "Sell it out and come on up here."

"Is this a proposition?" I said.

"All right. Come on up here and be the landlord. The beer and drinks is already on the house and you wouldn't need much but cigarettes and clothes and a little jack to rattle in your pocket and I can afford that and I wouldn't have to be always watching you about the girls, just like Mr Binford because I could always trust him too, always—" She was looking at me. There was something in her eyes or somewhere I never had seen before or expected either for that matter. "I nee— A man can do what a woman can't. You know: paying off protection, handling drunks, checking up on the son-a-bitching beer and whiskey peddlers that mark up prices and miscount bottles if you ain't watching day and night like a god-damn hawk." Sitting there looking at me, one fat hand with that diamond the size of a piece of gravel holding the beer glass. "I need . . . I . . . not jazzing; I done outgrowed that too long a time ago. It's—it's . . . Three years ago he died, yet even now I still can't quite believe it." It shouldn't have been there: the fat raddled face and body that had worn themselves out with the simple hard physical work of being a whore and making a living at it like an old prize fighter or football player or maybe an old horse until they didn't look like a man's or a woman's either in spite of the cheap rouge and too much of it and the big diamonds that were real enough even if you just did not believe that colour, and the eyes with something in or behind them that shouldn't have been there; that, as they say, shouldn't happen to a dog. Minnie passed the door going back down the hall. The tray was empty now. "For fourteen years we was like two doves." She looked at me. Yes, not even to a dog. "Like two doves," she roared and lifted the glass of beer then banged it down hard and shouted at the door: "Minnie!" Minnie came back to the door. "Bring the gin," Reba said.

"Now, Miss Reba, you don't want to start that," Minnie said. "Don't you remember, last time you started grieving about Mr Binford we had po-lice in here until four o'clock in the morning. Drink your beer and forget about gin."

"Yes," Reba said. She even drank some of the beer. Then she set the glass down. "You said something about a favour. It can't be money—I ain't talking about your nerve: I mean your good sense. So it might be interesting—"

"Expect it is money," I said. I took out the fifty dollars and separated ten from it and pushed the ten across to her. "I'm going away for a couple of years. That's for you to remember me by." She didn't touch it. She wasn't even looking at it, though Minnie was. She just looked at me. "Maybe Minnie can help too," I said. "I want to make a present of forty dollars to the poorest son of a bitch I can find. Who is the poorest son of a bitch anywhere at this second that you and Minnie know?"

They were both looking at me, Minnie too from under the hat. "How do you mean, poor?" Reba said.

"That's in trouble or jail or somewhere that maybe wasn't his fault."

"Minnie's husband is a son of a bitch and he's in jail all right," Reba said. "But I wouldn't call him poor. Would you, Minnie?"

"Nome," Minnie said.

"But at least he's out of woman trouble for a while," Reba told Minnie. "That ought to make you feel a little better."

"You don't know Ludus," Minnie said. "I like to see any place, chain gang or not, where Ludus can't find some fool woman to believe him."

"What did he do?" I said.

"He quit his job last winter and laid around here ever since, eating out of my kitchen and robbing Minnie's pocket-book every night after she went to sleep, until she caught him actually giving the money to the other woman, and when she tried to ask him to stop he snatched the flatiron out of her hand and damn near tore her ear off with it. That's why she has to wear a hat

F

all the time even in the house. So I'd say if any—if anybody deserved them forty dollars it would be Minnie—"

A woman began screaming at the top of the stairs in the upper hall. Minnie and Reba ran out. I picked up the money and followed. The woman screaming the curses was the new girl, Thelma, standing at the head of the stairs in a flimsy kimono, or more or less of it. Captain Strutterbuck was halfway down the stairs, wearing his hat and carrying his coat in one hand and trying to button his fly with the other. Minnie was at the foot of the stairs. She didn't outshout Thelma nor even shout her silent: Minnie just had more volume, maybe more practice:

"Course he never had no money. He ain't never had more than two dollars at one time since he been coming here. Why you ever let him get on the bed without the money in your hand first, I don't know. I bet he never even took his britches off. A man won't take his britches off, don't never have no truck with him a-tall; he done already shook his foot, no matter what his mouth still saying."

"All right," Reba told Minnie. "That'll do." Minnie stepped back; even Thelma hushed; she saw me or something and even pulled the kimono back together in front. Strutterbuck came on down the stairs, still fumbling at the front of his pants; maybe the last thing he did want was for both his eyes to look at the same thing at the same time. But I don't know; according to Minnie he had no more reason to be alarmed and surprised now at where he was than a man walking a tightrope. Concerned of course and damned careful, but not really alarmed and last of all surprised. He reached the downstairs floor. But he was not done yet. There were still eight or ten feet to the front door.

But Reba was a lady. She just held her hand out until he quit fumbling at his fly and took the folded money order out of whatever pocket it was in and handed it to her. A lady. She never raised her hand at him. She never even cursed him. She just went to the front door and took hold of the knob and turned and said, "Button yourself up. Ain't no man going to walk out of my house at just eleven o'clock at night with his pants still hanging open." Then she closed the door after him and locked it. Then she unfolded the money order. Minnie was right. It was for two dollars, issued at Lonoke, Arkansas. The sender's name was spelled Q'Milla Strutterbuck. "His sister or his daughter?" Reba said. "What's your guess?"

Minnie was looking too. "It's his wife," she said. "His sister or mama or grandma would sent five. His woman would sent fifty—if she had it and felt like sending it. His daughter would sent fifty cents. Wouldn't nobody but his wife sent two dollars."

She brought two more bottles of beer to the dining-room table. "All right," Reba said. "You want a favour. What favour?"

I took out the money again and shoved the ten across to her again, still holding the other forty. "This is for you and Minnie, to remember me until I come back in two years. I want you to send the other to my great-uncle in the Mississippi penitentiary at Parchman."

"Will you come back in two years?"

"Yes," I said. "You can look for me. Two years. The man I'm going to be working for says I'll be back in one, but I don't believe him."

"All right. Now what do I do with the forty?"

"Send it to my great-uncle Mink Snopes in Parchman."

"What's he in for?"

"He killed a man named Jack Houston back in 1908."

"Did Houston deserve killing?"

"I don't know. But from what I hear, he sure worked to earn it."

"The poor son of a bitch. How long is your uncle in for?"

"Life," I said.

"All right," she said. "I know about that too. When will he get out?"

"About 1948 if he lives and nothing else happens to him."

"All right. How do I do it?" I told her, the address and all.

"You could send it From another prisoner."

"I doubt it," she said. "I ain't never been in jail. I don't aim to be."

"Send it From a friend then."

"All right," she said. She took the money and folded it. "The poor son of a bitch," she said.

"Which one are you talking about now?"

"Both of them," she said. "All of us. Every one of us. The poor son of a bitches."

I hadn't expected to see Clarence at all until tomorrow morning. But there he was, a handful of crumpled bills scattered on the top of the dresser like the edge of a crap game and Clarence undressed down to his trousers standing looking at them and yawning and rooting in the pelt on his chest. This time they—Clarence—had found a big operator, a hot sport who, Virgil having taken on the customary two successfully, bet them he couldn't handle a third one without stopping, offering them the odds this time, which Clarence covered with Flem's other fifty since this really would be a risk; he said how he even gave Virgil a chance to quit and not hold it against him: " 'We're ahead now, you know; you done already proved yourself.' And do you know, the little sod never even turned a hair. 'Sure,' he says, 'Send her in.' And now my conscience hurts me," he said, yawning again. "It was Flem's money. My conscience says don't tell him a durn thing about it: the money just got spent like he thinks it was. But shucks, a man don't want to be a hog."

So we went back home. "Why do you want to go back to the jail?" Flem said. "It'll be three weeks yet."

"Call it for practice," I said. "Call it a dry run against my conscience." So now I had a set of steel bars between; now I was safe from the free world, safe and secure for a little while from the free Snopes world where Flem was parlaying his wife into the presidency of a bank and Clarence even drawing per diem as a state senator between Jackson and Gayoso Street to take the wraps off Virgil whenever he could find another Arkansas sport who refused to believe what he was looking at, and Byron in Mexico or wherever he was with whatever was still left of the bank's money, and mine and Clarence's father I.O. and all of our Uncle Wesley leading a hymn with one hand and fumbling the skirt of an eleven-year-old infant with the other; I don't count Wallstreet and Admiral Dewey and their father Eck, because they don't belong to us: they are only our shame.

Not to mention Uncle Murdering Mink six or seven weeks later (I had to wait a little while you see not to spook him too quick). "Flem?" he said. "I wouldn't a thought Flem wanted me out. I'd a thought he'd been the one wanted to keep me here longest."

"He must have changed," I said. He stood there in his barred overalls, blinking a little—a damn little worn-out dried-up shrimp of a man not as big as a fourteen-year-old boy. Until you wondered how in hell anything as small and frail could have held enough mad, let alone steadied and aimed a ten-gauge shotgun, to kill anybody.

"I'm obliged to him," he said. "Only, if I got out tomorrow, maybe I won't done changed. I been here a long time now. I ain't had much to do for a right smart while now but jest work in the field and think. I wonder if he knows to risk that? A man wants to be fair, you know."

"He knows that," I said. "He don't expect you to change inside here because he knows you can't. He expects you to change when you get out. Because he knows that as soon as the free air and sun shine on you again, you can't help but be a changed man even if you don't want to."

"But jest suppose I don't—" He didn't add *change in time* because he stopped himself.

"He's going to take that risk," I said. "He's got to. I mean, he's got to now. He couldn't have stopped them from sending you here. But he knows you think he didn't try. He's got to help you get out not only to prove to you he never put you here but so he can quit thinking and remembering that you believe he did. You see?"

He was completely still, just blinking a little, his hands hanging empty but even now shaped inside the palms like the handles of a plow and even his neck braced a little as though still braced against the loop of the ploughlines. "I just got five more years, then I'll get out by myself. Then won't nobody have no right to hold expectations against me. I won't owe nobody no help then."

"That's right," I said. "Just five more years. That's practically nothing to a man that has already put in fifteen years with a man with a shotgun watching him plow cotton that ain't his whether he feels like plowing that day or not, and another man with a shotgun standing over him while he eats grub that he either ate it or not whether he felt like eating or not, and another man with a shotgun to lock him up at night so he could either go to sleep or stay awake whether he felt like doing it or not. Just five years more, then you'll be out where the free sun and air can shine on you without any man with a shotgun's shadow to cut it off. Because you'll be free."

"Free," he said, not loud: just like that: "Free." That was all. It was that easy. Of course the guard I welshed to cursed me; I had expected that: it was a free country; every convict had a right to try to escape just as every guard and trusty had the right to shoot him in the back the first time he didn't halt. But no unprintable stool pigeon had the right to warn the guard in advance.

I had to watch it too. That was on the bill too: the promissory note of breathing in a world that had Snopeses in it. I wanted to turn my head or anyway shut my eyes. But refusing to not look was all I had left now: the last sorry lousy almost worthless penny—the damn little thing looking like a little girl playing mama in the calico dress and sun-bonnet that he believed was Flem's idea (that had been difficult; he still wanted to believe that a man should be permitted to run at his fate, even if that fate was doom, in the decency and dignity of pants; it took a little doing to persuade him that a petticoat and a woman's sunbonnet was all Flem could get). Walking; I had impressed that on him: not to run, but walk; as forlorn and lonely and fragile and alien in that empty penitentiary compound as a paper doll blowing across a rolling-mill; still walking even after he had passed the point where he couldn't come back and knew it; even still walking on past the moment when he knew that he had been sold and that he should have known all along he was being sold, not blaming anybody for selling him nor even needing to sell him because hadn't he signed—he couldn't read but he could sign his name—that same promissory note too to breathe a little while, since his name was Snopes?

So he even ran before he had to. He ran right at them before I even saw them, before they stepped out of the ambush. I was proud, not just to be kin to him but of belonging to what Reba called all of us poor son of a bitches. Because it took five of them striking and slashing at his head with pistol barrels and even then it finally took the blackjack to stop him, knock him out.

The Warden sent for me. "Don't tell me anything," he said. "I wish I didn't even know as much already as I suspect. In fact, if it was left to me, I'd like to lock you and him both in a

cell and leave you, you for choice in handcuffs. But I'm under a
bond too so I'm going to move you into solitary for a week or so,
for your own protection. And not from him."

"Don't brag or grieve," I said. "You had to sign one of them
too."

"What?" he said. "What did you say?"

"I said you don't need to worry. He hasn't got anything
against me. If you don't believe me, send for him."

So he came in. The bruises and slashes from the butts and the
blades of the sights were healing fine. The blackjack of course
never had showed. "Hidy," he said. To me. "I reckon you'll
see Flem before I will now."

"Yes," I said.

"Tell him he hadn't ought to used that dress. But it don't
matter. If I had made it out then, maybe I would a changed.
But I reckon I won't now. I reckon I'll jest wait."

So Flem should have taken that suggestion about the ten grand.
He could still do it. I could write him a letter: *Sure you can raise
ten thousand. All you need to do is swap Manfred de Spain a good jump
at your wife. No: that won't do: trying to peddle Eula Varner to Manfred
de Spain is like trying to sell a horse to a man that's already been feeding
and riding it for ten or twelve years. But you got that girl, Linda. She
ain't but eleven or twelve but what the hell, put smoked glasses and high
heels on her and rush her in quick and maybe De Spain won't notice it.*

Except that I wasn't going to. But it wasn't that that worried
me. It was knowing that I wasn't, knowing I was going to throw
it away—I mean my commission of the ten grand for contacting
the Chi syndicate for him. I don't remember just when it was, I
was probably pretty young, when I realised that I had come
from what you might call a family, a clan, a race, maybe even
a species, of pure sons of bitches. So I said, *Okay, okay, if that's the
way it is, we'll just show them. They call the best of lawyers, lawyers'
lawyers and the best of actors an actor's actor and the best of athletes a
ballplayer's ballplayer. All right, that's what we'll do: every Snopes
will make it his private and personal aim to have the whole world recognise
him as THE son of a bitch's son of a bitch.*

But we never do it. We never make it. The best we ever do is
to be just another Snopes son of a bitch. All of us, every one of
us—Flem, and old Ab that I don't even know exactly what kin

he is, and Uncle Wes and mine and Clarence's father I.O., then right on down the line: Clarence and me by what you might call simultaneous bigamy, and Virgil and Vardaman and Bilbo and Byron and Mink. I don't even mention Eck and Wallstreet and Admiral Dewey because they don't belong to us. I have always believed that Eck's mother took some extracurricular night work nine months before he was born. So the one true bitch we had was not a bitch at all but a saint and martyr, the one technically true pristine immaculate unchallengeable son of a bitch we ever produced wasn't even a Snopes.

FIVE

WHEN his nephew was gone, the Warden said, "Sit down."
He did so. "You got in the paper," the Warden said. It
was folded on the desk facing him:

TRIES PRISON BREAK

DISGUISED IN WOMEN'S CLOTHES

Parchman, Miss. Sept 8, 1923 M. C.
"Mink" Snopes, under life sentence for
murder from Yoknapatawpha County . . .

"What does the 'C' in your name stand for?" the Warden said.
His voice was almost gentle. "We all thought your name was
just Mink. That's what you told us, wasn't it?"

"That's right," he said. "Mink Snopes."

"What does the 'C' stand for? They've got it M. C. Snopes
here."

"Oh," he said. "Nothing. Just M. C. Snopes like I.C. Railroad.
It was them young fellers from the paper in the hospital that day.
They kept on asking me what my name was and I said Mink
Snopes and they said Mink ain't a name, it's jest a nickname.
What's your real name? And so I said M. C. Snopes."

"Oh," the Warden said. "Is Mink all the name you've got?"

"That's right. Mink Snopes."

"What did your mother call you?"

"I don't know. She died. The first I knowed my name was
just Mink." He got up. "I better go. They're likely waiting for
me."

"Wait," the Warden said. "Didn't you know it wouldn't
work? Didn't you know you couldn't get away with it?"

"They told me," he said. "I was warned." He stood, not
moving, relaxed, small and frail, his face downbent an little,
musing, peaceful, almost like faint smiling. "He hadn't ought
to fooled me to get caught in that dress and sunbonnet," he said.
"I wouldn't a done that to him."

"Who?" the Warden said. "Not your . . . is it nephew?"

"Montgomery Ward?" he said. "He was my uncle's grandson.

No. Not him." He waited a moment. Then he said again, "Well, I better—"

"You would have got out in five more years," the Warden said. "You know they'll probably add on another twenty now, don't you?"

"I was warned of that too," he said.

"All right," the Warden said. "You can go."

This time it was he who paused, stopped. "I reckon you never did find out who sent me them forty dollars."

"How could I?" the Warden said. "I told you that at the time. All it said was From a Friend. From Memphis."

"It was Flem," he said.

"Who?" the Warden said. "The cousin you told me refused to help you after you killed that man? That you said could have saved you if he had wanted to? Why would he send you forty dollars now, after fifteen years?"

"It was Flem," he said. "He can afford it. Besides, he never had no money hurt against me. He was jest getting a holt with Will Varner then and maybe he figgered he couldn't rest getting mixed up with a killing, even if hit was his blood kin. Only I wish he hadn't used that dress and sunbonnet. He never had to do that."

They were picking the cotton now; already every cotton county in Mississippi would be grooming their best fastest champions to pick against the best of Arkansas and Missouri for the championship picker of the Mississippi Valley. But he wouldn't be here. No champion at anything would ever be here because only failures wound up here: the failures at killing and stealing and lying. He remembered how at first he had cursed his bad luck for letting them catch him, but he knew better now: that there was no such thing as bad luck or good luck: you were either born a champion or not a champion, and if he had been born a champion Houston not only couldn't, he wouldn't have dared, misuse him about that cow to where he had to kill him; that some folks were born to be failures and get caught always, some folks were born to be lied to and believe it, and he was one of them.

It was a fine crop, one of the best he remembered, as though everything had been exactly right: season: wind and sun and

rain to sprout it, the fierce long heat of summer to grow and
ripen it. As though back there in the spring the ground itself
had said, *All right, for once let's confederate instead of fighting*—the
ground, the dirt which any and every tenant farmer and sharecropper knew to be his sworn foe and mortal enemy—the hard
implacable land which wore out his youth and his tools and then
his body itself. And not just his body but that soft mysterious
one he had touched that first time with amazement and reverence
and incredulous excitement the night of his marriage, now worn
too to such leather-toughness that half the time, it seemed to him
most of the time, he would be too spent with physical exhaustion
to remember it was even female. And not just their two, but those
of their children, the two girls to watch growing up and be able
to see what was ahead of that tender and elfin innocence; until
was it any wonder that a man would look at that inimical
irreconcilable square of dirt to which he was bound and chained
for the rest of his life, and say to it: *You got me, you'll wear me out
because you are stronger than me since I'm just bone and flesh. I can't
leave you because I can't afford to, and you know it. Me and what used to
be the passion and excitement of my youth until you wore out the youth
and I forgot the passion, will be here next year with the children of our
passion for you to wear that much nearer the grave, and you know it;
and the year after that, and the year after that, and you know that too.
And not just me, but all my tenant and cropper kind that have immolated
youth and hope on thirty or forty or fifty acres of dirt that wouldn't
nobody but our kind work because you're all our kind have. But we can
burn you. Every late February or March we can set fire to the surface of
you until all of you in sight is scorched and black, and there ain't one
god-damn thing you can do about it. You can wear out our bodies and dull
our dreams and wreck our stomachs with the sowbelly and corn meal and
molasses which is all you afford us to eat but every spring we can set you
afire again and you know that too.*

It was different now. He didn't own this land; he referred of
course to the renter's or cropper's share of what it made. Now,
what it produced or failed to produce—bumper or bust, flood or
drouth, cotton at ten cents a pound or a dollar a pound—would
make not one tittle of difference in his present life. Because now
(years had passed; the one in which he would have been free
again if he had not allowed his nephew to talk him into that

folly which anybody should have known—even that young fool
of a lawyer they had made him take back there at the trial when
he, Mink, could have run his case much better, that didn't have
any sense at all, at least knew this much and even told him so and
even what the result to him would be—not only wouldn't work,
it wasn't even intended to work, was now behind him) he had
suddenly discovered something. People of his kind never had
owned even temporarily the land which they believed they had
rented between one New Year's and the next one. It was the land
itself which owned them, and not just from a planting to its
harvest but in perpetuity; not the owner, the landlord who
evacuated them from one worthless rental in November, on to
the public roads to seek desperately another similar worthless
one two miles or ten miles or two counties or ten counties away
before time to seed the next crop in March, but the land, the
earth itself passing their doomed indigence and poverty from
holding to holding of its thralldom as a family or a clan does a
hopelessly bankrupt tenth cousin.

That was past now. He no longer belonged to the land even
on those sterile terms. He belonged to the government, the state
of Mississippi. He could drag dust up and down cotton middles
from year in to year out and if nothing whatever sprang up behind
him, it would make no difference to him. No more now to go
to a commissary store every Saturday morning to battle with the
landlord for every gram of the cheap bad meat and meal and
molasses and the tumbler of snuff which was his and his wife's
one spendthrift orgy. No more to battle with the landlord for
every niggard sack of fertiliser, then gather the poor crop which
suffered from that niggard lack and still have to battle the
landlord for his niggard insufficient share of it. All he had to do
was just to keep moving; even the man with the shotgun standing
over him neither knew nor cared whether anything came up
behind him or not just so he kept moving, any more than he
cared. At first he was ashamed, in shame and terror lest the
others find that he felt this way; until one day he knew (he could
not have said how) that all the others felt like this; that, given
time enough, Parchman brought them all to this; he thought in
a kind of musing amazement *Yes sir, a man can get used to jest
anything, even to being in Parchman, if you jest give him time enough.*

But Parchman just changed the way a man looked at what he saw after he got in Parchman. It didn't change what he brought with him. It just made remembering easier because Parchman taught him how to wait. He remembered back there that day even while the Judge was still saying "Life" down at him, when he still believed that Flem would come in and save him, until he finally realised that Flem wasn't, had never intended to, how he had pretty near actually said it out loud: *Just let me go long enough to get out to Frenchman's Bend or wherever he is and give me ten minutes and I'll come back here and you can go on and hang me if that's what you want to do.* And how even that time three or five or eight years or whenever it was back there when Flem had used that nephew—what was his name? Montgomery Ward—to trick him into trying to escape in a woman's dress and sunbonnet and they had given him twenty years more exactly like that young fool lawyer had warned him they would at the very beginning, how even while he was fighting with the five guards he was still saying the same thing: *Just let me go long enough to reach Jefferson and have ten minutes and I will come back myself and you can hang me.*

He didn't think things like that any more now because he had learned to wait. And, waiting, he found out that he was listening, hearing too; that he was keeping up with what went on by just listening and hearing even better than if he had been right there in Jefferson because like this all he had to do was just watch them without having to worry about them too. So his wife had gone back to her people they said and died, and his daughters had moved away too, grown girls now, likely somebody around Frenchman's Bend would know where. And Flem was a rich man now, president of the bank and living in a house he rebuilt that they said was as big as the Union Depot in Memphis, with his daughter, old Will Varner's girl's bastard, that was grown now, that went away and married and her and her husband had been in another war they had in Spain and a shell or cannon ball or something blew up and killed the husband but just made her stone deaf. And she was back home now, a widow, living with Flem, just the two of them in the big house where they claimed she couldn't even hear it thunder, the rest of the folks in Jefferson not thinking much of it because she was already mixed up in a

nigger Sunday school and they said she was mixed up in something called commonists, that her husband had belonged to and
that in fact they were both fighting on the commonists side in
that war.

Flem was getting along now. They both were. When he got
out in 1948 he and Flem would both be old men. Flem might
not even be alive for him to get out for in 1948 and he himself
might not even be alive to get out in 1948 and he could remember
how at one time that too had driven him mad: that Flem might
die, either naturally or maybe this time the other man wouldn't
be second class and doomed to fail and be caught, and it would
seem to him that he couldn't bear it: who hadn't asked for
justice since justice was only for the best, for champions, but at
least a man might expect a chance, anybody had a right to a
chance. But that was gone too now, into, beneath the simple
waiting; in 1948 he and Flem both would be old men and he
even said aloud: "What a shame we can't both of us jest come
out two old men setting peaceful in the sun or the shade, waiting
to die together, not even thinking no more of hurt or harm or
getting even, not even remembering no more about hurt or
harm or anguish or revenge"—two old men not only incapable
of further harm to anybody but even incapable of remembering
hurt or harm, as if whatever necessary amount of the money
which Flem no longer needed and soon now would not need at
all ever again, could be used to blot, efface, obliterate those
forty years which he, Mink, no longer needed now and soon also,
himself too, would not even miss. *But I reckon not* he thought. *Can't
neither of us help nothing now. Can't neither one of us take nothing back.*

So again he had only five more years and he would be free.
And this time he had learned the lesson which the fool young
lawyer had tried to teach him thirty-five years ago. There were
eleven of them. They worked and ate and slept as a gang, a unit,
living in a detached wire-canvas-and-plank hut (it was summer);
shackled to the same chain they went to the mess hall to eat,
then to the field to work and, chained again, back to the hut to
sleep again. So when the escape was planned, the other ten had
to take him into their plot to prevent his giving it away by simple
accident. They didn't want to take him in; two of them were
never converted to the idea. Because ever since his own abortive

attempt eighteen or twenty years ago he had been known as a sort of self-ordained priest of the doctrine of non-escape.

So when they finally told him simply because he would have to be in the secret to protect it, whether he joined them or not, the moment he said, cried, "No! Here now, wait! Wait! Don't you see, if any of us tries to get out they'll come down on all of us and won't none of us ever get free even when our forty years is up," he knew he had already talked too much. So when he said to himself, "Now I got to get out of this chain and get away from them," he did not mean *Because if dark catches me alone in this room with them and no guard handy, I'll never see light again* but simply *I got to get to the Warden in time, before they try it maybe tonight even and wreck ever body.*

And even he would have to wait for the very darkness he feared, until the lights were out and they were all supposed to have settled down for sleep, so that his murderers would make their move, since only during or because of the uproar of the attack on him could he hope to get the warning, his message, to a guard and be believed. Which meant he would have to match guile with guile: to lie rigid on his cot until they set up the mock snoring which was to lull him off guard, himself tense and motionless and holding his own breath to distinguish in time through the snoring whatever sound would herald the plunging knife (or stick or whatever it would be) in time to roll, fling himself off the cot and in one more convulsive roll underneath it, as the men—he could not tell how many since the spurious loud snoring had if anything increased—hurled themselves on to the vacancy where a split second before he had been lying.

"Grab him," one hissed, panted. "Who's got the knife?" Then another:

"I've got the knife. Where in hell is he?" Because he—Mink —had not even paused; another convulsive roll and he was out from under the cot, on all-fours among the thrashing legs, scrabbling, scuttling to get as far away from the cot as he could. The whole room was now in a sort of sotto-voce uproar. "We got to have a light," a voice muttered. "Just a second of light." Suddenly he was free, clear; he could stand up. He screamed, shouted: no word, cry: just a loud human sound; at once the voice muttered, panted: "There. Grab him," but he had already sprung, leaped, to carom from invisible body to body, shouting, bellowing steadily even after he realised he could see, the air beyond the canvas walls not only full of searchlights but the siren too, himself surrounded, enclosed by the furious silent faces which seemed to dart like fish in then out of the shoulder-high light which came in over the plank half-walls, through the wire mesh; he even saw the knife gleam once above him as he plunged, hurling himself among the surging legs, trying to get back under a cot, any cot, anything to intervene before the knife. But it was too late, they could also see him now. He vanished beneath them all. But it was too late for them too: the glaring and probing of all the searchlights, the noise of the siren itself, seemed to concentrate downward upon, into the flimsy ramshackle cubicle filled with cursing men. Then the guards were among them, clubbing at heads with pistols and shotgun barrels, dragging them off until he lay exposed, once more battered and bleeding but this time still conscious. He had even managed one last convulsive wrench and twist so that the knife which should have pinned him to it merely quivered in the floor beside his throat.

"Hit was close," he told the guard. "But looks like we made hit."

But not quite. He was in the infirmary again and didn't hear until afterward how on the very next night two of them—Stillwell, a gambler who had cut the throat of a Vicksburg prostitute (he had owned the knife), and another, who had been the two who had held out against taking him into the plot at all but advocated instead killing him at once—made the attempt anyway though only Stillwell escaped, the other having most of his head blown off by a guard's shotgun blast.

Then he was in the Warden's office again. This time he had needed little bandaging and no stitches at all; they had not had time enough, and no weapons save their feet and fists except Stillwell's knife. "It was Stillwell that had the knife, wasn't it?" the Warden said.

He couldn't have said why he didn't tell. "I never seen who had it," he answered. "I reckon hit all happened too quick."

"That's what Stillwell seems to think," the Warden said. He took from his desk a slitted envelope and a sheet of cheap ruled paper, folded once or twice. "This came this morning. But that's right: you can't read writing, can you?"

"No," he said. The Warden unfolded the sheet.

"It was mailed yesterday in Texarkana. It says, 'He's going to have to explain Jake Barron'" (he was the other convict, whom the guard had killed) "'to somebody someday so take good care of him. Maybe you better take good care of him anyway since there are some of us still inside.'" The Warden folded the letter back into the envelope and put it back into the drawer and closed the drawer. "So there you are. I can't let you go around loose inside here, where any of them can get at you. You've only got five more years; even though you didn't stop all of them, probably on a recommendation from me, the Governor would let you out tomorrow. But I can't do that because Stillwell will kill you."

"If Cap'm Jabbo" (the guard who shot) "had jest killed Stillwell too, I could go home tomorrow?" he said. "Couldn't you trace out where he's at by the letter, and send Cap'm Jabbo wherever that is?"

"You want the same man to kill Stillwell that kept Stillwell from killing you two nights ago?"

"Send somebody else then. It don't seem fair for him to get away when I got to stay here five more years." Then he said, "But hit's all right. Maybe we did have at least one champion here, after all."

"Champion?" the Warden said. "One what here?" But he didn't answer that. And now for the first time he began to count off the days and months. He had never done this before, not with that original twenty years they had given him at the start back there in Jefferson, nor even with the second twenty years they had added on to it after he let Montgomery Ward persuade him into that woman's mother hubbard and sunbonnet. Because nobody was to blame for that but himself; when he thought of Flem in connection with it, it was with a grudging admiration, almost pride that they were of the same blood; he would think, say aloud, without envy even: "That Flem Snopes. You can't beat him. There ain't a man in Missippi nor the U.S. and A. both put together that can beat Flem Snopes."

But this was different. He had tried himself to escape and had

failed and had accepted the added twenty years of penalty
without protest; he had spent fifteen of them not only never
trying to escape again himself, but he had risked his life to foil
ten others who planned to: as his reward for which he would
have been freed the next day, only a trained guard with a
shotgun in his hands let one of the ten plotters get free. So these
last five years did not belong to him at all. He had discharged
his forty years in good faith; it was not his fault that they actually
added up to only thirty-five, and these five extra ones had been
compounded on to him by a vicious, even a horseplayish,
gratuitor.

That Christmas his (now: for the first time) slowly diminishing
sentence began to be marked off for him. It was a Christmas
card, postmarked in Mexico, addressed to him in care of the
Warden, who read it to him; they both knew who it was from:
"Four years now. Not as far as you think." On Valentine's Day
it was home-made: the coarse ruled paper bearing, drawn
apparently with a carpenter's or a lumberman's red crayon, a
crude heart into which a revolver was firing. "You see?" the
Warden said. "Even if your five years were up . . ."

"It ain't five now," he said. "Hit's four years and six months
and nineteen days. You mean, even then you won't let me out?"

"And have you killed before you could even get home?"

"Send out and ketch him."

"Send where?" the Warden said. "Suppose you were outside
and didn't want to come back and knew I wanted to get you
back. Where would I send to catch you?"

"Yes," he said. "So there jest ain't nothing no human man
can do."

"Yes," the Warden said. "Give him time and he will do
something else the police somewhere will catch him for."

"Time," he said. "Suppose a man ain't got time jest to depend
on time."

"At least you have got your four years and six months and
nineteen days before you have to worry about it."

"Yes," he said. "He'll have that much time to work in."

Then Christmas again, another card with the Mexican
postmark: "Three years now. Not near as far as you think." He
stood there, fragile and small and durable in the barred overalls,

his face lowered a little, peaceful. "Still Mexico, I notice," he said. "Maybe He will kill him there."

"What?" the Warden said. "What did you say?"

He didn't answer. He just stood there, peaceful, musing, serene. Then he said: "Before I had that-ere cow trouble with Jack Houston, when I was still a boy, I used to go to church ever Sunday and Wednesday prayer meeting too with the lady that raised me until I—"

"Who were they?" the Warden said. "You said your mother died."

"He was a son of a bitch. She wasn't no kin a-tall. She was jest his wife—ever Sunday until I—"

"Was his name Snopes?" the Warden said.

"He was my paw—until I got big enough to burn out on God like you do when you think you are already growed up and don't need nothing from nobody. Then when you told me how by keeping nine of them ten fellers from breaking out I didn't jest add five more years to my time, I fixed it so you wasn't going to let me out a-tall, I taken it back."

"Took what back?" the Warden said. "Back from who?"

"I taken it back from God."

"You mean you've rejoined the church since that night two years ago? No you haven't. You've never been inside the chapel since you came here back in 1908." Which was true. Though the present Warden and his predecessor had not really been surprised at that. What they had expected him to gravitate to was one of the small violent irreconcilable nonconformist non-everything and -everybody else which existed along with the regular prison religious establishment in probably all Southern rural penitentiaries—small fierce cliques and groups (this one called themselves Jehovah's Shareholders) headed by self-ordained leaders who had reached prison through a curiously consistent pattern: by the conviction of crimes peculiar to the middle class, to respectability, originating in domesticity or anyway uxoriousness: bigamy, rifling the sect's funds for a woman: his wife or someone else's or, in an occasional desperate case, a professional prostitute.

"I didn't need no church," he said. "I done it in confidence."

"In confidence?" the Warden said.

"Yes," he said, almost impatiently. "You don't need to write God a letter. He has done already seen inside you long before He would even need to bother to read it. Because a man will learn a little sense in time even outside. But he learns it quick in here. That when a Judgment powerful enough to help you, will help you if you got to do is jest take back and accept it, you are a fool not to."

"So He will take care of Stillwell for you," the Warden said.

"Why not? What's He got against me?"

"Thou shalt not kill," the Warden said.

"Why didn't He tell Houston that? I never went all the way in to Jefferson to have to sleep on a bench in the depot jest to try to buy them shells, until Houston made me."

"Well I'll be damned," the Warden said. "I will be eternally damned. You'll be out of here in three more years anyway, but if I had my way you'd be out of here now, today, before whatever the hell it is that makes you tick starts looking cross-eyed at me. I don't want to spend the rest of my life even thinking somebody is thinking the kind of hopes about me you wish about folks that get in your way. Go on now. Get back to work."

So when it was only October, no holiday valentine or Christmas card month that he knew of, when the Warden sent for him, he was not even surprised. The Warden sat looking at him for maybe half a minute, with something not just aghast but almost respectful in the look, then said: "I will be damned." It was a telegram this time. "It's from the Chief of Police in San Diego, California. There was a church in the Mexican quarter. They had stopped using it as a church, had a new one or something. Anyway it had been deconsecrated, so what went on inside it since, even the police haven't quite caught up with yet. Last week it fell down. They don't know why: it just fell down all of a sudden. They found a man in it—what was left of him. This is what the telegram says: 'Fingerprints F.B.I. identification your man number 08213 Shuford H. Stillwell.'" The Warden folded the telegram back into the envelope and put it back into the drawer. "Tell me again about that church you said you used to go to before Houston made you kill him."

He didn't answer that at all. He just drew a long breath and exhaled it. "I can go now," he said. "I can be free."

"Not right this minute," the Warden said. "It will take a month or two. The petition will have to be got up and sent to the Governor. Then he will ask for my recommendation. Then he will sign the pardon."

"The petition?" he said.

"You got in here by law," the Warden said. "You'll have to get out by law."

"A petition," he said.

"That your family will have a lawyer draw up, asking the Governor to issue a pardon. Your wife—but that's right, she's dead. One of your daughters then."

"Likely they done married away too by now."

"All right," the Warden said. Then he said, "Hell, man, you're already good as out. Your cousin, whatever he is, right there in Jackson now in the legislature—Egglestone Snopes, that got beat for Congress two years ago?"

He didn't move, his head bent a little; he said, "Then I reckon I'll stay here after all." Because how could he tell a stranger: *Clarence, my own oldest brother's grandson, is in politics that depends on votes. When I leave here I won't have no vote. What will I have to buy Clarence Snopes's name on my paper?* Which just left Eck's boy, Wallstreet, whom nobody yet had ever told what to do. "I reckon I'll be with you them other three years too," he said.

"Write your sheriff yourself," the Warden said. "I'll write the letter for you."

"Hub Hampton that sent me here is dead."

"You've still got a sheriff, haven't you? What's the matter with you? Have forty years in here scared you for good of fresh air and sunshine?"

"Thirty-eight years this coming summer," he said.

"All right. Thirty-eight. How old are you?"

"I was born in eighty-three," he said.

"So you've been here ever since you were twenty-five years old."

"I don't know. I never counted."

"All right," the Warden said. "Beat it. When you say the word I'll write a letter to your sheriff."

"I reckon I'll stay," he said. But he was wrong. Five months later the petition lay on the Warden's desk.

"Who is Linda Snopes Kohl?" the Warden said.

He stood completely still for quite a long time. "Her paw's a rich banker in Jefferson. His and my grandpaw had two sets of chillen."

"She was the member of your family that signed the petition to the Governor to let you out."

"You mean the sheriff sent for her to come and sign it?"

"How could he? You wouldn't let me write the sheriff."

"Yes," he said. He looked down at the paper which he could not read. It was upside down to him, though that meant nothing either. "Show me where the ones signed to not let me out."

"What?" the Warden said.

"The ones that don't want me out."

"Oh, you mean Houston's family. No, the only other names on it are the District Attorney who sent you here and your Sheriff, Hubert Hampton, Junior, and V. K. Ratliff. Is he a Houston?"

"No," he said. He drew the slow deep breath again. "So I'm free."

"With one thing more," the Warden said. "Your luck's not even holding: it's doubling." But he handled that too the next morning after they gave him a pair of shoes, a shirt, overalls and jumper and a hat, all brand new, and a ten-dollar bill and the three dollars and eighty-five cents which were still left from the forty dollars Flem had sent him eighteen years ago, and the Warden said, "There's a deputy here today with a prisoner from Greenville. He's going back tonight. For a dollar he'll drop you off right at the end of the bridge to Arkansas, if you want to go that way."

"Much obliged," he said. "I'm going by Memphis first. I got some business to tend to there."

It would probably take all of the thirteen dollars and eighty-five cents to buy a pistol even in a Memphis pawn shop. He had planned to beat his way to Memphis on a freight train, riding the rods underneath a boxcar or between two of them, as he had once or twice as a boy and a youth. But as soon as he was outside the gate, he discovered that he was afraid to. He had been shut too long, he had forgotten how; his muscles might have lost the agility and co-ordination, the simple bold quick temerity for physical risk. Then he thought of watching his chance to scramble safely into an empty car and found that he didn't dare that either, that in thirty-eight years he might even have forgotten the unspoken rules of the freemasonry of petty lawbreaking without knowing it until too late.

So he stood beside the paved highway which, when his foot touched it last thirty-eight years ago, had not even been gravel but instead was dirt marked only by the prints of mules and the iron tyres of wagons; now it looked and felt as smooth and hard as a floor, what time you could see it or risk feeling it either for the cars and trucks rushing past on it. In the old days any passing wagon would have stopped to no more than his raised hand. But these were not wagons so he didn't know what the new regulations for this might be either; in fact if he had known any-thing else to do but this he would already be doing it instead of standing, frail and harmless and not much larger than a child in the new overalls and jumper still showing their off-the-shelf creases and the new shoes and the hat, until the truck slowed in toward him and stopped and the driver said, "How far you going, dad?"

"Memphis," he said.

"I'm going to Clarksdale. You can hook another ride from there. As good as you can here, anyway."

It was fall, almost October, and he discovered that here was something else he had forgotten about during the thirty-eight years: seasons. They came and went in the penitentiary too, but for thirty-eight years the only right he had to them was the privilege of suffering because of them: from the heat and sun of summer whether he wanted to work in the heat of the day or not, and the rain and icelike mud of winter whether he wanted to be in it or not. But now they belonged to him again: October next week, not much to see in this flat Delta country which he had misdoubted the first time he laid eyes on it from the train window that day thirty-eight years ago; just cotton stalks and cypress needles. But back home in the hills, all the land would be gold and crimson with hickory and gum and oak and maple, and the old fields warm with sage and splattered with scarlet sumac; in thirty-eight years he had forgotten that.

When suddenly, somewhere deep in memory, there was a

tree, a single tree. His mother was dead; he couldn't remember her nor even how old he was when his father married again. So the woman wasn't even kin to him and she never let him forget it: that she was raising him not from any tie or claim and not because he was weak and helpless and a human being, but because she was a Christian. Yet there was more than that behind it. He knew that at once—a gaunt harried slattern of a woman whom he remembered always either with a black eye or holding a dirty rag to her bleeding where her husband had struck her. Because he could always depend on her, not to do anything for him because she always failed there, but for constancy, to be always there and always aware of him, surrounding him always with that shield which actually protected, defended him from nothing but on the contrary seemed actually to invite more pain and grief. But simply to be there, lachrymose, harassed, yet constant.

She was still in bed, it was midmorning; she should have been hours since immolated into the ceaseless drudgery which composed her days. She was never ill, so it must have been the man had beat her this time even harder than he knew, lying there in bed talking about food—the fatback, the coarse meal, the molasses which as far as he knew was the only food all people ate except when they could catch or kill something else; evidently this new blow had been somewhere about her stomach. "I can't eat hit," she whimpered. "I need to relish something else. Maybe a squirrel." He knew now; that was the tree. He had to steal the shotgun: his father would have beat him within an inch of his life—to lug the clumsy weapon even taller than he was, into the woods, to the tree, the hickory, to ambush himself beneath it and crouch, waiting, in the drowsy splendour of the October afternoon, until the little creature appeared. Whereupon he began to tremble (he had but the one shell) and he remembered that too: the tremendous effort to raise the heavy gun long enough, panting against the stock, "Please God please God," into the shock of the recoil and the reek of the black powder until he could drop the gun and run and pick up the still warm small furred body with hands that trembled and shook until he could barely hold it. And her hands trembling too as she fondled the carcass. "We'll dress hit and cook hit now," she said. "We'll relish hit together right now." The hickory itself was of course gone now, chopped into firewood or wagon spokes or single trees years ago; perhaps the very place where it had stood was eradicated now into ploughed land—or so they thought who had felled and destroyed it probably. But he knew better: unaxed in memory and unaxeable, inviolable and immune, golden and splendid with October. *Why yes* he thought *it ain't a place a man wants to go back to; the place don't even need to be there no more. What aches a man to go back to is what he remembers.*

Suddenly he craned his neck to see out the window. "Hit looks like—" and stopped. But he was free; let all the earth know where he had been for thirty-eight years. "—Parchman," he said.

"Yep," the driver said. "P.O.W. camp."

"What?" he said.

"Prisoners from the war."

"From the war?"

"Where you been the last five years, dad?" the driver said. "Asleep?"

"I been away," he said. "I mind one war they fit with the Spaniards when I was a boy, and there was another with the Germans after that one. Who did they fight this time?"

"Everybody." The driver cursed. "Germans, Japanese, Congress too. Then they quit. If they had let us lick the Russians too, we might a been all right. But they just licked the Krauts and Japs and then decided to choke everybody else to death with money."

He thought *Money.* He said: "If you had twenty-five dollars and found thirty-eight more, how much would you have?"

"What?" the driver said. "I wouldn't even stop to pick up just thirty-eight dollars. What the hell you asking me? You mean you got sixty-three dollars and can't find nothing to do with it?"

Sixty-three he thought. *So that's how old I am.* He thought quietly. *Not justice; I never asked that; jest fairness, that's all.* That was all; not to have anything for him: just not to have anything against him. That was all he wanted, and sure enough, here it was.

LINDA

SIX

V. K. Ratliff

"You ain't even going to meet the train?" Chick says. Lawyer never even looked up, setting there at the desk with his attention (his nose anyway) buried in the papers in front of him like there wasn't nobody else in the room. "Not just a new girl coming to town," Chick says, "but a wounded female war veteran. Well, maybe not a new girl," he says. "Maybe that's the wrong word. In fact maybe 'new' is the wrong word all the way round. Not a new girl in Jefferson, because she was born and raised here. And even if she was a new girl in Jefferson or new anywhere else once, that would be just once because no matter how new you might have been anywhere once, you wouldn't be very new anywhere any more after you went to Spain with a Greenwich Village poet to fight Hitler. That is, not after the kind of Greenwich Village poet that would get you both blown up by a shell anyhow. That is, provided you were a girl. So just say, not only an old girl that used to be new, coming back to Jefferson, but the first girl old or new either that Jefferson ever had to come home wounded from a war. Men soldiers yes, of course yes. But this is the first female girl soldier we ever had, not to mention one actually wounded by the enemy. Naturally we don't include rape for the main reason that we ain't talking about rape." Still his uncle didn't move. "I'd think you'd have the whole town down there at the depot to meet her. Out of simple sympathetic interest, not to mention pity: a girl that went all the way to Spain to a war and the best she got out of it was to lose her husband and have both eardrums busted by a shell. Mrs Cole," he says.

Nor did Lawyer look up even then. "Kohl," he says.

"That's what I said," Chick says. "Mrs Cole."

This time Lawyer spelled it. "K-o-h-l," he says. But even before he spelled it, it had a different sound from the way Chick said it. "He was a sculptor, not a poet. The shell didn't kill him. It was an aeroplane."

"Oh well, no wonder, if he was just a sculptor," Chick says. "Naturally a sculptor wouldn't have the footwork to dodge machine-gun bullets like a poet. A sculptor would have to stay in one place too much of his time. Besides, maybe it wasn't Saturday so he didn't have his hat on."

"He was in the aeroplane," Lawyer says. "It was shot down. It crashed and burned."

"What?" Chick says. "A Greenwich Village sculptor named K-o-h-l actually in an aeroplane where it could get shot down by an enemy?" He was looking more or less at the top of his uncle's head. "Not Cole," he says: "K-o-h-l. I wonder why he didn't change it. Don't they, usually?"

Now Lawyer closed the papers without no haste a-tall and laid them on the desk and pushed the swivel chair back and set back in it and clasped his hands behind his head. His hair had done already started turning grey when he come back from the war in France in 1919. Now it was pretty near completely white, and him setting there relaxed and easy in the chair with that white mop of it and the little gold key he got when he was at Harvard on his watch chain and one of the cob pipes stuck upside down in his shirt pocket like it was a pencil or a toothpick, looking at Chick for about a half a minute. "You didn't find that at Harvard," he says. "I thought that maybe after two years in Cambridge, you might not even recognise it again when you came back to Mississippi."

"All right," Chick says. "I'm sorry." But Lawyer just sat there easy in the chair, looking at him. "Damn it," Chick says, "I said I'm sorry."

"Only you're not sorry yet," Lawyer says. "You're just ashamed."

"Ain't it the same thing?" Chick says.

"No," Lawyer says. "When you are just ashamed of something, you don't hate it. You just hate getting caught."

"Well, you caught me," Chick says. "I am ashamed. What more do you want?" Only Lawyer didn't even need to answer that. "Maybe I can't help it yet, even after two years at Harvard," Chick says. "Maybe I just lived too long a time among what us Mississippi folks call white people before I went there. You can't be ashamed of me for what I didn't know in time, can you?"

"I'm not ashamed of you about anything," Lawyer says.

"All right," Chick says. "Sorry, then."

"I'm not sorry over you about anything either," Lawyer says.

"Then what the hell is all this about?" Chick says.

So a stranger that never happened to be living in Jefferson or Yoknapatawpha County ten or twelve years ago might have thought it was Chick that was the interested party. Not only interested enough to be jealous of his uncle, but interested enough to already be jealous even when the subject or bone of contention not only hadn't even got back home yet, he wouldn't even seen her since ten years ago. Which would make him jealous not only over a gal he hadn't even seen in ten years, but that he wasn't but twelve or thirteen years old and she was already nineteen, a growed woman, when he seen her that last time—a insurmountable barrier of difference in age that would still been a barrier even with three or four more years added on to both of them, providing of course it was the gal that still had the biggest number of them. In fact you would think how a boy jest twelve or thirteen years old couldn't be man-jealous yet; wouldn't have enough fuel yet to fire jealousy and keep it burning very long or even a-tall over a gal nineteen years old or any other age between eight and eighty for that matter, except that how young does he have to be before he can dare to risk not having that fuel capable of taking fire and combusting? Jest how young must he be to be safe for a little while longer yet, as the feller says, from having his heart strangled as good as any other man by that one strand of Lilith's hair? Or how old either, for the matter of that. Besides, this time when she come back, even though she would still be the same six or seven years older, this time they would be jest six or seven years older than twenty-two or twenty-three instead of six or seven years older than twelve or thirteen, and that ain't no barrier a-tall. This time he wouldn't be no innocent infantile bystanding victim of that loop because this time he would be in there fighting for the right and privilege of being lassoed; fighting not jest for the right and privilege of being strangled too, but of being strangled first.

Which was exactly what he looked like he was trying to do: nudging and whetting at his uncle, reaching around for whatever stick or club or brickbat come to his hand like he was still jest twelve or thirteen years old or even less than that, grabbing up that one about Linda's husband being a Jew for instance, because even at jest twelve, if he had stopped long enough to think, he would a knowed that that wouldn't even be a good solid straw as far as his present opponent or rival was concerned.

Maybe that—swinging that straw at his uncle about how Lawyer had been the main one instrumental in getting Linda up there in New York where couldn't no homefolks look after her and so sho enough she had went and married a Jew—was what give Chick away. Because he ain't even seen her again yet; he couldn't a knowed all that other yet. I mean, knowed that even at jest twelve he already had all the jealousy he would ever need at twenty-two or eighty-two either. He would need to actively see her again to find out he had jest as much right as any other man in it to be strangled to death by this here new gal coming to town, and wasn't no man wearing hair going to interfere in the way and save him. When he thought about her now, he would have to remember jest what that twelve- or thirteen-year-old boy had seen: not a gal but a woman growed, the same general size and shape of his own maw, belonging to and moving around in the same alien human race the rest of the world except twelve-year-old boys belonged to. And, if it hadn't been for his uncle finally stopping long enough his-self to look at her and then you might say ketching Chick by the scruff of the neck and grinding his attention on to her by conscripting up half his out-of-school time toting notes back and forth to her for them after-school ice-cream-parlour dates her and Lawyer started to having, nowhere near as interesting.

So when Chick remembered her now, he would still have to see what twelve or thirteen years old had seen: *Hell fire, she's durn nigh old as maw.* He would have to actively look at her again to see what twenty-two or twenty-three would see: *Hell fire, suppose she is a year or two older than me, jest so it's me that's the man of the two of us.* So you and that stranger both would a thought how maybe it taken a boy of twelve or thirteen; maybe only a boy of twelve or thirteen is capable of pure and undefiled, what you might call virgin, jealousy toward a man of thirty over a gal of nineteen—or of any other age between eight and eighty for that matter, jest as it takes a boy of twelve or thirteen to know the true anguish and passion and hope and despair of love; you and that stranger both thinking that right up to that last final moment

when Chick give his-self away free-for-nothing by grabbing up
that one about Linda's husband being not only a poet but a
Jew too to hit at his uncle with. Then even that stranger would
a realised Chick wasn't throwing it at Linda a-tall: he was
throwing it at his uncle; that it wasn't his uncle he was jealous of
over Linda Snopes: he was jealous of Linda over his uncle. Then
even that stranger would a had to say to Chick in his mind:
*Maybe you couldn't persuade me on to your side at first, but we're sholy in
the same agreement now.*

Leastways if that stranger had talked to me a little. Because I
could remember, I was actively watching it, that time back
there when Lawyer first got involved into Linda's career as the
feller says. I don't mean when Lawyer thought her career got
mixed up into hisn, nor even when he first thought he actively
noticed her. Because she was already twelve or thirteen herself
then and so Lawyer had already knowed her all her life or
anyway since she was them one or two years old or whatever it is
when hit's folks begin to bring it out into the street in a baby
buggy or toting it and you first notice how it not only is beginning
to look like a human being, hit even begins to look like some
specific family of folks you are acquainted with. And in a little
town like Jefferson where not only ever body knows ever body else
but ever body has got to see ever body else in town at least once
in the twenty-four hours whether he wants to or not, except
for the time Lawyer was away at the war likely he had to see her
at least once a week. Not to mention having to know even before
he could recognise her to remember, that she was Eula Varner's
daughter that all Jefferson and Yoknapatawpha County both
that had ever seen Eula Varner first, couldn't help but look at
Eula Varner's child with a kind of amazement, like at some
minute-sized monster, since anybody, any man anyhow, that
ever looked at Eula once couldn't help but believe that all that
much woman in jest one simple normal-sized chunk couldn't a
possibly been fertilised by anything as frail and puny in comparison as jest one single man; that it would a taken that whole
generation of young concentrated men to seeded them, as the
feller says, splendid—no: he would a said magnificent—loins.

And I don't mean when Lawyer voluntarily went outen his
way and adopted Linda's career into a few spare extra years of

H

hisn like he thought he was doing. What I mean is, when Eula Varner taken that first one look of hern at Lawyer—or let him take that first one look of hisn at her, whichever way you want to put it—and adopted the rest of his life into that of whatever first child she happened to have, providing of course it's a gal. Like when you finally see the woman that had ought to been yourn all the time, only it's already too late. The woman that ought to been sixteen maybe at this moment and you not more than nineteen (which at that moment when he first seen Eula Lawyer actively was; it was Eula that was out of focus, being as she was already a year older than Lawyer to start with) and you look at her that first one time and in the next moment says to her: "You're beautiful. I love you. Let's don't never part again," and she says, "Yes, of course"—no more concerned than that: "Of course I am. Of course you do. Of course we won't." Only it's already too late. She is already married to somebody else. Except it wasn't too late. It ain't never too late and won't never be, providing, no matter how old you are, you still are that-ere nineteen-year-old boy that said that to that sixteen-year-old gal at that one particular moment outen all the moments you might ever call yourn. Because how can it ever be too late to that nineteen-year-old boy, because how can that sixteen-year-old gal you had to say that to ever be violated, it don't matter how many husbands she might a had in the meantime, providing she actively was the one that had to say "Of course" right back at you? And even when she is toting the active proof of that violation around in her belly or even right out in plain sight on her arm or dragging at the tail of her skirt, immolating hit and her both back into virginity wouldn't be no trick a-tall to that nineteen-year-old boy, since naturally that sixteen-year-old gal couldn't possibly be fertilised by no other seed except hisn, I don't care who would like to brag his-self as being the active instrument.

Except that Lawyer didn't know all that yet neither. Mainly because he was to busy. I mean, that day when Eula first walked through the Jefferson Square where not jest Lawyer but all Jefferson too would have to see her. That time back there when Flem had finally grazed up Uncle Billy Varner and Frenchman's Bend and so he would have to move on somewhere, and Jefferson was as good a place as any since, as the feller says, any spoke leads sooner or later to the rim. Or in fact maybe Jefferson was for the moment unavoidable, being as Flem had done beat me outen my half of that café me and Grover Winbush owned, and since there wasn't no easy quick practical way to get Grover out to Frenchman's Bend, Flem would simply have to make a stopover at least in Jefferson while he evicted Grover outen the rest of it.

Anyhow, Lawyer seen her at last. And there he was, entering not jest bare-handed but practically nekkid too, that engagement that he couldn't afford to do anything but lose it—Lawyer, a town-raised bachelor that was going to need a Master of Arts from Harvard and a Doctor of Philosophy from Heidelberg jest to stiffen him up to where he could cope with the natural normal Yoknapatawpha County folks that never wanted nothing except jest to break a few aggravating laws that was in their way or get a little free money outen the country treasury; and Eula Varner that never needed to be educated nowhere because jest what the Lord had already give her by letting her stand up and breathe and maybe walk around a little now and then was trouble and danger enough for ever male man in range. For Lawyer to win that match would be like them spiders, that the end of the honeymoon is when she finally finishes eating up his last drumstick. Which likely enough Lawyer knowed too, being nineteen years old and already one year at Harvard. Though even without Harvard, a boy nineteen years old ought to know that much about women jest by instinct, like a child or a animal knows fire is hot without having to actively put his hand or his foot in it. Even when a nineteen-year-old-boy says "You're beautiful and I love you," even he ought to know whether it's a sixteen-year-old gal or a tiger that says "Certainly" back at him.

Anyhow, there Lawyer was, rushing headlong into that engagement that not only the best he could expect and hope for but the best he could want would be to lose it, since losing it wouldn't do nothing but jest knock off some of his hide here and there. Rushing in with nothing in his hand to fight with but that capacity to say nineteen years old the rest of his life, to take on that McCarron boy that had not only cuckolded him before he ever seen Eula, but that was going to keep on cuckolding him in one or another different name and shape even after he would finally give up. Because maybe Flem never had no reason to pick out Jefferson to come to; maybe one spoke was jest the same as another to him since all he wanted was a rim. Or maybe he jest didn't know he had a reason for Jefferson. Or maybe married men don't even need reasons, being as they already got wives. Or maybe it's women that don't need reasons, for the simple reason that they never heard of a reason and wouldn't recognise it face to face, since they don't function from reasons but from necessities that couldn't nobody help nohow and that don't nobody but a fool man want to help in the second place, because he don't know no better; it ain't women, it's men that takes ignorance seriously, getting into a skeer over something for no more reason than that they don't happen to know what it is.

So it wasn't Grover Winbush and what you might call that dangling other half of mine and his café that brought Miz Flem Snopes to Jefferson so she could walk across the Square whatever that afternoon was when Lawyer had to look at her. It wasn't even Eula herself. It was that McCarron boy. And I seen some of that too and heard about all the rest of it. Because that was about all folks within five miles of Varner's store talked about that spring. The full unchallenged cynosure you might say of the whole Frenchman's Bend section, from sometime in March to the concluding dee-neweyment or meelee which taken place jest beyond the creek bridge below Varner's house one night in the following July—that McCarron boy coming in to French-man's Bend that day without warning out of nowhere like a cattymount into a sheep pen among them Bookwrights and Binfords and Quicks and Tulls that for about a year now had been hitching their buggies and saddle mules to Will Varner's fence. Like a wild buck from the woods jumping the patch fence and already trompling them tame domestic local carrots and squashes and eggplants that until that moment was thinking or leastways hoping that Eula's maiden citadel was actively being threatened and endangered, before they could even blench, let alone cover their heads. Likely—in fact, they had done a little local bragging to that effect—they called theirselves pretty unbitted too, until he come along that day, coming from nowhere jest exactly like a wild buck from the woods, like he had done located Eula from miles and even days away outen the hard unerring air itself and come as straight as a die to where she was waiting, not for him especially but maybe for jest any wild strong buck that was wild and strong enough to deserve and match her.

Yes sir. As the feller says, the big buck: the wild buck right off the mountain itself, with his tail already up and his eyes already flashing. Because them Bookwrights and Quicks and Tulls was pretty fair bucks theirselves, on that-ere home Frenchman's Bend range and reservation you might say, providing them outside boundary limits posted signs wasn't violated by these here footloose rambling uninvited strangers. In fact, they was pretty good at kicking and gouging and no holts barred and no bad feelings afterward, in all innocent friendliness and companionship not jest among one another but with that same friendly willingness to give and take when it was necessary to confederate up and learn him a lesson on some foreigner from four or five or six miles away that ought to stayed at home, had no business there, neither needed nor wanted, that had happened to see Eula somewhere once or maybe jest heard about her from somebody else that had watched her walk ten or fifteen feet. So he had to come crowding his buggy or mule up to Varner's picket fence some Sunday night, then coming innocently back down the road toward the gum and cypress thicket where the road crossed the creek bridge, his head still filled with female Varner dreams until the unified corporation stepped outen the thicket and bushwhacked them outen it and throwed creek water on him and put him back in the buggy or on the mule and wrapped the lines around the whipstock or the horn and headed him on toward wherever it was he lived and if he'd a had any sense he wouldn't a left it in the first place or at least in this direction.

But this here new one was a different animal. Because they—including them occasional volunteers—was jest bucks in the general—or maybe it's the universal—Frenchman's Bend pattern, while McCarron wasn't in nobody's pattern; he was unbitted not because he was afraid of a bit but simply because so fur he didn't prefer to be. So there not only wasn't nere a one of them would stand up to him alone, the whole unified confederated passel of them, that never hesitated one second to hide in that thicket against any other interloper that come sniffing at Varner's fence, never nerved their selves up to him until it was already too late. Oh sho, they had chances. They had plenty of chances. In fact, he give them so many chances that by the end of May they wouldn't even walk a Frenchman's Bend road after dark, even in sight of one of their own houses. without they was at least three of them. Because this here was a different kind of a buck, coming without warning right off the big mountain itself and doing what Lawyer would call arrogating to his-self what had been the gynecological cynosure of a whole section of north Missippi for going on a year or two now. Not ravishing Eula away: not riding up on his horse and snatching her up behind him and galloping off, but jest simply moving in and dispossessing them; not even evicting them but like he was keeping them on hand for a chorus you might say, or maybe jest for spice, like you keep five or six cellars of salt setting handy while you are eating the watermelon, until it was already too late, until likely as not, as fur as they or Frenchman's Bend either knowed, Eula was already pregnant with Linda.

Except I don't think that was exactly it. I don't think I prefer it to happen that way. I think I prefer it to happen all at once. Or that ain't quite right neither. I think what I prefer is, that them five timorous local stallions actively brought about the very exact thing they finally nerved their desperation up to try to prevent. There they all was, poised on the brink you might say of that-ere still intact maiden citadel, all seven of them: Eula and McCarron, and them five Tulls and Bookwrights and Turpins and Binfords and Quicks. Because what them Tulls and Quicks would a called the worst hadn't happened yet. I don't mean the worst in respects to Eula's chastity nor to the violated honour of Uncle Billy Varner's home, but in respects to them two years' investment of buggies and mules tied to the Varner fence when them and the five folks keeping them hitched there half the night both had ought to been home getting a little rest before going back to the field to plough at sunup, instead of having to live in a constantly shifting confederation of whatever four of them happened to believe that the fifth one was out in front in that-ere steeplechase, not to mention the need for all five of them having to gang up at a moment's notice maybe at almost any time on some stray interloper that turned up without warning with his head full of picket fence ideas too.

So I prefer to believe it didn't happen yet. I don't know what
Eula and McCarron was waiting on. I mean, what McCarron
was waiting on. Eula never done no waiting. Likely she never
even knowed what the word meant, like the ground, dirt, the
earth, whatever it is in it that makes seed sprout at the right
time, don't know nor need to know what waiting means. Since
to know what waiting means, you got to be skeered or weak or
self-doubtful enough to know what impatience or hurry means,
and Eula never needed them no more than that dirt does. All
she needed was jest to be, like the ground of the field, until the
right time come, the right wind, the right sun, the right rain;
until in fact that-ere single unique big buck jumped that tame
garden fence outen the big woods or the high mountain or the
tall sky, and finally got through jest standing there among the
sheep with his head up, looking proud. So it was McCarron
that put off that what long you might call that-ere inevitable.
Maybe that was why: having to jest stand there for a while
looking proud among the sheep. Maybe that was it: maybe he
was jest simply having too much fun at first, playing with them
Bookwright and Quick sheep, tantalising them up maybe to see
jest how much they would have to stand to forget for a moment
they was sheep, or to remember that maybe they was sheep but
at least there was five of them, until at last they would risk him
jest like he actively wasn't nothing but jest one more of them
natural occupational local hazards Eula had done already got
them accustomed to handling.

So maybe you can figger what they was waiting on. They
was church folks. I mean, they went to church a heap of Sundays,
and Wednesday night prayer meeting too, unless something
else come up. Because church was as good a place as any to
finish up one week and start another, especially as there wasn't no
particular other place to go on Sunday morning; not to mention
a crap game down back of the spring while the church was busy
singing or praying or listening; and who knowed but how on
almost any Wednesday night you might ketch some young gal
and persuade her off into the bushes before her paw or maw
noticed she was missing. Or maybe they never needed to ever
heard it, since likely it wasn't even Samson and Delilah that was
the first ones to invent that hair-cutting eupheemism neither. So

the whole idea might be what you would call a kind of last desperate instinctive hereditary expedient waiting handy for ever young feller (or old one either) faced with some form of man-trouble over his gal. So at least you knowed what they was waiting for. Naturally they would preferred to preserve that-ere maiden Varner citadel until one of them could manage to shake loose from the other four by luck or expedient long enough to ravage it. But now that this uninvited ringer had come in and wrecked ever thing anyhow, at least they could use that violation and rapine not only for revenge but to evict him for good from meddling around Frenchman's Bend.

Naturally not jest laying cravenly back to ketch him at a moment when he was wore out and exhausted with pleasure and success; they wasn't that bad. But since they couldn't prevent the victory, at least ketch him at a moment when he wasn't watching, when his mind was still fondly distracted and divided between what you might call bemusements with the recent past, which would a been last night, and aspirations toward the immediate future, which would be in a few minutes now as soon as the buggy reached a convenient place to hitch the horse. Which is what they—the ambushment—done. They was wrong of course; hadn't nothing happened yet. I mean, I prefer that even that citadel was still maiden right up to this moment. No: what I mean is, I won't have nothing else for the simple dramatic verities except that ever thing happened right there that night and all at once; that even that McCarron boy, that compared to them other five was a wild stag surrounded by a gang of goats— that even he wasn't enough by his-self but that it taken all six of them even to ravage that citadel, let alone seed them loins with a child: that July night and the buggy coming down the hill until they heard the horse's feet come off the creek bridge and the five of them, finally nerved up to even this last desperate gambit, piling outen that familiar bushwhacking thicket that up to this time had handled them local trespassing rams so simple and easy you wouldn't hardly need to dust off your hands afterward.

Naturally they never brought no bystanders with them and after the first two or three minutes there wasn't no witness a-tall left, since he was already laying out cold in the ditch. So my conjecture is jest as good as yourn, maybe better since I'm a interested party, being as I got what the feller calls a theorem to prove. In fact, it may not taken even three minutes, one of them jumping to ketch the horse's head and the other four rushing to snatch McCarron outen the buggy, providing of course he was still in the buggy by that time and not already blazing bushes up the creek, having chosen quick between discretion and valour, it don't matter a hoot who was looking, as had happened before with at least one of the invaders that had been quick enough.

Which, by the trompled evidence folks went to look at the next day, McCarron wasn't, though not for the already pre-cedented reason. Nor did the evidence explain jest what the wagon spoke was doing there neither that broke McCarron's arm: only that McCarron had the wagon spoke now in his remaining hand in the road while Eula was standing up in the buggy with that lead-loaded buggy whip reversed in both hands like a hoe or a axe, swinging the leaded butt of it at whatever head come up next.

Not over three minutes, at the outside. It wouldn't needed more than that. It wouldn't wanted more: it was all that simple and natural—a pure and simple natural circumstance as simple and natural and ungreedy as a tide-wave or a cloudburst, that didn't even want but one swipe—a considerable of trompling and panting and cussing and nothing much to see except a kind of moil of tangled shadows around the horse (It never moved. But then it spent a good part of its life ever summer right in the middle of Will's sawmill and it stood right there in the yard all the time Will was evicting Ab Snopes from a house he hadn't paid no rent on in two years, which was the nearest thing to a cyclone Frenchman's Bend ever seen; it was said that Will could drive up to a depot and get outen the buggy and not even hitch it while a train passed, and only next summer it was going to be tied to the same lot gate that them wild Texas ponies Flem Snopes brought back from Texas demolished right up to the hinges when they run over Frenchman's Bend) and buggy and the occasional gleam of that hickory wagon spoke interspersed among the mush-melon thumps of that loaded buggy whip handle on them Frenchman's Bend skulls.

And then jest the empty horse and buggy standing there in the road like the tree or rock or barn or whatever it was the tide-wave or cloudburst has done took its one rightful ungreedy swipe at and went away, and that-ere one remaining evidence —it was Theron Quick; for a week after it you could still see the print of that loaded buggy whip across the back of his skull; not the first time naming him Quick turned out to be what the feller calls jest a humorous allusion—laying cold in the weeds beside the road. And that's when I believe it happened. I don't even insist or argue that it happened that way. I jest simply decline to have it any other way except that one because there ain't no acceptable degrees between what has got to be right and what jest can possibly be.

So it never even stopped. I mean, the motion, movement. It was one continuous natural rush from the moment five of them busted outen that thicket and grabbed at the horse, on through the cussing and trompling and hard breathing and the final crashing through the bushes and the last rapid and fading footfall, since likely the other four thought Theron was dead; then jest the peaceful quiet and the dark road and the horse standing quiet in the buggy in the middle of it and Theron Quick sleeping peacefully in the weeds. And that's when I believe it happened: not no cessation a-tall, not even no active pausing; not jest that maiden bastion capitulate and overrun but them loins themselves seeded, that child, that girl, Linda herself created into life right there in the road with likely Eula to help hold him up offen the broke arm and the horse standing over them among the stars like one of them mounted big-game trophy heads sticking outen the parlour or the liberry or (I believe they call them now) den wall. In fact maybe that's what it was.

So in almost no time there was Will Varner with a pregnant unmarried daughter. I mean, there Frenchman's Bend was because even in them days when you said "Frenchman's Bend" you smiled at Uncle Billy Varner, or vice versa. Because if Eula Varner was a natural phenomenon like a cyclone or a tide-wave, Uncle Billy was one too even if he wasn't no more than forty yet: that had shaved notes and foreclosed liens and padded furnish bills and evicted tenants until the way Will Varner went Frenchman's Bend had done already left and the folks that composed it had damn sho better hang on and go too, unless they jest wanted to settle down in vacant space twenty-two miles south-east of Jefferson.

Naturally the McCarron boy was the man to handle the Varner family honour right there on the spot. After the first shock, folks all thought that's what he had aimed to do. He was the only child of a well-to-do widow maw up in Tennessee somewhere until he happened to be wherever it was his fate arranged for him to have his look at Eula Varner like theirn would do for Lawyer Stevens and Manfred de Spain about a year later. And, being the only child of a well-to-do maw and only educated in one of them fancy gentleman's schools, you would naturally expect him to lit out without even stopping to have his broke arm splinted up, let alone waiting for Will Varner to reach for his shotgun.

Except you would be wrong. Maybe you not only don't run outen the middle of a natural catastrophe—you might be flung outen it by centrifugal force or, if you had any sense, you might tried to dodge it. But you don't change your mind and plans in the middle of it. Or he might in his case even wanted to stay in the middle of that particular one until it taken the rest of his arms and legs too, as likely any number of them other Quicks and Tulls and Bookwrights would elected to do. Not to mention staying in that select school that even in that short time some of them high academic standards of honour and chivalry rubbed off on him by jest exposure. Anyhow it wasn't him that left that-ere now-flyspecked Varner family honour high and dry. It was Eula herself that done it. So now all you can do is try to figger. So maybe it was the McCarron boy that done it, after all. Like maybe that centrifugal force that hadn't touched him but that one light time and he had already begun to crumple. That simple natural phenomenon that maybe didn't expect to meet another phenomenon even a natural one, but at least expected or maybe jest hoped for something at least tough enough to crash back without losing a arm or a leg the first time they struck. Because next time it might be a head, which would mean the life along with it, and then all that force and power and unskeeredness and unskeerableness to give and to take and suffer the consequences it taken to be a female natural phenomenon in its phenomenal moment, would be wasted, throwed away. Because I ain't talking about love. Natural phenomenons ain't got no more concept of love than they have of the alarm and uncertainty and impotence you got to be capable of to know what waiting means. When she said to herself, and likely she did: *The next one of them creek-bridge episodes might destroy him completely*, it wasn't that McCarron boy's comfort she had in mind.

Anyhow, the next morning he was gone from Frenchman's Bend. I presume it was Eula that put what was left of the buggy whip back into the socket and druv the buggy back up the hill. Leastways they waked Will, and Will in his nightshirt (no shotgun: it would be anywhere up to twenty-eight days, give or take a few, before he would find out he needed the shotgun; it was jest his little grip of veterinary tools yet) patched up the arm to where he could drive on home or somewhere that more than a local cow-and-mule doctor could get a-holt of him. But he was back in Jefferson at least once about a month later, about the time when Eula likely found out if she didn't change her condition pretty quick now, it was going to change itself for her. And he even paid the mail rider extra to carry a special wrote-out private message to Eula. But nothing come of that neither, and at last he was gone. And sho enough, about sixty-five or seventy days after that-ere hors-de-combat creek-bridge evening—and if you had expected a roar of some kind to come up outen the Varner residence and environment, you would been wrong there too: it was jest a quick announcement that even then barely beat the wedding itself—Herman Bookwright and Theron Quick left Frenchman's Bend suddenly overnight too though it's my belief they was both not even bragging but jest wishing they had, and Eula and Flem was married; and after the one more week it taken Will to do what he thought was beating Flem down to accept that abandoned Old Frenchman place as full receipt for Eula's dowry, Eula and Flem left for Texas, which was fur enough away so that when they come back, that-ere new Snopes baby would look at least reasonably legal or maybe what I mean is orthodox. Not to mention as Texas would be where it had spent the presumable most of its prenatal existence, wouldn't nobody be surprised if it was cutting its teeth at three months old. And when they was back in Frenchman's Bend a year later,

anybody meddlesome enough to remark how it had got to be a
pretty good-size gal in jest them three possible months, all he
had to do was remind his-self that them three outside months
had been laid in Texas likewise.

Jest exactly fourteen months since that McCarron boy started
to crumple at the seams at that first encounter. But it wasn't
waiting. Not a natural phenomenon like Eula. She was jest being,
breathing, setting with that baby in a rocking chair on Varner's
front gallery while Flem changed enough money into them sixty
silver dollars and buried them in that Old Frenchman place
rose garden jest exactly where me and Henry Armstid and
Odum Bookwright couldn't help but find them. And still jest
being and breathing, setting with the baby in the wagon that
day they moved in to Jefferson so Flem could get a active holt on
Grover Winbush to evict him outen the other half of that café
me and Grover owned. And still jest being and breathing but
not setting now because likely even the tide-wave don't need to
be informed when it's on the right spoke to whatever rim it's due
at next, her and Flem and the baby living in that canvas tent
behind the café between when she would walk across the Square
until finally Manfred de Spain, the McCarron that wouldn't
start or break up when they collided together, would look up and
see her. Who hadn't had none of them select advantages of
being the only child of a well-to-do widowed maw living in
Florida hotels while he was temporarily away at them select
eastern schools, but instead had had to make out the best he
could with jest being the son of a Confederate cavalry officer,
that graduated his-self from West Point into what his paw would
a called the Yankee army and went to Cuba as a lieutenant and
come back with a long jagged scar down one cheek that the folks
trying to beat him for mayor rumoured around wasn't made by
no Spanish bayonet a-tall but instead by a Missouri sergeant
with a axe in a crap game: which, whether it was so or not,
never stood up long between him and getting elected mayor of
Jefferson, nor between him and getting to be president of
Colonel Sartoris's bank when that come up, not to mention
between him and Eula Varner Snopes when that come up.

I ain't even mentioning Lawyer. It wasn't even his bad luck
he was on that rim too because tide-waves ain't concerned with

luck. It was his fate. He jest got run over by coincidence, like a ant using the same spoke a elephant happened to find necessary or convenient. It wasn't that he was born too soon or too late or even in the wrong place. He was born at exactly the right time, only in the wrong envelope. It was his fate and doom not to been born into one of them McCarron separate covers too instead of into that fragile and what you might call gossamer-sinewed envelope of boundless and hopeless aspiration Old Moster give him.

So there he was, rushing headlong into that engagement that the best he could possibly hope would be to lose it quick, since any semblance or intimation of the most minorest victory would a destroyed him like a lightning bolt, while Flem Snopes grazed gently on up them new Jefferson pastures, him and his wife and infant daughter still living in the tent behind the café and Flem his-self frying the hamburgers now after Grover Winbush found out suddenly one day that he never owned one half of a café neither; then the Rouncewells that thought they still owned what Miz Rouncewell called the Commercial Hotel against all the rest of Yoknapatawpha County calling it the Rouncewell boarding house, found they was wrong too and the Flem Snopeses lived there now, during the month or so it taken him to eliminate the Rouncewells outen it, with the next Snopes from Frenchman's Bend imported into the tent behind the café and frying the hamburgers because Flem his-self was now superintendent of the power plant; Manfred de Spain had not only seen Eula, he was already mayor of Jefferson when he done it.

And still Lawyer was trying, even while at least once ever day he would have to see his mortal victorious rival and conqueror going in and out of the mayor's office or riding back and forth across the Square in that red brass-trimmed E.M.F. roadster that most of north Missippi, let alone jest Yoknapatawpha County, hadn't seen nothing like before; right on up and into that alley behind the Ladies' Cotillion Club Christmas ball where he tried to fight Manfred with his bare fists until his sister's husband drug him up outen the gutter and held him long enough for Manfred to get outen sight and then taken him home to the bathroom to wash him off and says to him: "What the hell do you mean? Don't you know you don't know how to fight?" And Lawyer leaning over the washbowl trying to stanch his nose with handfuls of tissue paper, saying, "Of course I know it. But can you suh-jest a better way than this for me to learn?"

And still trying, on up to that last desperate cast going all the way back to that powerhouse brass business. I mean, that pile of old wore-out faucets and valves and pieces of brass pipe and old bearings and such that had accumulated into the power plant until they all disappeared sometime during the second year of Flem's reign as superintendent, though there wasn't no direct evidence against nobody even after the brass safety valves vanished from both the boilers and was found to been replaced with screwed-in steel plugs; it was jest that finally the city auditors had to go to the superintendent and advise him as delicate as possible that that brass was missing and Flem quit chewing long enough to say "How much?" and paid them and then the next year they done the books again and found they had miscounted last year and went to him again and suh-jested they had made a mistake before and Flem quit chewing again long enough to say "How much?" and paid them that too. Going (I mean Lawyer) all the way back to them old by-gones even though Flem was not only long since resigned from being superintendent, he had even bought two new safety valves outen his own pocket as a free civic gift to the community; bringing all that up again, with evidence, in a suit to impeach Manfred outen the mayor's office until Judge Dukinfield recused his-self and appointed Judge Stevens, Lawyer's paw, to hear the case. Only we didn't know what happened then because Judge Stevens cleared the court and heard the argument in chambers as they calls it, jest Lawyer and Manfred and the judge his-self. And that was all; it never taken long; almost right away Manfred come out and went back to his mayor's office, and the tale, legend, report, whatever you want to call it, of Lawyer standing there with his head bent a little in front of his paw, saying, "What must I do now, Papa? Papa, what can I do now?"

But he was chipper enough the next morning when I seen him off on the train, that had done already graduated from Harvard and the University law school over at Oxford and was now on his way to a town in Germany to go to school some more.

Yes sir, brisk and chipper as you could want. "Here you are," he says. "This is what I want with you before I leave: to pass the torch on into your personal hand. You'll have to hold the fort alone now. You'll have to tote the load by yourself."

"What fort?" I says. "What load?"

"Jefferson," he says. "Snopeses. Think you can handle them alone for two years?" That's what he thought then: that he was all right now; he had done been disenchanted for good at last of Helen, and so now all he had to worry about was what them Menelaus-Snopeses might be up to in the Yoknapatawpha-Argive community while he had his back turned. Which was all right; it would ease his mind. He would have plenty of time after he come back to find out that ain't nobody yet ever lost Helen, since for the rest of not jest her life but hisn too she don't never get shut of him. Likely it's because she don't want to.

Except it wasn't two years. It was nearer five. That was in the early spring of 1914, and that summer the war come, and maybe that—a war—was what he was looking for. Not hoping for, let alone expecting to have one happen jest on his account, since like most other folks in this country he didn't believe no war was coming. But looking for something, anything, and certainly a war would do as well as another, since no matter what his brains might a been telling him once he had that much water between him and Eula Snopes, even his instincts likely told him that jest two years wasn't nowhere near enough for him or Helen either to have any confidence in that disenchantment. So even if he couldn't anticipate no war to save him, back in his mind somewhere he was still confident that Providence would furnish something, since like he said, God was anyhow a gentleman and wouldn't bollix up the same feller twice with the same trick, at least in the same original package.

So he had his war. Only you would a wondered—at least I did—why he never went into it on the German side. Not jest because he was already in Germany and the Germans handy right there surrounding him, but because he had already told me how, although it was the culture of England that had sent folks this fur across the water to establish America, right now it was the German culture that had the closest tie with the modern

virile derivations of the northern branch of the old Aryan stock.
Because he said that tie was mystical, not what you seen but what
you heard, and that the present-day Aryan, in America at least,
never had no confidence a-tall in what he seen, but on the
contrary would believe anything he jest heard and couldn't
prove; and that the modern German culture since the revolutions
of 1848 never had no concern with, and if anything a little
contempt for, anything that happened to man on the outside, or
through the eyes and touch, like sculpture and painting and
civil laws for his social benefit, but jest with what happened to
him through his ears, like music and philosophy and what was
wrong inside of his mind. Which he said was the reason why
German was such a ugly language, not musical like Italian and
Spanish nor what he called the epicene exactitude of French, but
was harsh and ugly, not to mention full of spit (like as the feller
says, you speak Italian to men, French to women, and German to
horses), so that there wouldn't be nothing to interfere and
distract your mind from what your nerves and glands was
hearing: the mystical ideas, the glorious music—Lawyer said,
the best of music, from the mathematical inevitability of Mozart
through the godlike passion of Beethoven and Bach to the
combination bawdy-house street-carnival uproar that Wagner
made—that come straight to the modern virile northern Aryan's
heart without bothering his mind a-tall.

Except that he didn't join the German army. I don't know
what lies he managed to tell the Germans to get out of Germany
where he could join the enemy fighting them, nor what lies he
thought up for the English and French to explain why a student
out of a German university was a safe risk to have around where
he might overhear somebody telling what surprise they was
fixing up next. But he done it. And it wasn't the English army
he joined neither. It was the French one: them folks that,
according to him, spent all their time talking about epicene
exactitudes to ladies. And I didn't know why even four years
later when I finally asked him: "After all you said about that-ere
kinship of German culture, and the German army right there
in the middle of you, or leastways you in the middle of it, you
still had to lie or trick your way to join the French one." Because
all he said was, "I was wrong." And not even another year after

I

that when I said to him, "Even despite that splendid glorious music and them splendid mystical ideas?" he jest says:

"They are still glorious, still splendid. It's the word *mystical* that's wrong. The music and the ideas both come out of obscurity, darkness. Not out of shadow: out of obscurity, obfuscation, darkness. Man must have light. He must live in the fierce full constant glare of light, where all shadow will be defined and sharp and unique and personal: the shadow of his own singular rectitude or baseness. All human evils have to come out of obscurity and darkness, where there is nothing to dog man constantly with the shape of his own deformity."

In fact, not until two or three years more and he was back home now, settled now; and Eula, still without having to do no more than jest breathe as far as he was concerned, had already adopted the rest of his life as long as it would be needed, into the future of that eleven- or twelve-year-old girl, and I said to him:

"Helen walked in light," And he says,

"Helen was light. That's why we can still see her, not changed, not even dimmer, from five thousand years away." And I says,

"What about all them others you talk about? Semiramises and Judiths and Liliths and Francescas and Isoldes?" And he says,

"But not like Helen. Not that bright, that luminous, that enduring. It's because the others all talked. They are fading steadily into the obscurity of their own vocality within which their passions and tragedies took place. But not Helen. Do you know there is not one recorded word of hers anywhere in existence, other than that one presumable Yes she must have said that time to Paris?"

So there they was. That gal of thirteen and fourteen and fifteen that wasn't trying to do nothing but jest get shut of having to go to school by getting there on time and knowing the lesson to make the rise next year, that likely wouldn't barely ever looked at him long enough to know him again except that she found out on a sudden that for some reason he was trying to adopt some of her daily life into hisn, or adopt a considerable chunk of his daily life into hern, whichever way you want to put it. And that bachelor lawyer twice her age, that was already more or less in the public eye from being county attorney, not to mention in a little town like Jefferson where ever time you had

your hair cut your constituency knowed about it by suppertime.
So that the best they knowed to do was to spend fifteen minutes
after school one or two afternoons a week at a table in the
window of Uncle Willy Christian's drugstore while she et a
ice-cream sody or a banana split and the ice melted into the
unteched Coca-Cola in front of him. Not jest the best but the only
thing, not jest for the sake of her good name but also for them
votes that two years from now might not consider buying ice-
cream for fourteen-year-old gals a fitting qualification for a
county attorney.

About twice a week meeting her by that kind of purely
coincidental accident that looked jest exactly as accidental as you
would expect: Lawyer ambushed behind his upstairs office
window across the street until the first of the let-out school
would begin to pass, which would be the kindergarden and the
first grade, then by that same accidental coincidence happening
to be on the corner at the exact time to cut her outen the seventh
or eighth or ninth grade, her looking a little startled and surprised the first time or two; not alarmed: jest startled a little,
wondering jest a little at first maybe what he wanted. But not
for long; that passed too and pretty soon Lawyer was even
drinking maybe a inch of the Coca-Cola before it got too luke-
warm to swallow. Until one day I says to him: "I envy you," and
he looked at me and I says, "Your luck," and he says,

"My which luck?" and I says,

"You are completely immersed twenty-four hours a day in
being busy. Most folks ain't. Almost nobody ain't. But you are.
Doing the one thing you not only got to do, but the one thing
in the world you want most to do. And if that wasn't already
enough, it's got as many or maybe even more interesting technical
complications in it than if you had invented it yourself instead
of jest being discovered by it. For the sake of her good name,
you got to do it right out in that very same open public eye
that would ruin her good if it ever found a chance, but maybe
wouldn't never even suspect you and she knowed one another's
name if you jest kept it hidden in secret. Don't you call that
keeping busy?"

Because he was unenchanted now, you see, done freed at last
of that fallen seraphim. It was Eula herself had give him a

salve, a ointment, for that bitter thumb the poets say ever man once in his life has got to gnaw at: that gal thirteen then fourteen then fifteen setting opposite him in Christian's drugstore maybe two afternoons a week in the intervals of them coincidental two or three weeks ever year while Miz Flem Snopes and her daughter would be on a holiday somewhere at the same coincidental time Manfred de Spain would be absent on hisn—not Mayor de Spain now but Banker de Spain since Colonel Sartoris finally vacated the presidency of the bank him and De Spain's paw and Will Varner had established, by letting his grandson run the automobile off into a ditch on the way to town one morning, and now Manfred de Spain was president of the bank, moving outen the mayor's office into the president's office at about the same more or less coincidental moment that Flem Snopes moved outen being the ex-superintendent of the power plant, into being vice-president of the bank, vacating simultaneously outen that little cloth cap he come to Jefferson in (jest vacated, not abandoned it, the legend being he sold it to a Negro boy for ten cents. Which wouldn't be a bad price, since who knows if maybe some of that-ere financial acumen might not a sweated off on to it.) into a black felt planter's hat suitable to his new position and avocation.

Oh yes, Lawyer was unenchanted now, even setting alone now and then in Christian's window while the ice melted into the Coca-Cola until they would get back home, maybe to be ready and in practice when them two simultaneous coincidences was over and school would open again on a whole fresh year of two afternoons a week—providing of course that sixteen- and seventeen-year-old gal never run into a Hoake McCarron or a Manfred de Spain of her own between two of them and Lawyer could say to you like the man in the book: *What you see ain't tears. You jest think that's what you're looking at.*

Sixteen and seventeen and going on eighteen now and Lawyer still lending her books to read and keeping her stallfed twice a week on ice-cream sundaes and banana splits, so anyhow Jefferson figgered it knowed what Lawyer was up to whether he admitted it out or not. And naturally Eula had already knowed for five or six years what she was after. Like there's a dog, maybe not no extra dog but leastways a good sound what you might

call a dog's dog, that don't seem to belong to nobody else, that
seems to show a preference for your vicinity, that even after the
five or six years you ain't completely convinced there won't
never be no other dog available, and that even them five or six
years back and even with another five or six years added on to
now, you never needed and you ain't going to need that dog
personally, there ain't any use in simply throwing away and
wasting its benefits and accomplishments, even if they ain't
nothing but fidelity and devotion, by letting somebody else
get a-holt of it. Or say you got a gal child coming along, that the
older and bigger she gets, the more of a nuisance she's bound to
be on your time and private occupations: in which case not only
won't that fidelity and devotion maybe come into handy use,
but even the dog itself might that could still be capable of them
long after even hit had give up all expectation of even one bone.

Which is what Jefferson figgered. But not me. Maybe even
though she got rid of Hoake McCarron, even after she knowed
she was pregnant, there is still moments when even female
physical phenomenons is female first whether they want to be
or not. So I believe that women ain't so different from men:
that if it ain't no trouble nor shock neither for a man to father
on to his-self the first child of the woman he loved and lost and
still can't rid outen his mind, no matter how many other men
holp to get it, it ain't no trouble neither for that woman to
father a dozen different men's chillen on to that man that lost
her and still never expected nothing of her except to accept his
devotion.

And since she was a female too, likely by the time Linda was
thirteen or fourteen or even maybe as soon as she got over that
first startle, which would a been at the second or third ice-cream
sody, she taken for granted she knowed what he was aiming at
too. And she would a been wrong. That wasn't Lawyer. Jest to
train her up and marry her wasn't it. She wouldn't a been
necessary for that—I mean, the simple natural normal following
lifetime up to the divorce of steady uxorious hymeneal conflict
that any female he could a picked outen that school crowd or
from Christian's sody counter would been fully competent for.
Jest that wouldn't a been worth his effort. He had to be the
sole one masculine feller within her entire possible circum-

ambience, not jest to recognise she had a soul still capable of being saved from what he called Snopesism: a force and power that stout and evil as to jeopardise it jest from her believing for twelve or thirteen years she was blood kin when she actively wasn't no kin a-tall, but that couldn't nobody else in range and reach but him save it—that-ere bubble-glass thing somewhere inside her like one of them shimmer-coloured balls balanced on the seal's nose, fragile yet immune too jest that one constant fragile inch above the smutch and dirt of Snopes as long as the seal don't trip or stumble or let her attention wander.

So all he aimed to do was jest to get her outen Jefferson or, better, safer still, completely outen Missippi, starting off with the nine months of the school year, until somebody would find her and marry her and she would be gone for good—a optimist pure and simple and undefiled if there ever was one since ever body knowed that the reason Flem Snopes was vice-president of De Spain's bank was the same reason he was ex-superintendent of the power plant: in the one case folks wanting to smile at Eula Varner had to at least be able to pronounce Flem Snopes, and in the other De Spain has to take Flem along with him to get the use of Will Varner's voting stock to get his-self president. And the only reason why Will Varner never used this chance to get back at Flem about that Old Frenchman homesite that Will thought wasn't worth nothing until Flem sold it to me and Odum Bookwright and Henry Armstid for my half of mine and Grover Winbush's café and Odum Bookwright's cash and the two-hundred-dollar mortgage on Henry's farm less them five or six dollars or whatever they was where Henry's wife tried to keep them buried from him behind the outhouse, was the same reason why Eula didn't quit Flem and marry De Spain: that staying married to Flem kept up a establishment and name for that gal that otherwise wouldn't a had either. So once that gal was married herself or leastways settled for good away from Jefferson so she wouldn't need Flem's name and establishment no more, and in consequence Flem wouldn't have no holt over her any more, Flem his-self would be on the outside trying to look back in and Flem knowed it.

Only Lawyer didn't know it. He believed right up to the last that Flem was going to let him get Linda away from Jefferson to where the first strange young man that happened by would marry her and then Eula could quit him and he would be finished. He—I mean Lawyer—had been giving her books to read ever since she was fourteen and then kind of holding examinations on them while the Coca-Cola ice melted. Then she was going on seventeen, next spring she would graduate from the high school and now he was ordering off for the catalogues from the extra-select girls' schools up there close to Harvard.

Now the part comes that don't nobody know except Lawyer, who naturally never told it. So as he his-self would say, you got to surmise from the facts in evidence: not jest the mind-improving books and the school catalogues accumulating into a dusty stack in his office, but the ice-cream sessions a thing of the past too. Because now she was going to and from school the back way, up alleys. Until finally in about a week maybe Lawyer realised that she was dodging him. And she was going to graduate from high school in less than two months now and there wasn't no time to waste. So that morning Lawyer went his-self to talk to her maw and he never told that neither so now we got to presume on a little more than jest evidence. Because my childhood too come out of that same similar Frenchman's Bend background and mill-yew that Flem Snopes had lifted his-self out of by his own unaided bootstraps, if you don't count Hoake McCarron. So all I had to do was jest to imagine my name was Flem Snopes and that the only holt I had on Will Varner's money was through his daughter, and if I ever lost what light holt I had on the granddaughter, the daughter would be gone. Yet here was a durn meddling outsider with a complete set of plans that would remove that granddaughter to where I wouldn't never see her again, if she had any sense a-tall. And since the daughter had evidently put up with me for going on eighteen years now for the sake of that granddaughter, the answer was simple: all I needed to do was go to my wife and say, "If you give that gal permission to go away to school, I'll blow up this-here entire Manfred de Spain business to where she won't have no home to have to get away from, let alone one to come back to for Christmas and holidays."

And for her first eighteen years Eula breathed that same

Frenchman's Bend mill-yew atmosphere too so maybe all I got to do is imagine my name is Eula Varner to know what she said back to Lawyer: "No, she can't go off to school but you can marry her. That will solve ever thing." You see? Because the kind of fidelity and devotion that could keep faithful and devoted that long without even wanting no bone any more, was not only too valuable to let get away, it even deserved to be rewarded. Because maybe the full rounded satisfaction and completeness of being Helen was bigger than a thousand Parises and McCarrons and De Spains could satisfy. I don't mean jest the inexhaustible capacity for passion, but of power: the power not jest to draw and enchant and consume, but the power and capacity to give away and reward; the power to draw to you, not more than you can handle because the words "can't-handle" and "Helen" ain't even in the same language, but to draw to you so much more than you can possibly need that you could even afford to give the surplus away, be that prodigal—except that you are Helen and you can't give nothing away that was ever yourn: all you can do is share it and reward its fidelity and maybe even, for a moment, soothe and assuage its grief. And cruel too, prodigal in that too, because you are Helen and can afford it; you got to be Helen to be that cruel, that prodigal in cruelty, and still be yourself unscathed and immune, likely calling him by his first name for the first time too: "Marry her, Gavin."

And saw in his face not jest startlement and a little surprise like he seen in Linda's that time, but terror, fright, not at having to answer "No" that quick nor even at being asked it because he believed he had done already asked and decided that suh-jestion forever a long while back. It was at having it suh-jested to him by her. Like, since he hadn't been able to have no hope since that moment when he realised Manfred de Spain had already looked at her too, he had found out how to live at peace with hoping since he was the only one alive that knowed he never had none. But now, when she said that right out loud to his face, it was like she had said right out in public that he wouldn't a had no hope even if Manfred de Spain hadn't never laid eyes on her. And if he could jest get that "No" out quick enough, it would be like maybe she hadn't actively said what she said, and he would still not be destroyed.

At least wasn't nobody, no outsider, there to hear it so maybe even before next January he was able to believe hadn't none of it even been said, like miracle: what ain't believed ain't seen. Miracle, pure miracle anyhow, how little a man needs to outlast jest about anything. Which—miracle—is about what looked like had happened next January: Linda graduated that spring from high school and next fall she entered the Seminary where she would be home ever night and all day Saturday and Sunday the same as before so Flem could keep his hand on her. Then jest after Christmas we heard how she had withdrawed from the Seminary and was going over to Oxford and enter the University. Yes sir, over there fifty miles from Flem day and night both right in the middle of a nest of five or six hundred bachelors under twenty-five years old any one of which could marry her that had two dollars for a licence. A pure miracle, especially after I run into Eula on the street and says,

"How did you manage it?" and she says,

"Manage what?" and I says,

"Persuade Flem to let her go to the University," and she says,

"I didn't. It was his idea. He gave the permission without even consulting me. I didn't know he was going to do it either." Only the Frenchman's Bend background should have been enough, without even needing the sixteen or seventeen years of Jefferson environment, to reveal even to blind folks that Flem Snopes didn't deal in miracles: that he preferred spot cash or at least a signed paper with a X on it. So when it was all over and finished, Eula dead and De Spain gone from Jefferson for good too and Flem was now president of the bank and even living in De Spain's rejuvenated ancestral home and Linda gone with her New York husband to fight in the Spanish war, when Lawyer finally told me what little he actively knowed, it was jest evidence I had already presumed on. Because of course all Helen's children would have to inherit something of generosity even if they couldn't inherit more than about one-millionth of their maw's bounty to be generous with. Not to mention that McCarron boy, that even if he wasn't durable enough to stand more than that-ere first creek bridge, was at least brave enough or rash enough to try to. So likely Flem already knowed in advance that he wouldn't have to bargain, swap, with her. That all he needed was jest to do what he probably done: ketching her after she had give up and then had had them three months to settle down into having give up, then saying to her: "Let's compromise. If you will give up them eastern schools, maybe you can go to the University over at Oxford." You see? Offering to give something that, in all the fourteen or fifteen years she could remember knowing him in, she had never dreamed he would do.

Then that day in the next April; she had been at the University over at Oxford since right after New Year's. I was jest leaving for Rockyford to deliver Miz Ledbetter's new sewing machine when Flem stopped me on the Square and offered me four bits extra to carry him by Varner's store a minute. Urgent enough to pay me four bits when the mail carrier would have took him for nothing; secret enough that he couldn't risk either public conveyance: the mail carrier that would a took him out and back free but would a needed all day, or a hired automobile that would had him at Varner's front gate in not much over a hour.

Secret enough and urgent enough to have Will Varner storming into his daughter's and son-in-law's house in Jefferson before daylight the next morning loud enough to wake up the whole neighbourhood until somebody (Eula naturally) stopped him. So we got to presume on a few known facts again: that Old Frenchman place that Will deeded to Flem because he thought it was worthless until Flem sold it to me and Odum Bookwright and Henry Armstid (less of course the active silver dollars Flem had had to invest into that old rose garden with a shovel where we—or any other Ratliffs and Bookwrights and Armstids that was handy—would find them). And that president's chair in the bank that we knowed now Flem had had his eye on ever since Manfred de Spain taken it over after Colonel Sartoris. And that gal that had done already inherited generosity from her maw and then was suddenly give another gob of it that she not only never in the world expected but that she probably never knowed how bad she wanted it until it was suddenly give to her free.

What Flem taken out to Frenchman's Bend that day was a will. Maybe when Linda finally got over the shock of getting permission to go away to school after she had long since give up any hope of it, even if no further away than Oxford, maybe when

she looked around and realised who that permission had come
from, she jest could not bear to be under obligations to him.
Except I don't believe that neither. It wasn't even that little of
bounty and generosity which would be all Helen's child could
inherit from her, since half of even Helen's child would have to
be corrupted by something less than Helen, being as even Helen
couldn't get a child on herself alone. What Linda wanted was not
jest to give. It was to be needed: not jest to be loved and wanted,
but to be needed too; and maybe this was the first time in her
life she ever had anything that anybody not jest wanted but
needed too.

It was a will; Eula of course told Lawyer. Flem his-self could
a suh-jested the idea to Linda; it wouldn't a been difficult.
Which I don't believe neither. He didn't need to; he knowed her
well enough to presume on that, jest like she knowed him
enough to presume too. It was Linda herself that evolved the
idea when she realised that as long as he lived and drawed
breath as Flem Snopes, he wasn't never going to give her permission to leave Jefferson for any reason. And her asking herself,
impotent and desperate: *But why? why?* until finally she answered
it—a answer that maybe wouldn't a helt much water but she
was jest sixteen and seventeen then, during which sixteen and
seventeen years she had found out that the only thing he loved
was money. Because she must a knowed something anyway about
Manfred de Spain. Jefferson wasn't that big, if in fact any place
is. Not to mention them two or three weeks of summer holiday
at the seashore or mountains or wherever, when here all of a
sudden who should turn up but a old Jefferson neighbour
happening by accident to take his vacation too from the bank at
the same time and place. So what else would she say? *It's grandfather's money, that his one and only chance to keep any holt on it is
through mama and me so he believes that once I get away from him his
holt on both of us will be broken and mama will leave too and marry
Manfred and any hope of grandfather's money will be gone forever.*

Yet here was this man that had had sixteen or seventeen
years to learn her he didn't love nothing but money and would
do anything you could suh-jest to get another dollar of it, coming
to her his-self, without no pressure from nobody and not asking
for nothing back, saying, *You can go away to school if you still want*

to; only, this first time anyhow stay at least as close to home as Oxford; saying in effect: *I was wrong. I won't no longer stand between you and your life, even though I am convinced I will be throwing away all hope of your grandpaw's money.*

So what else could she do but what she done, saying in effect back at him: *If you jest realised now that grandfather's money ain't as important as my life, I could a told you that all the time; if you had jest told me two years ago that all you was was jest skeered, I would a eased you then*—going (Lawyer his-self told me this) to a Oxford lawyer as soon as she was settled in the University and drawing up a will leaving whatever share she might ever have in her grandpaw's or her maw's estate to her father Flem Snopes. Sho, that wouldn't a held no water neither, but she was jest eighteen and that was all she had to give that she thought anybody wanted or needed from her; and besides, all the water it would need to hold would be what old Will Varner would sweat out when Flem showed it to him.

So jest after ten that morning I stopped not at the store where Will would be at this hour but at his front gate jest exactly long enough for Flem to get out and walk into the house until he coincided with Miz Varner I reckon it was and turn around and come back out and get back into the pickup and presumably at their two oclock a.m. morning family breakfast it occurred to Miz Varner or anyway she decided to or anyhow did hand Will the paper his son-in-law left yestiddy for him to look at. And by sunup Will had that whole Snopes street woke up hollering inside Flem's house until Eula got him shut up. And by our normal ee-feet Jefferson breakfast time Manfred de Spain was there too. And that done it. Will Varner, that Flem had done already tricked outen that Old Frenchman place, then turned right around and used him again to get his-self and Manfred de Spain vice-president and president respectively of Colonel Sartoris's bank, and now Flem had done turned back around the third time and somehow tricked his granddaughter into giving him a quit-claim to half of his active cash money that so far even Flem hadn't found no way to touch. And Flem, that all he wanted was for Manfred de Spain to resign from the bank so he could be president of it and would jest as lief done it quiet and discreet and all private in the family you might say by a simple friendly

suh-jestion from Will Varner to Manfred to resign from the
bank, as a even swap for that paper of Linda's, which should a
worked with anybody and would with anybody else except
Manfred. He was the trouble; likely Eula could a handled them
all except for him. Maybe he got that-ere scar on his face by
actively toting a flag up a hill in Cuba and running over a
cannon or a fort with it, and maybe it come from the axe in that
crap game that old mayor's-race rumour claimed. But leastways
it was on his front and not on his back and so maybe a feller
could knock him out with a piece of lead pipe and pick his
pocket while he was laying there, but couldn't no Snopes nor
nobody else pick it jest by pointing at him what the other feller
thought was a pistol.

And Eula in the middle of them, that likely could a handled
it all except for Manfred, that had even made Will shut up but
she couldn't make Manfred hush. That had done already spent
lacking jest a week of nineteen years holding together a home for
Linda to grow up and live in so she wouldn't never need to say,
Other children have got what I never had; there was Eula having to
decide right there right now, *If I was a eighteen-year-old gal, which
would I rather have: my mother publicly notarised as a suicide, or publicly
condemned as a whore?* and by noon the next day all Jefferson
knowed how the afternoon before she come to town and went to
the beauty parlour that hadn't never been in one before because
she never needed to, and had her hair waved and her fingernails
shined and went back home and presumably et supper or anyhow was present at it since it wasn't until about eleven o'clock
that she seemed to taken up the pistol and throwed the safety off.

And the next morning Lawyer and his sister drove over to
Oxford and brought Linda home; a pure misfortune coincidence
that all this had to happen jest a week before her nineteenth
birthday. But as soon as Flem received that will from her,
naturally he figgered Will Varner would want to see it as soon
as possible, being a interested party; it was Will that never had
no reason a-tall to pick out that special day to come bellering
in to town two hours after he first seen it. He could a jest as well
waited two weeks or even a month to come in, since wasn't
nobody hurrying him; Flem would certainly a waited on his
convenience.

And Lawyer that tended to the rest of it too: arranged for the funeral and sent out to Frenchman's Bend for Miz Varner and the old Methodist preacher that had baptised Eula, and then seen to the grave. Because naturally the bereaved husband couldn't be expected to break into his grief jest to do chores. Not to mention having to be ready to take over the bank after a decent interval, being as Manfred de Spain his-self had packed up and departed from Jefferson right after the burying. And then, after another decorious interval, a little longer this time being as a bank ain't like jest a house because a bank deals with active cash money and can't wait, getting ready to move into De Spain's house too since De Spain had give ever evident intention of not aiming to return to Jefferson from his last what you might still call Varner trip and there wasn't no use in letting a good sound well-situated house stand vacant and empty. Which—De Spain's house—was likely a part of that same swapping and trading between Flem and Will Varner that included Varner's bank-stock votes and that-ere financial Midsummer Night's Dream masque or rondeau that Linda and that Oxford lawyer composed betwixt them that had Linda's signature on it. Not to mention Lawyer being appointed by old man Will to be trustee of Linda's money since it was now finally safe from Flem until he thought up something that Lawyer would believe too this time. Will appointing Lawyer for the reason that likely he couldn't pass by Lawyer to get to no one else, Lawyer being not only in the middle of that entire monetary and sepulchrial crisis but all around ever part of it too, like one of them frantic water bugs skating and rushing immune and unwettable on top of a stagnant pond.

I mean, Lawyer was now busy over the headstone Flem had decided on. Because it would have to be made in Italy, which would take time, and so would demand ever effort on Lawyer's part before Linda could pack up and leave Jefferson too, being as Flem felt that that same filial decorum demanded that Linda wait until her maw's headstone was up and finished before leaving. Only I don't mean jest headstone: I mean monument: Lawyer combing and currying not jest Jefferson and Frenchman's Bend but most of the rest of Yoknapatawpha County too, hunting out ever photograph of Eula he could locate to send to Italy so they could carve Eula's face in stone to put on it. Which is when I noticed again how there ain't nobody quite as temerious as a otherwise timid feller that finds out that his moral standards and principles is now demanding him to do something that, if all he had to depend on was jest his own satisfaction and curiosity, he wouldn't a had the brass to do, penetrating into ever house that not only might a knowed Eula but that jest had a Brownie Kodak, thumbing through albums and intimate photographic family records, courteous and polite of course but jest a man obviously not in no condition to be said No to, let alone merely Please don't.

He could keep busy now. Because he was contented and happy now, you see. He never had nothing to worry him now. Eula was safely gone now and now he could be safe forevermore from ever again having to chew his bitter poetic thumbs over the constant anticipation of who would turn up next named McCarron or De Spain. And now Linda was not only safe for good from Flem, he, Lawyer, even had the full charge and control of her money from her maw and grandpaw, so that now she could go any-where she wanted—providing of course he could nag and harry them folks across the water to finish carving that face before the millennium or judgment day come, gathering up all the pictures of Eula he could find and sending them to Italy and then waiting until a drawing or a photograph of how the work was coming along would get back for him to see jest how wrong it was, and he would send me word to be at his office at a certain hour for the conference, with the newest fresh Italian sketch or photograph laid out on the desk with a special light on it and him saying, "It's the ear, or the line of the jaw, or the mouth—right here: see what I mean?" and I would say,

"It looks all right to me. It looks beautiful to me." And he would say,

"No. It's wrong right here. Hand me a pencil." Except he would already have a pencil, and he couldn't draw neither so he would have to rub that out and try again. Except that time was passing so he would have to send it back; and Flem and Linda living in De Spain's house now and now Flem had done bought a automobile that he couldn't drive but anyhow he had a daughter that could, leastways now and then; until at last even

that was over. It was October and Lawyer sent me word the
unveiling at the graveyard would be that afternoon. Except I
had done already got word to Chick, since from the state of
peace and contentment Lawyer had got his-self into by this
time, it might take both of us. So Chick stayed outen school that
afternoon so all three of us went out to the cemetery together in
Lawyer's car. And there was Linda and Flem too, in Flem's
car with the Negro driver that was going to drive her on to
Memphis to take the New York train with her packed grips
already in the car, and Flem leaning back in the seat with that
black hat on that even after five years still didn't look like it
actively belonged to him, chewing, and Linda beside him in her
dark going-away dress and hat with her head bent a little and
them little white gloves shut into fists on her lap. And there it
was: that-ere white monument with on the front of it that face
that even if it was carved outen dead stone, was still the same
face that ever young man no matter how old he got would still
never give up hope and belief that some day before he died he
would finally be worthy to be wrecked and ruined and maybe
even destroyed by it, above the motto that Flem his-self had
picked:

A Virtuous Wife Is a Crown to Her Husband
Her Children Rise and Call Her Blessed

Until at last Flem leaned out the window and spit and then set
back in the car and tells her: "All right. You can go now."

Yes sir, Lawyer was free now. He never had nothing to worry
him now: him and Chick and me driving back to the office and
him talking about how the game of football could be brought up
to date in keeping with the progress of the times by giving ever
body a football too so ever body would be in the game; or maybe
better still, keep jest one football but abolish the boundaries so
that a smart feller for instance could hide the ball under his
shirttail and slip off into the bushes and circle around town and
come in through a back alley and cross the goal before anybody
even missed he was gone; right on into the office where he set
down behind the desk and taken up one of the cob pipes and
struck three matches to it until Chick taken it away from him

and filled it from the tobacco jar and handed it back and Lawyer says, "Much obliged," and dropped the filled pipe into the wastebasket and folded his hands on the desk, still talking, and I says to Chick:

"Watch him. I won't be long," and went around into the alley; I never had much time so what was in the pint bottle was pretty bad but leastways it had something in it that for a moment anyhow would feel like alcohol. And I got the sugar bowl and glass and spoon from the cabinet and made the toddy and set it on the desk by him and he says,

"Much obliged," not even touching it, jest setting there with his hands folded in front of him, blinking quick and steady like he had sand in his eyes, saying: "All us civilised people date our civilisation from the discovery of the principle of distillation. And even though the rest of the world, at least that part of it in the United States, rates us folks in Mississippi at the lowest rung of culture, what man can deny that, even if this is as bad as I think it's going to be, we too grope toward the stars? Why did she do it, V.K.? That—all that—that she walked in, lived in, breathed in —it was only loaned to her; it wasn't hers to destroy and throw away. It belonged to too many. It belonged to all of us. Why, V.K.?" he says. "Why?"

"Maybe she was bored," I says, and he says:

"Bored. Yes, bored." And that was when he began to cry. "She loved, had the capacity to love, to give and to take it. Only she tried twice and failed twice not jest to find somebody strong enough to deserve it but even brace enough to accept it. Yes," he says, setting there bolt upright with jest the tears running down his face, at peace now, with nothing nowhere in the world any more to anguish or grieve him. "Of course she was bored."

SEVEN

V. K. Ratliff

So he was free. He had not only got shut of his sireen, he had even got shut of the ward he found out she had heired to him. Because I says, "Grinnich Village?" and he says,

"Yes. A little place without physical boundaries located as far as she is concerned in New York City, where young people of all ages below ninety go in search of dreams." Except I says,

"Except she never had to leave Missippi to locate that place." And then I said it, what Eula herself must have, had to have, said to him that day: "Why didn't you marry her?"

"Because she wasn't but nineteen," he says.

"And you are all of thirty-five, ain't you," I says. "When the papers are full of gals still carrying a doll in one hand marrying folks of sixty and seventy, providing of course they got a little extra money."

"I mean, she's got too much time left to run into something where she might need me. How many papers are full of people that got married because someday they might need the other one?"

"Oh," I says. "So all you got to do now is jest stay around close where you can hear the long-distance telephone or the telegram boy can find you. Because naturally you won't be waiting for her to ever come back to Missippi. Or maybe you are?"

"Naturally not," he says. "Why should she?"

"Thank God!" I says. He didn't answer. "Because who knows," I says, "she may done already found that dream even in jest these . . . two days, ain't it? three? Maybe he was already settled there when she arrived. That's possible in Grinnich Village, ain't it?"

Then he said it too. "Yes," he says, "thank God." So he was free. And in fact, when you had time to look around a little, he never had nothing no more to do but jest rest in peace and quiet and contentment. Because not only him but all Jefferson was free of Snopeses; for the first time in going on twenty years, Jefferson and Yoknapatawpha County too was in what you might call a kind of Snopes doldrum. Because at last even Flem seemed to be satisfied: setting now at last in the same chair the presidents

of the Merchants and Farmers Bank had been setting in ever
since the first one, Colonel Sartoris, started it twenty-odd years
ago, and actively living in the very house the second one of it was
born in, so that all he needed to do too after he had done locked
up the money and went home was to live in solitary peace and
quiet and contentment too, not only shut of the daughter that
had kept him on steady and constant tenterhooks for years
whether she might not escape at any moment to where he
couldn't watch her and the first male feller that come along
would marry her and he would lose her share of Will Varner's
money, but shut of the wife that at any time her and Manfred de
Spain would get publicly caught up with and cost him all the
rest of Varner's money and bank voting stock too.

In fact for the moment Flem was the only true Snopes actively
left in Jefferson. Old man Ab never had come no closer than
that hill two miles out where you could jest barely see the water
tank, where he taken the studs that day back about 1910 and
hadn't moved since. And four years ago Flem had ci-devanted
I.O. back to Frenchman's Bend for good. And even before that
Flem had eliminated Montgomery Ward into the penitentiary at
Parchman where Mink already was (Mink hadn't really resided
in Jefferson nohow except jest them few months in the jail
waiting for his life sentence to be awarded). And last month
them four half-Snopes Indians that Byron Snopes, Colonel
Sartoris's bank clerk that resigned by the simple practical
expedient of picking up as much of the loose money he could
tote and striking for the nearest U.S. border, sent back collect
from Mexico until somebody could get close enough to fasten
the return prepaid tags on them before whichever one had it
at the moment could get out that switch-blade knife. And as for
Eck's boys, Wall Street Panic and Admiral Dewey, they hadn't
never been Snopeses to begin with, since all Wall Street evidently
wanted to do was run a wholesale grocery business by the
outrageous un-Snopesish method of jest selling ever body
exactly what they thought they was buying, for exactly what
they thought they was going to pay for it.

Or almost satisfied that is. I mean Flem and his new house.
It was jest a house: two-storey, with a gallery for Major de Spain,
Manfred's paw, to set on when he wasn't fishing or hunting or

practising a little law, and it was all right for that-ere second president of the Merchants and Farmers Bank to live in, especially since he had been born in it. But this was a different president. His road to that chair and that house had been longer than them other two. Likely he knowed he had had to come from too fur away to get where he was, and had to come too hard to reach it by the time he did. Because Colonel Sartoris had been born into money and respectability too, and Manfred de Spain had been born into respectability at least even if he had made a heap of the money since. But he, Flem Snopes, had had to earn both of them, snatch and tear and scrabble both of them outen the hard enduring resisting rock you might say, not jest with his bare hands but with jest one bare hand since he had to keep the other bare single hand fending off while he tore and scrabbled with the first one. So the house the folks owning the money would see Manfred de Spain walk into ever evening after he locked the money up and went home, wouldn't be enough for Flem Snopes. The house they would see him walk into ever evening until time to unlock the money tomorrow morning, would have to be the physical symbol of all them generations of respectability and aristocracy that not only would a been too proud to mishandle other folks' money, but couldn't possibly ever needed to.

So there was another Snopes in Jefferson after all. Not transplanted in from Frenchman's Bend: jest imported in for temporary use. This was Wat Snopes, the carpenter, Watkins Products Snopes his full name was, like it was painted on both sides and the back of Doc Meeks's patent-medicine truck; evidently there was a Snopes somewhere now and then that could read reading, whether he could read writing or not. So during the next nine or ten months anybody that had or could think up the occasion, could pass along the street and watch Wat and his work gang of kinfolks and in-laws tearing off Major de Spain's front gallery and squaring up the back of the house and building and setting up them colyums to reach all the way from the ground up to the second-storey roof, until even when the painting was finished it still wouldn't be as big as Mount Vernon of course, but then Mount Vernon was a thousand miles away so there wasn't no chance of invidious or malicious eye-to-eye comparison.

So that when he locked up the bank and come home in the evening he could walk into a house and shut the door that the folks owning the money he was custodian of would some of them be jealous a little but all of them, even the jealous ones, would be proud and all of them would approve, laying down to rest undisturbed at night with their money that immaculate, that impeccable, that immune. He was completely complete, as the feller says, with a Negro cook and a yardboy that could even drive that-ere automobile now and then since he no longer had a only daughter to drive it maybe once a month to keep the battery up like the man told him he would have to do or buy a new one.

But it was jest the house that was altered and transmogrified and symbolised: not him. The house he disappeared into about four p.m. ever evening until about eight a.m. tomorrow, might a been the solid aristocratic ancestral symbol of Alexander Hamilton and Aaron Burr and Astor and Morgan and Harriman and Hill and ever other golden advocate of hard quick-thinking vested interest, but the feller the owners of that custodianed money seen going and coming out of it was the same one they had done got accustomed to for twenty years now: the same little snap-on bow tie he had got outen the Frenchman's Bend mule wagon in and only the hat was new and different; and even that old cloth cap, that maybe was plenty good enough to be Varner's clerk in but that wasn't to be seen going in and out of a Jefferson bank on the head of its vice-president—even the cap not throwed away or even give away, but sold, even if it wasn't but jest a dime because ten cents is money too around a bank, so that all the owners of that money that he was already vice-custodian of could look at the hat and know that, no matter how little they might a paid for one similar to it, hisn had cost him ten cents less. It wasn't that he rebelled at changing Flem Snopes: he done it by deliberate calculation, since the feller you trust ain't necessarily the one you never knowed to do nothing untrustable: its the one you have seen from experience that he knows exactly when being untrustable will pay a net profit and when it will pay a loss.

And that was jest the house on the outside too, up to the moment when he passed in and closed the front door behind him until eight o'clock tomorrow. And he hadn't never invited nobody in, and so far hadn't nobody been able to invent no way in, so the only folks that ever seen the inside of it was the cook and the yardman and so it was the yardman that told me: all them big rooms furnished like De Spain left them, plus them interior-decorated sweets the Memphis expert learned Eula that being vice-president of a bank he would have to have; that Flem never even went into them except to eat in the dining-room, except that one room at the back where when he wasn't in the bed sleeping he was setting in another swivel chair like the one in the bank, with his feet propped against the side of the fireplace: not reading, not doing nothing: jest setting with his hat on, chewing that same little mouth-sized chunk of air he had been chewing ever since he quit tobacco when he finally got to Jefferson and heard about chewing gum and then quit chewing gum too when he found out folks considered the vice-president of a bank rich enough not to have to chew anything. And how Wat Snopes had found a picture in a magazine how to do over all the fireplaces with colonial moulding and colyums and cornices too and at first Flem would jest set with his feet propped on the white paint, scratching it a little deeper ever day with the pegs in his heels. Until one day about a year after the house was finished over. Wat Snopes was there to eat dinner and after Wat finally left the yardman said how he went into the room and seen it: not a defiance, not a simple reminder of where he had come from but rather as the feller says a reaffirmation of his-self and maybe a warning to his-self too: a little wood ledge, not even painted, nailed to the front of that hand-carved hand-painted Mount Vernon mantelpiece at the exact height for Flem to prop his feet on it.

And time was when that first president, Colonel Sartoris, had come the four miles between his ancestral symbol and his bank in a surrey and matched pair drove by a Negro coachman in a linen duster and one of the Colonel's old plug hats; and time ain't so was when the second president still come and went in that fire-engine-coloured E.M.F. racer until he bought that black Packard and a Negro too except in a white coat and a showfer's cap to drive it. This here new third president had a black automobile too even if it wasn't a Packard, and a Negro that could drive it too even if he never had no white coat and showfer's cap yet and even if the president didn't ride back and forth to the bank or at least not yet. Them two previous presidents would ride around the county in the evening after the bank closed and on Sunday, in that surrey and pair or the black Packard, to look at the cotton farms they represented the mortgages on, while this new president hadn't commenced that neither. Which wasn't because he jest couldn't believe yet that he actively represented the mortgages. He never doubted that. He wasn't skeered to believe it, and he wasn't too meek to nor doubtful to. It was because he was watching yet and learning yet. It wasn't that he had learned two lessons while he thought he was jest learning that single one about how he would need respectability, because he had done already brought that second lesson in from Frenchman's Bend with him. That was humility, the only kind of humility that's worth a hoot: the humility to know they's a heap of things you don't know yet but if you jest got the patience to be humble and watchful long enough, especially keeping one eye on your back trail, you will. So now on the evenings and Sundays there was jest that house where you wasn't invited in to see him setting in that swivel chair in that one room he used, with his hat on and chewing steady on nothing and his feet propped on that little wooden additional ledge nailed in unpainted paradox to that hand-carved and painted mantel like one of them framed mottoes you keep hanging on the wall where you work or think, saying *Remember Death* or *Keep Smiling* or *-Working* or *God is Love* to remind not jest you but the strangers that see it too, that you got at least a speaking acquaintance with the fact that it might be barely possible it taken a little something more than jest you to get you where you're at.

But all that, footrest and all, would come later. Right now, Lawyer was free. And then—it wasn't no three days after Linda reached New York, but it wasn't no three hundred neither—he become, as the feller says, indeed free. He was leaning against the counter in the post-office lobby with the letter already open in his hand when I come in; it wasn't his fault neither that the lobby happened to be empty at the moment.

"His name is Barton Kohl," he says.

"Sho now," I says. "Whose name is?"

"That dream's name," he says.

"Cole," I says.

"No," he says. "You're pronouncing it Cole. It's spelled K-o-h-l."

"Oh," I says. "Kohl. That don't sound very American to me."

"Does Vladimir Kyrilytch sound very American to you?"

But the lobby was empty. Which, as I said, wasn't his fault. "Confound it," I says, "with one Ratliff in ever generation for them whole hundred and fifty years since your durn Yankee Congress banished us into the Virginia mountains, has had to spend half his life trying to live down his front name before somebody spoke it out loud where folks could hear it. It was Eula told you."

"All right," he says. 'I'll help you bury your family shame. —Yes," he says. "He's a Jew. A sculptor, probably a damned good one."

"Because of that?" I says.

"Probably, but not exclusively. Because of her."

"Linda'll make him into a good sculptor, no matter what he was before, because she married him?"

"No. He would have to be the best of whatever he was for her to pick him out."

"So she's married now," I says.

"What?" he says. "No. She just met him, I tell you."

"So you ain't—" I almost said *safe yet* before I changed it: "—sure yet. I mean, she ain't decided yet."

"What the hell else am I talking about? Don't you remember what I told you last fall? that she would love once and it would be for keeps"

"Except that you said 'doomed to'."

"All right," he says.

"Doomed to fidelity and grief, you said. To love once quick and lose him quick and for the rest of her life to be faithful and to grieve. But leastways she ain't lost him yet. In fact, she ain't even got him yet. That's correct, aint it?"

"Didn't I say all right?" he says.

That was the first six months, about. Another year after that, that-ere little footrest ledge was up on that hand-painted Mount

Vernon mantel—that-ere little raw wood step like out of a scrap pile, nailed by a country carpenter on to that what you might call respectability's virgin Matterhorn for the Al-pine climber to cling to panting, gathering his-self for that last do-or-die upsurge to deface the ultimate crowning pinnacle and peak with his own victorious initials. But not this one; and here was that humility again: not in public where it would be a insult to any and all that held Merchants and Farmers Bank Al-pine climbing in veneration, but in private like a secret chapel or a shrine: not to cling panting to it, desperate and indomitable, but to prop his feet on it while setting at his ease.

This time I was passing the office stairs when Lawyer come rushing around the corner as usual, with most of the law papers flying along loose in his outside pockets but a few of them still in his hand too as usual. I mean, he had jest two gaits: one standing more or less still and the other like his coat-tail was on fire. "Run back home and get your grip," he says. "We're leaving Memphis tonight for New York."

So we went up the stairs and as soon as we was inside the office he changed to the other gait as usual. He throwed the loose papers on to the desk and taken one of the cob pipes outen the dish and set down, only when he fumbled in his coat for the matches or tobacco or whatever it was he discovered the rest of the papers and throwed them on to the desk and set back in the chair like he had done already had all the time in the world and couldn't possibly anticipate nothing else happening in the next hundred years neither. "For the housewarming," he says.

"You mean the reception, don't you? Ain't that what they call it after the preacher has done collected his two dollars?" He didn't say anything, jest setting there working at lighting that pipe like a jeweller melting one exact drop of platinum maybe into a watch. "So they ain't going to marry," I says. "They're jest going to confederate. I've heard that: that that's why they call them Grinnich Village samples dreams: you can wake up without having to jump outen the bed in a dead run for the nearest lawyer."

He didn't move. He jest bristled, that lively and quick he never had time to change his position. He sat there and bristled like a hedgehog, not moving of course: jest saying cold and calm, since even a hedgehog, once it has got itself arranged and prickled out, can afford a cold and calm collected voice too: "All right. I'll arrogate the term 'marriage' to it then. Do you protest or question it? Maybe you would even suggest a better one?—Because there's not enough time left," he says. "Enough left? There's none left. Young people today don't have any left because only fools under twenty-five can believe, let alone hope, that there's any left at all—for any of us, anybody alive today—"

"It don't take much time to say We both do in front of a preacher and then pay whatever the three of you figger it's worth."

"Didn't I just say there's not even that much left if all you've had is just twenty-five or thirty years—"

"So that's how old he is," I says. "You stopped at jest twenty-five before."

He didn't stop at nowhere now: "Barely a decade since their fathers and uncles and brothers just finished the one which was to rid the phenomenon of government forever of the parasites —the hereditary properties, the farmers-general of the human dilemma who had just killed eight million human beings and ruined a forty-mile-wide strip down the middle of western Europe. Yet less than a dozen years later and the same old cynical manipulators not even bothering to change their names and faces but merely assuming a set of new titles out of the shibboleth of the democratic lexicon and its mythology, not even breaking stride to coalesce again to wreck the one doomed desperate hope—" *Now he will resume the folks that broke President Wilson's heart and killed the League of Nations* I thought, but he was the one that didn't even break stride: "That one already in Italy and one a damned sight more dangerous in Germany because all Mussolini has to work with are Italians while this other man has Germans. And the one in Spain that all he needs is to be let alone a little longer by the rest of us who still believe that if we just keep our eyes closed long enough it will all go away. Not to mention—"

"Not to mention the one in Russia," I said.

"—the ones right here at home: the organisations with the

fine names confederated in unison in the name of God against
the impure in morals and politics and with the wrong skin colour
and ethnology and religion: K.K.K. and Silver Shirts; not to
mention the indigenous local champions like Long in Louisiana
and our own Bilbo in Mississippi, not to mention our very own
Senator Clarence Egglestone Snopes right here in Yoknapatawpha County—"

"Not to mention the one in Russia," I says.

"What?" he says.

"So that's why," I says. "He ain't jest a sculptor. He's a
communist too."

"What?" Lawyer says.

"Barton Kohl. The reason they didn't marry first is that
Barton Kohl is a communist. He can't believe in churches and
marriage. They won't let him."

"He wanted them to marry," Lawyer says. "It's Linda that
won't." So now it was me that said What? and him setting there
fierce and untouchable as a hedgehog. "You don't believe that?"
he says.

"Yes," I says. "I believe it."

"Why should she want to marry? What could she have ever
seen in the one she had to look at for nineteen years, to make her
want any part of it?"

"All right," I says. "All right. Except that's the one I don't
believe. I believe the first one, about there ain't enough time
left. That when you are young enough, you can believe. When
you are young enough and brave enough at the same time,
you can hate intolerance and believe in hope and, if you are
sho enough brave, act on it." He still looked at me. "I wish it
was me," I says.

"Not just to marry somebody, but to marry anybody just
so it's marriage. Just so it's not adultery. Even you."

"Not that," I says. "I wish I was either one of them. To
believe in intolerance and hope and act on it. At any price.
Even at having to be under twenty-five again like she is, to do
it. Even to being a thirty-year-old Grinnich Village sculptor like
he is."

"So you do refuse to believe that all she wants is to cuddle up
together and be what she calls happy."

"Yes," I says. "So do I." So I didn't go that time, not even when he said:

"Nonsense. Come on. Afterward we will run up to Saratoga and look at that ditch or hill or whatever it was where your first immigrant Vladimir Kyrilytch Ratliff ancestor entered your native land."

"He wasn't no Ratliff then yet," I says. "We don't know what his last name was. Likely Nelly Ratliff couldn't even spell that one, let alone pronounce it. Maybe in fact neither could he. Besides, it wasn't even Ratliff then. It was Ratcliffe.—No," I says, "jest you will be enough. You can get cheaper corroboration than one that will not only need a round-trip ticket but three meals a day too."

"Corroboration for what?" he says.

"At this serious moment in her life when she is fixing to officially or leastways formally confederate or shack up with a gentleman friend of the opposite sex as the feller says, ain't the reason for this trip to tell her and him at last who she is? or leastways who she ain't?" Then I says, "Of course. She already knows," and he says,

"How could she help it? How could she have lived in the same house with Flem for nineteen years and still believe he could possibly be her father, even if she had incontrovertible proof of it?"

"And you ain't never told her," I says. Then I says, "It's even worse than that. Whenever it occurs to her enough to maybe fret over it a little and she comes to you and says maybe, 'Tell me the truth now. He ain't my father,' she can always depend on you saying, 'You're wrong, he is.' Is that the dependence and need you was speaking of?" Now he wasn't looking at me. "What would you do if she got it turned around backwards and said to you, 'Who is my father?'" No, he wasn't looking at me. "That's right," I says. "She won't never ask that. I reckon she has done watched Gavin Stevens too, enough to know there's some lies even he ought not to need to cope with." He wasn't looking at me a-tall. "So that there dependence is on a round-trip ticket too," I says.

He was back after ten days. And I thought how maybe if that sculptor could jest ketch her unawares, still half asleep maybe,

and seduce her outen the bed and up to a altar or even jest a
J.P. before she noticed where she was at, maybe he—Lawyer—
would be free. Then I knowed that wasn't even wishful thinking
because there wasn't nothing in that idea that could been called
thinking a-tall. Because once I got rid of them hopeful cobwebs I
realised I must a knowed for years what likely Eula knowed the
moment she laid eyes on him: that he wouldn't never be free
because he wouldn't never want to be free because this was his
life and if he ever lost it he wouldn't have nothing left. I mean,
the right and privilege and opportunity to dedicate forever his
capacity for responsibility to something that wouldn't have no
end to its appetite and that wouldn't never threaten to give him
even a bone back in recompense. And I remembered what he
said back there about how she was doomed to fidelity and
monogamy—to love once and lose him and then to grieve, and
I said I reckoned so, that being Helen of Troy's daughter was
kind of like being say the ex-Pope of Rome or the ex-Emperor
of Japan: there wasn't much future to it. And I knowed now he
was almost right, he jest had that word "doomed" in the wrong
place: that it wasn't her that was doomed, she would likely do
fine; it was the one that was recipient of the fidelity and the
monogamy and the love, and the one that was the proprietor of
the responsibility that never even wanted, let alone expected, a
bone back, that was the doomed one; and how even between
them two the lucky one might be the one that had the roof fall on
him while he was climbing into or out of the bed.

So naturally I would a got a fur piece quick trying to tell him
that, so naturally my good judgment told me not to try it. And so
partly by jest staying away from him but mainly by fighting like
a demon, like Jacob with his angel, I finally resisted actively
saying it—a temptation about as strong as a human man ever
has to face, which is to deliberately throw away the chance to
say afterward, "I told you so." So time passed. That little
additional mantelpiece footrest was up now that hadn't nobody
ever seen except that Negro yardman—a Jefferson legend after
he mentioned it to me and him (likely) and me both happened
to mention it in turn to some of our close intimates: a part of the
Snopes legend and another Flem Snopes monument in that
series mounting on and up from that water tank that we never

knowed yet if they had got out of it all that missing Flem Snopes regime powerhouse brass them two mad skeered Negro firemen put into it.

Then it was 1936 and there was less and less of that time left: Mussolini in Italy and Hitler in Germany and sho enough, like Lawyer said, that one in Spain too; Lawyer said, "Pack your grip. We will take the airplane from Memphis tomorrow morning. —No no," he says, "you don't need to fear contamination from association this time. They're going to be married. They're going to Spain to join the Loyalist army and apparently he nagged and worried at her until at last she probably said, 'Oh hell, have it your way then.' "

"So he wasn't a liberal emancipated advanced-thinking artist after all," I says. "He was jest another ordinary man that believed if a gal was worth sleeping with she was worth deserving to have a roof over her head and something to eat and a little money in her pocket for the balance of her life."

"All right," he says. "All right."

"Except we'll go on the train," I says. "It ain't that I'm jest simply skeered to go in a airplane: it's because when we go across Virginia I can see the rest of the place where that-ere first immigrant Vladimir Kyrilytch worked his way into the United States." So I was already on the corner with my grip when he drove up and stopped and opened the door and looked at me and then done what the moving pictures call a double take and says,

"Oh hell."

"It's mine," I says. "I bought it."

"You," he says, "in a necktie. That never even had one on before, let alone owned one, in your life."

"You told me why. It's a wedding."

"Take it off," he says.

"No," I says.

"I won't travel with you. I won't be seen with you."

"No," I says. "Maybe it ain't jest the wedding. I'm going back to let all them V. K. Ratliff beginnings look at me for the first time. Maybe it's them I'm trying to suit. Or leastways not to shame." So we taken the train to Memphis that night and the next day we was in Virginia—Bristol then Roanoke and Lynchburg and turned north-east alongside the blue mountains and

somewhere ahead, we didn't know jest where, was where that
first Vladimir Kyrilytch finally found a place where he could
stop, that we didn't know his last name or maybe he didn't even
have none until Nelly Ratliff, spelled Ratcliffe then, found him,
any more than we knowed what he was doing in one of them
hired German regiments in General Burgoyne's army that got
licked at Saratoga except that Congress refused to honour the
terms of surrender and banished the whole kit-and-biling of
them to struggle for six years in Virginia without no grub nor
money and the ones like that first V.K. without no speech
neither. But he never needed none of the three of them to escape
not only to the right neighbourhood but into the exact right
hayloft where Nelly Ratcliffe, maybe hunting eggs or such,
would find him. And never needed no language to eat the grub
she toted him; and maybe he never knowed nothing about
farming before the day when she finally brought him out where
her folks could see him; nor never needed no speech to speak of
for the next development, which was when somebody—her
maw or paw or brothers or whoever it was, maybe jest a neighbour—noticed the size of her belly; and so they married
and so that V.K. actively did have a active legal name of
Ratcliffe, and the one after him come to Tennessee and the one
after him moved to Missippi, except that by that time it was
spelled Ratliff, where the oldest son is still named Vladimir
Kyrilytch and still spends half his life trying to keep anybody
from finding it out.

The next morning we was in New York. It was early; not even
seven o'clock yet. It was too early. "Likely they ain't even
finished breakfast yet," I says.

"Breakfast hell," Lawyer says. "They haven't even gone to
bed yet. This is New York, not Yoknapatawpha County." So we
went to the hotel where Lawyer had already engaged a room.
Except it wasn't a room, it was three of them: a parlour and two
bedrooms. "We can have breakfast up here too," he says.

"Breakfast?" I says.

"They'll send it up here."

"This is New York," I says. "I can eat breakfast in the bedroom or kitchen or on the back gallery in Yoknapatawpha
County." So we went downstairs to the dining-room. Then I

says, "What time do they eat breakfast then? Sundown? Or is that jest when they get up?"

"No," he says. "We got a errand first.—No," he says, "we got two errands." He was looking at it again, though I will have to do him the justice to say he hadn't mentioned it again since that first time when I got in the car back in Jefferson. And I remember how he told me once how maybe New York wasn't made for no climate known to man but at least some weather was jest made for New York. In which case, this was sholy some of it: one of them soft blue drowsy days in the early fall when the sky itself seems like it was resting on the earth like a soft blue mist, with the tall buildings rushing up into it and then stopping, the sharp edges fading like the sunshine wasn't jest shining on them but kind of humming, like wires singing. Then I seen it: a store, with a shop window, a entire show window with not nothing in it but one necktie.

"Wait," I says.

"No," he says. "It was all right as long as just railroad conductors looked at it, but you can't face a preacher in it."

"No," I says, "wait." Because I had heard about these New York side-alley stores too. "If it takes that whole show window to deserve jest one necktie, likely they will want three or four dollars for it."

"We can't help it now," he says. "This is New York. Come on."

And nothing inside neither except some gold chairs and two ladies in black dresses and a man dressed like a congressman or at least a preacher, that knowed Lawyer by active name. And then a office with a desk and a vase of flowers and a short dumpy dark woman in a dress that wouldn't a fitted nobody, with grey-streaked hair and the handsomest dark eyes I ever seen even if they was popped a little, that kissed Lawyer and then he said to her, "Myra Allanovna, this is Vladimir Kyrilytch," and she looked at me and said something; yes, I know it was Russian, and Lawyer saying: "Look at it. Just once if you can bear it," and I says,

"Sholy it ain't quite as bad as that. Of course I had ruther it was yellow and red instead of pink and green. But all the same—" and she says,

"You like yellow and red?"

"Yessum," I says. Then I says, "In fact" before I could stop, and she says,

"Yes, tell me," and I says,

"Nothing. I was jest thinking that if you could jest imagine a necktie and then pick it right up and put it on, I would imagine one made outen red with a bunch or maybe jest one single sunflower in the middle of it," and she says,

"Sunflower?" and Lawyer says,

"Helianthe." Then he says, "No, that's wrong. Tournesol. Sonnenblume," and she says Wait and was already gone, and now I says Wait myself.

"Even a five-dollar necktie couldn't support all them gold chairs."

"It's too late now," Lawyer says. "Take it off." Except that when she come back, it not only never had no sunflower, it wasn't even red. It was jest dusty. No, that was wrong; you had looked at it by that time. It looked like the outside of a peach, that you know that in a minute, providing you can keep from blinking, you will see the first beginning of when it starts to turn peach. Except that it don't do that. It's still jest dusted over with gold, like the back of a sunburned gal. "Yes," Lawyer says, "send out and get him a white shirt. He never wore a white shirt before either."

"No, never," she says. "Always blue, not? And this blue, always? The same blue as your eyes?"

"That's right," I says.

"But how?" she says. "By fading them? By just washing them?"

"That's right," I says, "I jest washes them."

"You mean, you wash them? Yourself?"

"He makes them himself too," Lawyer says.

"That's right," I says. "I sells sewing machines. First thing I knowed I could run one too."

"Of course," she says. "This one for now. Tomorrow, the other one, red with sonnenblume." Then we was outside again. I was still trying to say Wait.

"Now I got to buy two of them," I says. "I'm trying to be serious. I mean, please try to believe I am as serious right now as ere a man in your experience. Jest exactly how much you reckon was the price on that one in that window?"

And Lawyer not even stopping, saying over his shoulder in the middle of folks pushing past and around us in both directions: "I don't know. Her ties run up to a hundred and fifty. Say, seventy-five dollars—" It was exactly like somebody had hit me a quick light lick with the edge of his hand across the back of the neck until next I knowed I was leaning against the wall back out of the rush of folks in a fit of weak trembles with Lawyer more or less holding me up. "You all right now?" he says.

"No I ain't," I says. "Seventy-five dollars for a necktie? I can't! I won't!"

"You're forty years old," he says. "You should a been buying at the minimum one tie a year ever since you fell in love the first time. When was it? eleven? twelve? thirteen? Or maybe it was eight or nine, when you first went to school—provided the first-grade teacher was female of course. But even call it twenty. That's twenty years, at one dollar a tie a year. That's twenty dollars. Since you are not married and never will be and don't have any kin close enough to exhaust and wear you out by taking care of you or hoping to get anything out of you, you may live another forty-five. That's sixty-five dollars. That means you will have an Allanovna tie for only ten dollars. Nobody else in the world ever got an Allanovna tie for ten dollars."

"I won't!" I says. "I won't!"

"All right. I'll make you a present of it then."

"I can't do that," I says.

"All right. You want to go back there and tell her you don't want the tie?"

"Don't you see I can't do that?"

"All right," he says. "Come on. We're already a little late." So when we got to this hotel we went straight to the saloon.

"We're almost there," I says. "Can't you tell me yet who it's going to be?"

"No," he says. "This is New York. I want to have a little fun and pleasure too." And a moment later, when I realised that Lawyer hadn't never laid eyes on him before, I should a figgered why he had insisted so hard on me coming on this trip. Except that I remembered how in this case Lawyer wouldn't need no help since you are bound to have some kind of affinity or out-ragement anyhow for the man that for twenty-five years has been as much a part and as big a part of your simple natural normal anguish of jest having to wake up again tomorrow, as this one had. So I says,

"I'll be durned. Howdy, Hoake." Because there he was, a little grey at the temples, with not jest a sunburned outdoors look but a rich sunburned outdoors look that never needed that-ere dark expensive-looking city suit, let alone two waiters jumping around the table where he was at, to prove it, already setting there where Lawyer had drawed him from wherever it was out west he had located him, the same as he had drawed me for this special day. No, it wasn't Lawyer that had drawed McCarron and me from a thousand miles away and two thousand more miles apart, the three of us to meet at this moment in a New York saloon: it was that gal that done it—that gal that never had seen one of us and fur as I actively heard it to take a oath, never had said much more than good-morning to the other two—that gal that likely not even knowed but didn't even care that she had inherited her maw's fatality to draw four men anyhow to that web, that one strangling hair; drawed all four of us without even lifting her hand—her husband, her father, the man that was still trying to lay down his life for her maw if he could jest find somebody that wanted it, and what you might call a by-standing family friend—to be the supporting cast while she said "I do" outen the middle of a matrimonial production line at the City Hall before getting on a ship to go to Europe to do whatever it was she figgered she was going to do in that war. So I was the one that said, "This is Lawyer Stevens, Hoake," with three waiters now (he was evidently that rich) bustling around helping us set down.

"What's yours?" he says to Lawyer. "I know what V.K. wants.—Bushmill's," he says to the waiter. "Bring the bottle.— You'll think you're back home," he says to me. "It tastes jest like that stuff Calvin Bookwright used to make—do you remember?" Now he was looking at it too. "That's an Allanovna, isn't it?" he says. "You've branched out a little since Frenchman's Bend too, haven't you?" Now he was looking at Lawyer. He taken his whole drink at one swallow though the waiter was already there with the bottle before he could a signalled. "Don't worry," he says. "You've got my word. I'm going to keep it."

"You stop worrying too," I says. "Lawyer's already got Linda. She's going to believe him first, no matter what anybody else might forget and try to tell her." And we could have et dinner there too, but Lawyer says,

"This is New York. We can eat dinner in Uncle Cal Bookwright's springhouse back home." So we went to that dining-room. Then it was time. We went to the City Hall in a taxicab. While he was getting out, the other taxicab come up and they got out. He was not big, he jest looked big, like a football player. No: like a prize fighter. He didn't look jest tough, and ruthless ain't the word neither. He looked like he would beat you or maybe you would beat him but you probably wouldn't, or he might kill you or you might kill him though you probably wouldn't. But he wouldn't never dicker with you, looking at you with eyes that was pale like Hub Hampton's but they wasn't hard: jest looking at you without no hurry and completely, missing nothing, and with already a pretty good idea beforehand of what he was going to see.

We went inside. It was a long hall, a corridor, a line of folks two and two that they would a been the last one in it except it was a line that never had no last: jest a next to the last and not that long: on to a door that said REGISTRAR and inside. That wasn't long neither; the two taxicabs was still waiting. "So this is Grinnich Village," I says. The door give right off the street but with a little shirt-tail of ground behind it you could a called a yard though maybe city folks called it a garden; It even had one tree in it, with three things on it that undoubtedly back in the spring or summer was leaves. But inside it was nice: full of folks of course, with two waiters dodging in and out with trays of glasses of champagne and three or four of the company helping too, not to mention the folks that was taking over the apartment while Linda and her new husband was off at the war in Spain—a young couple about the same age as them. "Is he a sculptor too?" I says to Lawyer.

"No," Lawyer says. "He's a newspaperman."

"Oh," I says. "Then likely they been married all the time."

It was nice: a room with plenty of window lights. It had a heap of stuff in it too but it looked like it was used—a wall full of books and a piano and I knowed they was pictures because they was hanging on the wall and I knowed that some of the other things was sculpture but the rest of them I didn't know what they was, made outen pieces of wood or iron or strips of tin and wires. Except that I couldn't ask then because of the rest of the poets and painters and sculptors and musicians, since he would still have to be the host until we—him and Linda and Lawyer and Hoake and me—could slip out and go down to where the ship was; evidently a heap of folks found dreams in Grinnich Village but evidently it was a occasion when somebody married in it. And one of them wasn't even a poet or painter or sculptor or musician or even jest a ordinary moral newspaperman but evidently a haberdasher taking Saturday evening off. Because we was barely in the room before he was not only looking at it too but rubbing it between his thumb and finger. "Allanovna," he says.

"That's right," I says.

"Oklahoma?" he says. "Oil?"

"Sir?" I says.

"Oh," he says. "Texas. Cattle then. In Texas you can choose your million between oil and cattle, right?"

"No sir," I says, "Missippi. I sell sewing machines."

So it was a while before Kohl finally come to me to fill my glass again.

"I understand you grew up with Linda's mother," he says.

"That's right," I says. "Did you make these?"

"These what?" he says.

"In this room," I says.

"Oh," he says. "Do you want to see more of them? Why?"

"I don't know yet," I says. "Does that matter?" So we shoved on through the folks—it had begun to take shoving by now—into a hall and then up some stairs. And this was the best of all: a loft with one whole side of the roof jest window lights—a room not jest where folks used but where somebody come off by his-self and worked. And him jest standing a little behind me, outen the way, giving me time and room both to look. Until at last he says,

"Shocked? Mad?" Until I says,

"Do I have to be shocked and mad at something jest because I never seen it before?"

"At your age, yes," he says. "Only children can stand surprise for the pleasure of surprise. Grown people can't bear surprise unless they are promised in advance they will want to own it."

"Maybe I ain't had enough time yet," I says.

"Take it then," he says. So he leaned against the wall with his arms folded like a football player, with the noise of the party where he was still supposed to be host at coming up the stairs from below, while I taken my time to look: at some I did recognise and some I almost could recognise and maybe if I had time enough I would, and some I knowed I wouldn't never quite recognise, until all of a sudden I knowed that wouldn't matter neither, not jest to him but to me too. Because anybody can see and hear and smell and feel and taste what he expected to hear and see and feel and smell and taste, and won't nothing much notice your presence nor miss your lack. So maybe when you can see and feel and smell and hear and taste what you never expected to and hadn't never even imagined until that moment, maybe that's why Old Moster picked you out to be the one of the ones to be alive.

So now it was time for that-ere date. I mean the one that Lawyer and Hoake had fixed up, with Hoake saying, "But what can I tell her—her husband—her friends?" and Lawyer says,

"Why do you need to tell anybody anything? I've attended to all that. As soon as enough of them have drunk her health, just take her by the arm and clear out. Just don't forget to be aboard the ship by eleven-thirty." Except Hoake still tried, the two of them standing in the door ready to leave, Hoake in that-ere dark expensive city suit and his derby hat in his hand, and Linda in a kind of a party dress inside her coat. And it wasn't that they looked alike, because they didn't. She was tall for a woman, so tall she didn't have much shape (I mean, the kind that folks whistle at), and he wasn't tall for a man and in fact kind of stocky. But their eyes was exactly alike. Anyhow, it seemed to me that anybody that seen them couldn't help but know they was kin. So he still had to try it: "A old friend of her mother's family. Her grandfather and my father may have been distantly related —" and Lawyer saying,

"All right, all right, beat it. Don't forget the time," and Hoake saying,

"Yes yes, we'll be at Twenty-One for dinner and afterward at

the Stork Club if you need to telephone." Then they was gone
and the rest of the company went too except three other men
that I found out was newspapermen too, foreign correspondents;
and Kohl his-self helped his new tenant's wife cook the spaghetti
and we et it and drunk some more wine, red this time, and they
talked about the war, about Spain and Ethiopia and how this
was the beginning: the lights was going off all over Europe soon
and maybe in this country too; until it was time to go to the
ship. And more champagne in the bedroom there, except
that Lawyer hadn't hardly got the first bottle open when Linda
and Hoake come in.

"Already?" Lawyer says. "We didn't expect you for at least a
hour yet."

"She—we decided to skip the Stork Club," Hoake says. "We
took a fiacre through the Park instead. And now," he says,
that hadn't even put the derby hat down.

"Stay and have some champagne," Lawyer says, and Kohl said
something too. But Linda had done already held out her hand.

"Good-bye, Mr McCarron," she says. "Thank you for the
evening and for coming to my wedding."

"Can't you say 'Hoake' yet?" he says.

"Good-bye, Hoake," she says.

"Wait in the cab then," Lawyer says. "We'll join you in a
minute."

"No," Hoake says. "I'll take another cab and leave that one
for you." Then he was gone. She shut the door behind him and
came toward Lawyer, taking something outen her pocket.

"Here," she says. It was a gold cigarette-lighter. "I know you
won't ever use it, since you say you think you can taste the fluid
when you light your pipe."

"No," Lawyer says. "What I said was, I know I can taste it."

"All right," she says. "Take it anyway." So Lawyer taken it.
"It's engraved with your initials: see?"

"G L S," Lawyer says. "They are not my initials. I just have
two: G S."

"I know. But the man said a monogram should have three so
I loaned you one of mine." Then she stood there facing him, as
tall as him almost, looking at him. "That was my father," she
says.

"No," Lawyer says.

"Yes," she says.

"You don't mean to tell me he told you that," Lawyer says.

"You know he didn't. You made him swear not to."

"No," Lawyer says.

"You swear then."

"All right," Lawyer says. "I swear."

"I love you," she says. "Do you know why?"

"Tell me," Lawyer says.

"It's because every time you lie to me I can always know you will stick to it."

Then the second sentimental pilgrimage. No, something else come first. It was the next afternoon. "Now we'll go pick up the necktie," Lawyer says.

"No," I says.

"You mean you want to go alone?"

"That's right," I says. So I was alone, the same little office again and her still in the same dress that wouldn't fitted nobody already looking at my empty collar even before I put the necktie and the hundred and fifty dollars on the desk by the new one that I hadn't even teched yet because I was afraid to. It was red jest a little under what you see in a black-gum leaf in the fall, with not no single sunflower nor even a bunch of them but little yellow sunflowers all over it in a kind of diamond pattern, each one with a little blue centre almost the exact blue my shirts gets to after a while. I didn't dare touch it. "I'm sorry," I says. "But you see I jest can't. I sells sewing machines in Missippi. I can't have it knowed back there that I paid seventy-five dollars apiece for neckties. But if I'm in the Missippi sewing-machine business and can't wear seventy-five dollar neckties, so are you in the New York necktie business and can't afford to have folks wear or order neckties and not pay for them. So here," I says. "And I ask your kindness to excuse me."

But she never even looked at the money. "Why did he call you Vladimir Kyrilytch?" she says. I told her.

"Except we live in Missippi now, and we got to live it down. Here," I says. "And I ask you again to ex—"

"Take that off my desk," she says. "I have given the ties to you. You cannot pay for them."

"Don't you see I can't do that neither?" I says. "No more than I could let anybody back in Missippi order a sewing machine from me and then say he had done changed his mind when I delivered it to him?"

"So," she says. "You cannot accept the ties, and I cannot accept the money. Good. We do this—" There was a thing on the desk that looked like a cream pitcher until she snapped it open and it was a cigarette-lighter. "We burn it then, half for you, half for me—" until I says,

"Wait! Wait!" and she stopped. "No," I says, "no. Not burn money," and she says,

"Why not?" and us looking at each other, her hand holding the lit lighter and both our hands on the money.

"Because it's money," I says. "Somebody somewhere at some time went to—went through—I mean, money stands for too much hurt and grief somewhere to somebody that jest the money wasn't never worth—I mean, that ain't what I mean . . ." and she says,

"I know exactly what you mean. Only the gauche, the illiterate, the frightened and the pastless destroy money. You will keep it then. You will take it back to—how you say?"

"Missippi," I says.

"Missippi. Where is one who, not needs: who cares about so base as needs? Who wants something that costs one hundred fifty dollar—a hat, a picture, a book, a jewel for the ear; something never never never anyhow just to eat—but believes he——she—will never have it, has even long ago given up, not the dream but the hope— This time do you know what I mean?"

"I know exactly what you mean because you jest said it," I says.

"Then kiss me," she says. And that night me and Lawyer went up to Saratoga.

"Did you tell Hoake better than to try to give her a lot of money, or did he jest have that better sense his-self?" I says.

"Yes," Lawyer says.

"Yes which?" I says.

"Maybe both," Lawyer says. And in the afternoon we watched the horses, and the next morning we went out to Bemis's Heights and Freeman's Farm. Except that naturally

F*

there wasn't no monument to one mercenary Hessian soldier that maybe couldn't even speak German, let alone American, and naturally there wasn't no hill or ditch or stump or rock that spoke up and said aloud: On this spot your first ancestral V.K. progenitor forswore Europe forever and entered the United States. And two days later we was back home, covering in two days the distance it taken that first V.K. four generations to do; and now we watched the lights go out in Spain and Ethiopia, the darkness that was going to creep eastward across all Europe and Asia too, until the shadow of it would fall across the Pacific islands until it reached even America. But that was a little while away yet when Lawyer says,

"Come up to the office," and then he says, "Barton Kohl is dead. The airplane—it was a worn-out civilian passenger carrier, armed with 1918 infantry machine guns, with home-made bomb bays through which the amateur crew dumped by hand the homemade bombs; that's what they fought Hitler's Luftwaffe with—was shot down in flames so she probably couldn't have identified him even if she could have reached the crash. She doesn't say what she intends to do now."

"She'll come back here," I says.

"Here?" he says. "Back here?" then he says, "Why the hell shouldn't she? It's home."

"That's right," I says. "It's doom."

"What?" he says. "What did you say?"

"Nothing," I says. "I jest said I think so too."

EIGHT

Charles Mallison

LINDA KOHL (Snopes that was, as Thackeray would say. Kohl that was too, since he was dead) wasn't the first wounded war hero to finally straggle back to Jefferson. She was just the first one my uncle bothered to meet at the station. I don't mean the railroad station; by 1937 it had been a year or so since a train had passed through Jefferson that a paid passenger could have got off of. And not even the bus depot because I don't even mean Jefferson. It was the Memphis airport we went to meet her, my uncle apparently discovering at the last minute that morning that he was not able to make an eighty-mile trip and back alone in his car.

She was not even the first female hero. For two weeks back in 1919 we had had a nurse, an authentic female lieutenant—not a denizen, citizen of Jefferson to be sure, but at least kin to (or maybe just interested in a member of) a Jefferson family, who had been on the staff of a base hospital in France and—so she said—had actually spent two days at a casualty clearing station within sound of the guns behind Montdidier.

In fact, by 1919 even the five-year-old Jeffersonians like I was then were even a little blasé about war heroes, not only un-scratched ones but wounded too getting off trains from Memphis Junction or New Orleans. Not that I mean that even the un-scratched ones actually called themselves heroes or thought they were or in fact thought one way or the other about it until they got home and found the epithet being dinned at them from all directions until finally some of them, a few of them, began to believe that perhaps they were. I mean, dinned at them by the ones who organised and correlated the dinning—the ones who hadn't gone to that war and so were already on hand in advance to organise the big debarkation-port parades and the smaller county-seat local ones, with inbuilt barbecue and beer; the ones that hadn't gone to that one and didn't intend to go to the next one nor the one after that either, as long as all they had to do to stay out was buy the tax-free bonds and organise the hero-dinning parades so that the next crop of eight- and nine- and ten-year-old males could see the divisional shoulder patches and the wound- and service-stripes and the medal ribbons.

Until some of them anyway would begin to believe that that many voices dinning it at them must be right, and they were heroes. Because, according to Uncle Gavin, who had been a soldier too in his fashion (in the American Field Service with the French army in '16 and '17 until we got into it, then still in France as a Y.M.C.A. secretary or whatever they were called), they had nothing else left: young men or even boys most of whom had only the vaguest or completely erroneous idea of where and what Europe was, and none at all about armies, let alone about war, snatched up by lot overnight and regimented into an expeditionary force, to survive (if they could) before they were twenty-five years old what they would not even recognise at the time to be the biggest experience of their lives. Then to be spewed, again willy-nilly and again overnight, back into what they believed would be the familiar world they had been told they were enduring disruption and risking injury and death so that it would still be there when they came back, only to find that it wasn't there any more. So that the bands and the parades and the barbecues and all the rest of the hero-dinning not only would happen only that once and was already fading even before they could get adjusted to it, it was already on the way out before the belated last of them even got back home, already saying to them above the cold congealing meat and the flat beer while the last impatient brazen chord died away: "All right, little boys; eat your beef and potato salad and drink your beer and get out of our way, who are already up to our necks in this new world whose single and principal industry is not just solvent but dizzily remunerative peace."

So, according to Gavin, they had to believe they were heroes even though they couldn't remember now exactly at what point or by what action they had reached, entered for a moment or a second, that heroic state. Because otherwise they had nothing left: with only a third of life over, to know now that they had already experienced their greatest experience, and now to find that the world for which they had so endured and risked was in their absence so altered out of recognition by the ones who had stayed safe at home as to have no place for them in it any more.

So they had to believe that at least some little of it had been true. Which (according to Gavin) was the why of the veterans' clubs and legions: the one sanctuary where at least once a week they could find refuge among the other betrayed and dispossessed reaffirming to each other that at least that one infinitesimal scrap had been so.

In fact (in Jefferson anyway) even the ones that came back with an arm or a leg gone, came back just like what they were when they left: merely underlined, italicised. There was Tug Nightingale. His father was the cobbler, with a little cubbyhole of a shop around a corner off the Square—a little scrawny man who wouldn't have weighed a hundred pounds with his last and bench and all his tools in his lap, with a fierce moustache which hid most of his chin too, and fierce undefeated intolerant eyes—a Hard-Shell Baptist who didn't merely have to believe it, because he knew it was so: that the earth was flat and that Lee had betrayed the whole South when he surrendered at Appomattox. He was a widower. Tug was his only surviving child. Tug had got almost as far as the fourth grade when the principal himself told Mr Nightingale it would be better for Tug to quit. Which Tug did, and now he could spend all his time hanging around the auction lot behind Dilazuck's livery stable, where he had been spending all his spare time anyhow, and where he now came into his own: falling in first with Lonzo Hait, our local horse and mule trader, then with Pat Stamper himself, who in the horse and mule circles not just in Yoknapatawpha County or north Mississippi but over most of Alabama and Tennessee and Arkansas too, was to Lonzo Hait what Fritz Kreisler would be to the fiddle player at a country picnic, and so recognised genius when he saw it. Because Tug didn't have any piddling mere affinity for and rapport with mules: he was an *homme fatal* to them, any mule, horse or mare either, being putty in his hands; he could do anything with them except buy and sell them for a profit. Which is why he never rose higher than a simple hostler and handy man and so finally had to become a house painter also to make a living: not a first-rate one, but at least he could stir the paint and put it on a wall or fence after somebody had shown him where to stop.

Which was his condition up to about 1916, when he was about

thirty years old, maybe more, when something began to happen
to him. Or maybe it had already happened and we—Jefferson—
only noticed it then. Up to now he had been what you might call
a standard-type provincial county-seat house painter: a bachelor,
living with his father in a little house on the edge of town, having
his weekly bath in the barbershop on Saturday night and then
getting a little drunk afterward—not too much so: only once
every two or three years waking up Sunday morning in the jail
until they would release him on his own recognisance; this not
for being too drunk but for fighting, though the fighting did
stem from the whiskey, out of that mutual stage of it when the
inevitable one (never the same one: it didn't need to be)
challenged his old fixed father-bequeathed convictions that
General Lee had been a coward and a traitor and that the earth
was a flat plane with edges like the shed roofs he painted—then
shooting a little dice in the big ditch behind the cemetery while
he sobered up Sunday afternoon to go back to his turpentine
Monday morning; with maybe four trips a year to the Memphis
brothels.

Then it happened to him. He still had the Saturday-night
barbershop bath and he still drank a little, though as far as
Jefferson knew, never enough any more to need to go to combat
over General Lee and Ptolemy and Isaac Newton, so that not
only the jail but the harassed night marshal too who at the
mildest would bang on the locked barbershop or poolroom door
at two o'clock Sunday morning, saying, "If you boys don't quiet
down and go home," knew him no more. Nor did the dice game
in the cemetery ditch; on Sunday morning now he would be
seen walking with his scrawny fiercely moustached miniature
father toward the little backstreet Hard-Shell church, and that
afternoon sitting on the minute gallery of their doll-sized house
poring (whom the first three grades of school rotationally licked
and the fourth one completely routed) over the newspapers and
magazines which brought us all we knew about the war in
Europe.

He had changed. Even we (Jefferson. I was only three then)
didn't know how much until the next April, 1917, after the
Lusitania and the President's declaration, and Captain (Mister
then until he was elected captain of it) McLendon organised

the Jefferson company to be known as the Sartoris Rifles in
honour of the original Colonel Sartoris (there would be no
Sartoris in it since Bayard and his twin brother John were
already in England training for the Royal Flying Corps), and
then we heard the rest of it: how Tug Nightingale, past thirty
now and so even when the draft came would probably escape it,
was one of the first to apply, and we—they—found out what his
dilemma was: which was simply that he did not dare let his
father find out that he planned to join the Yankee army, since
if his father ever learned it, he, Tug, would be disinherited and
thrown out. So it was more than Captain McLendon who said,
"What? What's that?" and McLendon and another—the one
who would be elected his First Sergeant—went home with Tug
and the sergeant-to-be told it:

"It was like being shut up in a closet with a buzz saw that had
jumped off the axle at top speed, or say a bundle of dynamite
with the fuse lit and snapping around the floor like a snake, that
you not only can't get close enough to step on it, you don't want
to: all you want is out, and Mack saying, 'Wait, Mr Nightingale,
it ain't the Yankee army: it's the army of the United States:
your own country,' and that durn little maniac shaking and
seething until his moustache looked like it was on fire too,
hollering, 'Shoot the sons of bitches! Shoot em! Shoot em!'
and then Tug himself trying it: 'Papa, papa, Captain McLendon
and Crack here both belong to it,' and old man Nightingale
yelling, 'Shoot them then. Shoot all the blue-bellied sons of
bitches,' and Tug still trying, saying 'Papa, papa, if I don't join
now, when they pass that draft they will come and get me
anyway,' and still that little maniac hollering, 'Shoot you all!
Shoot all you sons of bitches!' Yes sir. Likely Tug could join the
German army or maybe even the French or British, and had his
blessing. But not the one that General Lee betrayed him to that
day back in 1865. So he threw Tug out. The three of us got out
of that house as fast as we could, but before we even reached the
sidewalk he was already in the room that was evidently Tug's.
He never even waited to open the door: just kicked the window
out, screen and all, and started throwing Tug's clothes out into
the yard."

So Tug had crossed his Rubicon, and should have been safe

now. I mean, Captain McLendon took him in. He—McLendon
—was one of a big family of brothers in a big house with a
tremendous mother weighing close to two hundred pounds, who
liked to cook and eat both so one more wouldn't matter; maybe
she never even noticed Tug. So he should have been safe now
while the company waited for orders to move. But the others
wouldn't let him alone; his method of joining the colours was a
little too unique, not to mention *East Lynne*; there was always
one to say:

"Tug, is it really so that General Lee didn't need to give up
when he did?" and Tug would say,

"That's what papa says. He was there and seen it, even if he
wasn't but seventeen years old." And the other would say:

"So you had to go clean against him, clean against your own
father, to join the Rifles?" And Tug sitting there quite still now,
the hands that never would be able to paint more than the
roughest outhouse walls and finesseless fences but which could do
things to the intractable and unpredictable mule which few
other hands dared, hanging quiet too between his knees, because
by now he would know what was coming next. And the other—
and all the rest of them within range—watching Tug with just
half an eye since the other three halves would be watching
Captain McLendon across the room; in fact they usually waited
until McLendon had left, was actually out.

"That's right," Tug would say; then the other:

"Why did you do it, Tug? You're past thirty now, safe from
the draft, and your father's an old man alone here with nobody
to take care of him."

"We can't let them Germans keep on treating folks like they're
doing. Somebody's got to make them quit."

"So you had to go clean against your father to join the army
to make them quit. And now you'll have to go clean against him
again to go round to the other side of the world where you can
get at them."

"I'm going to France," Tug would say.

"That's what I said: halfway round. Which way are you
going? east or west? You can pick either one and still get there.
Or better still, and I'll make you a bet. Pick out east, go on east
until you find the war, do whatever you aim to do to them

Germans and then keep right on going east, and I'll bet you a hundred dollars to one that when you see Jefferson next time, you'll be looking at it right square across Miss Joanna Burden's mailbox one mile west of the courthouse." But by that time Captain McLendon would be there; probably somebody had gone to fetch him. He may have been such a bad company commander that he was relieved of his command long before it ever saw the lines, and a few years after this he was going to be the leader in something here in Jefferson that I anyway am glad I don't have to lie down with in the dark every time I try to go to sleep. But at least he held his company together (and not by the bars on his shoulders since, if they had been all he had, he wouldn't have had a man left by the first Saturday night, but by simple instinctive humanity, of which even he, even in the middle of that business he was going to be mixed up in later, seemed to have had a little, like now) until a better captain could get hold of it. He was already in uniform. He was a cotton man, a buyer for one of the Memphis export houses, and he spent most of his commissions gambling on cotton futures in the market, but he never had looked like a farmer until he put on the uniform.

"What the hell's going on here?" he said. "What the hell do you think Tug is? a damn ant running around a damn orange or something? He ain't going *around* anything: he's going straight *across* it, across the water to France to fight for his country, and when they don't need him in France any longer he's coming back across the same water, back here to Jefferson the same way he went out of it, like we'll all be damn glad to get back to it. So don't let me hear any more of this" (excrement: my word) "any more."

Whether or not Tug would continue to need Captain McLendon, he didn't have him much longer. The company was mustered that week and sent to Texas for training; whereupon, since Tug was competent to paint any flat surface provided it was simple enough, with edges and not theoretical boundaries, and possessed that gift with horses and mules which the expert Pat Stamper had recognised at once to partake of that inexplicable quality called genius, naturally the army made him a cook and detached him the same day, so that he was not only

M

the first Yoknapatawpha County soldier (the Sartoris boys didn't count since they were officially British troops) to go overseas, he was among the last of all American troops to get back home, which was in late 1919, since obviously the same military which would decree him into a cook, would mislay where it had sent him (not lose him; my own experience between '42 and '45 taught me that the military never loses anything: it merely buries it).

So now he was back home again, living alone now (old Mr Nightingale had died in that same summer of 1917, killed, Uncle Gavin said, by simple inflexibility, having set his intractable and contemptuous face against the juggernaut of history and science both that April day in 1865 and never flinched since), a barn and fence painter once more, with his Saturday-night bath in the barbershop and again drinking and gambling again within his means, only with on his face now a look, as V. K. Ratliff put it, as if he had been taught and believed all his life that the fourth dimension was invisible, then suddenly had seen one. And he didn't have Captain McLendon now. I mean, McLendon was back home too but they were no longer commander and man. Or maybe it was that even that natural humanity of Captain McLendon's, of which he should have had a pretty good supply since none of it seemed to be within his reach on his next humanitarian crises after that one when he shielded Tug from the harsh facts of cosmology, would not have sufficed here.

This happened in the barbershop too (no, I wasn't there; I still wasn't old enough to be tolerated in the barbershop at ten o'clock on Saturday night even if I could have got away from Mother; this was hearsay from Ratliff to Uncle Gavin to me). This time the straight man was Skeets McGowan, Uncle Willy Christian's soda jerker—a young man with a swagger and dash to him, who probably smelled more like toilet water than just water, with a considerable following of fourteen- and fifteen-year-old girls at Uncle Willy's fountain, who we realised afterward had been just a little older than we always thought and, as Ratliff said, even ten years later would never know as much as he —Skeets—figured he had already forgotten ten years ago; he had just been barbered and scented, and Tug had finished his bath

and was sitting quietly enough while the first drink or two began
to take hold.

"So when you left Texas, you went north," Skeets said.

"That's right," Tug said.

"Come on," Skeets said. "Tell us about it. You left Texas
going due north, to New York. Then you got on the boat, and
it kept right on due north too."

"That's right," Tug said.

"But suppose they fooled you a little. Suppose they turned the
boat, to the east or west or maybe right back south—"

"God damn it," Tug said. "Don't you think I know where
north is? You can wake me up in the bed in the middle of the
night and I can point my hand due north without even turning
on the light."

"What'll you bet? Five dollars? Ten?"

"I'll bet you ten dollars to one dollar except that any dollar
you ever had you already spent on that shampoo or that silk
shirt."

"All right, all right," Skeets said. "So the boat went straight
north, to France. And you stayed in France two years and then
got on another boat and it went straight north too. Then you
got off that boat and got on a train and it—"

"Shut up," Tug said.

"—went straight north too. And when you got off, you were
back in Jefferson."

"Shut up, you goddam little bastard," Tug said.

"So don't you see what that means? Either one of two things:
either they moved Jefferson—" Now Tug was on his feet though
even now apparently Skeets knew no better: "—which all the
folks that stayed around here and didn't go to that war can tell
you they didn't. Or you left Jefferson going due north by way of
Texas and come back to Jefferson still going due north without
even passing Texas again—" It took all the barbers and customers
and loafers too and finally the night marshal himself to immobilise
Tug. Though by that time Skeets was already in the ambulance
on his way to the hospital.

And there was Bayard Sartoris. He got back in the spring of
'19 and bought the fastest car he could find and spent his time
ripping around the country or back and forth to Memphis until

(so we all believed) his aunt, Mrs Du Pre, looked over Jefferson and picked out Narcissa Benbow and then caught Bayard between trips with the other hand long enough to get them married, hoping that would save Bayard's neck since he was now the last Sartoris Mohican (John had finally got himself shot down in July of '18), only it didn't seem to work. I mean, as soon as he got Narcissa pregnant, which must have been pretty quick, he was back in the car again until this time Colonel Sartoris himself stepped into the breach, who hated cars yet gave up his carriage and pair to let Bayard drive him back and forth to the bank, to at least slow the car down during that much of the elapsed mileage. Except that Colonel Sartoris had a heart condition, so when the wreck came it was him that died: Bayard just walked out of the crash and disappeared, abandoned pregnant wife and all, until the next spring when he was still trying to relieve his boredom by seeing how much faster he could make something travel than he could invent a destination for; this time another aeroplane: a new experimental type at the Dayton testing field: only this one fooled him by shedding all four of its wings in midair.

That's right: boredom, Uncle Gavin said—that war was the only civilised condition which offered any scope for the natural blackguardism inherent in men, that not just condoned and sanctioned it but rewarded it, and that Bayard was simply bored: he would never forgive the Germans not for starting the war but for stopping it, ending it. But Mother said that was wrong. She said that Bayard was frightened and ashamed: not ashamed because he was frightened but terrified when he discovered himself to be capable of, vulnerable to being ashamed. She said that Sartorises were different from other people. That most people, nearly all people, loved themselves first, only they knew it secretly and maybe even admitted it secretly; and so they didn't have to be ashamed of it—or if they were ashamed, they didn't need to be afraid of being ashamed. But that Sartorises didn't even know they loved themselves first, except Bayard. Which was all right with him and he wasn't ashamed of it until he and his twin brother reached England and got into flight training without parachutes in aeroplanes made out of glue and baling wire; or maybe not even until they were at the front, where even for the ones that had lived that far the odds were near zero against scout pilots surviving the first three weeks of active service. When suddenly Bayard realised that, unique in the squadron and, for all he knew, unique in all the R.F.C. or maybe all military air forces, he was not one individual creature at all but there was two of him since he had a twin engaged in the same risk and chance. And so in effect he alone out of all the people flying in that war had been vouchsafed a double indemnity against those odds (and vice versa of course since his twin would enjoy the identical obverse vouchsafement)—and in the next second, with a kind of terror, discovered that he was ashamed of the idea, knowledge, of being capable of having thought it even.

That was what Mother said his trouble was — why he apparently came back to Jefferson for the sole purpose of trying, in that sullen and pleasureless manner, to find out just how many different ways he could risk breaking his neck that would keep the most people anguished or upset or at least annoyed: that completely un-Sartoris-like capacity for shame which he could neither live with nor quit; could neither live in toleration with it nor by his own act repudiate it. That was why the risking, the chancing, the fatalism. Obviously the same idea—twinship's double indemnity against being shot down—must have occurred to the other twin at the same moment, since they were twins. But it probably hadn't worried John any more than the things he had done in his war (Uncle Gavin said—and in about five years I was going to have a chance to test it myself—that no man ever went to a war, even in the Y.M.C.A., without bringing back something he wished he hadn't done or anyway would stop thinking about) worried that old original Colonel Sartoris who had been their great-grandfather; only he, Bayard, of all his line was that weak, that un-Sartoris.

So now (if Mother was right) he had a double burden. One was anguish over what base depths of imagination and selfish hope he knew himself to be, not so much capable of as doomed to be ashamed of; the other, the fact that if that twinship double indemnity did work in his favour and John was shot down first, he—Bayard—would, no matter how much longer he survived, have to face his twin some day in the omniscience of the mutual immortality, with the foul stain of his weakness now beyond concealment. The foul stain being not the idea, because the same idea must have occurred to his twin at the same instant with himself although they were in different squadrons now, but that of the two of them, John would not have been ashamed of it. The idea being simply this: John had managed to shoot down three huns before he himself was killed (he was probably a better shot than Bayard or maybe his flight commander liked him and set up targets) and Bayard himself had racked up enough ninths and sixteenths, after the British method of scoring (unless somebody was incredible enough to say "Not me; I was too damn scared to remember to pull up the cocking handles") to add up to two and maybe an inch over; now that John was gone and no longer needed his, suppose, just suppose he could wangle, bribe, forge, corrupt the records and whoever kept them, into transferring all the Sartoris bumf under one name, so that one of them anyway could come back home an ace—an idea not base in itself, because John had not only thought of it too but if he had lived and Bayard had died, would have managed somehow to accomplish it, but base only after he, Bayard, had debased and befouled it by being ashamed of it. And he could not quit it of his own volition, since when he faced John's ghost some day in the course of simple fatality, John would be just amused and contemptuous; where if he did it by putting the pistol barrel in his mouth himself, that ghost would be not just risible and contemptuous but forever unreconciled, irreconcilable.

But Linda Snopes—excuse me: Snopes Kohl—would be our first female one. So you would think the whole town would turn out, or at least be represented by delegates: from the civic clubs and churches, not to mention the American Legion and the V.F.W., which would have happened if she had been elected Miss America instead of merely blown up by a Franco shell or land mine or whatever it was that went off in or under the ambulance she was driving and left her stone deaf. So I said, "What does she want to come back home for? There's nothing for her to join. What would she want in a Ladies' Auxiliary, raffling off home-made jam and lamp-shades. Even if she could make jam, since obviously cooking is the last thing a sculptor would demand of his girl. Who was just passing time anyway between Communist meetings until somebody started a Fascist war he could get into. Not to mention the un-kosher stuff she would have had to learn in Jefferson, Mississippi. Especially if where she learned to cook was in that Dirty Spoon her papa beat Ratliff out of back there when they first came to town." But I was wrong. It wouldn't be municipal: only private: just three people only incidentally from Jefferson because they were mainly out of her mother's past: my uncle, her father, and Ratliff. Then I saw there would be only two. Ratliff wouldn't even get in the car.

"Come on," Uncle Gavin said. "Go with us."

"I'll wait here," Ratliff said. "I'll be the local committee. Until next time," he said at me.

"What?" Uncle Gavin said.

"Nothing," Ratliff said. "Jest a joke Chick told me that I'm reminding him of."

Then I saw it wasn't going to be even two out of her mother's past. We were not even going by the bank, let alone stop at it. I said, "What the hell would Mr Snopes want, throwing away at least six hours of good usury to make a trip all the way to Memphis to meet his daughter, after all the expense he had to go to get her out of Jefferson—not only butchering up De Spain's house, but all that imported Italian marble over her mother's grave to give her something worth going away from or not coming back to if you like that better."

I said: "So it's my fault I wasn't born soon enough either to defend Das Democracy in your war or Das Kapital in hers. Meaning there's still plenty of time for me yet. Or maybe what you mean is that Hitler and Mussolini and Franco all three working together cannot get an authentic unimpeachable paid-up member of the Harvard R.O.T.C. into really serious military trouble. Because I probably won't make Porcellian either; F.D.R. didn't."

I said: "That's it. That's why you insisted on me coming along this morning: although she hasn't got any eardrums now and can't hear you say No or Please No or even For God's sake No, at least she can't marry you before we get back to Jefferson with me right here in the car too. But there's the rest of the afternoon when you can chase me out, not to mention the eight hours of the night when Mother likes to believe I am upstairs asleep. Not to mention I've got to go back to Cambridge next month— unless you believe your . . . is it virginity or just celibacy? is worth even that sacrifice? But then why not, since it was your idea to send me all the way to Cambridge, Mass, for what we laughingly call an education. Being as Mother says she's been in love with you all her life, only she was too young to know it and you were too much of a gentleman to tell her. Or does Mother really always know best?"

By this time we had reached the airport; I mean Memphis. Uncle Gavin said, "Park the car and let's have some coffee. We've probably got at least a half-hour yet." We had the coffee in the restaurant; I don't know why they don't call it the Skyroom here too. Maybe Memphis is still off quota. Ratliff said she would have to marry somebody sooner or later, and every day that passed made it that much sooner. No, that wasn't the way he put it: that he—Uncle Gavin—couldn't escape forever, that almost any day now some woman would decide he was mature and dependable enough at last for steady work in place of merely an occasional chore; and that the sooner this happened the better, since only then would he be safe. I said, "How safe? He seems to me to be doing all right; I never knew anybody that scatheless."

"I don't mean him," Ratliff said. "I mean us, Yoknapatawpha County; that he would maybe be safe to live with then because he wouldn't have so much time for meddling."

In which case, saving us would take some doing. Because he —Gavin—had one defect in his own character which always saved him, no matter what jeopardy it left the rest of us in. I mean, the fact that people get older, especially young girls of fifteen or sixteen, who seem to get older all of a sudden in six months or one year than they or anybody else ever does in about ten years. I mean, he always picked out children, or maybe he was just vulnerable to female children and they chose him, whichever way you want it. That the selecting or victim-falling was done at an age when the oath of eternal fidelity would have ceased to exist almost before the breath was dry on it. I'm thinking now of Melisandre Backus naturally, before my time and Linda Snopes's too. That is, Melisandre was twelve and thirteen and fourteen several years before she vacated for Linda to take her turn in the vacuum, Gavin selecting and ordering the books of poetry to read to Melisandre or anyway supervise and check on, which was maybe how by actual test, trial and error, he knew which ones to improve Linda's mind and character with when her turn came, or anyway alter them.

Though pretty soon Melisandre committed the irrevocable error of getting a year older and so quitting forever that fey unworld of Spenser and the youth Milton, for the human race where even the sort of girl that he picked out or that picked out him, when a man talked about fidelity and devotion to her, she was in a position to tell him either to put up or shut up. Anyway, he was saved that time. Though I wasn't present to remember exactly what the sequence was: whether Gavin went off to Harvard first or maybe it was between Harvard and Heidelberg, or whether she got married first. Anyway, when he got back from his war, she was married. To a New Orleans underworld big shot named Harriss with two esses. And how in the world or where on earth she ever managed to meet him—a shy girl, motherless and an only child, who lived on what used to be one of our biggest plantations two or three miles from town but that for years had been gradually going to decay, with her widowered father who spent all his time on the front gallery in summer and in the library in winter with a bottle of whiskey and a volume of Horace. Who (Melisandre) had as far as we knew never been away from it in her life except to be driven daily in to town by a Negro coachman in a victoria while she graduated from the grammar school then the high school then the Female Academy. And a man about whom all we knew was what he said: that his name was Harriss with two esses, which maybe it was, and that he was a New Orleans importer. Which we knew he was, since (this was early 1919, before Uncle Gavin got back home) even Jefferson recognised when it saw one a bullet-proof Cadillac that needed two chauffeurs, both in double-breasted suits that bulged a little at the left armpit.

Not to mention the money. Mr Backus died about then and of course there were some to say it was with a broken heart over his only child marrying a bootleg czar. Though apparently he waited long enough to make sure his son-in-law was actually a

czar or anyway the empire a going and solvent one, since the
money had already begun to show a little before he died—the
roofs and galleries patched and shored up even if Mr Backus
evidently balked at paint on the house yet, and gravel in the
drive so that when she came home to spend that first Christmas,
she and the nurse and the czarevitch could go back and forth
to town in an automobile instead of the old victoria drawn by a
plough team. Then Mr Backus died and the house and outbuildings
too got painted. And now Harriss with both his esses began to
appear in Jefferson, making friends even in time though most of
Yoknapatawpha County was unsold still, just neutral, going out
there in the Model T's and on horses and mules, to stand along
the road and watch what had been just a simple familiar red-ink
north Mississippi cotton plantation being changed into a Virginia
or Long Island horse farm, with miles of white panel fence where
the rest of us were not a bit too proud for what we called bobwire
and any handy sapling post, and white stables with electric
light and steam heat and running water and butlers and footmen
for the horses where a lot of the rest of us still depended on coal-oil
lamps for light and our wives to tote firewood and water from the
nearest woodlot and spring or well.

Then there were two children, an heir and a princess too,
when Harriss died with his two esses in a New Orleans barber's
chair of his ordinary thirty-eight-calibre occupational disease.
Whereupon the horses and their grooms and valets became sold
and the house closed except for a caretaker, vacant now of
Mrs Harriss with her two esses and the two children and the
five maids and couriers and nannies and secretaries, and now
Mother and the other ones who had been girls with her in the
old Academy days would get the letters and post cards from the
fashionable European cities telling how just the climate at first
but presently, in time, the climate and the schools both were
better for the children and (on Mother's naturally) she hoped
Gavin was well and maybe even married. "So at least he's safe
from that one," I told Ratliff, who said,

"Safe?"

.. "Why the hell not? She not only got too big for the fairy tale,
she's got two children and all that money: what the hell does she
want to marry anybody for? Or not Gavin anyway; he don't

want money: all he wants is just to meddle and change. Why the hell isn't he safe now?"

"That's right," Ratliff said. "It looks like he would almost have to be, don't it? At least until next time." Joke. And still worth repeating two hours ago when he declined to come with us. And Gavin sitting there drinking a cup of what whoever ran the airport restaurant called coffee, looking smug and inscrutable and arrogant and immune as a louse on a queen's arse. Because maybe Linda Kohl (pardon me, Snopes Kohl) had plenty of money too, not only what her mother must have left her but what Uncle Gavin, as her guardian, had managed to chisel out of old Will Varner. Not chiselled out of her father too because maybe old Snopes was glad to stump up something just to have what Gavin or Ratliff would call that reproachless virgin rectitude stop looking at him. But she didn't have two children so all Ratliff and I had to trust, depend on this time was that old primary condition founded on simple evanescence, that every time a moment occurred they would be one moment older: that they had to be alive for him to notice them, and they had to be in motion to be alive, and the only moment of motion which caught his attention, his eye, was that one at which they entered puberty like the swirl of skirt or flow or turn of limb when entering, passing through a door, slowed down by the camera trick but still motion, still a moment, irrevocable.

That was really what saved him each time: that the moment had to be motion. They couldn't stop in the door, and once through it they didn't stop either; sometimes they didn't even pause long enough to close it behind them before going on to the next one and through it, which was into matrimony—from maturation to parturition in one easy lesson you might say. Which was all right. Uncle Gavin wouldn't be at that next door. He would still be watching the first one. And since life is not so much motion as an inventless repetition of motion, he would never be at that first door long before there would be another swirl, another unshaped vanishing adolescent leg. So I should have thought to tell Ratliff that, while I was in Memphis helping Uncle Gavin say good-bye to this one, he might be looking around the Square to see who the next one was going to be, as Linda had already displaced Melisandre Backus probably before Melisandre even knew she had been dispossessed. Then in the next moment I knew that would not be necessary; obviously Uncle Gavin had already picked her out himself, which was why he could sit there placid and composed, drinking coffee while we waited for the plane to be announced.

Which it was at last. We went out to the ramp. I stopped at the rail. "I'll wait here," I said. "You'll want a little privacy while you can still get it even if it's only anonymity and not solitude. Have you got your slate ready? or maybe she'll already have one built in on her cuff, or maybe strapped to her leg like aviators carry maps." But he had gone on. Then the plane taxied up, one of the new DC 3's, and in time there she was. I couldn't see her eyes from this distance, but then it wasn't them, it was just her ears the bomb or shell or mine or whatever it was blew up—the same tall girl too tall to have a shape but then I don't know: women like that and once you get their clothes off they surprise you even if she was twenty-nine years old now. Then I could see her eyes, so dark blue that at first you thought they were black. And I for one never did know how or where she got them or the black hair either since old Snopes's eyes were the colour of stagnant pond water and his hair didn't have any colour at all, and her mother had had blue eyes too but her hair was blonde. So that when I tried to remember her, she always looked like she had just been raided out of a brothel in the Scandinavian Valhalla and the cops had just managed to fling a few garments on her before they hustled her into the wagon. Fine eyes too, that probably if you were the one to finally get the clothes off you would have called them beautiful too. And she even had the little pad and pencil in her hand while she was kissing Gavin. I mean, kissing him. Though evidently he would need a little time to get used to using it or depending on it because he said aloud, just like she was anybody else:

"Here's Chick too," and she remembered me; she was as tall as Gavin and damn near as tall as me, as well as a nail-biter though maybe that had come after the shell or perhaps after the bereavement. And when she shook hands she really had driven that ambulance and apparently changed the tyres on it too, speaking not loud but in that dry harsh quacking voice that deaf people learn to use, even asking about Mother and Father

as if she really cared, like any ordinary Jefferson woman that
never dreamed of going to wars and getting blown up. Though
Uncle Gavin remembered now, or at least was learning fast,
taking the pad and pencil and scrawling something on it, baggage
I reckon, since she said, "Oh yes," just like she could hear too,
and got the checks out of her handbag.

I brought the car up while they untangled the bags. So she
had lived with the guy for years before they married but it didn't
show on her. And she had gone to Spain to the war and got
blown up at the front, and that didn't show on her either. I
said, "Why don't you let her drive? Then maybe she won't be so
nervous because she can't talk to you."

"Maybe you'd better drive then," he said. So we did, and
brought the hero home, the two of them in the back. And
somebody may have said, "Why don't we all ride in front? the
seat's wide enough." Though I don't remember it. Or at least
nobody did. Or anyway at least they got into the back seat. So
I don't remember that either: only Uncle Gavin: "You can
relax now. You're quite safe. I'm holding her hand."

Which they were, she holding his hand in both hers on her
lap and every mile or so the duck voice would say, "Gavin,"
and then after a mile or so, "Gavin." And evidently she hadn't
had the pad and pencil long enough to get used to them either
or maybe when you lose hearing and enter real silence you forget
everything does not take place in that privacy and solitude. Or
maybe after he took the pencil from her to answer on the pad,
she couldn't wait to get the pencil back so both should have had
slates: "Yes it does. I can feel it, somewhere in my skull or the
back of my mouth. It's an ugly sound. Isn't it?" But evidently
Gavin was learning because it was still the duck voice: "Yes it is.
I can feel it, I tell you." And still the duck voice: "How? If I
try to practise, how can I know when it's right?" Which I agree
with myself: if you're going to take time out from your law
practice and being county attorney to restore to your deaf girl
friend the lost bridehead of her mellifluity, how would you go
about it. Though what a chance for a husband: to teach your
stone-deaf wife that all she needed to make her tone and pitch
beautiful was merely to hold her breath while she spoke. Or
maybe what Uncle Gavin wrote next was simply Jonson (or

some of that old Donne or Herrick maybe or even just Suckling maybe—any or all of them annotated to that one ear—eye now —by that old Stevens) *Vale not these cherry lips with vacant speech But let her drink instead thy tender Yes.* Or maybe what he wrote was simpler still: *Hold it till we get home. This is no place to restore your voice. Besides, this infant will have to go back to Cambridge next month and then we'll have plenty of time, plenty of privacy.*

Thus we brought the hero home. Now we could see Jefferson, the clock on the courthouse, not to mention her father's water tank, and now the duck voice was saying Ratliff. "Bart liked him. He said he hadn't expected to like anybody from Mississippi, but he was wrong." What Gavin wrote this time was obvious, since the voice said: "Not even you. He made me promise—I mean, whichever one of us it was, would give Ratliff one of his things. You remember it—the Italian boy that you didn't know what it was even though you had seen sculpture before, but Ratliff that had never even seen an Italian boy, nor anything else beyond the Confederate monument in front of the court-house, knew at once what it was, and even what he was doing?" And I would have liked the pad myself long enough to write *What was the Italian boy doing?* only we were home now, the hero; Gavin said:

"Stop at the bank first. He should have some warning; simple decency commands it. Unless he has had his warning and has simply left town for a little space in which to wrestle with his soul and so bring it to the moment which it must face. Assuming of course that even he has realised by now that he simply cannot foreclose her out of existence like a mortgage or a note."

"And have a public reception here in the street before she has had a chance to fix her makeup?" I said.

"Relax," he said again. "When you are a little older you will discover that people really are much more gentle and considerate and kind than you want right now to believe."

I pulled up at the bank. But If I had been her I wouldn't even have reached for the pencil, duck quack or not, to say, "What the hell? Take me on home." She didn't. She sat there, holding his hand in both hers, not just on her lap but right against her belly, looking around at the Square, the duck voice saying, "Gavin. Gavin." Then: "There goes Uncle Willy, coming back from dinner." Except it wasn't old man Christian: he was dead. But then it didn't really matter whether anybody wrote that on the pad or not. And Gavin was right. Nobody stopped. I watched two of them recognise her. No, I mean they recognised juxtaposition: Gavin Stevens's car at the curb before the bank at twenty-two minutes past one in the afternoon with me at the wheel and Gavin and a woman in the back seat. Who had all heard about Linda Kohl I mean Snopes Kohl, anyhow that she was female and from Jefferson and had gone near enough to a war for it to bust her eardrums. Because he is right: people are kind and gentle and considerate. It's not that you don't expect them to be, it's because you have already made up your mind they are not and so they upset you, throw you off. They didn't even stop, just one of them said Howdy Gavin and went on.

I got out and went into the bank. Because what would I do myself if I had a daughter, an only child, and her grandfather had plenty of money for it and I could have afforded myself to let her go away to school. Only I didn't and nobody knew why I wouldn't, until suddenly I let her go, but only as far as the University which was only fifty miles away; and nobody knew why for that either: only that I aimed to become president of the bank that the president of it now was the man everybody believed had been laying my wife ever since we moved to town. That is, nobody knew why until three months later, when my wife went to the beauty parlour for the first time in her life and that night shot herself carefully through the temple so as not to disarrange the new permanent, and when the dust finally settled sure enough that fornicating bank president had left town and now I was not only president of his bank but living in his house and you would have thought I wouldn't need the daughter any more and she could go wherever the hell she wanted provided it wasn't ever Jefferson, Mississippi, again. Except I wouldn't even let her do that until we could both sit in the car and see the monument over her mother's grave unveiled, sitting there defenceless before the carved face and the carved defenceless taunt:

A Virtuous Wife Is a Crown to Her Husband
Her Children Rise and Call Her Blessed

and then I said, "All right. You can go now." And I came back out.

"Mr Snopes has taken the afternoon off," I said. "To go home and wait there for his daughter." So we went there, on to the colonial monstrosity which was the second taunt. He had three monuments in Jefferson now: the water tank, the gravestone, and the mansion. And who knows at which of the windows he lurked his wait or waited out his lurk, whichever way you prefer. "Maybe I should come in too," I said.

"Maybe we should each have a pad and pencil," Uncle Gavin said. "Then everybody could hear." We were expected. Almost at once the Negro yardman-chauffeur came out the front door. I got the luggage out on to the sidewalk while they still stood there, she as tall as him and Gavin in her arms just as much as she was in his, kissing right on the street in the broad daylight, the duck voice saying "Gavin Gavin" not so much as if she still couldn't believe it was him at last but as if she still hadn't got used to the new sound she was convinced she made. Then she turned him loose and he said, "Come on," and we got back in the car, and that was all. The hero was home. I turned in the middle of the block and looked not back, I would have liked to say, if it had been true: the houseman still scuttling up the walk with the bags and she still standing there, looking at us, a little too tall for my taste, immured, inviolate in silence, invulnerable, serene.

That was it: silence. If there were no such thing as sound. If it only took place in silence, no evil man has invented could really harm him: explosion, treachery, the human voice.

That was it: deafness. Ratliff and I couldn't beat that. Those others, the other times had flicked the skirt or flowed or turned the limb at and into mere puberty; beyond it and immediately, was the other door immediately beyond which was the altar and the long line of drying diapers: fulfilment, the end. But she had beat him. Not in motion continuous through a door, a moment, but immobilised by a thunderclap into silence, herself the immobile one while it was the door and the walls it opened which fled away and on, herself no moment's child but the inviolate bride of silence, inviolable in maidenhead, fixed, forever safe from change and alteration. Finally I ran Ratliff to ground; it took three days.

"Her husband is sending you a present," I said. "It's that sculpture you liked: the Italian boy doing whatever it was you liked that Gavin himself who has not only seen Italian boys before but maybe even one doing whatever this one is doing, didn't even know where first base was. But it's all right. You don't have a female wife nor any innocent female daughters either. So you can probably keep it right there in the house.— She's going to marry him," I said.

"Why not?" he said. "I reckon he can stand it. Besides, if somebody jest marries him, maybe the rest of us will be safe."

"The rest of them, you mean?" I said.

"I mean jest what I said," Ratliff answered. "I mean the rest of all of us."

NINE

Charles Mallison

GAVIN was right. That was late August. Three weeks later I was back in Cambridge again, hoping, I mean trying, or maybe what I mean is I belonged to the class that would, or anyway should, graduate next June. But I had been in Jefferson three weeks, plenty long enough even if they had insisted on having banns read: something quite unnecessary for a widow who was not only a widow but a wounded war hero too. So then I thought maybe they were waiting until they would be free of me. You know: the old road-company drammer reversed in gender: the frantic child clinging this time to the prospective broom's coat-tail, crying "Papa papa papa" (in this case Uncle uncle uncle) "please don't make us marry Mrs Smith."

Then I thought (it was Thanksgiving now; pretty soon I would be going home for Christmas) *Naturally it won't occur to any of them to bother to notify me way up here in Massachusetts.* So I even thought of writing and asking, not Mother of course and certainly not Uncle Gavin, since if it had happened he would be too busy to answer, and if it hadn't he would still be too busy either dodging for his life if he was the one still saying No, or trying to learn her enough language to hear Please if he was the one saying Yes. But to Ratliff, who would be an interested bystander even if you couldn't call that much curiosity about other people's affairs which he possessed merely innocent— maybe even a wire: *Are they bedded formally yet or not? I mean is it rosa yet or still just sub, assuming you assume the same assumption they teach us up here at Harvard that once you get the clothes off those tall up-and-down women you find out they ain't all that up-and-down at all.*

Then it was Christmas and I thought *Maybe I wronged them. Maybe they have been waiting for me all along, not to interrupt my education by an emergency call but for the season of peace and good will to produce me available to tote the ring or bouquet or whatever it is.* But I didn't even see her. Uncle Gavin and I even spent most of one whole day together. I was going out to Sartoris to shoot quail with Benbow (he wasn't but seventeen but he was considered one of the best bird shots in the county, second only to Luther Biglin, a half farmer, half dog trainer, half market hunter, who shot left-handed, not much older than Benbow, in fact about my age, who lived up near Old Wyottsport on the river) and Uncle Gavin invited himself along. He—Gavin—wouldn't be much of a gun even if he stopped talking long enough, but now and then he would go with me. And all that day, nothing; it was me that finally said:

"How are the voice lessons coming?"

"Mrs Kohl? Fair. But your fresh ear would be the best judge," and I said:

"When will that be?" and he said:

"Any time you're close enough to hear it." And again on Christmas day, it was me. Ratliff usually had Christmas dinner with us, Uncle Gavin's guest though Mother liked him too, whether or not because she was Uncle Gavin's twin. Or sometimes Uncle Gavin ate with Ratliff and then he would take me because Ratliff was a damned good cook, living alone in the cleanest little house you ever saw, doing his own housework and he even made the blue shirts he always wore. And this time too it was me.

"What about Mrs Kohl for dinner too?" I asked Mother, and Uncle Gavin said:

"My God, did you come all the way down here from Cambridge to spend Christmas too looking at that old fish-blooded son—" and caught himself in time and said, "Excuse me, Maggie," and Mother said:

"Certainly she will have to take her first Christmas dinner at home with her father." And the next day I left. Spoade—his father had been at Harvard back in 1909 with Uncle Gavin—had invited me to Charleston to see what a Saint Cecilia ball looked like from inside. Because we always broke up then anyway; the day after Christmas Father always went to Miami to spend a week looking at horses and Mother would go too, not that she was interested in running horses but on the contrary: because of her conviction that her presence or anyway adjacence or at least contiguity would keep him from buying one.

Then it was 1938 and I was back in Cambridge. Then it was September 1938, and I was still or anyway again in Cambridge, in law school now. Munich had been observed or celebrated or consecrated, whichever it was, and Uncle Gavin said, "It won't

be long now." But he had been saying that back last spring. So
I said:

"Then what's the use of me wasting two or three more years
becoming a lawyer when if you're right nobody will have time
for civil cases any more, even if I'm still around to prosecute or
defend them?" and he said:

"Because when this one is over, all humanity and justice will
have left will be the law," and I said:

"What else is it using now?" and he said:

"These are good times, boom halcyon times when what do
you want with justice when you've already got welfare? Now the
law is the last resort, to get your hand into the pocket which so
far has resisted or foiled you."

That was last spring, in June when he and Mother (they had
lost Father at Saratoga though he had promised to reach Cambridge in time for the actual vows) came up to see me graduate
in Ack. And I said, "What? No wedding bells yet?" and he said:

"Not mine anyway," and I said:

"How are the voice lessons coming? Come on," I said, "I'm
a big boy now; I'm a Harvard A.M. too even if I won't have
Heidelberg. Tell me. Is that really all you do when you are all
cosy together? practise talking?" and he said:

"Hush and let me talk awhile now. You're going to Europe for
the summer; that's my present to you. I have your tickets and
your passport application; all you need do is go down to the
official photographer and get mugged."

"Why Europe? and Why now? Besides, what if I don't want
to go?" and he said:

"Because it may not be there next summer. So it will have to
be this one. Go and look at the place; you may have to die in it."

"Why not wait until then, then?" and he said:

"You will go as a host then. This summer you can still be a
guest." There were three of us; by fast footwork and pulling all
the strings we could reach, we even made the same boat. And
that summer we—I: two of us at the last moment found themselves incapable of passing Paris—saw a little of Europe on a
bicycle. I mean, that part still available: that presumable
corridor of it where I might have to do Uncle Gavin's dying:
Britain, France, Italy—the Europe which Uncle Gavin said

would be no more since the ones who survived getting rid of Hitler and Mussolini and Franco would be too exhausted and the ones who merely survived them wouldn't care anyway.

So I did try to look at it, to see, since even at twenty-four I still seemed to believe what he said just as I believed him at fourteen and (I presume: I can't remember) at four. In fact, the Europe he remembered or thought he remembered was already gone. What I saw was a kind of composed and collected hysteria: a frenetic holiday in which everybody was a tourist, native and visitor alike. There were too many soldiers. I mean, too many people dressed as, and for the moment behaving like, troops, as if for simple police or temporary utility reasons they had to wear masquerade and add to the Maginot Line (so that they—the French ones anyway—seemed to be saying, "Have a heart; don't kid us. We don't believe it either.") right in the middle of the fight for the thirty-nine-hour week; the loud parliamentary conclaves about which side of Piccadilly or the Champs-Elysées the sandbags would look best on like which side of the room to hang the pictures; the splendid glittering figure of Gamelin still wiping the soup from his moustache and saying, "Be calm. I am here"—as though all Europe (oh yes, us too; the place was full of Americans too) were saying, "Since Evil is the thing, not only *de rigueur* but successful too, let us all join Evil and so make it the Good."

Then me too in Paris for the last two weeks, to see if the Paris of Hemingway and the Paris of Scott Fitzgerald (they were not the same ones; they merely used the same room) had vanished completely or not too; then Cambridge again, only a day late: all of which, none of which that is, ties up with anything but only explains to me why it was almost a year and a half before I saw her again. And so we had Munich: that moment of respectful silence, then once more about our affairs; and Uncle Gavin's letter came saying "It won't be long now." Except that it was probably already too late for me. When I had to go—no, I don't mean that: when the time came for me to go—I wanted to be a fighter pilot. But I was already twenty-four now; in six years I would be thirty and even now it might be too late; Bayard and John Sartoris were twenty when they went to England in '16 and Uncle Gavin told me about one R.F.C. (I mean R.A.F. now) child who was a captain with such a record that the British government sent him back home and grounded him for good so that he might at least be present on the day of his civilian majority. So I would probably wind up as a navigator or engineer on bombers, or maybe at thirty they wouldn't let me go up at all.

But still no wedding bells. Maybe it was the voice. My spies —I only needed one of course: Mother—reported that the private lessons were still going on, so maybe she felt that the Yes would not be dulcet enough yet to be legal. Which—legality— she would of course insist on, having tried cohabitation the first time *au naturel* you might say, and it blew up in her face. No, that's wrong. The cohabitation didn't blow up until after it became legal, until whichever one it was finally said, "Oh hell then, get the licence and the preacher but please for sweet please sake shut up." So now she would fear a minister or a J.P. like Satan or the hangman, since to appear before one in the company of someone of the opposite sex would be the same as a death warrant. Which she certainly would not wish for Uncle Gavin, since not only was the Yes to him going to be tender enough to have brought her all the way back to Jefferson to say it, he wouldn't leave enough money to make it worth being his widow in case that Yes wasn't so tender.

No, that's wrong too. If she had to shack up with a man for five years before he would consent to marry her, I mean, with a sculptor so advanced and liberal that even Gavin couldn't recognise what he sculpted, made, he must have been pretty advanced in liberalism. And if he had to quit anything as safe and pleasant as being a Greenwich Village sculptor living with a girl that could afford and wanted to pay the rent and buy the grub whether he married her or not—if he had to quit all this to go to Spain to fight on what anybody could have told him would be the losing side, he must have been advanced even beyond just liberalism. And if she loved him enough to wait five years for him to say All right, dammit, call the parson, and then went to Spain to get blown up herself just to be with him, she must be one of them too since apparently you can't even be moderate about communism: you either violently are or violently are not. (I asked him; I mean of course Uncle Gavin. "Suppose she is," he said. "All right," I said. "So what the hell?" he said. "All right, all right," I said. "What the hell's business is it of yours anyway?" he said. "All right, all right, all right," I said.) And just being blown up wouldn't cure it. So there would be no wedding bells; that other one had been a mere deviation due to her youth, not to happen again; she was only for a moment an enemy of the people, and paid quickly for it.

So there would be no preacher. They were just going to practise people's democracy, where everybody was equal no matter what you looked like when he finally got your clothes off, right here in Jefferson. So all you had to figure out was, how the bejesus they would manage it in a town no bigger and equal than Jefferson. Or not they: he, Gavin, I mean, it would be his trouble, problem, perhaps need. Not hers. She was free, absolved of mundanity; who knows, who is not likewise castrate of sound, circumcised from having to hear, of need too. She had the silence: that thunderclap instant to fix her forever inviolate and private in solitude; let the rest of the world blunder in all the loud directions over its own feet trying to find first base at the edge of abyss like one of the old Chaplin films.

He would have to find the ways and means; all she would bring would be the capability for compliance, and what you might call a family precedence. Except that she wasn't her mother, not to mention Gavin not being Manfred de Spain. I mean—I was only thirteen when Mrs Snopes shot herself that night so I still don't know how much I saw and remembered and how much was compelled onto or into me from Uncle Gavin, being, as Ratliff put it, as I had spent the first eleven or twelve years of my existence in the middle of Uncle Gavin, thinking what he thought and seeing what he saw, not because he taught me to but maybe just because he let me, allowed me to. I mean, Linda and Uncle Gavin wouldn't have that one matchless natural advantage which her mother and Manfred de Spain had, which was that aura, nimbus, condition, whatever the word is, in which Mrs Snopes not just existed, lived, breathed, but created about herself by just existing, living, breathing. I don't know what word I want: an aura not of licence, unchastity, because (this may even be Ratliff; I don't remember now) little petty moral conditions like restraint and purity had no more connection with a woman like Mrs Snopes—or rather, a woman like her had no more concern with or even attention for them—than conventions about what force you use or when or how or where have to do with wars or cyclones. I mean, when a community suddenly discovered that it has the sole ownership of Venus for however long it will last, she cannot, must not be a chaste wife or even a faithful mistress whether she is or not or really wants to be or not. That would be not only intolerable, but a really criminal waste; and for the community so accoladed to even condone, let alone abet, the chastity, continence, would be an affront to the donors deserving their godlike vengeance. Like having all miraculous and matchless season—wind, sun, rain, heat and frost—concentrated into one miraculous instant over the county, then us to try to arrogate to ourselves the puny right to pick and choose and select instead of every man woman and child that could walk turning out to cultivate to the utmost every seed the land would hold. So we—I mean the men and the women both—would not even ask to escape the anguish and uproar she would cause by breathing and existing among us and the jealousy we knew ourselves to be unworthy of, so long as we did have one who could match and cope with her in fair combat and so be our champion and pride like the county ownership of the fastest horse in the country. We would all be on hers and De Spain's side; we would even engineer and guard the trysts; only the preachers would hate her because they would be afraid of her since the god she represented without even trying to, for the men to pant after and even the women to be proud that at least one of their sex was its ambassador, was a stronger one than the pale and desperate Galilean who was all they had to challenge with.

Because Linda didn't have that quality; that one was not transferable. So all that remained for her and Gavin was continence. To put it crudely, morality. Because where could they go. Not to her house because between her and her father, the wrong one was deaf. And not to his because the house he lived in wasn't his but Mother's and one of the earliest (when the time came of course) principles he taught me was that a gentleman does not bring his paramour into the home of: in this order: His wife. His mother. His sister. His mistress. And they couldn't make the coincidental trips to the available places in Memphis or New Orelans or maybe as far away as St Louis and Chicago that (we assumed) her mother and Manfred de Spain used to make, since even police morality, not to mention that of that semi-underworld milieu to which they would have had to resort, would have revolted at the idea of seducing a stone-deaf woman from the safety and innocence of her country home town, to such a purpose. So that left only his automobile, concealed desperately and frantically behind a bush—Gavin Stevens, aged fifty, M.A. Harvard, Ph.D. Heidelberg, Ll.B. Mississippi, American Field Service and Y.M.C.A., France, 1915-1918, County Attorney; and Linda Kohl, thirty, widow, wounded in action with the communist forces in Spain, fumbling and panting in a parked automobile like they were seventeen years old.

Especially when the police found out (I mean if, of course, if somebody came and told them) that she was a communist. Or Jefferson either, for that matter. We had two Finns who had escaped by the skin of their teeth from Russia in 1917 and from Europe in 1919 and in the early twenties wound up in Jefferson; nobody knew why—one the cobbler who had taken over Mr Nightingale's little shop, the other a tinsmith—who were not professed communists nor confessed either since they still spoke too little English by the time Mr Roosevelt's N.R.A. and the labour unions had made "communist" a dirty word referring mostly to John L. Lewis's C.I.O. In fact, there was no need as they saw it to confess or profess either. They simply took it for granted that there was a proletariat in Jefferson as specific and obvious and recognisable as the day's climate, and as soon as they learned English they would find it and, all being proletarians together, they would all be communists together too as was not only their right and duty but they couldn't help themselves. That was fifteen years ago now, though the big one, the cobbler, the one slower at learning English, was still puzzled and bewildered, believing it was simply the barrier of language instead of a condition in which the Jefferson proletariat declined not only to know it was the proletariat but even to be content as the middle class, being convinced instead that it was merely in a temporary interim state toward owning in its turn Mr Snopes's bank or Wall Street, Snopes's wholesale grocery chain or (who knows?) on the way to the governor's mansion in Jackson or even the White House in Washington.

The little one, the tinsmith, was quicker than that. Maybe, as distinct from the cobbler's sedentary and more meditative trade, he got around more. Anyway he had learned some time ago that any proletariat he became a member of in Jefferson he would have to manufacture first. So he set about it. The only means he had was to recruit, convert communists, and the only material he had were Negroes. Because among us white male Jeffersons there was one concert of unanimity, no less strong and even louder at the bottom, extending from the operators of Saturday curb-side peanut- and popcorn-vending machines, through the side-street and back-alley grocers, up to the department store owners and automobile and gasoline agencies, against everybody they called communists now—Harry Hopkins, Hugh Johnson and everybody else associated with N.R.A., Eugene Debs, the I.W.W., the C.I.O.—any and everybody who seemed even to question our native-born Jefferson right to buy or raise or dig or find anything as cheaply as cajolery or trickery or threat or force could do it, and then sell it as dear as the necessity or ignorance or timidity of the buyer would stand. And that was what Linda had, all she had in our alien capitalist waste this far from home if she really was a communist and communism really is not just a political ideology but a religion which has to be practised in order to stay alive—two Arctic Circle immigrants: one practically without human language, a troglodyte, the other a little quick-tempered irreconcilable hornet because of whom both of them were already well advanced outside the Jefferson pale, not by being professed communists (nobody would have cared how much of a communist the little one merely professed himself to be so long as he didn't actually interfere with local wage scales, just as they could have been Republicans so long as they didn't try to interfere with our Democratic town and county elections or Catholics as long as they didn't picket churches or break up prayer meetings) but Negro lovers: consorters, political affiliators with Negroes. Not social consorters: we would not have put up with that from even them and the little one anyway knew enough Jefferson English to know it. But association of any sort was too much; the local police were already looking cross-eyed at them even though we didn't really believe a foreigner could do any actual harm among our own loyal coloured.

So, you see, all they—Gavin and Linda—had left now was marriage. Then it was Christmas 1938, the last one before the lights began to go out, and I came home for the holidays and she came to supper one night. Not Christmas dinner. I don't know what happened there: whether Mother and Gavin decided it would be more delicate to ask her and let her decline, or not ask her at all. No, that's wrong. I'll bet Mother invited them both—her and old Snopes too. Because women are marvellous. They stroll perfectly bland and serene through a fact that the men have been bloodying their heads against for years; whereupon you find that the fact not only wasn't important, it wasn't really there. She invited them both, exactly as if she had been doing it whenever she thought of it maybe at least once a month for the last hundred years, whenever she decided to give them a little pleasure by having them to a meal, or whenever she decided it would give her pleasure to have them whether they thought so or not; and Linda declined for both of them in exactly the same way.

So you can imagine that Christmas dinner in that house that nobody I knew had seen the inside of except Mother (oh yes, she would have by now, with Linda home again) and Uncle Gavin: the dining-room—table, chairs, sideboard, cabinets, chandeliers and all—looking exactly as it had looked in the Memphis interior decorator's warehouse when he—Snopes— traded in Major de Spain's mother's furniture for it, with him at one end of the table and Linda at the other and the yardman in a white coat serving them—the old fish-blooded son of a bitch who had a vocabulary of two words, one being No and the other Foreclose, and the bride of silence more immaculate in that chastity than ever Caesar's wife because she was invulnerable too, forever safe, in that chastity forever pure, that couldn't have heard him if he had had anything to say to her, any more than he could have heard her, since he wouldn't even recognise the language she spoke in. The two of them sitting there face to face through the long excruciating ritual which the day out of all the days compelled; and nobody to know why they did it, suffered it, why she suffered and endured it, what ritual she served or compulsion expiated—or who knows? what portent she postulated to keep him reminded. Maybe that was why. I mean, why she came back to Jefferson. Evidently it wasn't to marry Gavin Stevens. Or at least not yet.

So it would be just an ordinary supper, though Mother would have said (and unshakably believed) that it was in honour of me being at home again. And didn't I just say that women are wonderful? She—Linda: a present from Guess Who—had a little pad of thin ivory leaves just about big enough to hold three words at a time, with gold corners, on little gold rings to turn the pages, with a little gold stylus thing to match, that you could write on and then efface it with a handkerchief or a piece of tissue or, in a mere masculine emergency, a little spit on your thumb and then use it again (sure, maybe he gave it to her in return for that gold cigarette-lighter engraved G L S when he didn't have L for his middle initial or in fact any middle initial at all, that she gave him about five years ago that he never had used because nobody could unconvince him he could taste the fluid through his cob pipe). And though Mother used the pad like the rest of us, it was just coincidental, like any other gesture of the hands while talking. Because she was talking to Linda at the same time, not even watching her hand but looking at Linda instead, so that she couldn't have deciphered the marks she was making even provided she was making marks, just talking away at Linda exactly as she did to the rest of us. And be damned if Linda wouldn't seem to understand her, the two of them chattering and babbling away at one another like women do, so that maybe no women ever listen to the other one because they don't have to, they have already communicated before either one begins to speak.

Because at those times Linda would talk. Oh yes, Gavin's voice lessons had done some good because they must have, there had been too many of them or anyway enough of them, assuming they did spend some of the time together trying to soften down her voice. But it was still the duck's voice: dry, lifeless, dead. That was it: dead. There was no passion, no heat in it; and, what was worse, no hope. I mean, in bed together in the dark and to have more of love and excitement and ecstasy

than just one can bear and so you must share it, murmur it, and
to have only that dry and lifeless quack to murmur, whisper
with. This time (there were other suppers during the next
summer but this was the first one when I was at table too) she
began to talk about Spain. Not about the war. I mean, the lost
war. It was queer. She mentioned it now and then, not as if it
had never happened but as if their side hadn't been licked. Some
of them like Kohl had been killed and a lot of the others had had
the bejesus blown out of the eardrums and arms and legs like
her, and the rest of them were scattered (and in no time now
would begin to be proscribed and investigated by the F.B.I., not
to mention harried and harassed by the amateurs, but we
hadn't quite reached that yet) but they hadn't been whipped
and hadn't lost anything at all. She was talking about the people
in it, the people like Kohl. She told about Ernest Hemingway
and Malraux, and about a Russian, a poet that was going to be
better than Pushkin only he got himself killed; and Mother
scribbling on the pad but not paying any more attention to
what she thought she was writing than Linda was, saying,

"Oh, Linda, no!"—you know: how tragic, to be cut off so
young, the work unfinished, and Gavin taking the pad away from
Mother but already talking too:

"Nonsense. There's no such thing as a mute inglorious Milton.
If he had died at the age of two, somebody would still write it
for him."

Only I didn't bother with the pad; I doubt if I could have
taken it away from them. "Named Bacon or Marlowe," I said.

"Or maybe a good sound synthetic professional name like
Shakespeare," Uncle Gavin said.

But Linda hadn't even glanced at the pad. I tell you, she and
Mother didn't need it.

"Why?" she said. "What line or paragraph or even page can
you compose and write to match giving your life to say No to
people like Hitler and Mussolini?" and Gavin not bothering
with the pad either now:

"She's right. She's absolutely right, and thank God for it.
Nothing is ever lost. Nothing. Nothing." Except Linda of
course. Gavin said how Kohl had been a big man, I don't mean
just a hunk of beef, but virile, alive; a man who loved what the

old Greeks meant by laughter, who would have been a match for, competent to fulfil, any woman's emotional and physical life too. And Linda was just thirty now and oh yes, the eyes were beautiful, and more than just the eyes; maybe it never mattered to Kohl what was inside her clothes, nor would to anyone else lucky enough to succeed him, including Uncle Gavin. So now I understood at last what I was looking at: neither Mother nor Linda either one needed to look at what Mother thought she was scribbling on that damned ivory slate, since evidently from the second day after Linda got home Mother had been as busy and ruthless and undevious as one of the old Victorian head-hunting mamas during the open season at Bath or Tunbridge Wells in Fielding or Dickens or Smollett. Then I found out something else. I remembered how not much more than a year ago we were alone in the office and Ratliff said,

"Look-a-here, what you want to waste all this good weather being jealous of your uncle for? Somebody's bound to marry him sooner or later. Someday you're going to outgrow him and you'll be too busy yourself jest to hang around and protect him. So it might jest as well be Linda." You see what I mean? that evidently it was transferable. I mean, whatever it was her mother had had. Gavin had seen her once when she was thirteen years old, and look what happened to him. Then Barton Kohl saw her once when she was nineteen years old, and look where he was now. And now I had seen her twice, I mean after I was old enough to know what I was looking at: once at the Memphis airport last summer, and here tonight at the supper table, and now I knew it would have to be me to take Uncle Gavin off to the library or den or wherever such interview happen, and say:

"Look here, young man. I know how dishonourable your intentions are. What I want to know is, how serious they are." Or if not him, at least somebody. Because it wouldn't be him. Ratliff had told me how Gavin said her doom would be to love once and lose him and then to mourn. Which could have been why she came back to Jefferson: since if all you want is to grieve, it doesn't matter where you are. So she was lost; she had even lost that remaining one who should have married her for no other reason than that he had done more than anybody else while she was a child to make her into what she was now. But it wouldn't be him; he had his own prognosis to defend, make his own words good no matter who anguished and suffered.

Yes, lost. She had been driving that black country-banker-cum-Baptist-deacon's car ever since she got home; apparently she had assumed at first that she would drive it alone, until old Snopes himself objected because of the deafness. So each afternoon she would be waiting in the car when the bank closed and the two of them would drive around the adjacent country while he could listen for the approaching horns if any. Which—the country drives—was in his character since the county was his domain, his barony—the acres, the farms, the crops—since even where he didn't already hold the mortgage, perhaps already in process of foreclosure even, he could measure and calculate with his eye the ones which so far had escaped him.

That is, except one afternoon a week, usually Wednesday. Old Snopes neither smoked nor drank nor even chewed tobacco; what his jaws worked steadily on was, as Ratliff put it, the same little chunk of Frenchman's Bend air he had brought in his mouth when he moved to Jefferson thirty years ago. Yes, lost: it wasn't even to Uncle Gavin: it was Ratliff she went to that afternoon and said, "I can't find who sells the whiskey now." No, not lost so much, she had just been away too long, explaining to Ratliff why she hadn't gone to Uncle Gavin: "He's the County Attorney; I thought—" and Ratliff patting her on the back right there in the street, saying for anybody to hear it since obviously she couldn't:

"You been away from home too long. Come on. We'll go git him."

So the three of them in Gavin's car drove up to Jakeleg Wattman's so-called fishing camp at Wyott's Crossing so she would know where and how herself next time. Which was to drive up to Jakeleg's little unpainted store (Jakeleg kept it unpainted so that whenever a recurrent new reform-administration sheriff would notify him he had to be raided again, Jakeleg wouldn't have a lot of paint to scratch up in drawing the nails and dismantling the sections and carrying them another mile deeper into the bottom until the reform reached its ebb and he could move back convenient to the paved road and the automobiles) and get out of the car and step inside where the unpainted shelves were crowded with fishhooks and sinkers and lines and tobacco and flashlight batteries and coffee and canned beans and shotgun shells and the neat row of United States Internal Revenue Department liquor licences tacked on the wall and Jakeleg in the flopping rubber hip boots he wore winter and summer with a loaded pistol in one of them, behind the chicken-wire-barricaded counter, and you would say, "Howdy, Jake. What you got today?" And he would tell you: the same one brand like he didn't care whether you liked that brand or not, and the same one price like he didn't give a damn whether that suited you either. And as soon as you said how many the Negro man (in the flopping hip boots Jakeleg had worn last year) would duck out or down or at least out of sight and reappear with the bottles and stand holding them until you had given Jakeleg the money and got your change (if any) back and Jakeleg would open the wicket in the wire and shove the bottles through and you would return to your car and that was all there was to it; taking (Uncle Gavin) Linda right on in with him, saying as likely as not: "Howdy, Jake. Meet Mrs Kohl. She can't hear but there's nothing wrong with her taste and swallowing." And maybe Linda said,

"What does he have?" and likely what Uncle Gavin wrote on the pad for that was *That's fighting talk here This is a place where you take it or leave it Just give him eight dollars or sixteen if you want 2.* So next time maybe she came alone. Or maybe Uncle Gavin himself walked into the bank and on to that little room at the back and said, "Look here, you old fish-blooded son of a bitch, are you going to just sit here and let your only female daughter that won't even hear the trump of doom, drive alone up yonder to Jakeleg Wattman's bootleg joint to buy whiskey?" Or maybe it was simple coincidence: a Wednesday afternoon and he—Mr Snopes—can't say, "Here, hold on; where the hell you going? This ain't the right road." Because she can't hear him and in fact I don't know how he did talk to her since I can't imagine his hand writing anything except adding a percent symbol or an expiration date; maybe they just had a county road map he could point to that worked up until this time. So now he had not one dilemma but three: not just the bank president's known recognisable car driving up to a bootleg joint, but with him in it; then the dilemma of whether to let every prospective mortgagee in Yoknapatawpha County hear how he would sit there in the car and let his only female child walk into a notorious river-bottom joint to buy whiskey, or go in himself and with his own Baptist deacon's hand pay out sixteen dollars' worth of his own life's blood.

Lost. Gavin told me how over a year ago the two Finn communists had begun to call on her at night (at her invitation of course) and you can imagine this one. It would be the parlour. Uncle Gavin said she had fixed up a sitting-room for herself upstairs, but this would be in the parlour diagonally across the hall from the room where old Snopes was supposed to spend all his life that didn't take place in the bank. The capitalist parlour and the three of them, the two Finnish immigrant labourers and the banker's daughter, one that couldn't speak English and another that couldn't hear any language, trying to communicate through the third one who hadn't yet learned to spell, talking of hope, millennium, dream: of the emancipation of man from his tragedy, the liberation at last and forever from pain and hunger and injustice, of the human condition. While two doors away in the room where he did everything but eat and keep the bank's cash money, with his feet propped on that little unpainted ledge nailed to his Adam fireplace and chewing steadily at what Ratliff called his little chunk of Frenchman's Bend air—the capitalist himself who owned the parlour and the house, the very circumambience they dreamed in, who had begun life as a nihilist and then softened into a mere anarchist and now was not only a conservative but a tory too: a pillar, rock-fixed, of things as they are.

Lost. Shortly after that she began what Jefferson called meddling with the Negroes. Apparently she went without invitation or warning, into the different classrooms of the Negro grammar and high school, who couldn't hear thunder, mind you, and so all she could do was watch—the faces, expressions, gestures of the pupils and teachers both who were already spooked, perhaps alarmed, anyway startled and alerted to cover, by the sudden presence of the unexplained white woman who was presently talking to the teacher in the quacking duck's voice of the deaf and then holding out a tablet and pencil for the teacher to answer. Until presently, as quick as the alarmed messenger could find him I suppose, the principal was there—a college-bred man, Uncle Gavin said, of intelligence and devotion too—and then she and the principal and the senior woman teacher were in the principal's office, where it probably was not so much that she, the white woman, was trying to explain, as that they, the two Negroes, had already divined and maybe understood even if they did not agree with her. Because they, Negroes, when the problems are not from the passions of want and ignorance and fear—gambling, drink—but are of simple humanity, are a gentle and tender people, a little more so than white people because they have had to be; a little wiser in their dealings with white people than white people are with them, because they have had to survive in a minority. As if they already knew that the ignorance and superstition she would have to combat—the ignorance and superstition which would counteract, cancel her dream and, if she remained bullheaded enough in perseverance, would destroy her—would not be in the black race she proposed to raise but in the white one she represented.

So finally the expected happened, anticipated by everyone except her apparently, maybe because of the deafness, the isolation, the solitude of living not enclosed with sound but merely surrounded by gestures. Or maybe she did anticipate it but, having been through a war, she just didn't give a damn. Anyway, she bulled right ahead with her idea. Which was to establish a kind of competitive weekly test, the winners, who would be the top students for that week in each class, to spend the following week in a kind of academy she would establish, with white teachers, details to be settled later but for temporary they would use her sitting-room in her father's house for a sort of general precept, the winners of each week to be replaced by next week's winners; these to embrace the whole school from kindergarden to seniors, her theory being that if you were old enough to be taught at eighteen you were old enough at eight too when learning something new would be even easier. Because she couldn't hear, you see, not just the words but the tones, over- and under-tones of alarm, fright, terror in which the black voice would have to say Thank you. So it was the principal

himself who finally came to see Uncle Gavin at the office—the
intelligent dedicated man with his composed and tragic face.

"I've been expecting you," Uncle Gavin said. "I know what
you want to say."

"Thank you," the principal said. "Then you know yourself
it won't work. That you are not ready for it yet and neither are
we."

"Not many of your race will agree with you," Uncle Gavin
said.

"None of them will," the principal said. "Just as none of them
agreed when Mr Washington said it."

"Mr Washington?"

"Booker T.," the principal said. "Mr Carver too."

"Oh," Uncle Gavin said. "Yes?"

"That we have got to make the white people need us first.
In the old days your people did need us, in your economy
if not your culture, to make your cotton and tobacco and indigo.
But that was the wrong need, bad and evil in itself. So it couldn't
last. It had to go. So now you don't need us. There is no place
for us now in your culture or economy either. We both buy the
same instalment-plan automobiles to burn up the same gasoline
in, and the same radios to listen to the same music and the same
iceboxes to keep the same beer in, but that's all. So we have got
to make a place of our own in your culture and economy too.
Not you to make a place for us just to get us out from under
your feet, as in the South here, or to get our votes for the
aggrandisement of your political perquisites, as in the North,
but *us* to make a place for ourselves by compelling you to need us,
you cannot do without us because nobody else but us can fill
that place in your economy and culture which only we can fill
and so that place will have to be ours. So that you will not just
say Please to us, you will need to say Please to us, you will want
to say Please to us. Will you tell her that? Say we thank her and
we won't forget this. But to leave us alone. Let us have your
friendship all the time, and your help when we need it. But keep
your patronage until we ask for it."

"This is not patronage," Uncle Gavin said. "You know that
too."

"Yes," the principal said. "I know that too. I'm sorry. I am ashamed that I . . ." Then he said: "Just say we thank her and will remember her, but to let us alone."

"How can you say that to someone who will face that much risk, just for justice, just to abolish ignorance?"

"I know," the principal said. "It's difficult. Maybe we can't get along without your help for a while yet, since I am already asking for it.—Good-day, sir," he said, and was gone. So how could Uncle Gavin tell her either. Or anybody else tell her, everybody else tell her, white and black both. Since it wasn't that she couldn't hear: she wouldn't listen, not even to the unified solidarity of No in the Negro school itself—that massive, not resistance but immobility, like the instinct of the animal to lie perfectly still, not even breathing, not even thinking. Or maybe she did hear that because she reversed without even stopping, from the school to the board of education itself: if she could not abolish the ignorance by degrees of individual cases, she would attempt it wholesale by putting properly educated white teachers in the Negro school, asking no help, not even from Gavin, hunting down the school board then, they retreating into simple evaporation, the county board of supervisors in their own sacred lair, armed with no petty ivory tablet and gold stylus this time but with a vast pad of yellow foolscap and enough pencils for everybody. Evidently they committed the initial error of letting her in. Then Gavin said it went something like this:

The president, writing: *Assuming for the moment just for argument you understand that we substitute white teachers in the negro school what will become of the negro teachers or perhaps you plan to retire them on pensions yourself*

The duck's voice: "Not exactly. I will send them North to white schools where they will be accepted and trained as white teachers are."

The pencil: *Still assuming for the sake of argument we have got the negro teachers out where will you find white teachers to fill vacancies left by negroes in Mississippi and how long do you think they will be permitted to fill negro vacancies in Mississippi*

The duck's voice: "I will find them if you will protect them."

The pencil: *Protect them from who Mrs Kohl* Only she didn't need to answer that. Because it had already started: the words

Nigger Lover scrawled huge in chalk on the sidewalk in front of
the mansion the next morning for her father to walk steadily
through them in his black banker's hat and his little snap-on
bow tie, chewing his steady chunk of Frenchman's Bend air.
Sure he saw it. Gavin said nobody could have helped seeing it,
that by noon a good deal of the rest of Jefferson had managed
to happen to pass by to look at it. But what else—a banker,
THE banker—could he do? spit on his handkerchief and get
down on his knees and rub it out? And later Linda came out on
her way back to the courthouse to badger the rest of the county
authorities back behind their locked doors. And maybe, very
likely, she really didn't see it. Anyway, it wasn't either of them
nor the cook nor the yardman either. It was a neighbour, a
woman, who came with a broom and at least obscured it,
viciously, angrily, neither to defend Linda's impossible dream
nor even in instinctive female confederation with another female,
but because she lived on this street. The words could have been
the quick short primer-bald words of sex or excrement, as
happened now and then even on sidewalks in this part of town,
and she would have walked through them too since to pause
would have been public admission that a lady knew what they
meant. But nobody was going to write *Nigger Lover* nor *-Hater*
either, delineate in visible taunting chalk that ancient subterrene
atavistic ethnic fear on the sidewalk of the street she (and her
husband of course) lived and owned property on.

Until at last the president of the board of supervisors crossed
the Square to the bank and on to that back room where old
Snopes sat with his feet propped on that mantelpiece between
foreclosures, and I would have liked to hear that: the outsider
coming in and saying, more or less: Can't you for God's sake
keep your daughter at home or at least out of the courthouse. In
desperation, because what change could he have hoped to get
back, she was not only thirty years old and independent and a
widow, she was a war veteran too who had actually—Ratliff
would say, actively—stood gunfire. Because she didn't stop; it
had got now to where the board of supervisors didn't dare
unlock their door while they were in session even to go home at
noon to eat, but instead had sandwiches from the Dixie Café
passed in through the back window. Until suddenly you were

thinking how suppose she were docile and amenable and would have obeyed him, but it was he, old Snopes, that didn't dare ask, let alone order, her to quit. You didn't know why of course. All you could do was speculate: on just what I.O.U. or mortgage bearing his signature she might have represented out of that past which had finally gained for him that back room in the bank where he could sit down and watch himself grow richer by lending and foreclosing other people's I.O.U.s.

Because pretty soon he had something more than just that unsigned *Nigger Lover* to have to walk through practically any time he came out his front door. One night (this was while I was in Europe) a crude cross soaked in gasoline blazed suddenly on the lawn in front of the mansion until the cops came and put it out, outraged and seething of course, but helpless; who—the cops—would still have been helpless even if they hadn't been cops. You know: if she had only lived alone, or had been the daughter of a mere doctor or lawyer or even a minister, it would have been one thing, and served them both—her and her old man—right. Instead, she had to be the daughter of not just *a* banker but THE banker, so that what the cross really illuminated was the fact that the organisation which put it there were dopes and saps: if the sole defence and protection of its purity rested in hands which didn't—or what was worse, couldn't—distinguish a banker's front yard, the white race was in one hell of a fix.

Then the next month was Munich. Then Hitler's and Stalin's pact and now when he came out of his house in the morning in his black banker's hat and bow tie and his little cud of Ratliff's Frenchman's Bend air, what he walked through was no longer anonymous and unspecific, the big scrawled letters, the three words covering the sidewalk before the house in their various mutations and combinations:

KOHL
COMMUNIST
JEW

JEW
KOHL
COMMUNIST

COMMUNIST
KOHL
JEW

and he, the banker, the conservative, the tory who had done more than any other man in Jefferson or Yoknapatawpha County either to repeal time back to 1900 at least, having to walk through them as if they were not there or were in another language and age which he could not be expected to understand, with all Jefferson watching him at least by proxy, to see if his guard would ever drop. Because what else could he do. Because now you knew you had figured right and it actually was *durst not*, with that record of success and victory behind him which already had two deaths in it: not only the suicide which left her motherless, but if he had been another man except the one whose wife would finally have to shoot herself, he might have raised the kind of daughter whose Barton Kohl wouldn't have been a Jewish sculptor with that Spanish war in his horoscope. Then in the very next second you would find you were thinking the exact opposite: that those words on his sidewalk he had to walk through every time he left home were no more portents and threats of wreckage and disaster to him than any other loan he had guessed wrong on would be an irremediable disaster, as long as money itself remained unabolished. That the last thing in the world he was thinking to himself was *This is my cross; I will bear it* because what he was thinking was *All I got to do now is keep folks thinking this is a cross and not a gambit.*

Then Poland. I said, "I'm going now," and Gavin said, "You're too old. They wouldn't possibly take you for flight training yet," and I said, "Yet?" and he said, "Finish one more year of law. You don't know what will be happening then, but it won't be what you're looking at now." So I went back to Cambridge and he wrote me how the F.B.I. was investigating her now and he wrote me: *I'm frightened. Not about her. Not at what they will find out because she would tell them all that herself if it only occurred to them that the simple thing would be to come and ask her.* And told me the rest of it: how she had at last quit beating on the locked door behind which the board of supervisors and the school board crouched holding their breath, and now she was merely meeting a class of small children each Sunday at one of the Negro churches, where she would read aloud in the dry inflectionless quacking, not the orthodox Biblical stories perhaps but at least the Mesopotamian folklore and the Nordic fairy tales which the Christian religion has arrogated into its seasonal observances, safe now since even the white ministers could not go on record against this paradox. So now there was no more *Jew Communist Kohl* on the sidewalk and no more *Nigger Lover* either (you would like to think, from shame) to walk through in order to be seen daily on the Square: the bride of quietude and silence striding inviolate in the isolation of unhearing, immune, walking still like she used to walk when she was fourteen and fifteen and sixteen years old: exactly like a young pointer bitch just about to locate and pin down a covey of birds.

So that when I got home Christmas I said to Gavin: "Tell her to tear up that god-damn party card, if she's got one. Go on. Tell her. She can't help people. They are not worth it. They don't want to be helped any more than they want advice or work. They want cake and excitement, both free. Man stinks. How the hell can she have spent a year in a war that not only killed her husband and blew the bejesus out of the inside of her skull, but even at that price the side she was fighting for still lost, without finding that out? Oh sure, I know, I know, you and Ratliff both have told me often enough; if I've heard Ratliff one time I've heard him a hundred: 'Man ain't really evil, he jest ain't got any sense.' But so much the more reason, because that leaves him completely hopeless, completely worthless of anybody's anguish and effort and trouble." Then I stopped, because he had put his hand on my head. He had to reach up to do it now, but he did it exactly as he used to when I was half as tall and only a third as old, gentle and tender and stroking it a little, speaking quiet and gentle too:

"Why don't you tell her?" he said. Because he is a good man, wise too except for the occasions when he would aberrate, go momentarily haywire and take a wrong turn that even I could see was wrong, and then go hell-for-leather, with absolutely no deviation from logic and rationality from there on, until he wound us up in a mess of trouble or embarrassment that even I would have had sense enough to dodge. But he is a good man.

Maybe I was wrong sometimes to trust and follow him, but I never was wrong to love him.

"I'm sorry," I said.

"Don't be," he said. "Just remember it. Don't ever waste time regretting errors. Just don't forget them."

So I ran Ratliff to earth again. No: I just took advantage of him. It was the regular yearly Christmas-season supper that Ratliff cooked himself at his house and invited Uncle Gavin and me to eat it with him. But this time Gavin had to go to Jackson on some drainage-district business so I went alone, to sit in Ratliff's immaculate little kitchen with a cold toddy of old Mr Calvin Bookwright's corn whiskey that Ratliff seemed to have no trouble getting from him, though now, in his old age, with anybody else Mr Cal might sell it to you or give it to you or order you off his place, you never knew which; sipping the cold toddy as Ratliff made them—first the sugar dissolved into a little water, then the whiskey added while the spoon still stirred gently, then rain water from the cistern to fill the glass—while Ratliff in a spotless white apron over one of the neat tieless faded blue shirts which he made himself, cooked the meal, cooking it damned well, not just because he loved to eat it but because he loved the cooking, the blending up to perfection's ultimate moment. Then he removed the apron and we ate it at the kitchen table, with the bottle of claret Uncle Gavin and I always furnished. Then with the coffee and the decanter of whiskey we moved (as always) to the little immaculate room he called his parlour, with the spotlessly waxed melodeon in the corner and the waxed chairs and the fireplace filled with fluted green paper in the summer but with a phony gas log in the winter, now that progress had reached, whelmed us, and the waxed table in the centre of the room on which, on a rack under a glass bell, rested the Allanovna necktie—a rich not-quite-scarlet, not-quite-burgundy ground patterned with tiny yellow sunflowers each with a tiny blue centre of almost the exact faded blue of his shirts, that he had brought home from New York that time three or four years ago when he and Gavin went to see Linda married and off to Spain, that I would have cut my tongue out before I would have told him it probably cost whoever (Gavin I suppose) paid for it around seventy-five dollars; until that day when I inadvertently said something to that effect and Ratliff said, "I know how much. I paid it. It was a hundred and fifty dollars." "What?" I said. "A hundred and fifty?" "There was two of them," he said. "I never saw but one," I said. "I doubt if you will," he said. "The other one is a private matter."— and beside it, the piece of sculpture that Barton Kohl had bequeathed him that, if Gavin was still looking for first base, I had already struck out because I didn't even know what it was, let alone what it was doing.

"All it needs is that gold cigarette-lighter she gave him," I said. "The Linda Snopes room."

"No," he said. "The Eula Varner room. It ought to have more in it, but maybe this will do. Leastways it's something. When a community is lucky enough to be the community that every thousand years or so has a Eula Varner to pick it out to do her breathing in, the least we can do is for somebody to set up something; a . . . monument ain't quite the word I want."

"Shrine," I said.

"That's it," he said. "A shrine to mark and remember it, for the folks that wasn't that lucky, that was already doomed to be too young. . . ." He stopped. He stood there quite still. Except that you would think of him as being quizzical, maybe speculative, but not bemused. Then I said it:

"You were wrong. They aren't going to."

"What?" he said. "What's that?"

"She's not going to marry Gavin."

"That's right," he said. "It will be worse than that."

Now it was me that said, "What? What did you say?" But he was already himself again, bland, serene, inscrutable.

"But I reckon Lawyer can stand that too," he said.

TEN

Gavin Stevens

I COULD have suggested that, told her to do that, and she would have done it—torn the card up at once, quickly, immediately, with passion and exultation. She was like her mother in one thing at least: needing, fated to need, to find something competent enough, strong enough (in her case, this case, not tough enough because Kohl was tough enough: he happened to be mere flesh and bones and so wasn't durable enough) to take what she had to give; and at the same time doomed to fail, in this, her case, not because Barton failed her but because he also had doom in his horoscope. So if the Communist party, having already proved itself immune to bullets and therefore immortal, had replaced him, not again to bereave her, of course she would have torn her card up, with passion and exultation and joy too. Since what sacrifice can love demand more complete than abasement, abnegation, particularly at the price of what the unknowing materialist world would in its crass insensitive ignorance dub cowardice and shame? I have always had a sneaking notion that that old Christian martyr actually liked, perhaps even loved, his aurochs or his lion.

But I did suggest something else. It was 1940 now. The Nibelung maniac had destroyed Poland and turned back west where Paris, the civilised world's eternal and splendid courtesan, had been sold to him like any whore and only the English national character turned him east again; another year and Lenin's Frankenstein would be our ally but too late for her; too late for us too, too late for all the western world's peace for the next hundred years, as a tubby little giant of a man in England was already saying in private, but needs must when the devil etcetera.

It began in my office. He was a quiet, neat, almost negative man of no particular age between twenty-five and fifty, as they all appear, who showed me briefly the federal badge (his name was Gihon) and accepted the chair and said Thank you and opened his business quietly and impersonally, as they do, as if they are simply delivering a not-too-important message. Oh yes, I was doubtless the last, the very last on his list since he would have checked thoroughly on or into me without my knowing it as he had days and maybe months ago penetrated and resolved and sifted all there was to be learned about her.

"We know that all she has done, tried to do, has been done quite openly, where everybody would have a chance to hear about it, know about it—"

"I think you can safely say that," I said.

"Yes," he said. "—quite openly. Quite harmless. With the best of intentions, only not very . . . practical. Nothing in fact that a lady wouldn't do, only a little . . ."

"Screwy," I suggested.

"Thank you. But there you are. I can tell you in confidence that she holds a Communist party card. Naturally you are not aware of that."

Now I said, "Thank you."

"And, once a communist—I grant you, that's like the old saying (no imputation of course, I'm sure you understand that), Once a prostitute. Which anyone after calm reflection knows to be false. But there you are. This is not a time of calmness and reflection; to ask or expect, let alone hope for, that from the government and the people too, faced with what we are going to have to meet sooner probably than we realise—"

"Yes," I said. "What do you want me to do? What do you assume I can do?"

"She . . . I understand, have been informed, that you are her earliest and still are her closest friend—"

"No imputation of course," I said. But he didn't say Thank you in his turn. He didn't say anything, anything at all. He just sat there watching me through his glasses, grey, negative as a chameleon, terrifying as the footprint on Crusoe's beach, too negative and neuter in that one frail articulation to bear the terrible mantle he represented. "What you want then is for me to use my influence—"

"—as a patriotic citizen who is intelligent enough to know that he too will be in this war within five years—I set five years as an outside maximum since it took the Germans only three years before to go completely mad and defy us into that one— with exactly who for our enemy we may not know until it is already too late—"

"—to persuade her to surrender that card quietly to you and swear whatever binding oath you are authorised to give her," I said. "Didn't you just say yourself that Once a whore (with no imputations) always a whore?"

"I quite agree with you," he said. "In this case, not the one with the imputations."

"Then what do you want of me—her?"

He produced a small notebook and opened it; he even had the days of the week and the hours: "She and her husband were in Spain, members of the Loyalist communist army six months and twenty-nine days until he was killed in action; she herself remained, serving as an orderly in the hospital after her own wound, until the Loyalists evacuated her across the border into France—"

"Which is on record even right here in Jefferson."

"Yes," he said. "Before that she lived for seven years in New York City as the common-law wife—"

"—which of course damns her not only in Jefferson, Mississippi, but in Washington too." But he had not even paused.

"—of a known registered member of the Communist party, and the close associate of other known members of the Communist party, which may not be in your Jefferson records."

"Yes," I said. "And then?"

He closed the notebook and put it back inside his coat and sat looking at me again, quite cold, quite impersonal, as if the space between us were the lens of a microscope. "So she knew people, not only in Spain but in the United States too, people who so far are not even in our records—Communists members and agents, important people, who are not as noticeable as Jewish sculptors and Columbia professors and other such intelligent amateurs—" Because that was when I finally understood.

"I see," I said. "You offer a swap. You will trade her immunity for names. Your bureau will whitewash her from an enemy into a simple stool pigeon. Have you a warrant of any sort?"

"No," he said. I got up.

"Then good-day, sir." But he didn't move yet.

"You won't suggest it to her?"

"I will not," I said.

"Your country is in danger, perhaps in jeopardy."

"Not from her," I said. Then he rose too and took his hat from the desk.

"I hope you won't regret this, Mr Stevens."

"Good-day, sir," I said.

Or that is, I wrote it. Because it was three years now and she had tried, really tried to learn lip reading. But I don't know. Maybe to live outside human sound is to live outside human time too, and she didn't have time to learn, to bother to learn. But again I don't know. Maybe it didn't take even three years of freedom, immunity from it to learn that perhaps the entire dilemma of man's condition is because of the ceaseless gabble with which he has surrounded himself, enclosed himself, insulated himself from the penalties of his own folly, which otherwise—the penalties, the simple red ink—might have enabled him by now to have made his condition solvent, workable, successful. So I wrote it

Leave here Go away

"You mean, move?" she said. "Find a place of my own? an apartment or a house?"

I mean leave Jefferson I wrote. *Go completely away for good Give me that damn card & leave Jefferson*

"You said that to me before."

"No I didn't," I said. I even spoke it, already writing, already planning out the whole paragraph it would take: *We've never even mentioned that card or the Communist party either. Even back there three years ago when you first tried to tell me you had one and show it to me and I wouldn't let you, stopped you, refused to listen: don't you remember?* But she was already talking again:

"I mean back there when I was fifteen or sixteen and you said I must get away from Jefferson."

So I didn't even write the other; I wrote *But you couldn't then Now you can Give me the card & go* She stood quietly for a moment, a time. We didn't even try to use the ivory tablet on occasions of moment and crisis like this. It was a bijou, a gewgaw, a bangle, feminine; really almost useless: thin ivory sheets bound with gold and ringed together with more of it, each sheet about the size of a playing card so that it wouldn't really contain more than about three words at a time, like an anagram, an acrostic at the level of children—a puzzle say or maybe a continued story ravished from a primer. Instead, we were in her upstairs sitting-room she had fitted up, standing at the mantel which she had designed at the exact right height and width to support a foolscap pad when he had something to discuss that there must be no mistake about or something which wasn't worth not being explicit about, like money, so that she could read the words as my hand formed them, like speech, almost like hearing.

"Go where?" she said. "Where could I go?"

Anywhere New York Back to Europe of course but in New York some of the people still you & Barton knew the friends your own age She looked at me. With the pupils expanded like this, her eyes looked almost black; blind too.

"I'm afraid," she said.

I spoke; she could read single words if they were slow: "You? Afraid?" She said:

"Yes. I don't want to be helpless. I won't be helpless. I won't have to depend."

I thought fast, like that second you have to raise or draw or throw in your hand, while each fraction of the second effaces another pip from your hole card. I wrote quite steadily while she watched *Then why am I here* and drew my hand back so she could read it. Then she said, in that dry, lifeless, what Chick calls duck's quack:

"Gavin." I didn't move. She said it again: "Gavin." I didn't move. She said: "All right. I lied. Not the depend part. I won't depend. I just must be where you are." She didn't even add *Because you're all I have now.* She just stood, our eyes almost level, looking at me out of, across, something—abyss, darkness; not abject, not questioning, not even hoping; in a moment I would know it; saying again in the quacking voice: "Gavin."

I wrote rapidly, in three- or four-word bursts, gaggles, clumps, whatever you want to call them, so she could read as I wrote *Its all right don't Be afraid I Refuse to marry you 20 years too much Difference for it To work besides I Don't want to*

"Gavin," she said.

I wrote again, ripping the yellow sheets off the pad and shoving them aside on the mantel *I don't want to*

"I love you," she said. "Even when I have to tell a lie, you have already invented it for me."

I wrote *No lie nobody Mentioned Barton Kohl*

"Yes," she said.

I wrote *No*

"But you can   me," she said. That's right. She used the explicit word, speaking the hard brutal guttural in the quacking duck's voice. That had been our problem as soon as we undertook the voice lessons: the tone, to soften the voice which she herself couldn't hear. "It's exactly backward," she told me. "When you say I'm whispering, it feels like thunder inside my head. But when I say it this way, I can't even feel it." And this time it would be almost a shout. Which is the way it was now, since she probably believed she had lowered her voice, I standing there while what seemed to me like reverberations of thunder died away.

"You're blushing," she said.

I wrote *that word*

"What word?"

that you just said

"Tell me another one to use. Write it down so I can see it and remember it."

I wrote *There is no other thats the right one only one I am old fashioned it still shocks me a little No what shocks is when a woman uses it & is not shocked at all until she realises I am* Then I wrote *that's wrong too what shocks is that all that magic passion excitement be summed up & dismissed in that one bald unlovely sound*

"All right," she said. "Don't use any word then."

I wrote *Do you mean you want to*

"Of course you can," she said. "Always. You know that."

I wrote *That's not what I asked you* She read it. Then she didn't move. I wrote *Look at me* She did so, looking at me from out or across what it was that I would recognise in a moment now.

"Yes," she said.

I wrote *Didn't I just tell you you don't ever have to be afraid* and this time I had to move the pad slightly to draw her attention to it, until she said, not looking up:

"I don't have to go away either?"

I wrote *No* under her eyes this time, then she looked up, at me, and I knew what it was she looked out of or across: the immeasurable loss, the appeaseless grief, the fidelity and the enduring, the dry quacking voice saying, "Gavin. Gavin. Gavin." while I wrote

because we are the 2 in all the world who can love each other without having to the end of it tailing off in a sort of violent rubric as she clasped me, clinging to me, quite hard, the dry clapping voice saying,

"Gavin. Gavin. I love you. I love you," so that I had to break free to reach the pad and write

Give me the card

She stared down at it, her hands arrested in the act of leaving my shoulders. "Card?" she said. Then she said, "I've lost it."

Then I knew: a flash, like lightning. I wrote *your father* even while I was saying out loud: "Oh the son of a bitch, the son of a bitch," saying to myself *Wait. Wait! He had to. Put yourself in his place. What else could he do, what other weapon did he have to defend his very existence before she destroyed it—the position he had sacrificed everything for—wife home friends peace—to gain the only prize he knew since it was the only one he could understand since the world itself as he understood it assured him that was what he wanted because that was the only thing worth having.* Of course: his only possible weapon: gain possession of the card, hold the threat of turning it in to the F.B.I. over her and stop her before she destroyed him. Yet all this time I was telling myself *You know better. He will use it to destroy her. It was he himself probably who scrawled Jew Communist Kohl on his own sidewalk at midnight to bank a reserve of Jefferson sympathy against the day when he would be compelled to commit his only child to the insane asylum.* I wrote

Ransacked your room drawers desk

"Somebody did," she said. "It was last year. I thought—" I wrote

It was your father

"Was it?" Yes, it was exactly that tone. I wrote

Don't you know it was

"Does it matter? They will send me another one I suppose. But that doesn't matter either. I haven't changed. I don't have to have a little printed card to show it."

This time I wrote slowly and carefully *You don't have to go I won't ask any more but when I do ask you again to go will you just believe me & go at once I will make all plans will you do that*

P

"Yes," she said.

I wrote *Swear*

"Yes," she said. "Then you can marry." I couldn't have written anyway; she had caught up both my hands, holding them between hers against her chest. "You must. I want you to. You mustn't miss that. Nobody must never have had that once. Nobody. Nobody." She was looking at me. "That word you didn't like. My mother said that to you once too, didn't she." It wasn't even a question. "Did you?"

I freed my hands and wrote *You know we didn't*

"Why didn't you?"

I wrote *Because she felt sorry for me when you do things for people just because you feel sorry for them what you do is probably not very important to you*

"I don't feel sorry for you. You know that. Don't you know it will be important to me?"

I wrote *Then maybe it was because I wasn't worthy of her & we both knew it but I thought if we didn't maybe she might always think maybe I might have been* and ripped the sheet off and crumpled it into my pocket and wrote *I must go now*

"Don't go," she said. Then she said, "Yes, go. You see, I'm all right now, I'm not even afraid any more."

I wrote *why should you ever have been* then on the same sheet *My hat* and she went and got it while I gathered up the rest of the used sheets into my pocket and took the hat and went toward the door, the quacking voice saying "Gavin" until I turned. "How did we say it? the only two people in the world that love each other and don't have to? I love you, Gavin," in that voice, tone which to her was whispering, murmuring perhaps but to anyone tragic enough to still have ears was as penetrating and shocking almost as an old-time klaxon automobile horn.

And out, fast and quick out of his house, his mansion, his palace, on to his bank fast and quick too, right on back into that little room and bump, nudge, startle the propped feet off the fireplace, my hand already out: "I will now take that card, if you please." Except that would be wantonly throwing away an opportunity, a gift actually; why let him pick his moment to surrender, produce the evidence on his side, to the F.B.I.? Why not strike first, sic the F.B.I. on him before he could, as Ratliff would say, snatch back: that mild neutral grey man flashing that badge on him, saying, "We have it on authority, Mr Snopes, that you have a Communist party card in your possession. Do you care to make a statement?"

But I didn't know where Gihon would be now and, his declared enemy, he wouldn't believe me. So the F.B.I. as represented by him was out; I would have to go straight to that vast Omnipotence called Govment; the stool-pigeoning itself must be unimpeachable; it must stem from the milieu and hold rigidly to the vernacular. A post card of course, a penny post card. I thought first of addressing it to the President of the United States but with the similar nut mail Mr Roosevelt was probably already getting, mine would be drowned in that flood. Which left the simple military. But although the military never loses any piece of paper once it has been written on and signed (anything else yes, it will abandon or give away or destroy, but a piece of signed paper never, though it have to subsidise and uniform a thousand people to do nothing else but guard it); it would inevitably reappear someday even if it took a hundred years, but that would be too long also. Whereupon I suddenly overheard myself asking, What's wrong with your first idea of the F.B.I.? to which the only answer was, Nothing. So I could even see the completed card. The vernacular was an informed one, it knew there were two Hoovers: one a carpet sweeper and the other had been President, and that the head of the F.B.I. was said to be named Hoover. So I could see it:

Herbert Hoover
F.B.I. Department

then paused, because not Washington; this vernacular was not only knowledgeable but consistent too so I thought first of Parchman, Mississippi, the State Penitentiary, except that the mail clerk there would probably be a trusty possibly in for life so what would a span of time computable in mere days, especially in regard to a piece of mail, be to him? and again it would be lost. Then I had the answer: Jackson, the Capital. It would be perfect: not really a big city, so that the agents there would be

just bored and idle enough to leap at this opportunity; besides
not being far. So that's what it would be:

> *Herbert Hoover*
> *F B & I Depment*
> *Jackson Miss*
>
> > *If you will come up to*
> > *Jefferson Miss and serch warant the bank and*
> > *home of Flem Snopes you will fined a commonist*
> > *part Card*
>
> > > *Patriotic Citizen*

Whereupon you will object that "search warrant" is a little
outside this writer's vernacular and that the spelling of "find"
is really going a little too far. Whereupon I rebut you that this
writer knows exactly what he is talking about; that "search
warrant" and "fined" are the two words of them all which he
would never make any mistake regarding, no matter how he
might spell them: the one being constantly imminent in his
(by his belief, in yours too) daily future and the other or its
synonym "jailed" being its constant co-adjutant.

If I only dared. You see? even if I burgled his house or bank
vault and found the card and erased her name and substituted
his to pass their gimlet muster, she herself would be the first to
leap, spring, deny, refute, claim and affirm it for her own; she
would probably have gone to Gihon or any else available before
this and declared her convictions if it had occurred to her they
might be interested. Whereupon, from then until even the
stronger alliance of cosmic madmen had finally exhausted
themselves into peace and oblivion, she would be harried and
harassed and spied upon day and night, waking and eating and
sleeping too. So finally I had to fall back, not on her innocent
notion that it wasn't important, really wouldn't matter anyway,
but on my own more evil or—and/or—legal conviction that it
was his only weapon of defence and he wouldn't use it until he
was frightened into it.

Or hope perhaps. Anyway, that's how it stood until in fact
the Battle of Britain saved her; otherwise all that remained was

simply to go to him and say, "I want that card," which would
be like walking up to a stranger and saying Did you steal my
wallet. So the Battle of Britain saved her, him too for a time. I
mean, the reports, stories now coming back to us of the handful
of children fighting it. Because during the rest of that spring and
summer and fall of 1940 she was getting more and more restless.
Oh, she was still doing her Negro Sunday school classes, still
"meddling" as the town called it, but after a fashion condoned
now, perhaps by familiarity and also that no one had discovered
yet any way to stop her.

This, until June when Chick came home from Cambridge.
Whereupon I suddenly realised—discovered—two things: that
it was apparently Chick now who was our family's representative
in her social pattern; and that she knew more than even he of the
R.A.F. names and the machines they flew: Malan and Aitken
and Finucane and Spitfire and Beaufighter and Hurricane and
Buerling and Deere and the foreigners too like the Americans
who wouldn't wait and the Poles and Frenchmen who declined
to be whipped: Daymond and Wzlewski and Clostermann;
until that September, when we compromised: Chick agreed to
take one more year of law and we agreed to let it be the University over at Oxford instead of Cambridge. Which was perhaps
the reason: when he left, she no longer had anyone to swap the
names with. So I should not have been surprised when she came
to the office. Nor did she say I must do something to help, I've
got to do something, I can't just sit here idle; she said:

"I'm going away. I've got a job, in a factory in California
where they make aircraft to be sent to Europe," and I scribbling,
scrawling *Wait*. "It's all right," she said. "It's all settled. I
wrote them that I couldn't hear but that I was familiar enough
with truck engines and gears to learn what they needed. And
they said for me to come on out, just bring a few papers with me.
You know: letters saying you have known me long enough to
assure them she is moral and doesn't get too tight and nobody
has caught her stealing yet. That's what you are to do because
you can even sign them Chairman of the Yoknapatawpha
County, Mississippi, Draft Board," and I still scrawling Wait,
or no, not writing it again because I already had: just gripping
her with one hand and holding the pad up with the other until

she read it and stopped or stopped long enough to read it or at least hushed and I could write:

at this factory all factories an individual of limitless power called Security whose job position is the 1 thing on earth between him & being drafted into the and ripped that sheet off, already writing again, her hand, her arm across my shoulder so I could feel her breathing and feel smell her hair against my cheek *army which naturally he will defend with his life by producing not too far apart provable subversives so that sooner or later he will reach you & fire you you re* and ripped that one off, not stopping *member the Mississippi coast Biloxi Ocean Springs you were there*

"Yes. With Mother and"—and now I thought she would stop but she didn't even pause—"Manfred. I remember."

I wrote *Pascagoula a shipyard where they are building ships to carry airplanes guns tanks if California will take you so will they will you go there*

"Yes," she said. She said, "Russia." She drew a long breath. "But the Security will be there too."

I wrote *yes but that's close I could come there quick & even if Security I could probably find you something else*

"Yes," she said, breathing quiet and slow at my shoulder. "Close. I could come home on week-ends."

I wrote *you might have to work weekends they need ships*

"Then you can come there. The draft board is closed on week-ends, isn't it?"

I wrote *we will see*

"But together sometimes now and then. That's why I was afraid about California, because it's so far. But Pascagoula is close. At least occasionally now and then."

I wrote *Of course*

"All right," she said. "Of course I'll go."

Which she did, right after New Year's, 1941 now. I know a lawyer there so she had a small apartment with its own entrance in a private home. And apparently her belief was that, once she was free of Jefferson, at least twelve hours away from interdiction by Snopes or me or either or both, nobody could challenge her intention to buy a small car and run it herself, until I threatened to tell the Pascagoula police myself that she was deaf the first time I heard about it. So she agreed to refrain and my lawyer friend arranged for her in a car pool and presently she was at work as a tool checker, though almost at once she wrote that she had almost got them to agree to let her become a riveter, where the deafness would be an actual advantage. Anyway, she could wear overalls again, once more minuscule in that masculine or rather sexless world engaged, trying to cope with the lethal mechanical monstrosities which war has become now, and perhaps she was even at peace again, if peace is possible to anyone. Anyway, at first there were the letters saying *When you come we will* and then *If you come don't forget* and then several weeks and just a penny post card saying *I miss you* and nothing more—that almost inarticulate paucity of the picture cards saying *Wish you were here* or *This is our room* which the semiliterate send back, until the last one, a letter again. I mean, in an envelope: *It's all right. I understand. I know how busy the draft board has to be. Just come when you can because I have something to ask you.* To which I answered at once, immediately (I was about to add, Because I don't know what I thought. Only I know exactly what I thought) *Ask me or tell me?* so that I already knew beforehand what her answer would be: *Yes. Ask you.*

So (it was summer again now) I telegraphed a date and she answered *Have booked room will meet what train love* and I answered that (who had refused to let her own one) *Coming by car will pick you up at shipyard Tuesday quitting time love* and I was there. She came out with the shift she belonged in, in the overall, already handing me the tablet and stylus before she kissed me, clinging to me, hard, saying, "Tell me everything," until I could free myself to write, restricted again to the three- or four-word bursts and gaggles before having to erase:

You tell me what It is

"Let's go to the beach." And I:

You don't want to Go home first & Change

"No. Let's go to the beach." We did. I parked the car and it seemed to me I had already written *Now tell me* but she was already out of the car, already waiting for me, to take the tablet and stylus from me and thrust them into her pocket, then took my near arm in both her hands, we walking so, she clinging with both hands to my arm so that we would bump and stagger every few steps, the sun just setting and our one shadow along

the tide-edge before us and I thinking *No, no, that can't be it*
when she said, "Wait," and released me, digging into the other
overall pocket from the tablet. "I've got something for you. I
almost forgot it." It was a shell; we had probably trodden on a
million of them since we left the car two hundred yards back, I
still thinking *It can't be that. That can't be so* "I found it the first
day. I was afraid I might lose it before you got here, but I
didn't. Do you like it?"

"It's beautiful," I said.

"What?" she said, already handing me the tablet and stylus. I
wrote

Damn fine now Tell me

"Yes," she said. She clung, gripping my arm hard and strong
in both hands again, we walking again and I thinking *Why not,
why shouldn't it be so, why should there not be somewhere in the world
at least one more Barton Kohl or at least a fair substitute, something to
do, at least something a little better than grief* when she said, "Now,"
and stopped and turned us until we faced the moment's pause
before the final plunge of the sun, the tall and ragged palms and
pines fixed by that already fading explosion until the night
breeze would toss and thresh them. Then it passed. Now it was
just sunset. "There," she said. "It's all right now. We were here.
We saved it. Used it. I mean, for the earth to have come all this
long way from the beginning of the earth, and the sun to have
come all this long way from the beginning of time, for this one
day and minute and second out of all the days and minutes and
seconds, and nobody to use it, no two people who are finally
together at last after all the difficulties and waiting, and now they
are together at last and are desperate because of all the long
waiting, they are even running along the beach toward where the
place is, not far now, where they will finally be alone together at
last and nobody in the world to know or care or interfere so that
it's like the world itself wasn't except you so now the world that
wasn't even invented yet can begin." And I thinking *Maybe it's
the fidelity and the enduring which must be so at least once in your lifetime,
no matter who suffers. That you have heard of love and loss and grief and
fidelity and enduring and you have seen love and loss and maybe you
have even seen love and loss and grief but not all five of them—or four
of them since the fidelity and enduring I am speaking of were inextricable:*

one—this, even while she was saying, "I don't mean just—" and stopped herself before I could have raised the hand to clap to on her lips—if I had been going to, saying: "It's all right, I haven't forgotten; I'm not going to say that one any more." She looked at me. "So maybe you already know what I'm going to ask you."

"Yes," I said; she could read that. I wrote *marriage*

"How do you know?"

What does it Matter I wrote *I'm glad*

"I love you," she said. "Let's go eat. Then we will go home and I can tell you."

I wrote *Not home first To change*

"No," she said. "I won't need to change where we're going."

She didn't. Among the other female customers, she could have worn anything beyond an ear trumpet and a G-string, and even then probably the ear trumpet would have drawn the attention. It was a joint. By midnight on Saturday (possibly any other night in such boom ship-building times) it would be bedlam, jumping as they say; with the radio going full blast, it already was to me. But then, I was not deaf. But the food—the flounder and shrimp—was first rate and the waitress produced glasses and ice to match the flask I had brought; and with all the other uproar her voice was not so noticeable. Because she used it, as if by premeditation, about things I would need only Yes and No for, babbling actually, about the shipyard, the work, the other people, sounding almost like a little girl home on her first holiday from school, eating rapidly too, not chewing it enough, until we had done and she said, "We can go now."

She hadn't told me yet where I was to stay, nor did I know where her place was either. So when we were in the car again I snapped on the dash light so she could see the tablet and wrote *Where*. "That way," she said. It was back toward the centre of town and I drove on until she said, "Turn here," and I did; presently she said, "There it is," so that I had to pull in to the curb to use the tablet

Which is

"The hotel," she said. "Right yonder." I wrote

We want to talk Havent you got a Sitting room your place Quiet & private

"We're going to both stay there tonight. It's all arranged. Our rooms are next door with just the wall between and I had both beds moved against it so after we talk and are in bed any time during the night I can knock on the wall and you can hear it and if I hold my hand against the wall I can feel you answer.—I know, I won't knock loud enough to disturb anybody, for anybody to hear it except you."

The hotel had its own parking lot. I took my bag and we went in. The proprietor knew her, perhaps by this time everybody in the town knew or knew of the young deaf woman working in the shipyard. Anyway, nobody stopped us, he called her by name and she introduced me and he gave me the two keys and still nobody stopped us, on to her door and unlocked it, her overnight bag was already in the room and there were flowers in a vase too and she said, "Now I can have a bath. Then I will knock on the wall," and I said,

"Yes," since she could read that and went to my room; yes, why should there have to be fidelity and enduring too just because you imagined them? If mankind matched his dreams too, where would his dreams be? Until presently she knocked on the wall and I went out one door, five steps, into the other one and closed it behind me. She was in bed, propped on both pillows, in a loose jacket or robe, her hair (evidently she had cut it short while she was driving the ambulance but now it was long enough again to bind in a ribbon dark blue like her eyes) brushed or dressed for the night, the tablet and stylus in one hand on her lap, the other hand patting the bed beside her for me to sit down.

"You won't really need this," she said, raising the tablet slightly then lowering it again, "since all you'll need is just to say Yes and I can hear that. Besides, since you already know what it is, it will be easy to talk about. And maybe if I tell you I want you to do it for me, it will be even easier for you to do. So I do say that. I want you to do it for me." I took the tablet

Of course I will Do what

"Do you remember back there at the beach when the sun finally went down and there was nothing except the sunset and the pines and the sand and the ocean and you and me and I said how that shouldn't be wasted after all that waiting and

distance, there should be two people out of all the world desperate
and anguish for one another to deserve not to waste it any longer
and suddenly they were hurrying, running toward the place at
last not far now, almost here now and no more the desperation
and the anguish no more, no more—" when suddenly, as I
watched, right under the weight of my eyes you might say, her
face sprang and ran with tears, though I had never seen her cry
before and apparently she herself didn't even know it was
happening. I wrote

Stop it

"Stop what?" And I

you're crying

"No I'm not." And I

look at your Face

There was the customary, the standard, hand-glass and box of
tissue on the table but instead I took my handkerchief and held
it out. But instead she simply set the heels of her palms to her
face, smearing the moisture downward and outward like you do
sweat, even snapping, flicking the moisture away at the end of the
movement as you do sweat.

"Don't be afraid," she said. "I'm not going to say that word.
Because I don't even mean that. That's not important, like
breathing's not important as long as you don't even have to
think about it but just do it when it's necessary. It's important
only when it becomes a question or a problem or an issue, like
breathing's important only when it becomes a question or a
problem of whether or not you can draw another one. It's the
rest of it, the little things: it's this pillow still holding the shape of
the head, this necktie still holding the shape of the throat that
took it off last night even just hanging empty on a bedpost, even
the empty shoes on the floor still sit with the right one turned
out a little like his feet were still in them and even still walking
the way he walked, stepping a little higher with one foot than
the other like the old-time Negroes say a proud man walks—"
And I

stop it stop It you're crying Again

"I can't feel it. I can't feel anything on my face since that day,
not heat nor cold nor rain nor water nor wind nor anything."
This time she took the handkerchief and used it, but when I

handed her the mirror and even started to write *where's your compact* she didn't even take the mirror. "I'll be careful now.— So that's what I want you to have too. I love you. If it hadn't been for you, probably I wouldn't have got this far. But I'm all right now. So I want you to have that too. I want you to do it for me." And I

But what for you You never have Told me yet

"Marry," she said. "I thought you knew. Didn't you tell me you knew what it was?" And I

Me marry You mean me

"Who did you think I meant? Did you think I was—Gavin."

"No," I said.

"I read that. You said No. You're lying. You thought I meant me."

"No," I said.

"Do you remember that time when I told you that any time you believe you had to lie for my sake, I could always count on you sticking to it, no matter how bad you were disproved?"

"Yes," I said.

"So that's settled, then," she said. "No, I mean you. That's what I want you to do for me. I want you to marry. I want you to have that too. Because then it will be all right. We can always be together no matter how far apart either one of us happens to be or has to be. How did you say it? the two people in all the earth out of all the world that can love each other not only without having to but we don't even have to not say that word you don't like to hear? Will you promise?"

"Yes," I said.

"I know you can't just step outdoors tomorrow and find her. It may take a year or two. But all you've got to do is just stop resisting the idea of being married. Once you do that it's all right because the rest of it will happen. Will you do that?"

"I swear," I said.

"Why, you said Swear, didn't you?"

"Yes," I said.

"Then kiss me." I did so, her arms quite hard, quite strong around my neck; a moment, then gone. "And early tomorrow morning, go back home." And I, writing

I was going to Stay all day

"No. Tomorrow. Early. I'll put my hand on the wall and when you're in bed knock on it and if I wake up in the night I can knock and if you're awake or still there you can knock back and if I don't feel you knock you can write me from Jefferson tomorrow or the next day. Because I'm all right now. Good-night, Gavin."

"Good-night, Linda," I said.

"I read that too. I love you."

"I love you," I said.

"I read that too but write it on the tablet anyway and I can have that for a—what do you call it?—eye opener in the morning."

"Yes," I said, extending my hand for the tablet.

ELEVEN

Charles Mallison

THIS time, I was in uniform. So now all I need is to decide, find out, what this-time I mean or time for what I mean. It wasn't the next time I saw Linda, because she was still in Pascagoula building ships for Russia too now. And it wasn't the next time I was in Jefferson, because I passed through home en route to the brown suit. So maybe I mean the next time I ran Ratliff to earth. Though maybe what I really mean is that the next time I saw Uncle Gavin after his marriage, he was a husband.

Because it was 1942 and Gavin was married now, to Melisandre Harriss (Backus that was as Thackeray said); that pitcher had went to that well jest that one time too many, as Ratliff said, provided of course he had said it. One Sunday morning there was Pearl Harbour and I wired Gavin by return mail you might say from Oxford *This is it am gone now.* I wired Gavin because otherwise I would have had to talk to Mother on the telephone and on long distance Mother ran into money, so by wiring Gavin for forty-two cents the telephone call from Mother would be on Father's bill in Jefferson.

So I was at home in time to be actually present at the first innocent crumblings of what he had obviously assumed to be his impregnable bastions; to "stand up" with him, be groomsman to his disaster. It happened like this. I was unable to get into the government flight-training programme course at the University but they told me that anybody with a college degree and any number of hours from one up of flying time, especially solo, would have about as good a chance of going straight into military training for a commission. So there was a professional crop-duster operating from the same field and he took me on as a student, on even bigger aircraft, one of (he claimed) the actual type of army primary training, than the little fifty h.p. popguns the official course used.

So when I sent Uncle Gavin the wire I had around fifteen logged hours, three of which were solo, and when Mother rang my telephone I was already packed up and the car already pointed toward Jefferson. So I was there to see the beginning of it whether Gavin recognised it as banns or not. I mean the

Long Island horse farm that Miss Melisandre Harriss Backus
that was used to bring the two children (they were grown now;
Gavin was marrying not stepchildren but in-laws) back home to
now and then from Europe until the Germans began to blow up
Americans in actual sight of the Irish coast. So after that it had
to be South America, this last time bringing the Argentine
steeplechasing cavalry officer that that maniac boy of the two
Harriss children (I don't mean that both Aunt Melisandre's
children were maniacs but that only one of them was a boy)
believed was trying to marry the money his mother was still
trustee of instead of just his sister who just had an allowance like
him. So he (the maniac of course) set out to murder the Argentine
steeplechaser with that wild stallion of Rafe McCallum's that he
(the maniac) bought or tricked or anyway got inside that stall
where the innocent Argentine would have walked up in the
dark and opened the door on what he (the innocent Argentine)
thought was going to be not only a gentle horse but a partly
blind one too. Except that Gavin read his tea leaves or used his
second sight or divining rod or whatever it was he did in cases
like this, and got hold of Rafe in time to reach the stall door
first and stop him.

So the Argentine was saved, and that night the maniac took
his choice between the army recruiting station in Memphis, and
Uncle Gavin, and chose the army so he was safe, and that
afternoon the Argentine and the maniac's sister were married
and left Jefferson and they were safe. But Uncle Gavin remained,
and the next day I had to go on to ground school, preflight, so
when I got home next time I was in uniform and Gavin was not
only a husband but father too of a stepson who would have been
as neat a by-standing murderer as you could hope to see except
for a stroke of arrant meddling which to a dog shouldn't happen,
and a stepdaughter married to an Argentine steeplechasing
son-in-law. (By which time I was married too, to a bombsight
—I hadn't made pilot but at least I would be riding up front—
allotted to me by a government which didn't trust me with it and
so set spies to watch what I did with it, which before entrusting
it to me had trained me not to trust my spies nor anybody else
respecting it, in a locked black case which stayed locked by a
chain to me even while I was asleep—a condition of constant

discomfort of course but mainly of unflagging mutual suspicion and mutual distrust and in time mutual hatred which you even come to endure, which is probably the best of all training for successful matrimony.)

So when I saw Jefferson next I was in uniform, long enough to call on the squire and his dame among his new ancestral white fences and electric-lit stables and say Bless you my children and then run Ratliff once more to earth.

"He can't marry her now," I said. "He's already got a wife."

And you never thought of *soberly* in connection with Ratliff either. Anyway, not before now, not until this time. "That's right," he said. "She ain't going to marry him. It's going to be worse than that."

FLEM

TWELVE

WHEN the pickup truck giving him the ride onward from
Clarksdale turned off at a town called Lake Cormorant and
he had to get out, he had to walk. And he was apparently still
nowhere near Memphis. He was realising now that this was the
biggest, in a way terrifying, thing that had happened to him in
the thirty-eight years: he had forgotten distance. He had forgot
how far one place could be from another. And now he was going
to have to eat too. Because all he had was the ten-dollar bill
they had given him along with the new overalls and hat and
shoes at the Parchman gate, plus the three dollars and eighty-five
cents still left out of the forty dollars his cousin Flem—it must
have been Flem; after he finally realised that Flem wasn't going
to come or even send in from Frenchman's Bend to help him and
he quit calling down from the jail window to anybody passing
that would send word out to Flem, nobody else but Flem and
maybe the judge knew or even bothered to care what became of
him, where he was—had sent him back there eighteen years
ago just before Flem sent Montgomery Ward to trick him into
trying to escape in that woman's wrapper and sunbonnet and
he got caught of course and they gave him the other twenty
years.

It was a small tight neatly cluttered store plastered with
placards behind a gasoline pump beside the highway; a battered
dust- and mud-stained car was parked beside it and inside were
only the proprietor and a young Negro man in the remnants of
an army uniform. He asked for a loaf of bread and suddenly he
remembered sardines, the taste of them from almost forty years
ago; he could afford another nickel one time, when to his shock
and for the moment unbelief, possibly in his own hearing, he
learned that the tin would now cost him twenty-six cents—the
small flat solid-feeling tin ubiquitous for five cents through all
his previous days until Parchman—and even while he stood in
that incredulous shock the proprietor set another small tin
before him, saying, "You can have this one for eleven."

"What is it?" he said.

"Lunch meat," the proprietor said.

"What is lunch meat?" he said.

"Don't ask," the proprietor said. "Just eat it. What else can you buy with eleven cents?"

Then he saw against the opposite wall a waist-high stack of soft-drink cases and something terrible happened inside his mouth and throat—a leap, a spring of a thin liquid like fire or the myriad stinging of ants all the way down to his stomach; with a kind of incredulous terror, even while he was saying *No! No! That will cost at least a quarter too*, his voice was saying aloud: "I reckon I'll have one of them."

"A whole case?" the proprietor said.

"You can't jest buy one bottle?" he said, counting rapidly, thinking *At least twenty bottles. That would take all the ten dollars. Maybe that will save me.* Nor, when the proprietor set the uncapped coldly sweating bottle on the counter before him, did he even have time to tell himself *I'm going to pick it up and put my mouth on it before I ask the price because otherwise I might not be able to touch it* because his hand had already picked up the bottle, already tilting it, almost ramming the neck into his mouth, the first swallow coldly afire and too fast to taste until he could curb, restrain the urgency and passion so he could taste and affirm that he had not forgot the taste at all in the thirty-eight years: only how good it was, draining that bottle in steady controlled swallows now and only then removing it and in horror hearing his voice saying, "I'll have another one," even while he was telling himself *Stop it! Stop it!* then stood perfectly calm and perfectly composed while the proprietor uncapped the second sweating bottle and took that one up and closed his eyes gently and drank it steadily empty and fingered one of the bills loose in the pocket where he carried the three dollar ones (the ten-dollar note was folded carefully beneath a wad of newspaper and safety-pinned inside the fob pocket of the overall bib) and put it on the counter, not looking at it nor at anything while he waited for the proprietor to ask for a second bill or maybe two more; until the proprietor laid sixty-eight cents in coins on the counter and picked up the bill.

Because the two empty bottles were still sitting on the counter in plain sight, he thought rapidly *If I could jest pick up the change and git outside before he notices them*—if not an impossibility, certainly a gamble he dared not take, had not time to risk: to gamble perhaps two dollars against a shout, a leap over the counter to bar the door until another sheriff came for him. So he said, not touching the change: "You never taken out for the sody."

"What's that?" the proprietor said. He scattered the coins on the counter. "Lunch meat, eleven; bread—" He stopped and as suddenly huddled the coins into a pile again. "Where did you say you come from?"

"I never said," Mink said. "Down the road."

"Been away a long time, have you?"

"That's right," he said.

"Much obliged," the proprietor said. "I sure forgot about them two Cokes. Damn labour unions have even run Coca-Cola up out of sight like everything else. You had two of them, didn't you?" taking the half-dollar from the change and shoving the rest of it across to him. "I don't know what folks are going to do unless somebody stops them somewhere. Looks like we're going to have to get shut of these damn Democrats to keep out of the poorhouse. Where'd you say you were headed? Memphis?"

"I ain't said," he started to say. But the other was already, or still, speaking to the Negro now, already extending toward the Negro another opened soda.

"This is on the house. Jump in your car and run him up to the crossroads; he'll have double chance to catch a ride there, maybe someone from the other highway."

"I wasn't fixing to leave yet," the Negro said.

"Yes you are," the proprietor said. "Just a half a mile? You got plenty of time. Don't let me see you around here until you get back. All right," he said to Mink. "You'll sure catch a ride there."

So he rode again, in the battered mud-stained car; just for a moment the Negro slid his eyes toward him, then away. "Where down the road did you come from?" the Negro said. He didn't answer. 'It was Parchman, wasn't it?" Then the car stopped. "Here's the crossroads," the Negro said. "Maybe you can catch a ride."

He got out. "Much obliged," he said.

"You done already paid him," the Negro said. So now he walked again. But mainly it was to be out of the store; he must not stop at one again. If the bottles had been a dollar apiece, there was a definite limit beyond which temptation, or at least his lack of will power, could no longer harm him. But at only a quarter apiece, until he could reach Memphis and actually have the pistol in his hand, there was no foreseeable point within the twelve remaining dollars where he would have peace; already, before he was even outside the store, he was saying *Be a man, Be a man. You got to be a man, you got too much to do, too much to resk* and, walking again, he was still sweating a little, not panting so much as simply breathing deeply like one who has just blundered unwarned into then out of the lair, the arms, of Semiramis or Messalina, still incredulous, still aghast at his own temerity and still amazed that he has escaped with his life.

And now he was discovering something else. For most of the twenty-odd years before he went to Parchman, and during the thirty-eight since, he had walked only on soft dirt. Now he walked on concrete; not only were his feet troubling him but his bones and muscles ached all the way up to his skull, until presently he found a foul puddle of water among rank shadeless weeds at the end of a culvert and removed the new stiff brogans they had given him with the new overalls and sat with his feet in the water, eating the tinned meat and the bread, thinking *I got to watch myself. Maybe I dassent to even go inside where they sell hit* thinking, not with despair really: still indomitable *Likely hit will cost the whole ten-dollar bill, maybe more. That jest leaves three dollars and eighty-five cents and I done already spent eighty-two of that* and stopped and took the handful of coins from his pocket and spread them carefully on the ground beside him; he had had three one-dollar bills and the eighty-five cents and he counted slowly the eighty-five cents, a half-dollar, a quarter, and two nickels, and set them aside. He had given the man at the store one of the dollar bills and the man had given him back change for bread, eleven cents, lunch meat eleven cents, which was twenty-two cents, then the man had taken up the half-dollar for the sodas, which was seventy-two cents, which should have left twenty-eight cents; counting what remained slowly over coin by coin again, then counting the coins he had already set aside to be sure they were right. And still it was only eighteen cents instead of twenty-eight. A dime was gone somewhere. And the lunch meat was just eleven cents, he remembered that because there had been a kind of argument about it. So it was the bread, it would have to be the bread. *It went up another dime right while I was standing there* he thought. *And if bread could jump up ten cents right while I was looking at it, maybe I can't buy a pistol even for the whole thirteen dollars. So I got to stop somewhere and find a job.*

The highway was dense with traffic, but going fast now, the automobiles big ones, brand new, and the trucks were big as railroad cars; no more the dusty pickups which would have offered him a lift, but vehicles now of the rich and hurried who would not even have seen a man walking by himself in overalls. Or probably worse: they probably would have hedged away with their own size and speed and shining paint any other one of them which might have stopped for him, since they would not have wanted him under their feet in Memphis either. Not that it mattered now. He couldn't even see Memphis yet. And now he couldn't even say when he was going to see it, thinking *So I may need as much as ten dollars more before I even get to where I can buy one.* But at least he would have to reach Memphis before that became an actual problem, obstacle; at least when he did reach Memphis the thirteen dollars and three cents he still had must be intact, no matter how much more he might have to add to it to get there. So he would have to get more money some way, who knew he could not be trusted in another roadside store where they sold soda pop. *So I will have to stop somewhere and ask for work and I ain't never asked no man for work in my life so maybe I don't even know how* thinking *And that will add at least one more day, maybe even more than one* thinking quietly but still without despair *I'm too old for this. A feller sixty-three years old ought not to have to handle such as this* thinking, but without despair: quite indomitable still *But a man that's done already had to wait thirty-eight years, one more day or two or even three ain't going to hurt.*

The woman was thick but not fat and not old, a little hard-looking, in a shapeless not very clean dress, standing in a small untidy yard pulling dead clematis vines from a frame beside a small house. "Are you a man of God?" she said.

"Ma'am?" he said.

"You look like a preacher."

"Nome," he said. "I been away."

"What kind of work can you do?"

"I kin do that. I kin rake the yard."

"What else?"

"I been a farmer. I reckon I can do most anything."

"I reckon first you want something to eat," she said. "All right. We're all God's creatures. Finish pulling down these vines. Then you'll find a rake by the kitchen door. And remember. I'll be watching you."

Perhaps she was, from behind the curtains. He couldn't tell. He didn't try to. Though evidently she was, already standing on the minuscule front gallery when he put the last rake-full on the pile, and told him where the wheelbarrow was and gave him three kitchen matches and stood watching while he wheeled the trash into the adjoining vacant lot and set fire to it. "Put the wheelbarrow and rake back where you got them and come in the kitchen," she said. He did so—a stove, sink, refrigerator, a table and chair set and on the table a platter of badly cooked greens and livid pork lumps in it and two slices of machine-made bread on a saucer and a glass of water; he standing for a time quite still, his hands hanging quietly at his sides, looking at it. "Are you too proud to eat it?" she said.

"It ain't that," he said. "I ain't hungry. I needed the money to get on. I got to get to Memphis and then back to Missippi."

"Do you want that dinner, or don't you?" she said.

"Yessum," he said. "Much obliged," and sat down, she watching him a moment, then she opened the refrigerator and took out an opened tin and set it on the table before him. It contained one half of a canned peach.

"Here," she said.

"Yessum," he said. "Much obliged." Perhaps she was still watching him. He ate what he could (it was cold) and had carried the plate and knife and fork to the sink to wash them when she came suddenly in again.

"I'll do that," she said. "You go on up the road four miles. You'll come to a mailbox with Brother Goodyhay on it. You can read, can't you?"

"I'll find it," he said.

"Tell him Beth Holcomb sent you."

He found it. He had to. He thought *I got to find it* thinking how maybe he would be able to read the name on the mailbox simply

because he would have to read it, would have to penetrate
through the inscrutable hieroglyph; thinking while he stood
looking at the metal hutch with the words *Bro J C Goodyhay* not
stencilled but painted on it, not sloven nor careless but impatiently, with a sort of savage impatience: thinking, either
before or at least simultaneous with his realisation that someone
near by was shouting at him *Maybe I could read all the time and
jest never knowed it until I had to*. Anyway, hearing the voice and
looking up the tiny savagely untended yard, to another small
frame house on that minuscule gallery of which a man stood
waving one arm and shouting at him: "This is it. Come on."—
a lean quick-moving man in the middle thirties with coldly
seething eyes and the long upper lip of a lawyer or an orator
and the long chin of the old-time comic-strip Puritan, who
said,

"Hell, you're a preacher."

"No," he said. "I been away. I'm trying to get to—"

"All right, all right," the other said. "I'll meet you round
back," and went rapidly back into the house. He, Mink, went
around it into the back yard, which if anything was of an even
more violent desolation than the front, since the back yard
contained another house not dismantled so much as collapsed—
a jumble of beams, joists, window- and door-frames and even
still-intact sections of siding, among which moved or stood
rather a man apparently as old as he, Mink, was, although he
wore a battle jacket of the type which hadn't been copied from
the British model until after Pearl Harbour, with the shoulder
patch of a division which hadn't existed before then either, who
when Mink came in sight began to chop rapidly with the axe in
his hand among the jumble of lumber about him; barely in
time as the back door of the house crashed open and the first
man came out, carrying a buck saw; now Mink saw the sawbuck
and a small heap of sawn lengths. "All right, all right " the
first man said, handing Mink the saw. "Save all the sound
pieces. Don't split the nails out, pull them out. Saw up all the
scraps, same length. Dad is in charge. I'll be in the house," and
went back into it; even doors which he barely released seemed to
clap to behind him violently, as though his passage had sucked
them shut.

"So they caught you too did they, mac?" the man in the battle jacket (he would be Dad) said.

Mink didn't answer that. He said: "Is that the reverend?"

"That's Goodyhay," the other said. "I ain't heard him preach yet, but even if he hadn't opened his mouth he would be a better preacher than he is a cook. But then, somebody's got to scorch the biscuits. They claim his wife ran off with a sonabitching Four-F potato-chip salesman before he even got back from fighting in the Pacific. They were all doing it back then and what I notice, they ain't quit, even without any war to blame it on. But what the hell, I always say there's still a frog in the puddle for every one that jumps out. So they caught you too, huh?"

This time he answered. "I got to get to Memphis and then back down to Missippi. I'm already behind. I got to get on tonight. How much does he pay here?"

"That's what you think," the other said. "That's what I thought three days ago: pick up a dollar or so and move on. Because you're building a church this time, bully boy. So maybe we both better hope the bastard can preach since we ain't going to get our money until they take up the collection Sunday."

"Sunday?" he said.

"That's right," the other said. "This is Thursday; count it."

"Sunday," he said. "That's three days."

"That's right," the other said. "Sunday's always three days after Thursday around here. It's a law they got."

"How much will we get on Sunday?"

"It may be as much as a dollar cash; you're working for the Lord now, not mammon, jack. But anyway you'll be fed and slept—"

"I can't work that long for jest a dollar," he said. "I ain't got the time."

"It may be more than a dollar. What I hear around here, he seems to have something. Anyway, he gets them. It seems he was a Marine sergeant on one of them landing barges out in the Pacific one day when a Jap dive bomber dove right at them and everybody tried to jump off into the water before the bomb hit, except one mama's boy that got scared or tangled up in something so he couldn't jump and the reverend (except he hadn't turned reverend then, not for the next few minutes yet) went

back to try and untangle him, when the whole barge blew up
and took the reverend and the mama's boy both right on down
to the bottom with it before the reverend could get them both
loose and up to the top again. Which is just the official version
when they gave him the medal, since according to the reverend
or leastways his congregation— What I hear, the rest of them
are mostly ex-soldiers too or their wives or the other broads they
just knocked up without marrying, mostly young, except for a
few old ones that seem to got dragged in by the passing suction
you might say; maybe the moms and pops of soldiers that got
killed, or the ones like that Sister Holcomb one that caught you
down the road, that probably never thawed enough to have a
child of any kind and God help the husband either if she ever
had one, that wasn't even sucked in but flagged the bus herself
because the ride looked like it was free—" He stopped. Then he
said: "No, I know exactly why she come: to listen to some of
the words he uses doing what he calls preaching. Where was I?
Oh yes: that landing barge. According to the reverend, he was
already safe and dead and peacefully out of it at last on the
bottom of the Pacific Ocean when all of a sudden Jesus Himself
was standing over him saying Fall in and he did it and Jesus said
TenSHUN, about-FACE and assigned him to this new permanent
hitch right down here on the edge of Memphis, Tennessee. He's
got something, enough of whatever it took to recruit this new-
faith boot camp to need a church to hold it. And I be damned if
I don't believe he's even going to get a carpenter to nail it
together. What did he say when he first saw you?"

"What?" Mink said.

"What were his first words when he looked at you?"

"He said, 'Hell, you're a preacher.' "

"You see what I mean? He's mesmerised enough folks to scour
the country for any edifice that somebody ain't actually sitting
on the front porch of, and knocking it down and hauling it over
here to be broke up like we're doing. But he ain't got a master
carpenter yet to nail it together into a church. Because master
carpenters belong to unions, and deal in cash money per diem
on the barrel-head, where his assignment come direct from
Jesus Christ Who ain't interested in money or at least from the
putting-out angle. So him and his outpost foxholes up and down

the road like that Sister Holcomb that snagged you are sifting for one."

"Sifting?" he said.

"Sivving. Like flour. Straining folks through this back yard until somebody comes up that knows how to nail that church together when we get enough boards and planks and window frames ripped a-loose and stacked up. Which maybe we better get at it. I ain't actually caught him spying behind a window shade yet, but likely an ex-Marine sergeant even reformed into the ministry is no man to monkey with too far."

"You mean I can't leave?"

"Sure you can. All the outdoors is yours around here. You ain't going to get any money until they take up that collection Sunday though. Not to mention a place to sleep tonight and what he calls cooking if you ain't particular."

In fact, this house had no shades nor curtains whatever to be spied from behind. Indeed, as he really looked about it for the first time, the whole place had an air of violent transience similar to the indiscriminate jumble of walls and windows and doors among which he and the other man worked: merely still nailed together and so standing upright; from time to time, as the stack of reclaimed planks and the pile of fire-lengths to which his saw was reducing the spoiled fragments slowly rose, Mink could hear the preacher moving about inside the intact one, so that he thought *If he jest went back inside to compose up his sermon, it sounds like getting ready to preach takes as much activity and quickness as harnassing up a mule.* Now it was almost sunset; he thought *This will have to be at least a half a dollar. I got to have it. I got to get on. I can't wait till Sunday* when the back door jerked, burst open and the preacher said, "All right. Supper's ready. Come on."

He followed Dad inside. Nothing was said by anyone about washing. "I figgered—" he began. But it was already too late. This was a kitchen too, but not Spartan so much as desolate, like a public camp site in a roadside park, with what he called another artermatic stove since he had never seen a gas or electric stove until he saw Mrs Holcomb's, Goodyhay standing facing it in violent immobility enclosed in a fierce sound of frying; Mink said again. "I figgered—" as Goodyhay turned from the stove with three platters bearing each a charred splat of something

which on the enamel surfaces looked as alien and solitary and
not for eating as the droppings of cows. "I done already et,"
Mink said. "I figgered I would jest get on."

"What?" Goodyhay said.

"Even after I get to Memphis, I still ain't hardly begun," he
said. "I got to get on tonight."

"So you want your money now," Goodyhay said, setting the
platters on the table where there already sat a tremendous bottle
of tomato ketchup and a plate of machine-sliced bread and a
sugar bowl and a can of condensed milk with holes punched in
the top. "Sit down," Goodyhay said, turning back to the stove,
where Mink could smell the coffee overboiled too with that same
violent impatience of the fried hamburger and the woodpiles in
the yard and the lettering on the mailbox; until Goodyhay
turned again with the three cups of coffee and said again, "Sit
down." Dad was already seated. "I said, sit down," Goodyhay
said. "You'll get your money Sunday after the collection."

"I can't wait that long."

"All right," Goodhay said, dashing ketchup over his plate.
"Eat your supper first. You've already paid for that." He sat
down; the other two were already eating. In fact Goodyhay had
already finished, rising in the same motion with which he put
his fork down, still chewing, and went and swung inward an
open door (on the back of which was hanging what Mink did
not recognise to be a camouflaged battle helmet worn by Marine
troops on the Pacific beachheads and jungles because what he
was looking at was the automatic-pistol butt projecting from
its webbing belt beneath the helmet) and from the refrigerator
behind it took a tin also of canned peach halves and brought it to
the table and dealt, splashed the halves and the syrup with
exact impartiality on to the three greasy plates and they ate
that too, Goodyhay once more finishing first; and now, for the
first time since Mink had known him, sitting perfectly motionless, almost as though asleep, until they had finished also. Then
he said, "Police it," himself leading the way to the sink with his
plate and utensils and cup and washed them beneath the tap,
then stood and watched while the other two followed suit and
dried and racked them as he had done. Then he said to Mink:
"All right. You going or staying?"

"I got to stay," Mink said. "I got to have the money."

"All right," Goodyhay said. "Kneel down," and did so first again, the other two following, on the kitchen floor beneath the hard dim glare of the single unshaded low-watt bulb on a ceiling cord, Goodyhay on his knees but no more, his head up, the coldly seething desert-hermit's eyes not even closed, and said, "Save us, Christ, the poor sons of bitches," and rose and said, "All right. Lights out. The truck'll be here at seven oclock."

The room was actually a lean-to, a little larger than a closet. It had one small window, a door connecting with the house, a single bulb on a drop cord, a thin mattress on the floor with a tarpaulin cover but no pillows nor sheets, and nothing else, Goodyhay holding the door for them to enter and then closing it. They were alone.

"Go ahead," Dad said. "Try it."

"Try what?" Mink said.

"The door. It's locked. Oh, you can get out any time you want; the window ain't locked. But that door leads back into the house and he don't aim to have none of us master-carpenter candidates maybe ramshagging the joint as a farewell gesture on the way out. You're working for the Lord now, buster, but there's still a Marine sergeant running the detail." He yawned. "But at least you will get your two dollars Sunday—three, if he counts today as a day too. Not to mention hearing him preach. Which may be worth even three dollars. You know: one of them special limited editions they can charge ten prices for because they never printed but two or three of." He blinked at Mink. "Because why. It ain't going to last much longer." He blinked at Mink. "Because they ain't going to let it."

"They won't even pay me two dollars?" Mink said.

"No no," the other said. "I mean the rest of the folks in the neighbourhood he ain't converted yet, ain't going to put up with no such as this. The rest of the folks that already had to put up with that damn war for four-five years now and want to forget about it. That've already gone to all that five years of trouble and expense to get shut of it, only just when they are about to get settled back down again, be damned if here ain't a passel of free-loading government-subsidised exdrafted sons of bitches acting like whatever had caused the war not only actually happened but was still going on, and was going to keep on going on until somebody did something about it. A passel of mostly non-taxpaying folks that like as not would have voted for Norman Thomas even ahead of Roosevelt, let alone Truman, trying to bring Jesus Christ back alive in the middle of 1946. So it may be worth three dollars just to hear him in the free outside air. Because next time you might have to listen through a set of jail bars." He yawned again, prodigiously, beginning to remove the battle jacket. "Well, we ain't got a book to curl up with in here even if we wanted to. So all that leaves is to go to bed."

Which they did. The lights was off, he lay breathing quietly on his back, his hands folded on his breast. He thought *Sholy it will be three dollars. Sholy they will count today too* thinking *And Sunday will make three days lost because even if I go to Memphis Sunday after we are paid off the stores where I can buy one will still be closed until Monday morning* thinking *But I reckon I can wait three more days* a little wryly now *Likely because I can't figger out no way to help it* and almost immediately was asleep, peacefully, sleeping well because it was daylight when he knew next, lying there peacefully for a little time yet before he realised he was alone. It seemed to him afterward that he still lay there peaceful and calm, his hand still playing idly with the safety pin it had found lying open on his chest, for the better part of a minute after he knew what had happened; then sitting, surging up, not even needing to see the open window and the dangling screen, his now frantic hand scrabbling from the bib pocket of the overalls the wad of newspaper beneath which the ten-dollar bill had been pinned, his voice making a puny whimpering instead of the cursing he was trying for, beating his fists on the locked door until it jerked open and Goodyhay stood in it, also taking one look at the ravished window.

"So the son of a bitch robbed you," Goodyhay said.

"It was ten dollars," Mink said. "I got to ketch him. Let me out."

"Hold it," Goodyhay said, still barring the doorway. "You can't catch him now."

"I got to," he said. "I got to have that ten dollars."

"You mean you've got to have ten dollars to get home?"

"Yes!" he said, cursing again. "I can't do nothing without it. Let me out."

"How long since you been home?" Goodyhay said.

"Thirty-eight years. Tell me which way you figger he went."

"Hold it," Goodyhay said, still not moving. "All right," he said. "I'll see you get your ten dollars back Sunday. Can you cook?"

"I can fry eggs and meat," Mink said.

"All right. You cook breakfast and I'll load the truck. Come on." Goodyhay showed him how to light the stove and left him; he filled up last night's coffee-pot with water as his tradition was until the grounds had lost all flavour and colour too, and sliced the fatback and dusted it with meal into the skillet in his tradition also, and got eggs out to fry, standing for a while with the door in his hand while he looked, mused, at the heavy holstered pistol beneath the helmet, thinking quietly *If I jest had that for two days I wouldn't need no ten dollars* thinking *I done been robbed in good faith without warning; why ain't that enough to free me to rob in my turn. Not to mention my need being ten times, a hundred times, a thousand times more despaired than ara other man's need for jest ten dollars* thinking quietly peacefully indeed now *No. I ain't never stole. I ain't never come to that and I won't never.*

When he went to the door to call them, Goodyhay and another man had the truck loaded with intact sections of wall and disassembled planks; he rode on top of the load, once more on the highway toward Memphis; he thought *Maybe they'll even go through Memphis and if I jest had the ten dollars* and then quit, just riding, in motion, until the truck turned into a side road; now they were passing, perhaps entering, already on, a big place, domain, plantation—broad cotton fields still white for the pickers; presently they turned into a farm road across a field and came to a willow-grown bayou and another pickup truck and another stack of dismembered walls and a group of three or four men all curiously similar somehow to Goodyhay and the driver of his—their—truck; he, Mink, couldn't have said how nor why, and not even speculating: remarking without attention another battle jacket, remarking without much attention either a rectangle of taut string between driven stakes in the dimensions of whatever it was they were going to build, where they unloaded the truck and Goodyhay said, "All right. You and Albert go back of another load."

So he rode in the cab this time, back to the parsonage or whatever it was, where he and Albert loaded the truck and they returned to the bayou, where by this time, with that many folks working—if any of the other four worked half as fast and as hard as Goodyhay did—they would probably have one wall already up. Instead, the other truck and Goodyhay and the stake-and-string rectangle were gone and only three men sat quietly beside the pile of lumber. "Well?" Albert said.

"Yep," one of the others said. "Somebody changed his mind."

"Who?" Mink said. "Changed what? I got to get on. I'm already late."

"Fellow that owns this place," Albert said. "That gave us permission to put the chapel here. Somebody changed his mind for him. Maybe the bank that holds his mortgage. Maybe the Legion."

"What Legion?" he said.

"The American Legion. That's still holding the line at 1918. You never heard of it?"

"Where's Reverend Goodyhay?" he said. "I got to get on."

"All right," Albert said. "So long." So he waited. Now it was early afternoon when the other truck returned, being driven fast, Goodyhay already getting out of it before it stopped.

"All right," he said. "Load up." Then they were on the Memphis highway again, going fast now to keep at least in sight of Goodyhay, as fast as any of the traffic they dashed among, he thinking *If I jest had the ten dollars, even if we ain't going all the way to Memphis this time neither.* They didn't. Goodyhay turned off and they ran again, faster than they dared except that Goodyhay in the front truck would have lost them, into a region of desolation, the lush Delta having played out now into eroded barren clay hills; into a final, the uttermost of desolation, where Goodyhay stopped—a dump, a jumbled plain of rusted auotmobile bodies and boilers and gin machinery and brick and concrete rubble; already the stakes had been re-driven and the rectangular string tautened rigid between them, Goodyhay standing beside his halter truck beckoning his arm, shouting, "All right. Here we are. Let's go."

R

So there was actual work again at last. But it was already late: most of the day was gone and tomorrow was Saturday, only one more full day. But Goodyhay didn't even give him a chance to speak. "Didn't I tell you you'd get your ten dollars Sunday? All right then." Nor did Goodyhay say, "Can you cook supper?" He just jerked, flung open the refrigerator door and jerked out the bloodstained paper of hamburger meat and left the kitchen. And now Mink remembered from somewhere that he had cooked grits once and found grits and the proper vessel. And tonight Goodyhay didn't lock the door; he, Mink, tried it to see, then closed it and lay down, again peacefully on his back, his hands folded on his breast like a corpse, until Goodyhay waked him to fry the side meat and the eggs again. The pickup truck was already there and a dozen men on hand this time and now you could begin to see what the chapel (they called it) was going to look like; until dark. He said: "It ain't cold tonight and besides I can lay under that-ere roofing paper and get started at daylight until the rest of them—"

"We don't work on Sunday," Goodyhay said. "Come on. Come on." Then it was Sunday. It was raining: the thin steady drizzle of early fall. A man and his wife called for them, not a pickup this time but a car, hard-used and a little battered. They turned again into a crossroad, not into desolate country this time but simply empty, coming at last to an unpainted box of a building which somebody somewhere back before the thirty-eight years in the penitentiary recognised, remembered. *It's a nigger schoolhouse* he thought, getting out among five or six other stained and battered cars and pickup trucks and a group of people already waiting, a few older ones but usually men and women about the age of Goodyhay or a little younger; again he sensed that identity, similarity among them even beyond the garments they wore—more battle jackets, green army slickers, one barracks cap still showing where the officer's badge had been removed; someone said, "Howdy," at his elbow. It was Albert and now he, Mink, recognised the Miss or Mrs Holcomb whose yard he had raked, and then he saw a big Negro woman— a woman no longer young, who looked at the same time gaunt yet fat too. He stopped, not quite startled: just watchful.

"You all take niggers too?" he said.

"We do this one," Albert said. Goodyhay had already entered the house. The rest of them now moved slowly toward the door, clotting a little. "Her son had it too just like she was a white woman, even if they didn't put his name on the same side of the monument with the others. See that woman yonder with the yellow hat?" The hat was soiled now but still flash, the coat below it had been white once too, a little flash too; the face between could have been twenty-five and probably at one time looked it, thin now, not quite raddled. "That's right," Albert said. "She still looks a little like a whore yet but you should have seen her last spring when she came out of that Catalpa Street house. Her husband commanded an infantry platoon back there when the Japs were running us out of Asia, when we were falling back all mixed up together—Aussies, British, French from Indo-China—not trying to hold anything any more except a line of foxholes after dark, fell long enough to get the stragglers up and move again tomorrow, including the ones in the foxholes too if any of them were still there by daylight. His platoon was the picket that night, him in one foxhole and his section strung out, when the nigger crawled up with the ammunition. He was new, you see. I mean, the nigger. This was as close as he had been to a Jap yet.

"So you know how it is: crouched in the stinking pitch dark in a stinking sweating hole in the ground with your eyes and ears both strained until in another minute they will pop right out of your head like marbles, and all around in front of you the chirping voices like crickets in a hayfield until you realise they ain't crickets because pretty soon what they are chirping is English: 'Maline. Tonigh youdigh. Maline. Tonigh youdigh.' So here comes the nigger with his sack of grenades and Garand clips and the lieutenant tells him to get down into the hole and puts the nigger's finger on the trigger of the Garand and tells him to stay there while he crawls back to report to the p.c. or something.

"You know how it is. A man can stand just so much. He don't even know when it will be, but all of a sudden a moment comes and he knows that's all, he's already had it; he hates it as much as you do but he didn't ask for it and he can't help it. That's the trouble; you don't know beforehand, there's nothing to warn you, to tell you to brace. Especially in war. It makes you think that just something no tougher than men ain't got any business in war, don't it? that if they're going to keep on having them, they ought to invent something a little more efficient to fight them with. Anyway, it's the next morning, first light, when the first of the cut-off heads that maybe last night you split a can of dog ration with, comes tumbling down among you like somebody throwing a basketball. Only this time it's that black head. Because why not? a nigger bred up on a Arkansas plantation, that a white man, not just a lieutenant but talking Arkansas to boot, says, 'Take a-holt of this here hoe or rifle and stay here till I get back." So as soon as we finished fighting the Japs far enough back to get organised to spend another day dodging the strafing planes, the lieutenant goes around behind the dump of stuff we can tote with us and are trying to set fire to it and make it burn— It's funny about jungles. You're sweating all the time, even in the dark, and you are always parched for water because there ain't any in a jungle no matter what you thought, and when you step into a patch of sun you blister before you can even button your shirt. Until you believe that if you so much as drop a canteen or a bayonet or even strike a boot calk against a root a spark will jump out and set the whole country afire. But just try to start one. Just try to burn something up and you'll see different. Anyway, the lieutenant went around behind the dump where he would have a little privacy and put his pistol barrel in his mouth. Sure, she can get in here."

Now they were all inside, and he recognised this from thirty-eight years back too—how the smell of Negroes remained long after the rooms themselves were vacant of them—the smell of poverty and secret fear and patience and enduring without enough hope to deodorise it—they (he supposed they would call themselves a congregation) filing on to the backless benches, the woman in the yellow hat on the front one, the big Negress alone on the back one, Goodyhay himself facing them at the end of the room behind a plank laid across two sawhorses, his hands resting, not clenched: just closed into fists, on the plank until everybody was quiet.

"All right," Goodyhay said. "Anybody that thinks all he's got to do is sit on his stern and have salvation come down on him

like a cloudburst or something, don't belong in here. You got to
get up on your feet and hunt it down until you can get a-hold of
it and then hold it, even fighting off if you have to. And if you
can't find it, then by God make it. Make a salvation. He will
pass and then earn the right to grab it and hold on and fight off
too if you have to but anyway hold it, hell and high water be
damned—" when a voice, a man, interrupted:

"Tell it again, Joe. Go on. Tell it again."

"What?" Goodyhay said.

"Tell it again," the man said. "Go on."

"I tried to," Goodyhay said. "You all heard me. I can't tell
it."

"Yes you can," the man said; now there were women's voices
too:

"Yes, Joe. Tell it," and he, Mink, still watching the hands not
clenched but just closed on the plank, the coldly seething
anchorite's eyes—the eyes of a fifth-century hermit looking at
nothing from the entrance of his Mesopotamian cave—the body
rigid in an immobility like a tremendous strain beneath a
weight.

"All right," Goodyhay said. "I was laying there. I was all
right, everything snafu so I was all right. You know how it is in
water when you don't have any weight at all, just laying there
with the light coming way down from up on top like them lattice
blinds when they shake and shiver slow in a breeze without
making any sound at all. Just laying there watching my hands
floating along without me even having to hold them up, with the
shadow of them lattice blinds winking and shaking across them,
and my feet and legs too, no weight at all, nowhere to have to
go or march, not even needing to breathe, not even needing to
be asleep or nothing: just all right. When there He was standing
over me, looking like any other shavetail just out of a foxhole,
maybe a little older, except he didn't have a hat, bucket: just
standing there bareheaded with the shadow of the lattice
running up and down him, smoking a cigarette. 'Fall in, soldier,'
He said.

" 'I can't,' I says. Because I knew that as long as I laid still,
I would be all right. But that once I let myself start thinking
about moving, or tried to, I would find out I couldn't. But what

the hell, why should I? I was all right. I had had it. I had it made. I was sacked up. Let them do whatever they ....ing wanted to with their ....ing war up on top.

" 'That's once,' He said. 'You ain't got but three times. You, the Top Soldier, saying can't. At Château-Thierry and St-Mihiel the company would have called you the Top Soldier. Do they still do that in the Corps on Guadalcanal?'

" 'Yes,' I says.

" 'All right, Top Soldier,' He said. 'Fall in.' So I got up. 'At ease,' He said. 'You see?' He said.

" 'I thought I couldn't,' I says. 'I don't believe I could.'

" 'Sure,' He said. 'What else do we want with you. We're already full up with folks that know they can but don't, since because they already know they can, they don't have to do it. What we want are folks that believe they can't, and then do it. The other kind don't need us and we don't need them. I'll say more: we don't even want them in the outfit. They won't be accepted; we won't even have them under our feet. If it ain't worth that much, it ain't worth anything. Right?'

" 'Yes sir,' I says.

" 'You can say Sir up there too if you want,' He said. 'It's a free country. Nobody gives a damn. You all right now?'

" 'Yes sir,' I says.

" 'TenSHUN!' He said. And I made them pop, mud or no mud. 'About-FACE!' He said. And He never saw one smarter than that one neither. 'Forward MARCH!' He said. And I had already stepped off when He said, 'Halt!' and I stopped. 'You're going to leave him laying there,' He said. And there he was, I had forgot about him, laying there as peaceful and out of it too as you please—the damned little bastard that had gone chicken at the exact wrong time, like they always do, turned the wheel a-loose and tried to duck and caused the whole damn mess; luck for all of us he never had a ...ing bar on his shoulder so he could have ...ed up the whole detail and done for all of us.

" 'I can't carry him too,' I says.

" 'That's two times,'' He said. 'You've got one more. Why not go on and use it now and get shut of it for good?''

" 'I can't carry him too,' I says.

" 'Fine,' He said. 'That's three and finished. You won't ever

have to say can't again. Because you're a special case; they
gave you three times. But there's a general order coming down
today that after this nobody has but one. Pick him up.' So I did.
'Dismiss,' He said. And that's all. I told you I can't tell it. I was
just there. I can't tell it." He, Mink, watching them all, himself
alien, not only unreconciled but irreconcilable: not contemptuous, because he was just waiting, not impatient because even if
he were in Memphis right this minute, at ten or eleven or whatever o'clock it was on Sunday morning, he would still have almost
twenty-four hours to get through somehow before he could move
on to the next step. He just watched them: the two oldish couples,
man and wife of course, farmers obviously, without doubt
tenant farmers come up from the mortgaged bank- or syndicate-
owned cotton plantation from which the son had been drafted
three or four or five years ago to make that far from home that
sacrifice, old, alien too, too old for this, unreconciled by the
meagre and arid tears which were less of tears than blisters;
none of the white people actually watching as the solitary Negro
woman got up from her back bench and walked down the aisle
to where the young woman's soiled yellow hat was crushed into
the crook of her elbow like a child in a child's misery and
desolation, the white people on the bench making way for the
Negro woman to sit down beside the young white woman and
put her arm around her; Goodyhay still standing, his arms
propped on the closed fists on the plank, the cold seething eyes
not even closed, speaking exactly as he had spoken three nights
ago while the three of them knelt on the kitchen floor: "Save us,
Christ. The poor sons of bitches." Then Goodyhay was looking
at him. "You, there," Goodyhay said. "Stand up." Mink did
so. "He's trying to get home. He hasn't put in but one full day,
but he needs ten dollars to get home on. He hasn't been home
in thirty-eight years. He needs nine bucks more. How about
it?"

"I'll take it," the man in the officer's cap said. "I won thirty-
four in a crap game last night. He can have ten of that."

"I said nine," Goodyhay said. "He's got one dollar coming.
Give him the ten and I'll give you one. He says he's got to go to
Memphis first. Anybody going in tonight?"

"I am," another said.

"All right," Goodyhay said. "Anybody want to sing?"

That was how he saw Memphis again under the best, the matchless condition for one who hadn't seen it in . . . He could figure that. He was twenty years old when he got married. Three times before that he had wrenched wrung enough money from the otherwise unpaid labour he did on the tenant farm of the kinsman who had raised him from orphanhood, to visit the Memphis brothels. The last visit was in the same year of his marriage. He was twenty-six years old when he went to Parchman. Twenty dollars from twenty-six dollars was six dollars. He was in Parchman thirty-eight years. Six dollars and thirty-eight dollars was forty-four dollars to see Memphis again not only after forty-four years but under the matchless condition: at night, the dark earth on either hand and ahead already random and spangled with the neon he had never seen before, and in the distance the low portentous glare of the city itself, he sitting on the edge of the seat as a child sits, almost as small as a child, peering ahead as the car rushed, merging into one mutual spangled race bearing toward, as though by the acceleration of gravity or suction, the distant city; suddenly off to the right a train fled dragging a long string of lighted windows as rapid and ephemeral as dream; he became aware of a convergence like the spokes of a gigantic dark wheel lying on its hub, along which sped dense and undeviable as ants, automobiles and what they told him were called buses as if all the earth was hurrying, plunging, being sucked, decked with diamond and ruby lights, into the low glare on the sky as into some monstrous, frightening, unimaginable joy or pleasure.

Now the converging roads themselves were decked with globular lights as big and high in the trees as roosting turkeys. "Tell me when we get close," he said.

"Close to what?" the driver said.

"Close to Memphis."

"We're already in Memphis," the driver said. "We crossed the city limits a mile back." So now he realised that if he had still been walking, alone, with none to ask or tell him, his troubles would have really begun only after he reached Memphis. Because the Memphis he remembered from forty-four years back no longer existed; he thought *I been away too long; when you*

*got something to handle like I got to handle, and by yourself and not no
more to handle it with than I got, not to mention eighty more miles to go
yet, a man jest can't afford to been away as long as I had to be.* Back then
you would catch a ride in somebody's wagon coming in from
Frenchman's Bend or maybe two or three of you would ride
plough mules in to Jefferson, with a croker sack of corn behind the
borrowed saddle, to leave the mules in the lot behind the Commercial Hotel and pay the nigger there a quarter to feed them
until you got back, and get on the train at the depot and change
at the Junction to one that went right into the middle of Memphis,
the depot there almost in the centre of town.

But all that was changed now. They had told him four days
ago that most of the trains were gone, quit running, even if he
had had that much extra money to spend just riding. They had
told him how they were buses now but in all the four days he
had yet to see anything that looked like a depot where he could
buy a ticket and get on one. And as for the edge of Memphis
that back there forty-four years ago a man could have walked
in from in an hour, he, according to the driver, had already
crossed it over a mile back yet still all he could see of it was just
that glare on the sky. Even though he was actually in Memphis,
he was apparently still as far from the goal he remembered and
sought as from Varner's store to Jefferson; except for the car
giving him a ride and the driver of it who knew in general where
he needed to go, he might have had to spend even the ten dollars
for food wandering around inside Memphis before he ever
reached the place where he could buy the pistol.

Now the car was wedged solid into a rushing mass of other
vehicles all winking and glittering and flashing with coloured
lights; all circumambience in fact flashed and glared luminous
and myriad with colour and aloud with sound: suddenly a
clutch of winking red green and white lights slid across the high
night itself; he knew, sensed what they were but was much too
canny to ask, telling, hissing to himself *Remember. Remember. It
won't hurt you long as don't nobody find out you don't know it.*

Now he was in what he knew was the city. For a moment it
merely stood glittering and serried and taller than stars. Then it
engulfed him; it stooped soaring down, bearing down upon him
like breathing the vast concrete mass and weight until he himself

was breathless, having to pant for air. Then he knew what it was. It's un-sleeping, he thought. It ain't slept in so long now it's done forgot how to sleep and now there ain't no time to stop long enough to try to learn how again; the car rigid in its rigid mass, creeping then stopping then creeping again to the ordered blink and change of coloured lights like the railroads used to have, until at last it drew out and could stop.

"Here's the bus station," the driver said. "This was where you wanted, wasn't it?"

"It's fine," he said.

"Buses leave here for everywhere. You want me to come in with you and find out about yours?"

"Much obliged," he said. "It's jest fine."

"So long then," the driver said.

"I thank you kindly," he said. "So long." Sure enough, it was a bus depot at last. Only if he went inside, one of the new laws he had heard about in Parchman—laws that a man couldn't saw boards and hammer nails unless he paid money to an association that would let him, couldn't even raise cotton on his own land unless the government said he could—might be that he would have to get on the first bus that left, no matter where it was going. So there was the rest of the night, almost all of it since it wasn't even late yet. But it would only be twelve hours and for that time he could at least make one anonymous more among the wan anonymous faces thronging about him, hurrying and myriad beneath the coloured glare, passionate and gay and unsleeping. Then something happened. Without warning the city spun, whirled, vertiginous, infinitesimal and dizzying, then as suddenly braked and immobilised again and he not only knew exactly where he was, but how to pass the twelve hours. He would have to cross the street, letting the throng itself enclot and engulf him as the light changed; once across he could free himself and go on. And there it was: the Confederate Park they called it—the path- and flower-bed-crisscrossed vacancy exactly as he remembered it, the line of benches along the stone parapet in the gaps of which the old iron cannon from the War squatted and beyond that the sense and smell of the River, where forty-four and -five and -six years ago, having spent half his money in the brothel last night and the other half saved for

tonight, after which he would have nothing left but the return
ticket to Jefferson, he would come to watch the steamboats.

The levee would be lined with them bearing names like
Stacker Lee and *Ozark Belle* and *Crescent Queen*, come from as far
apart as Cairo and New Orleans, to meet and pass while he
watched them, the levee clattering with horse- and mule-drawn
drays and chanting stevedores while the cotton bales and the
crated machinery and the rest of the bags and boxes moved up
and down the gangplanks, and the benches along the bluff
would be crowded with other people watching them too. But
now the benches were vacant and even when he reached the
stone parapet among the old cannon there was nothing of the
River but the vast and vacant expanse, only the wet dark cold
blowing, breathing up from across the vast empty River so that
already he was buttoning the cotton jumper over his cotton
shirt; no sound here at all: only the constant unsleeping murmur
of the city behind him, no movement save the minute crawl of
the automobiles on the bridge far down the River, hurrying,
drawn also toward and into that unceasing murmur of passion
and excitement, into this backwash of which he seemed to have
blundered, strayed, and then abandoned, betrayed by having
had to be away from it so long. And cold too, even here behind
one of the old cannon, smelling the cold aged iron too, huddled
into the harsh cotton denim too new to have acquired his own
body's shape and so warm him by contact; it was going to be
cold here before much longer even though he did have peace and
quiet to pass the rest of the twelve hours in. But he had already
remembered the other one, the one they called Court Square,
where he would be sheltered from the River air by the tall
buildings themselves provided he waited a little longer to give
the people who might be sitting on the benches there time to
get sleepy and go home.

So when he turned back toward the glare and the murmur,
the resonant concrete hum, though unsleeping still, now had a
spent quality like rising fading smoke or steam, so that what
remained of it was now high among the ledges and cornices; the
random automobiles which passed now, though gleaming with
coloured lights still, seemed now as though fleeing in terror, in
solitude from solitude. It was warmer here. And after a while he

was right: there was nobody here save himself; on a suitable
bench he lay down, drawing and huddling his knees up into the
buttoned jumper, looking no larger than a child and no less waif,
abandoned, when something hard was striking the soles of his
feet and time, a good deal of it, had passed and the night itself
was now cold and vacant. It was a policeman; he recognised
that even after forty-four years of change and alteration.

"Damn Mississippi," the policeman said. "I mean, where are
you staying in town here? You mean, you haven't got anywhere
to sleep? You know where the railroad station is? Go on down
there; you can find a bed for fifty cents. Go on now." He didn't
move, waiflike and abandoned true enough but no more pitiable
than a scorpion. "Hell, you're broke too. Here." It was a half-
dollar. "Go on now. Beat it. I'm going to stand right here and
watch you out of sight."

"Much obliged," he said. A half a dollar. So that was another
part of the new laws they had been passing; come to remember,
he had heard about that in Parchman too; they called it Relief
or W P and A: the same government that wouldn't let you raise
cotton on your own land would turn right around and give you a
mattress or groceries or even cash money, only first you had to
swear you didn't own any property of your own and even had to
prove it by giving your house or land or even your wagon and
team to your wife or children or any kinfolks you could count on,
depend on, trust. And who knew? even if second-hand pistols
had gone up too like everything else, maybe the one fifty cents
more would be enough without another policeman.

Though he found another. Here was the depot. It at least
hadn't changed: the same hollowly sonorous rotunda through
which he had passed from the Jefferson train on the three other
times he had seen Memphis—that first unforgettable time (he
had figured it now: the last time had been forty-four years ago
and the first time was three dollars on to that, which was forty-
seven years) with the niggard clutch of wrenched and bitter
dollars and the mentor and guide who had told him about the
houses in Memphis for no other purpose, filled with white women
any one of which he could have if he had the money: whose
experiences until then had been furious unplanned episodes as
violent as vomiting, with no more preparation than the ripping of

buttons before stooping downward into the dusty roadside weeds
or cotton middle where the almost invisible unwashed Negro
girl lay waiting. But different in Memphis: himself and his
guide stepping out into the street where the whole city lay
supine to take him into itself like embrace, like arms, the very
meagre wad of bills in his pocket on fire too which he had wrung,
wrested from between-crops labour at itinerant sawmills, or
from the implacable rented ground by months behind a plough,
his pittance of which he would have to fight his father each time
to get his hands on a nickel of it. It was warm here too and almost
empty and this time the policeman had jerked him awake before
he even knew he was going to sleep. Though this one was not in
uniform. But he knew about that kind too.

"I said, what train are you waiting for?" the policeman said.

"I ain't waiting for no train," he said.

"All right," the policeman said. "Then get out of here. Go on
home." Then, exactly like the other one: "You ain't got anywhere to sleep? Okay, but you damn sure got some place to
leave from, whether you go to bed or not. Go on now. Beat it."
And then, since he didn't move: "Go on, I said. What're you
waiting for?"

"The half a dollar," he said.

"The what?" the policeman said. "The half a— Why, you—"
so that this time he moved, turned quickly, already dodging,
not much bigger than a small boy and therefore about as hard
for a man the size of the policeman to catch in a place as big as
this. He didn't run: he walked, just fast enough for the policeman
to be not quite able to touch him, yet still not have cause to
shout at him, through the rotunda and out into the street, not
looking back at the policeman standing in the doorway shouting
after him: "And don't let me catch you in here again neither."

He was becoming more and more oriented now. There was
another depot just down a cross street, but then the same thing
would happen there; evidently the railroad policemen who just
wore clothes like everybody else didn't belong to the W P and A
free-relief laws. Besides, the night was moving toward its end
now; he could feel it. So he just walked, never getting very far
away because he knew where he was now; and now and then in
the vacant side streets and alleys he could stop and sit down, in a

doorway or behind a cluster of garbage or trash cans and once more be waking up before he knew he had gone to sleep. Then he would walk again, the quiet and empty city—this part of it anyway—his impeachless own, thinking, with the old amazement no less fresh and amazed for being almost as old as he *A man can get through anything if he can jest keep on walking*.

Then it was day, not waking the city; the city had never slept, not resuming but continuing back into visibility the faces pallid and wan and unsleeping, hurrying, passionate and gay, toward the tremendous, the unimaginable pleasures. He knew exactly where he was now; this pavement could have shown his print from forty-four years ago; for the first time since he had come out the Parchman gate five mornings ago he was confident, invulnerable and immune. *I could even spend a whole dollar of it now and hit wouldn't stop me* he thought, inside the small dingy store where a few Negroes were already trafficking. A Negro man seemed to be running it or anyway serving the customers. Maybe he even owned it; maybe the new laws even said a nigger could even own a store, remembering something else from thirty-eight years back.

"Animal crackers," he said. Because he was there now, safe, immune and invulnerable. "I reckon they done jumped them up ten or fifteen cents too, ain't they?" looking at the small cardboard box coloured like a circus wagon itself and blazoned with beasts like a heraldry.

"Ten cents," the Negro said.

"Ten cents more than what?" he said.

"It's ten cents," the Negro said. "Do you want it or don't you?"

"I'll take two of them," he said. He walked again, in actual sunlight now, himself one with the hurrying throng, eating his minute vanilla menagerie; there was plenty of time now since he was not only safe but he knew exactly where he was; by merely turning his head (which he did not) he could have seen the street, the actual housefront (he didn't know it of course and probably wouldn't have recognised her either, but his younger daughter was now the madam of it) which he had entered with his mentor that night forty-seven years ago, where waited the glittering arms of women not only shaped like Helen and Eve and Lilith, not only functional like Helen and Eve and Lilith, but coloured white like them too, where he had said No not just to all the hard savage years of his hard and barren life, but to Death too in the bed of a public prostitute.

The window had not changed: the same unwashed glass behind the wire grillework containing the same tired banjos and ornate clocks and trays of glass jewelry. "I want to buy a pistol," he said to one of the two men blue-jowled as pirates behind the counter.

"You got a permit?" the man said.

"A permit?" he said. "I jest want to buy a pistol. They told me before you sold pistols here. I got the money."

"Who told you we sold pistols here?" the man said.

"Maybe he don't want to buy one but just reclaim one," the second man said.

"Oh," the first said. "That's different. What sort of pistol do you want to reclaim, dad?"

"What?" he said.

"How much money have you got?" the first said. He removed the wadded paper from the bib of his overalls and took out the ten-dollar bill and unfolded it. 'That all you got?"

"Let me see the pistol," he said.

"You can't buy a pistol for ten dollars, grandpaw," the first said. "Come on. Try them other pockets."

"Hold it," the second said. "Maybe he can reclaim one out of my private stock." He stooped and reached under the counter.

"That's an idea," the first said. "Out of your private stock, he wouldn't need a permit." The second man rose and laid an object on the counter. Mink looked at it quietly.

"Hit looks like a cooter," he said. It did: snub-nosed, short-barrelled, swollen of cylinder and rusted over, with its curved butt and flat reptilian hammer it did resemble the fossil relic of some small antediluvian terrapin.

"What are you talking about?" the first said. "That's a genuine bulldog detective special forty-one, the best protection a man could have. That's what you want, ain't it—protection? Because it it's more than that; if you aim to take it back to Arkansaw and start robbing and shooting folks with it, the Law ain't going to like it. They'll put you in jail for that even in Arkansaw. Even right down in Missippi you can't do that."

"That's right," Mink said. "Protection." He put the bill on the counter and took up the pistol and broke it and held the barrel up to the light. "Hit's dirty inside," he said.

"You can see through it, can't you?" the first said. "Do you think a forty-one-calibre bullet can't go through any hole you can see through?" Mink lowered the pistol and was in the act of closing it again when he saw that the bill was gone.

"Wait," he said.

"Sure, sure," the first said, putting the bill back on the counter. "Give me the pistol. We can't reclaim even that one to you for just ten dollars."

"How much will you have to have?"

"How much have you got?"

"I got jest three more. I got to get home to Jefferson."

"Sure he's got to get home," the second said. "Let him have it for eleven. We ain't robbers."

"It ain't loaded," he said.

"There's a store around the corner on Main where you can buy all the forty-ones you want at four dollars a box," the first said.

"I ain't got four dollars," he said. "I won't have but two now. And I got to get—"

"What does he want with a whole box, just for protection?" the second said. "Tell you what. I'll let you have a couple out of my private stock for another dollar."

"I got to have at least one bullet to try it with," he said. "Unless you will guarantee it."

"Do we ask you to guarantee you ain't going to rob or shoot anybody with it?" the first said.

"Okay, okay, he's got to try it out," the second said. "Give him another bullet for a— You could spare another quarter, couldn't you? Them forty-one bullets are hard to get, you know."

"Could it be a dime?" he said. "I got to get home yet."

"Okay, okay," the second said. "Give him the pistol and three bullets for twelve dollars and a dime. He's got to get home. To hell with a man that'll rob a man trying to get home."

So he was all right; he stepped out into the full drowsing sunlight of early fall, into the unsleeping and passionate city. He was all right now. All he had to do now was to get to Jefferson and that wasn't but eighty miles.

THIRTEEN

WHEN Charles Mallison got home in September of 1945, there was a new Snopes in Jefferson. They had got shot down ("of course," Charles always added, telling it) though it wasn't a crash. Plexiglass was the pilot. Plex. His name was Harold Baddrington, but he had an obsession on the subject of cellophane, which he called plexiglass, amounting to a phobia; the simple sight or even the mere idea of a new pack of cigarettes or a new shirt or handkerchief as you had to buy them now pre-encased in an invisible impenetrable cocoon, threw him to the sort of virulent almost hysterical frenzy which Charles had seen the idea of Germans or Japanese throw some civilians, especially ones around fifty years old. He—Plex—had a scheme for winning the war with cellophane: instead of bombs, the seventeens and twenty-fours and the British Lancasters and Blenheims would drop factory-vulcanised packs of tobacco and new shirts and underclothes, and while the Germans were queued up waiting turns at the ice pick, they could be strafed en masse or even captured without a shot by paratroop drops.

It wasn't even a bailout; Plex made a really magnificent one-engine landing. The trouble was, he picked out a farm that a German patrol had already selected that morning to practise a new occupation innovation or something whose directive had just come down, so in almost no time the whole crew of them were in the P.O.W. camp at Limbourg, which almost immediately turned out to be the most dangerous place any of them had been in during the war; it was next door to the same marshalling yard that the R.A.F. bombed regularly every Wednesday night from an altitude of about thirty or forty feet. They would spend six days watching the calendar creep inexorably toward Wednesday, when as regular as clockwork the uproar of crashes and thuds and snarling engines would start up, and the air full of searchlights and machine-gun bullets and whizzing fragments of AA, the entire barracks crouching under bunks or anything else that would interpose another inch of thickness, no matter what, with that frantic desire, need, impulse to rush outdoors waving their arms and shouting up at the pandemonium over-head: "Hey, fellows! For Christ's sake have a heart! It's us! It's us!" If it had been a moving picture or a book instead of a war, Charles said they would have escaped. But he himself didn't know and never knew anyone who ever actually escaped from a genuine authentic stalag, so they had to wait for regular routine liberation before he came back home and found there was already another Snopes in Jefferson.

But at least they—Jefferson—were holding their own. Because in that same summer, 1945, when Jefferson gained the new Snopes, Ratliff eliminated Clarence. Not that Ratliff shot him or anything like that: he just simply eliminated Clarence as a factor in what Charles's Uncle Gavin also called their constant Snopes-fear and -dread, or you might say, Snopes-dodging. It happened during the campaign which ended in the August primary election; Charles hadn't got back home yet by a month, nor was his Uncle Gavin actually present at the picnic where it actually happened, where Clarence Snopes was actually defeated in the race for Congress which, being a national election, wouldn't even take place until next year. That's what he, Charles, meant by Ratliff doing it. He was in the office when his Uncle Gavin this time ran Ratliff to earth and bayed him and said, "All right. Just exactly what did happen out there that day?"

Senator Clarence Egglestone Snopes, pronounced "Cla'-nce" by every free white Yoknapatawpha American whose right and duty it was to go to the polls and mark his X each time old man Will Varner told him to; just Senator Clarence Snopes for the first few years after old Varner ordained or commanded—anyway, translated—him into the upper house of the state legislature in Jackson; beginning presently to put on a little flesh (he had been a big, hulking youth and young man but reasonably hard and active in an awkward kind of way until the sedentary brain work of being one of the elected fathers and guardians and mentors of the parliamentary interests of Yoknapatawpha County began to redden his nose and pouch his eyes and paunch his belt a little) until one hot July day in the middle twenties when no other man in Jefferson or Yoknapatawpha County either under sixty years of age had on a coat, Clarence appeared on the Square in a complete white linen suit with a black Windsor tie, and either just before or just after or maybe it was that same simultaneous start or shock brought it to their

notice, they realised that he was now signing himself Senator
C. E. Snopes, and Charles's Uncle Gavin said, "Where did the
'E' come from?" and Ratliff said,

"Maybe he picked it up along with that-ere white wedding
suit going and coming through Memphis to get back and forth
to Jackson to work. Because why not? Ain't even a elected
legislative senator got a few private rights like any free ordinary
voter?"

What Charles meant was that Clarence already had them all
a little off balance like a prize fighter does his opponent without
really hitting him yet. So their emotion was simple docility
when they learned that their own private Cincinnatus was not
even C. any longer but was Senator Egglestone Snopes; his
Uncle Gavin merely said, "Egglestone? Why Egglestone?" and
Ratliff merely said,

"Why not?" and even his Uncle Gavin merely said,

"Yes, why not?" So they didn't really mark it when one day
the C. was back again—Senator C. Egglestone Snopes now,
with a definite belly and the pouched eyes and a lower lip now
full from talking, forensic. Because Clarence was making speeches,
anywhere and everywhere, at bond rallies and women's clubs,
any place or occasion where there was a captive audience,
because Charles was still in the German prison camp when his
Uncle Gavin and Ratliff realised that Clarence intended to run
for Congress in Washington and that old Will Varner might
quite possibly get him elected to it—the same Clarence Snopes
who had moved steadily onward and upward from being old
Varner's privately appointed constable in Varner's own private
Beat Two, then supervisor of the Beat and then elected out of the
entire county by means of old Will's diffused usurious capacity
for blackmail, to be the county representative in Jackson; and
now, 1945, tapped by all the mutually compounding vote-
swapping Varners of the whole congressional district for the
House of Representatives in Washington itself, where in the
clutches not of a mere neighbourhood or sectional Will Varner
but of a Will Varner of really national or even international
scope, there would be no limit to what he might be capable of
unless somebody did something about it. This, until that day in
July at the annual Varner's Mill picnic where by custom and

tradition not only the local candidates for county and state offices but even the regional and sectional ones for national offices, like Clarence, even though the election itself would not happen until next year, started the ball rolling. Whereupon Clarence had not only failed to appear on the speakers' platform to announce his candidacy, he disappeared from the picnic grounds before the dinner was even served. And the next day word went over the county that Clarence had not only decided not to run for Congress, he was even withdrawing from public life altogether when his present term in the state senate was up.

So what Charles's Uncle Gavin really wanted to know was not so much what had happened to Clarence, as what had happened to old Will Varner. Because whatever eliminated Clarence from the congressional race would have to impact not on Clarence but on old Will; it wouldn't have needed to touch Clarence at all in fact. Because nobody really minded Clarence just as you don't mind a stick of dynamite until somebody fuses it; otherwise he was just so much sawdust and greasy paper that wouldn't even burn good set on fire. He was unprincipled and without morals of course, but without a guiding and prompting and absolving hand or intelligence, Clarence himself was anybody's victim since all he had was his blind instinct for sadism and overreaching, and was himself really dangerous only to someone he would have the moral and intellectual ascendency of, which out of the entire world's population couldn't possibly be anybody except another Snopes, and out of the entire Snopes population couldn't possibly be more than just one of them. In this case it was his youngest brother Doris—a hulking youth of seventeen who resembled Clarence not only in size and shape but the same mentality of a child and the moral principles of a wolverine, the only difference being that Doris hadn't been elected to the state legislature yet. Back in the late twenties Byron Snopes, who looted Colonel Sartoris's bank and fled to Texas, sent back C.O.D. four half-Snopes half-Apache Indian children which Clarence, spending the summer at home between two legislative sessions, adopted into a kind of peonage of practical jokes. Only, being a state senator now, Clarence had to be a little careful about his public dignity, not for the sake of his constituency but because even he knew a damn sight better than to take chances with old Will Varner's standards of *amour-propre*. So he would merely invent the jokes and use his brother Doris to perpetrate them, until the four Indian children finally caught Doris alone in no man's land and captured him and tied him to a stake in the woods and even had the fire burning when someone heard his screams and got there in time to save him.

But Clarence himself was in his late twenties then, already a state senator; his career had begun long before that, back when he was eighteen or nineteen years old out at Varner's store and became leader of a subjugated (he was big and strong and Ratliff said really liked fighting, provided the equality in size was enough in his favour) gang of cousins and toadies who fought and drank and gambled and beat up Negroes and terrified women and young girls around Frenchman's Bend until (Ratliff said) old Varner became irritated and exasperated enough to take him out of the public domain by ordering the local J.P. to appoint Clarence his constable. That was where and when Clarence's whole life, existence, destiny, seemed at last to find itself like a rocket does at the first touch of fire.

Though his career didn't go quite that fast, not at first anyway. Or maybe it wasn't his career so much as his exposure, revealment. At first it was almost like he was just looking around, orienting himself, learning just where he now actually was; and only then looking in a sort of amazed incredulity at the vista opening before him. Merely amazed at first, before the exultation began, at the limitless prospect which nobody had told him about. Because at first he even behaved himself. At first everybody thought that, having been as outrageous as he had been with no other backing than the unanimity of his old lawless pack, he would be outrageous indeed now with the challengeless majesty of organised law according to Will Varner to back him. But he fooled them. Instead, he became the champion and defender of the civic mores and the public peace of Frenchman's Bend. Of course the first few Negroes who ran afoul of his new official capacity suffered for it. But there was now something impersonal even to the savaging of Negroes. Previous to his new avatar, he and his gang had beaten up Negroes as a matter of principle. Not chastising them as individual Negroes nor even, Charles's Uncle Gavin said, warring against them as representatives of a race which was alien because it was of a different appearance and therefore enemy *per se*, but (and his Uncle Gavin said Clarence and his gang did not know this because they dared not know it was so) because they were afraid of that alien race. They were afraid of it not because it was black but because they—the white man—had taught the black one how to threaten the white economy of material waste, when the white man compelled the black man to learn how to do more with less and worse if the black man wanted to survive in the white economy—less and worse of tools to farm and work with, less of luxury to be content with, less of waste to keep alive with. But not any more now. Now when Clarence manhandled a Negro with the blackjack he carried or with the butt of the pistol which he now officially wore, it was with a kind of detachment, as if he were using neither the man's black skin nor even his human flesh, but simply the man's present condition of legal vulnerability as testing ground or sounding board on which to prove again, perhaps even reassure himself from day to day, just how far his official power and legal immunity actually went and just how physically strong, even with the inevitable passage of time, he actually remained.

Because they were not always Negroes. In fact, one of the first victims of Clarence's new condition was his lieutenant, his second-in-command, in the old gang; if anything, Clarence was even more savage this time because the man had tried to trade on the old relationship and the past; it was as if Clarence had now personally invested a kind of incorruptibility and integrity into his old natural and normal instinct and capacity for violence and physical anguish; had had to borrow them—the incorruptibility and the integrity—at so high a rate that he had to defend them with his life. Anyway, he had changed. And, Charles's Uncle Gavin said, since previous to his elevation to grace, everybody had believed Clarence incapable of change, now the same people believed immediately that the new condition was for perpetuity, for the rest of his life. They still believed this even after they found out—it was no rumour; Clarence himself bragged, boasted quietly of it—that he was a member of the Ku Klux Klan when it appeared in the country (it never got very far and didn't last very long; it was believed that it wouldn't have lasted at all except for Clarence), taken in because the Klan needed him or could use him, or, as Charles's Uncle Gavin said, probably because there was no way under heaven that they could have kept him out since it was his dish just as he was its. This was before he became constable of Frenchman's Bend; his virgin advent from private life you might say, his initial accolade of public recognition, comparatively harmless yet, since even a Ku Klux Klan would have more sense than to depend on Clarence very far; he remained just one more obedient integer, muscle man—what in a few more years people would mean by "goon"—until the day came when old Will Varner's irritation or exasperation raised him to constable, whereupon within the year it was rumoured that he was now an officer in the Klavern or whatever they called it; and in two more years was himself the local Dragon or Kleagle: who having been designated by old Varner custodian of the public peace, had now decreed himself arbiter of its morals too.

Which was probably when he really discerned at last the breadth and splendour of his rising destiny; with amazement and incredulity at that apparently limitless expanse and, who knows? maybe even humility too that he should have been chosen, found worthy—that limitless field for his capacity and talents: not merely to beat, hammer men into insensibility and submission, but to use them; not merely to expend their inexhaustible numbers like ammunition or consume them like hogs or sheep, but to use, employ them like mules or oxen, with one eye constant for the next furrow tomorrow or next year; using not just their competence to mark an X whenever and wherever old Will Varner ordered them to, but their capacity for passion and greed and alarm as well, as though Clarence had been in the business of politics all his life instead of those few mere years as a hick constable. And, as Charles's uncle said, doing it all by simple infallible instinct, without preceptor or example. Because this was even before Huey Long had risen far enough to show their own Mississippi Bilbo just what a man with a little brass and courage and no inhibitions could really accomplish.

So when Clarence announced for the state legislature, they —the County—knew he would need no other platform than

Uncle Billy Varner's name. In fact they decided immediately that his candidacy was not even Clarence's own idea but Uncle Billy's; that Uncle Billy's irritation had simply reached a point where Clarence must be removed completely from his sight. But they were wrong. Clarence had a platform. Which was the moment when some of them, a few of them like Charles's uncle and Ratliff and a few more of the young ones like Charles (he was only eight or ten then) who would listen (or anyway had to listen, like Charles) to them, discovered that they had better fear him, tremble and beware. His platform was his own. It was one which only his amoral temerity would have dared because it set him apostate to his own constituency; the thin deciding margin of his vote came from sources not only beyond the range of Will Varner's autocracy, it came from people who under any other conditions would have voted for almost any other member of the human race first: he came out publicly against the Ku Klux Klan. He had been the local Kleagle, Dragon, whatever the title was, right up to the day he announced his candidacy— or so the County thought. But now he was its mortal enemy, stumping the county apparently only coincidentally to win an office, since his dedication was to destroy a dragon, winning the race by that scant margin of votes coming mostly from Jefferson itself—school-teachers, young professional people, women—the literate and liberal innocents who believed that decency and right and personal liberty would prevail simply because they were decent and right; who until Clarence offered them one, had had no political unanimity and had not even bothered always to vote, until at last the thing they feared and hated seemed to have produced for them a champion. So he went to Jackson not as the successful candidate for a political office but as the dedicated paladin of a cause, walking (Charles's uncle said) into the legislative halls in an aura half the White Knight's purity and half the shocked consternation of his own kind whom he had apparently wrenched himself from and repudiated. Because he did indeed destroy the Ku Klux Klan in Yoknapatawpha County; as one veteran klansman expressed it: "Durn it, if we can't beat a handful of schoolteachers and editors and Sunday-school superintendents, how in hell can we hope to beat a whole race of niggers and catholics and jews?"

So Clarence was in. Now he had it made, as Charles's generation would say. He was safe now for the next two years, when
there would be another election, to look around, find out where
to go next like the alpinist on his ledge. That's what Charles's
uncle said it was: like the mountain climber. Except that the
climber climbs the mountain not just to get to the top. He would
try to climb it even if he knew he would never get there. He
climbs it simply because he can have the solitary peace and
contentment of knowing constantly that only his solitary nerve,
will and courage stand between him and destruction, while
Clarence didn't even know it was a mountain because there
wasn't anything to fall off, you could only be pushed off; and
anybody that felt himself strong enough or quick enough to
push Clarence Snopes off anything was welcome to try it.

So at first what the County thought Clarence was doing now
was simply being quiet while he watched and listened to learn
the rules of the new trade. They didn't know that what he was
teaching himself was how to recognise opportunities when they
occurred; that he was still doing that even after he began at
last to talk, address the House, himself still the White Knight who
had destroyed bigotry and intolerance in Yoknapatawpha County
in the eyes of the innocent illusionees whose narrow edge of
additional votes had elected him, long after the rest of the County
realised that Clarence was preaching the same hatred of Negroes
and Catholics and Jews that had been the tenet of the organisation by wrecking which he had got where he now was; when the
Silver Shirts appeared, Clarence was one of the first in Mississippi
to join it, joining, his uncle said, not because of the principles
the Silver Shirts advocated but simply because Clarence probably
decided that it would be more durable than the merely county-
autonomous Klan which he had wrecked. Because by this time
his course was obvious: to join things, anything, any organisation
to which human beings belonged, which he might compel or
control or coerce through the emotions of religion or patriotism
or just simple greed, political gravy-hunger; he had been born
into the Baptist Church in Frenchman's Bend; he was now
affiliated in Jackson, where (he had been re-elected twice now) he
now taught a Sunday-school class; in that same summer the
County heard that he was contemplating resigning his seat in the

legislature long enough to do a hitch in the army or navy to be eligible for the American Legion.

Clarence was in now. He had it made. He had—Charles was about to say "divided the county" except that "divided" implied balance or at least suspension even though the lighter end of the beam was irrevocably in the air. Where with Clarence and Yoknapatawpha County, the lesser end of that beam was not in suspension at all but rather in a condition of aerial banishment, making now only the soundless motions of vociferation in vacuum; Clarence had engorged the county whole as whales and owls do and, as owls do, disgorged onto that airy and harmless pinnacle the refuse of bones and hair he didn't need—the doomed handful of literate liberal underpaid white-collar illusionees who had elected him into the state senate because they thought he had destroyed the Ku Klux Klan, plus the other lesser handful of other illusionees like Charles's Uncle Gavin and Ratliff, who had voted for Clarence that time as the lesser of two evils because he had come out against the Klan and hence were even more doomed since where the school- and music-teachers and the other white-collar innocents who learned by heart President Roosevelt's speeches, could believe anew each time that honour and justice and decency would prevail just because they were honourable and just and decent, his uncle and Ratliff never had believed this and never would.

Clarence didn't destroy them. There were not enough of them. They were so few of them in fact that he could continue to send them year after year the mass-produced Christmas cards which it was said he obtained from the same firm he was instrumental in awarding the yearly contract for automobile licence plates. As for the rest of the county voters, they only waited for Clarence to indicate where he wanted the X marked to elect him to any office he wanted, right up to the ultimate one which the County (including for a time even Charles's uncle's branch of the illusioned) believed was his goal: governor of the state. Huey Long now dominated the horizon of every Mississippi politician's ambition; it seemed only natural to the County that their own should pattern on him; even when Clarence took up Long's soak-the-rich battle cry as though he, Clarence, had invented it, even Charles's Uncle Gavin and Ratliff still believed that

Clarence's sights were set no higher than the governor's mansion. Because, though at that time—1930-'35—Mississippi had no specific rich to soak—no industries, no oil, no gas to speak of— the idea of taking from anybody that had it that which they deserved no more than he did, being no more intelligent or industrious but simply luckier, struck straight to the voting competence of every sharecropper and tenant farmer not only in Yoknapatawpha County but in all the rest of Mississippi too; Clarence could have been elected governor of Mississippi on the simple platform of soaking the rich in Louisiana or Alabama, or for that matter in Maine or Oregon.

So their (his uncle's and Ratliff's little forlorn cell of un-reconstructed purists) shock at the rumour that Clarence had contemplated for a moment taking over the American Legion in Mississippi was nothing to the one when they learned three years ago (Charles himself was not present; he had already departed from Yoknapatawpha County to begin training for his ten months in the German P.O.W. camp) that the most potent political faction in the state, the faction which was sure to bring their man in as governor, had offered to run Clarence for lieutenant-governor, and Clarence had declined. He gave no reason but then he didn't need to because now all the county— not just Charles's uncle's little cell, but everybody—knew what Clarence's aim, ambition was and had been all the time: Washington, Congress. Which was horror only among the catacombs behind the bestiarium; with everyone else it was triumph and exultation: who had already ridden Clarence's coat-tails to the (comparatively) minor-league hog trough at Jackson and who saw now the clear path to that vast and limit-less one in Washington.

And not just shock and horror, but dread and fear too of the man who had used the Ku Klux Klan while he needed it and then used their innocence to wreck the Klan when he no longer did, who was using the Baptist Church as long as he believed it would serve him; who had used W.P.A. and N.R.A. and A.A.A. and C.C.C. and all the other agencies created in the dream or hope that people should not suffer or, if they must, at least suffer equally in times of crisis and fear; being either for them or against them as the political breeze indicated, since in the late thirties he turned against the party which had fathered them, ringing the halls which at least occasionally had echoed the voices of statesmen and humanitarians, with his own voice full of racial and religious and economic intolerance (once the strongest plank in his political creed had been soaking the rich; now the loudest one was the menace of organised labour), with nothing to intervene between him and Congress but that handful of innocents still capable of believing that evil could be destroyed simply because it was evil, whom Clarence didn't even fear enough to stop sending them the cheap Christmas cards.

"Which won't be enough," Charles's uncle said, "as it never has been enough in the country, even if they could multiply themselves by the ten-thousand. Because he would only fool them again."

"Maybe," Ratliff said. (This was Charles's Uncle Gavin telling him what had happened when he got back home in September after it was all over and whatever it was had licked Clarence, caused him to withdraw from the race, at old Will Varner's annual picnic in July; this was back in April when his uncle and Ratliff were talking.) "What you need is to have the young folks back for at least a day or two between now and the seventeenth of next August. What a shame the folks that started this war and drafted all the young voters away never had sense enough to hold off at least long enough to keep Clarence Snopes outen Congress, ain't it?"

"*You* need?" Charles's uncle said. "What do you mean, *you?*"

"I thought you jest said how the old folks like you and me can't do nothing about Clarence but jest fold our hands and feel sorry," Ratliff said.

"No more we can," his uncle said. "Oh, there are enough of us. It was the ones of your and my age and generation who carried on the good work of getting things into the shape they're in now. But it's too late for us now. We can't now; maybe we're just afraid to stick our necks out again. Or if not afraid, at least ashamed. No: not afraid: we are just too old. Call it just tired, too tired to be afraid any longer of losing. Just to hate evil is not enough. You—somebody—has got to do something about it. Only now it will have to be somebody else, and even if the Japs should quit too before the August primary, there still won't be enough somebody elses here. Because it won't be us."

"Maybe," Ratliff said. And his uncle was right. And then, maybe Ratliff was right too. One of the first to announce for the race to challenge Clarence from the district was a member of his uncle's somebody elses—a man from the opposite end of the district, who was no older than Charles: only—as Charles put it —braver. He announced for Congress even before Clarence did. The election for Congress wouldn't be until next year, 1946, so there was plenty of time. But then, Clarence always did it this way: waited until the other candidate or candidates had announced and committed or anyway indicated what their platforms would be. And Clarence had taught Yoknapatawpha County to know why: that by waiting to be the last, he didn't even need to invent a platform because by that time his chief, most dangerous opponent had supplied him with one. As happened now, Clarence using this one in his turn, using his valour as an instrument to defeat him with.

His name was Devries; Yoknapatawpha County had never heard of him before 1941. But they had since. In 1940 he had been Number One in his R.O.T.C. class at the University, had graduated with a regular army commission and by New Year's 1942 was already overseas; in 1943 when he was assigned back to the United States to be atmosphere in bond drives, he was a major with (this is Charles telling it) enough ribbons to make a four-in-hand tie which he had acquired while commanding Negro infantry in battle, having been posted to Negro troops by some brass-hatted theorist in Personnel doubtless on the premise that, being a Southerner, he would indubitably "understand" Negroes; and (Charles supposed) just as indubitably commanded them well for the same reason: that, being a Southerner, he knew that no white man understood Negroes and never would so long as the white man compelled the black man to be first a Negro and only then a man, since this, the impenetrable dividing wall, was the black man's only defence and protection for survival. Maybe he couldn't sell bonds. Anyway apparently he didn't really put his back into it. Because the story was that almost before his folks knew he was home he was on his way back to the war and when he came out this time, in 1944, he was a full bird colonel with next to the last ribbon and a tin leg; and while he was on his way to Washington to be given the last one, the top one, the story came out how he had finished the second tour up front and was already posted stateside when the general pinned the next to the last medal on him. But instead he dropped the medal into his foot locker and put back on the battle fatigues and worried them until they let him go back up the third time, and one night he turned the rest of the regiment over to the second and with a Negro sergeant and a runner crawled out to where what was left of the other battalion had been trapped by a barrage and sent them back with the runner for guide, he and the sergeant holding off one attack single-handed until they were clear, then he, Devries, was carrying the sergeant back when he took one too and this time a hulking giant of an Arkansas Negro cotton-field hand crawled out and picked them both up and brought them in. And when he, Devries, came out of the ether with the remaining leg he worried enough people until they sent in the field hand and he, Devries, had the nurse dig the medal out of the foot locker and said to the field hand, "Lift me up, you big bastard," and pinned the medal on him.

That was Clarence's opponent for Congress. That is, even if the army hadn't anyone else at all for the experts to assume he understood Negroes, Devries (this is Charles talking) couldn't have talked himself back up front with one leg missing. So all he had now to try to persuade to send him somewhere where civilians, and apparently the only place he could think of was Congress. So (this is still Charles) maybe it would take somebody with no more sense than to volunteer twice for the same war, to have the temerity to challenge a long-vested interest like Clarence Snopes. Because even if they had arranged things better, more practical: either for 1944 to have happened in 1943 or have the election year itself moved forward one, or in fact if the Japs quit in 1945 too and all the ruptured ducks in the congressional district were back home in time, there still would not be enough of them and in the last analysis all Devries would have would be the heirs of the same unco-ordinated political illusionees innocent enough to believe still that demagoguery and bigotry and intolerance must not and cannot and will not endure simply because they are bigotry and demagoguery and intolerance, that Clarence himself had already used up and thrown away twenty-odd years ago; Charles's uncle said to Ratliff:

"They'll always be wrong. They think they are fighting Clarence Snopes. They're not. They're not faced with an individual nor even a situation: they are beating their brains out against one of the foundation rocks of our national character itself. Which is the premise that politics and political office are not and never have been the method and means by which we can govern ourselves in peace and dignity and honour and security, but instead are our national refuge for our incompetents who have failed at every other occupation by means of which they might make a living for themselves and their families; and whom as a result we would have to feed and clothe and shelter out of our own private purses and means. The surest way to be elected to office in America is to have fathered seven or eight children and then lost your arm or leg in a sawmill accident: both of which—the reckless optimism which begot seven or eight children with nothing to feed them by but a sawmill, and the incredible ineptitude which would put an arm or a leg in range of a moving saw—should already have damned you from any form of public trust. They can't beat him. He will be elected to Congress for the simple reason that if he fails to be elected, there is nothing else he can do that anybody on earth would pay him for on Saturday night; and old Will Varner and the rest of the interlocked Snopes kin and connections have no intention whatever of boarding and feeding Clarence for the rest of his life. You'll see."

It looked like he was going to be right. It was May now almost time for the political season to open; a good one again after four years, now that the Germans had collapsed too. And still Clarence hadn't announced his candidacy in actual words. Everybody knew why of course. What they couldn't figure out yet was just how Clarence planned to use Devries's military record for his, Clarence's, platform; exactly how Clarence intended to use Devries's military glory to beat him for Congress with it. And when the pattern did begin to appear at last, Yoknapatawpha County—some of it anyway—found out something else about the Clarence they had lived in innocence with for twenty and more years. Which was just how dangerous

Clarence really was in his capacity to unify normal—you might even say otherwise harmless—human baseness and get it to the polls. Because this time he compelled them whose champion he was going to be, to come to him and actually beg him to be their champion; not just beg him to be their knight, but themselves to invent or anyway establish the cause for which they would need him.

Charles's Uncle Gavin told him how suddenly one day in that May or early June, the whole county learned that Clarence was not only not going to run for Congress, he was going to retire from public life altogether; this not made as a formal public announcement but rather breathed quietly from sheep to sheep of old Will Varner's voting flock which had been following Clarence to the polls for twenty-five years now; gently, his Uncle Gavin said, even a little sadly, with a sort of mild astonishment that it was not self-evident:

"Why, I'm an old man now," Clarence (he was past forty) said. "It's time I stepped aside. Especially since we got a brave young man like this Captain Devries—"

"Colonel Devries," they told him.

"Colonel Devries—to represent you, carry on the work which I tried to do to better our folks and our country—"

"You mean, you're going to endorse him? You going to support him?"

"Of course," Clarence said. "Us old fellows have done the best we could for you, but now the time has come for us to step down. What we need in Congress now is the young men, especially the ones that were brave in the war. Of course General Devries—"

"Colonel Devries," they told him.

"Colonel Devries—is a little younger maybe than I would have picked out myself. But time will cure that. Of course he's got some ideas that I myself could never agree with and that lots of other old fogies like me in Missippi and the South won't never agree with either. But maybe we are all too old now, out of date, and the things we believed in and stood up for and suffered when necessary, ain't true any more, ain't what folks want any more, and his new ideas are the right ones for Yoknapatawpha County and Missippi and the South—"

And then of course they asked it: "What new ideas?"

And that was all. He told them: this man, Colonel Devries (no trouble any more about the exactness of his rank), who had become so attached to Negroes by commanding them in battle that he had volunteered twice, possibly even having to pull a few strings (since everyone would admit that he had more than done his share of fighting for his country and democracy and was entitled to—more: had earned the right to—be further excused) to get back into the front lines in order to consort with Negroes; who had there risked his life to save one Negro and then had his own life saved by another Negro. A brave man (had not his government and country recorded and affirmed that by the medals it gave him, including that highest one in its gift?) and an honourable one (that medal meant honour too; did not its very designation include the word?), what course would—could—dared he take, once he was a member of that Congress already passing legislation to break down forever the normal and natural (natural? God Himself had ordained and decreed them) barriers between the white man and the black one. And so on. And that was all; as his uncle said, Clarence was already elected, the county and the district would not even need to spend the money to have the ballots cast and counted; that Medal of Honor which the government had awarded Devries for risking death to defend the principles on which that government was founded and by which it existed, had destroyed forever his chance to serve in the Congress which had accoladed him.

"You see?" Charles's uncle said to Ratliff. "You can't beat him."

"You mean, even you can't think of nothing to do about it?" Ratliff said.

"Certainly," his uncle said. "Join him."

"Join him?" Ratliff said.

"The most efficacious, the oldest—oh yes, without doubt the first, the very first, back to the very dim moment when two cave men confederated against the third one—of all political maxims."

"Join—*him?*" Ratliff said.

"All right," his uncle said. "You tell me then. I'll join you." His uncle told how Ratliff blinked at him awhile. "There

T

must be some simpler way than that. It's a pure and simple proposition; there must be a pure and simple answer to it. Clarence jest purely and simply wants to get elected to Congress, he don't keer how; there must be some pure and simple way for the folks that purely and simply don't want him in Congress to say No to him, they don't keer how neither."

His uncle said again, "All right. Find it. I'll join you." But evidently it wasn't that pure and simple to Ratliff either: only to Clarence. His uncle said that after that Clarence didn't even need to make a campaign, a race; that all he would need to do would be to get up on the speakers' platform at the Varner's Mill picnic long enough to be sure that the people who had turned twenty-one since old Will Varner had last told them who to vote for, would know how to recognise the word Snopes on the ballot. In fact, Devries could have quit now, and his uncle said there were some who thought he ought to. Except how could he, with that medal—all five or six of them—for guts and valour in the trunk in the attic or wherever he kept them. Devries even came to Jefferson, into Clarence's own bailiwick, and made his speech as if nothing were happening. But there you were. There were not enough soldiers back yet who would know what the medal meant. And even though the election itself would not happen until next year, nobody could know now that the Japs would cave this year too. To the others, the parents and Four-F cousins and such to whom they had sent their voting proxies, Devries was a nigger lover who had actually been decorated by the Yankee government for it. In fact, the story now was that Devries had got his Congressional Medal by choosing between a Negro and a white boy to save, and had chosen the Negro and left the white boy to die. Though Charles's uncle said that Clarence himself did not start this one: they must do him that justice at least. Not that Clarence would have flinched from starting it: he simply didn't need that additional ammunition now, having been, not so much in politics but simply a Snopes long enough now to know that only a fool would pay two dollars for a vote when fifty cents would buy it.

It must have been even a little sad: the man who had already been beaten in advance by the very medal which wouldn't let him quit. It was more than just sad. Because his Uncle Gavin

told him how presently even the ones who had never owned a
mechanical leg and, if the odds held up, never would, began to
realise what owning, having to live with one, let alone stand up
and walk on it, must have meant. Devries didn't sit in the car
on the Square or even halted on the road, letting the constituency,
the votes, do the standing and walking out to the car to shake his
hand and listen to him as was Clarence's immemorial and
successful campaigning method. Instead, he walked himself,
swinging that dead mechanical excrescence or bracing it to stand
for an hour on a platform to speak, rationalising for the votes
which he already knew he had lost, while trying to keep all
rumour of the chafed and outraged stump out of his face while
he did it. Until at last Charles's uncle said how the very ones
who would vote for him would dread having to look at him and
keep the rumour of that stump out of their faces too; until they
themselves began to wish the whole thing was over, the debacle
accomplished, wondering (his uncle said) how they themselves
might end it and set him free to go home and throw the tin leg
away, chop it up, destroy it, and be just peacefully maimed.

Then the day approached for Uncle Billy Varner's election-
year picnic, where by tradition all county aspirants for office,
county state or national, delivered themselves and so Clarence
too would have to announce formally his candidacy, his Uncle
Gavin saying how they clutched even at that straw: that once
Clarence had announced for Congress, Devries might feel he
could withdraw his name and save his face.

Only he didn't have to. After the dinner was eaten and the
speakers gathered on the platform, Clarence wasn't even among
them; shortly afterward the word spread that he had even left
the grounds and by the next morning the whole county knew
that he had not only withdrawn from the race for Congress, he
had announced his retirement from public life altogether. And
that this time he meant it because it was not Clarence but old
man Will Varner himself who had sent the word out that Clarence
was through. That was July 1945; a year after that, when the
election for Congress finally came around, the Japanese had
quit too and Charles and most of the rest of them who knew what
Devries's medal meant, were home in person with their votes.
But they merely increased Devries's majority; he didn't really

need the medal because Ratliff had already beat Clarence
Snopes. Then it was September, Charles was home again and
the next day his uncle ran Ratliff to earth on the Square and
brought him up to the office and said,

"All right. Tell us just exactly what did happen out there that
day."

"Out where what day?" Ratliff said.

"You know what I mean. At Uncle Billy Varner's picnic when
Clarence Snopes withdrew from the race for Congress."

"Oh, that," Ratliff said. " Why, that was what you might call
a kind of a hand of God, holp a little of course by them two twin
boys of Colonel Devries's sister."

"Yes," his uncle said. "That too: why Devries brought his
sister and her family all the way over here from Cumberland
County just to hear him announce for a race everybody knew
he had already lost."

"That's that hand of God I jest mentioned," Ratliff said.
"Because naturally otherwise Colonel Devries couldn't a possibly
heard away over there in Cumberland County about one little
old lonesome gum thicket behind Uncle Billy Varner's water
mill now, could he?"

"All right, all right," his uncle said. "Thicket. Twin boys.
Stop now and just tell us."

"The twin boys was twin boys and the thicket was a dog
thicket," Ratliff said. "You and Chick both naturally know
what twin boys is and I was about to say you and Chick both of
course know what a dog thicket is too. Except that on second
thought I reckon you don't because I never heard of a dog
thicket neither until I seen this clump of gum and ash and
hickory and pin-oak switches on the bank jest above Varner's
millpond where it will be convenient for the customers like them
city hotels that keeps a reservoy of fountain-pen ink open to
anybody that needs it right next to the writing-room—"

"Hold it," his uncle said. "Dog thicket. Come on now. I'm
supposed to be busy this morning even if you're not."

"That's what I'm trying to tell you," Ratliff said. "It was a
dog way-station. A kind of a dog post office you might say.
Every dog in Beat Two uses it at least once a day, and every dog
in the congressional district, let alone jest Yoknapatawpha

County, has lifted his leg there at least once in his life and left his visiting card. You know: two dogs comes trotting up and takes a snuff and Number One says   'I be dawg if here ain't that old bobtail Bluetick from up at Wyott's Crossing. What you reckon he's doing away down here?' 'No it ain't,' Number Two says. 'This here is that-ere fyce that Res Grier swapped Solon Quick for that half a day's work shingling the church that time, don't you remember?' and Number One says, 'No, that fyce come afterward. This here is that old Wyott's Crossing Bluetick. I thought he'd a been skeered to come back here after what that Littlejohn half-Airedale done to him that day.' You know: that sort of thing."

"All right," his uncle said. "Go on."

"That's all," Ratliff said, "Jest that-ere what you might call select dee-butant Uncle Billy Varner politics coming-out picnic and every voter and candidate in forty miles that owned a pickup or could bum a ride in one or even a span of mules either if wasn't nothing else handy, the sovereign votes theirselves milling around the grove where Senator Clarence Egglestone Snopes could circulate among them until the time come when he would stand up on the platform and actively tell them where to mark the X. You know: ever thing quiet and peaceful and ordinary and law-abiding as usual until this-here anonymous underhanded son-of-a-gun—I won't say scoundrel because evidently it must a been Colonel Devries his-self couldn't nobody else a knowed who them two twin boys was, let alone what they was doing that far from Cumberland County; leastways not them particular two twin boys and that-ere local dog thicket in the same breath you might say—until whoever this anonymous underhanded feller was, suh-jested to them two boys what might happen say if two folks about that size would shoo them dogs outen that thicket long enough to cut off a handful of them switches well down below the dog target level and kind of walk up behind where Senator C. Egglestone Snopes was getting out the vote, and draw them damp switches light and easy, not to disturb him, across the back of his britches legs. Light and easy, not to disturb nobody, because apparently Clarence nor nobody else even noticed the first six or eight dogs until maybe Clarence felt his britches legs getting damp or maybe jest cool, and looked over his shoulder to see the waiting line-up of his political fate with one eye while already breaking for the nearest automobile or pickup you could roll the windows up in with the other, with them augmenting standing-room-only customers strung out behind him like the knots in a kite's tail until he got inside the car with the door slammed and the glass rolled up, them frustrated dogs circling round and round the automobile like the spotted horses and swan boats on a flying jenny, except the dogs was travelling on three legs, being already loaded and cocked and aimed you might say. Until somebody finally located the owner of the car and got the key and druv Clarence home, finally outdistancing the last dog in about two miles, stopping at last in the ex-Senator's yard where he was safe, the Snopes dogs evidently having went to the picnic too, while somebody went into the house and fetched out a pair of dry britches for the ex-Senator to change into in the automobile. That's right. Ex-Senator. Because even with dry britches he never went back to the picnic; likely he figgered that even then it would be too much risk and strain. I mean, the strain of trying to keep your mind on withdrawing from a political race and all the time having to watch over your shoulder in case some dog recollected your face even if your britches did smell fresh and uninteresting."

"Well I'll be damned," his uncle said. "It's too simple. I don't believe it."

"I reckon he figgered that to convince folks how to vote for him and all the time standing on one foot trying to kick dogs away from his other leg, was a little too much to expect of even Missippi voters," Ratliff said.

"I don't believe you, I tell you," his uncle said. "That wouldn't be enough to make him withdraw even if everybody at the picnic had known about it, seen it. Didn't you just tell me they got him into a car and away almost at once?" Then his uncle stopped. He looked at Ratliff, who stood blinking peacefully back at him. His uncle said: "Or at least—"

"That's right," Ratliff said. "That was the trade."

"What trade?" his uncle said.

"It was likely that same low-minded anonymous scoundrel again," Ratliff said. "Anyhow, somebody made the trade that

if Senator Snopes would withdraw from this-here particular
race for Congress, the folks that had seen them pro-Devries dogs
would forget it, and the ones that hadn't wouldn't never need to
know about it."

"But he would have beat that too," his uncle said. "Clarence
Snopes stopped or even checked just because a few dogs raised
their legs against him? Hell, he would have wound up having
every rabies tag in Yoknapatawpha County counted as an
absentee ballot."

"Oh, you mean Clarence," Ratliff said. "I thought you meant
Uncle Billy Varner."

"Uncle Billy Varner?" his uncle said.

"That's right," Ratliff said. "It was Uncle Billy his-self that
that low-minded rascal must a went to. Leastways Uncle Billy
his-self sent word back that same afternoon that Senator Clarence
Egglestone Snopes had withdrawed from the race for Congress;
Uncle Billy never seemed to notified the ex-Senator a-tall. Oh
yes, they told Uncle Billy the same thing you jest said: how it
wouldn't hurt Clarence none in the long run; they even used
your same words about the campaign tactics of the dogs, only a
little stronger. But Uncle Billy said No, that Clarence Snopes
wasn't going to run for nothing in Beat Two.

" 'But he ain't running in jest Beat Two," they said. 'He ain't
even running in jest Yoknapatawpha County now. He's running
in a whole one-eighth of the state of Missippi.' " And Uncle
Billy said:

" 'Durn the whole hundred eighths of Missippi and Yoknapatawpha County too. I ain't going to have Beat Two and
Frenchman's Bend represented nowhere by nobody that ere a
son-a-bitching dog that happens by can't tell from a fence post.' "

His uncle was looking at Ratliff. He had been looking at
Ratliff for some time. "So this anonymous meddler you speak
of not only knew the twin nephews and that dog thicket, he
knew old Will Varner too."

"It looks like it," Ratliff said.

"So it worked," his uncle said.

"It looks like it," Ratliff said.

Both he and his uncle looked at Ratliff sitting neat and easy,
blinking, bland and inscrutable in one of the neat blue shirts

he made himself, which he never wore a tie with though Charles
knew he had two at home he had paid Allanovna seventy-five
dollars apiece for that time his uncle and Ratliff went to New
York ten years ago to see Linda Snopes married, which Ratliff
had never had on. "O Cincinnatus," his uncle said.

"What?" Ratliff said.

"Nothing," his uncle said. "I was just wondering who it was
that told those twin boys about that dog thicket."

"Why, Colonel Devries, I reckon," Ratliff said. "A soldier in
the war with all them medals, after three years of practice on
Germans and I-talians and Japanese, likely it wasn't nothing to
him to think up a little political strategy too."

"They were mere death worshippers and simple pre-absolved
congenital sadists," his uncle said. "This was a born bred and
trained American professional ward-level politician."

"Maybe ain't neither of them so bad, providing a man jest
keeps his eyes open and uses what he has, the best he knows,"
Ratliff said. Then he said, "Well," and rose, lean and easy,
perfectly bland, perfectly inscrutable, saying to Charles now:
"You mind that big oat field in the bend below Uncle Billy's
pasture, Major? It stayed full of geese all last winter they say.
Why don't you come out when the season opens and shoot a
few of them? I reckon Uncle Billy will let us."

"Much obliged," Charles said.

"It's a trade then," Ratliff said. "Good-day, gentlemen."
Then Ratliff was gone. Now Charles was looking at his uncle,
whereupon his uncle drew a sheet of paper to him and began to
write on it, not fast: just extremely preoccupied, absorbed.

"So, quote," Charles said, "it will have to be you, the young
people unquote. I believe that's about how it went, wasn't it?—
that summer back in '37 when us moralists were even having
to try to beat Roosevelt himself in order to get to Clarence
Snopes?"

"Good-day, Charles," his uncle said.

"Because quote it won't be us," Charles said. "We are too
old, too tired, have lost the capacity to believe in ourselves—"

"Damn it," his uncle said, "I said good-day."

"Yes sir," Charles said. "In just a moment. Because quote the
United States, America: the greatest country in the world if we

can just keep on affording it unquote. Only, let 'afford' read
'depend on God'. Because He saved you this time, using V. K.
Ratliff of course as His instrument. Only next time Ratliff may
be off somewhere selling somebody a sewing machine or a radio"
—That's right, Ratliff now had a radio agency too, the radio
riding inside the same little imitation house on the back of his
pickup truck that the demonstrator sewing machine rode in;
two years more and the miniature house would have a miniature
TV stalk on top of it—"and God may not be able to put His
hand on him in time. So what you need is to learn how to trust
in God without depending on Him. In fact, we need to fix things
so He can depend on us for a while. Then He won't need to
waste Himself being everywhere at once." Now his uncle looked
up at him and suddenly Charles thought *Oh yes, I liked Father
too all right but Father just talked to me while Uncle Gavin listened to
me, no matter how foolish what I was saying finally began to sound even to
me, listening to me until I had finished, then saying,* "Well, I don't know
whether it will hold together or not but I know a good way to find out.
Let's try it." *Not* YOU *try it but* US *try it.*

"Yes," his uncle said. "So do I."

FOURTEEN

THOUGH by the time Ratliff eliminated Clarence back into private life in Frenchman's Bend, there had already been a new Snopes living in Jefferson for going on two years. So Jefferson was merely holding its own in what Charles's uncle would call the Snopes condition or dilemma.

This was a brand-new one, a bachelor named Orestes, called Res. That's right, Orestes. Even Charles's Uncle Gavin didn't know how either. His uncle told him how back in 1943 the town suddenly learned that Flem Snopes now owned what was left of the Compson place. Which wasn't much. The tale was they had sold a good part of it off back in 1909 for the municipal golf course in order to send the oldest son, Quentin, to Harvard, where he committed suicide at the end of his freshman year; and about ten years ago the youngest son, Benjy, the idiot, had set himself and the house both on fire and burned up in it. That is, after Quentin drowned himself at Harvard and Candace's, the sister's, marriage blew up and she disappeared, nobody knew where, and her daughter, Quentin, that nobody knew who her father was, climbed down the rainpipe one night and ran off with a carnival, Jason, the middle one, finally got rid of Benjy too by finally persuading his mother to commit him to the asylum only it didn't stick, Jason's version being that his mother whined and wept until he, Jason, gave up and brought Benjy back home, where sure enough in less than two years Benjy not only burned himself up but completely destroyed the house too.

So Jason took the insurance and borrowed a little more on the now vacant lot and built himself and his mother a new brick bungalow up on the main street to the Square. But the lot was a valuable location; Jefferson had already begun to surround it; in fact the golf links had already moved out to the country club back in 1929, selling the old course back to Jason Compson. Which was not surprising. While he was still in high school Jason had started clerking after school and on Saturdays in Uncle Ike McCaslin's hardware store, which even then was run by a man named Earl Triplett that Uncle Ike got from somewhere, everybody supposed off a deer stand or a Delta fishing lake, since that was where Uncle Ike spent most of his time. For

which reason it was not surprising for the town to assume
presently that Triplett had long since gently eliminated Uncle Ike
from the business even though Uncle Ike still loafed in the store
when he wasn't hunting or fishing and without doubt Triplett
still let him have his rifle and shotgun ammunition and fishing
tackle at cost. Which without doubt the town assumed Jason did
too when Jason had eliminated Triplett in his turn back to his
deer stand or trotline or minnow bucket.

Anyhow, for all practical purposes Jason Compson was now
the McCaslin Hardware Company. So nobody was surprised
when it was learned that Jason had bought back into the original
family holding the portion which his father had sacrificed to
send his older brother to Harvard—a school which Jason held in
contempt for the reason that he held all schools beyond the
tenth grade to be simply refuges for the inept and the timid.
Charles's uncle said that what surprised him was when he went
to the courthouse and looked at the records and saw that,
although Jason had apparently paid cash for the abandoned
golf course, he had not paid off the mortgage on the other part
of the property on which he had raised the money to build his
new bungalow, the interest on which he had paid promptly in
to Flem Snopes's bank ever since, and apparently planned to
continue. This, right up to Pearl Harbour. So that you would
almost believe Jason had a really efficient and faithful spy in the
Japanese Diet. And then in the spring of 1942, another spy just
as efficient and loyal in the U.S. Cabinet too; his uncle said that
to listen to Jason, you would believe he not only had advance
unimpeachable information that an air-training field was to be
located in Jefferson, he had an unimpeachable promise that it
would be located nowhere else save on that old golf links; his
uncle said how back then nobody in Jefferson knew or had
thought much about airfields and they were willing to follow
Jason in that anything open enough to hit golf balls in was open
enough to land airplanes on.

Or anyway the right one believed him. The right one being
Flem Snopes, the president of the bank which held the mortgage
on the other half of Jason's property. His Uncle Gavin said it
must have been like a two-handed stud game when both have
turned up a hole-ace and by mutual consent decreed the other

two aces dead cards. Gavin said that of course nobody knew what really happened. All they knew was what they knew about Jason Compson and Flem Snopes; Gavin said there must have come a time when Flem, who knew all along that he didn't know as much about airfields as Jason did, must have had a terrifying moment when he believed maybe he didn't know as much about money either. So Flem couldn't risk letting Jason draw another card and maybe raise him; Flem had to call.

Or (Gavin said) so Jason thought. That Jason was simply waving that imaginary airfield around the Square to spook Mr Snopes into making the first move. Which was evidently what Snopes did: he called in the note his bank held on Jason's mortgage. All amicable and peaceful of course, which was the way Jason expected it, inviting him (Jason) into that private back room in the bank and saying, "I'm just as sorry about this as you can ever be, Mr Compson. But you can see how it is. With our country fighting for its very life and existence on both sides of the world, it's every man's duty and privilege too to add his little mite to the battle. So my board of directors feel that every possible penny of the bank's resources should go into matters pertaining directly to the war effort."

Which was just what Jason wanted: "Why certainly, Mr Snopes. Any patriotic citizen will agree whole-heartedly with you. Especially when there is a direct war effort right here in Jefferson, like this airfield I understand they have practically let the contract for, just as soon as the title to the land is cleared:" naming his price for the ex-golf course, out of which sum naturally the mortgage note would be paid. Or, if Mr Snopes and his directors preferred, he, Jason, would name a lump sum for the entire Compson property, including the mortgage, and so leave the bank's directors or some patriotic civic body representing the town itself to deal with the government for the airfield; Jason reserving only the right to hope that the finished flying field might be christened Compson Field as a monument not to him, Jason, but to the hope that his family had had a place in the history of Jefferson at least not to be ashamed of, including as it did one governor and one brigadier-general, whether it was worth commemorating or not. Because Charles's uncle said that Jason was shrewd too in his way, enough to speculate that the

man who had spent as much as Snopes had to have his name on a
marble monument over the grave of his unfaithful wife, might
spend some more to have an airfield named for him too.

Or so Jason thought. Because in January '43 Jefferson learned
that Mr Snopes—not the bank: Mr Private Individual Snopes
—now owned the Compson place. And now his Uncle Gavin
said how Jason exposed his hand a little from triumph. But then,
who could really blame him since until now nobody but the
Italian marble syndicate had ever managed to sell Flem Snopes
anything as amorphous as prestige. And what the Italians had
sold him was respectability, which was not a luxury but a
necessity: referring (Jason did) to his old home property as
Snopes Field, even (Charles's uncle said) waylaying, ambushing
Mr Snopes himself now and then on the street when there was
an audience, to ask about the progress of the project; this after
even the ones who didn't know what an airfield really was, had
realised there would not be one here since the government had
already designated the flatter prairie land to the east near
Columbus, and the perfectly flat Delta land to the west near
Greenville, as the only acceptable terrain for flight training.
Because then Jason began to commiserate with Mr Snopes in
reverse, by delivering long public tirades on the government's
stupidity; that Mr Snopes in fact was ahead of his time but that
inevitably, in the course of time as the war continued and we all
had to tighten our belts still further, the Snopes concept of a
flying field composed of hills would be recognised as the only
practical one and would become known throughout the world
as the Snopes Airport Plan, since under it runways that used to
have to be a mile long could be condensed into half that distance,
since by simply bulldozing away the hill beneath it both sides of
the runway could be used for each takeoff and landing, like a
fly on a playing card wedged in a crack.

Or maybe Jason was whistling in the dark, Gavin said, saying
No in terror to terrified realisation, already too late. Because
Jason was shrewd in his way, having had to practise shrewdness
pretty well to have got where he now was without any outside
help and not much of a stake either. That maybe as soon as he
signed the deed and before he even cashed the cheque, it may have
occurred to him that Flem Snopes had practised shrewdness

pretty well too, to be president of a bank now from even less of a stake than he, Jason, who at least had had a house and some land where Flem's had been only a wife. That Jason may have divined, as through some prescience bequeathed him by their mutual master, the Devil, that Flem Snopes didn't want and didn't intend to have a flying field on that property. That it was only Jason Compson who assumed that that by-product of war would go on forever which condemned and compelled real estate to the production and expension of airplanes and tanks and cannon, but that Flem Snopes knew better. Flem Snopes knew that the airplanes and tanks and guns were self-consuming in their own nihilism and inherent obsolescence, and that the true by-product of the war which was self-perpetuating and -compounding and would prevail and continue to self-compound into perpetuity, was the children, the birth rate, the space on which to build walls to house it from weather and temperature and contain its accumulating junk.

Too late. Because now Snopes owned it and all he had to do was just to sit still and wait while the war wore itself out. Since whether America, Jefferson, won it or lost it wouldn't matter; in either case population would compound and government or somebody would have to house it, and the houses would have to stand on something somewhere—a plot of land extending a quarter of a mile in both directions except for a little holding in one corner owned by a crotchety old man named Meadowfill, whom Flem Snopes would take care of in ten or fifteen minutes as soon as he got around to needing it, which even before Pearl Harbour had already begun to be by-passed and surrounded and enclosed by the town. So what Jason did next didn't surprise anyone; Charles's uncle said the only surprising thing was why Jason chose him, Gavin Stevens, to try to bribe either to find a flaw in the title he had conveyed to Mr Snopes; or if he, Stevens, couldn't find one, to invent one into it. His uncle said Jason answered that one himself: "Hell, ain't you supposed to be the best-educated lawyer in this section? Not only Harvard but that German place too?"

"That is, if Harvard can't trick your property back from Flem Snopes, Heidelberg should," his uncle said. "Get out of here, Jason."

"That's right," Jason said. "You can afford virtue, now that you have married money, can't you?"

"I said get out of here, Jason," his uncle said.

"Okay, okay," Jason said. "I can probably find a lawyer somewhere that ain't got enough money in Flem Snopes's bank to be afraid of him."

Except that Jason Compson shouldn't have needed anybody to tell him that Flem Snopes wasn't going to buy a title from anybody capable of having a flaw in it, or anything else in it to make it vulnerable. But Jason continued to try; Charles's uncle told him about it: Jason going about the business of trying to find some way, any way to overturn or even just shake Snopes's title, with a kind of coldly seething indefatigable outrage like that of a revivalist who finds that another preacher has stepped in behind his back and converted the client or patient he had been working on all summer, or a liar or a thief who has been tricked or robbed by another liar or thief. But he failed each time: Snopes's title to the entire old Compson place stood, so that even Jason gave up at last; and that same week the same Wat Snopes who had transformed the old De Spain house into Flem's antebellum mansion twenty years ago, came in again and converted the Compson carriage house (it was detached from the main house so Benjy had failed to burn it) into a small two-storey residence, and a month later the new Jefferson Snopes, Orestes, was living in it. And not merely as Flem Snopes's agent in actual occupation against whatever machinations Jason might still discover or invent. Because by summer Res had fenced up the adjacent ground into lots and was now engaged in the business of buying and selling scrubby cattle and hogs. Also, by that time he was engaged in an active kind of guerrilla feud with old man Meadowfill, whose orchard boundary was Res Snopes's hog-lot fence.

Even before the war old Meadowfill had a reputation in Jefferson: he was so mean as to be solvent and retired even from the savings on a sawmill. He had been active as a mill owner and timber dealer for a year or so after he bought his little corner of the Compson place and built his little unwired un-plumbing-ed house, until he sold his mill and retired into the house with his grey drudge of a wife and their one child; where, since it was obvious to anyone that a man retiring still alive and with all his limbs from a sawmill could not possibly possess one extra dollar for anyone to borrow or sell him anything for, he could devote his full time to gaining and holding the top name for curmudgeonry in all Jefferson and probably all Yoknapatawpha County too.

Charles remembered the daughter—a quiet modest mousy girl nobody even looked at twice until suddenly in 1942 she graduated not only valedictorian of her high school class but with the highest grades ever made in it, plus a five-hundred-dollar scholarship offered by the president of the Bank of Jefferson (not Snopes's bank: the other one) as a memorial to his only son, a navy pilot who had been killed in one of the first Pacific battles. She refused the scholarship. She went to Mr Holland and told him she had already taken a job with the telephone company and wouldn't need the scholarship but instead she wanted to borrow five hundred dollars from the bank against her future salary, and, pressed, finally divulged the reason for it: to put a bathroom in her home; how once a week, on Saturday night, winter and summer, the mother would heat water on the kitchen stove and fill a round galvanised washtub in the middle of the floor, in which single filling all three of them bathed in turn: the father, then the child, then last of all the mother: at which point Mr Holland himself took over, had the bathroom installed despite old Meadowfill's outraged fury (he didn't intend to have his house meddled with at all by outsiders and strangers but if it was he wanted the cash money instead) and gave Essie a job for life in his bank.

Whereupon, now that the only child was not only secure but was actually contributing to the family budget, old Meadowfill soared to heights of outrageousness of which even he hadn't dreamed. Up to this time he had done the grocery shopping himself, walking to town each morning with an empty jute feed sack, to haggle in the small dingy back- and side-street stores which catered mostly to Negroes, for wilted and damaged leftovers of food which even Negroes would have scorned. The rest of the day he would spend, not lurking exactly but certainly in wait, ambushed, about his yard to shout and curse at the stray dogs which crossed his unfenced property, and the small boys

who had a game of raiding the few sorry untended fruit trees
which he called his orchard. Now he stopped that. He waited
exactly one year, as though to be really sure Essie had her job
for good. Then on the morning following the death of a paralytic
old lady neighbour, he went and bought from the family the
wheel chair she had inhabited for years, not even waiting until
the funeral had left the house, and pushed the chair home along
the street for his last appearance on it, and retired into the chair.
Not completely at first. Although Charles's uncle said that Essie
now did the daily shopping, Meadowfill could still be seen in
the yard, still snarling and cursing at the small boys or throwing
rocks (he kept a small pile handy, like the cannon balls of a
war memorial) at the stray dogs. But he never left his own
premises any more and presently he seemed to have retired
permanently into the wheel chair, sitting in it like it was a
rocking chair in a window which looked out over the vegetable
patch he no longer worked at all now, and the scraggy fruit trees
he had always been either too stingy or too perverse to spray and
tend enough to produce even an edible crop, let alone a saleable
one.

Then Flem Snopes let Jason Compson overreach himself out
of his ancestral acres, and Res Snopes built a hog lot along the
boundary of old Meadowfill's orchard and made a new man of
old Meadowfill. Because the trespassing of little boys merely
broke a limb now and then, and stray dogs merely dug up flower
beds if he had had flower beds. But one rooting hog could foul and
sour and make sterile the very dirt itself. So now Meadowfill
had a reason for staying alive. He even abandoned the wheel
chair temporarily, it would have been in his way now, spending
all day while Res and a hired Negro built the wire fence along
his boundary, watching the digging of every post hole and the
setting and tamping of the post, grasping the post in both hands
to shake and test it, on the verge of apoplexy, a little mad by this
time, shouting at Snopes and his helper as they stretched the
wire: "Tighter! Tighter! Hell fire, what do you figger you're
doing? hanging a hammock?" until Snopes—a lean gangling
man with a cast in one sardonic eye—would say,

"Now, Mr Meadowfill, don't you worry a-tall. Before I
would leave a old broke-down wheel-chair gentleman like you

to have to climb this fence by hand, I aim to put slip bars in it that you could even get down and crawl under when you don't feel like opening them," with Meadowfill almost past speech now, saying,

"If ara one of them hogs—if jest ara durn one of them hogs—" and Snopes:

"Then all you got to do is jest ketch it and shut it up in your kitchen or bedroom or any other handy place and the pound law will make me pay you a dollar for it. In fact, that might even be good easy work for a retired wheel-chair old gentleman—" By which time Meadowfill would be in such a state that Snopes would call toward the kitchen, from the window or door of which by this time the grey wife would be watching or anyway hovering: "Maybe you better come and git him away from here."

Which she would do—until the next day. But at last the fence was finished. Or at least Snopes was no longer where Meadowfill could curse at him: only the hogs rooting and rubbing along the new fence which did hold them, or anyway so far. But only so far, only up to the moment it got too dark to see the orchard last night. So now he had something to stay alive for, to get up in the morning for, hurry out of bed and across to the window as soon as darkness thinned, to see if perhaps darkness itself hadn't betrayed him in which he couldn't have seen a hog in his orchard even if he had been able to stay awake twenty-four hours a day watching for it; to get into his chair and wheel himself across to the window and see his orchard for one more night anyway unravished; for one more night at least he had been spared. Then to begrudge the very time he would have to spend at table eating, since this would leave the orchard unguarded, unwatched of course he meant. Because, as Charles's uncle said, Meadowfill wasn't worrying at all about what he would do next when he did look out the window and actually see a hog on his property—an old bastard who, as Charles himself remembered, had already alienated all his neighbours before he committed himself to invalidism and the wheel chair, so that not one of them would have raised a hand to eject the hog for him or do anything else for him except maybe hide the body if and when his grey drab of a wife did what she should have done years ago: murdered him some night. Meadowfill hadn't thought about

what to do with the hog at all. He didn't need to. He was happy,
for the first time in his life probably, Charles's Uncle Gavin said:
that you are happy when your life is filled, and any life is filled
when it is so busy living from moment to moment that it has no
time over to remember yesterday or dread tomorrow. Which of
course couldn't last, his uncle said. That in time Meadowfill
would reach the point where if he didn't look out that window
some morning and see a hog in his orchard, he would die of
simply hope unbearably deferred; and if he did some morning
look out and see one, he would surely die because he would have
nothing else left.

The atom bomb saved him. Charles meant that at last the
Japs quit too and now the troops could come home from all
directions, back to the women they had begun to marry before
the echo of the first Pearl Harbour bomb had died away, and
had been marrying ever since whenever they could get two days'
leave, coming back home now either to already going families or
to marry the rest of the women they hadn't got around to yet,
the blood money already in the hands of the government housing
loan (as his Uncle Gavin put it: "The hero who a year ago was
rushing hand grenades and Garand clips up to front-line foxholes,
is now rushing baskets of soiled didies out of side- and back-street
Veterans Administration tenements.") and now Jason Compson
was undergoing an anguish which he probably believed not only
no human should suffer, but no human could really bear.
Because when Charles reached home in September of '45,
Jason's old lost patrimony was already being chopped up into a
subdivision of standardised Veterans' Housing matchboxes;
within the week Ratliff came to the office and told him and his
uncle the official name of the subdivision: Eula Acres. Not
Jason's old triumphant jeering gibe of Snopes Field, Snopes's
Demolitional Jump-off, but Eula Acres, Eula's Uxorious Nest-
place. And Charles didn't know whether old Flem Snopes had
named it that himself or not but he would remember his uncle's
face while Ratliff was telling them. But even without that he,
Charles, would still prefer to believe it was not really Flem but
his builder and (the town assumed) partner Wat Snopes who
thought of it, maybe because Charles still wanted to believe
that there are some things, at least one thing, that even Flem

Snopes wouldn't do, even if the real reason was that Flem himself never thought of naming it anything because to him it couldn't matter whether it had a name or not. By Christmas it was already dotted over with small brightly painted pristinely new hutches as identical (and about as permanent) as squares of gingerbread or teacakes, the ex-soldier or -sailor or -marine with his ruptured duck pushing the perambulator with one hand and carrying the second (or third) infant in the other arm, waiting to get inside almost before the last painter could gather up his dropcloth. And by New Year's a new arterial highway had been decreed and surveyed which would run the whole length of Mr Snopes's subdivision, including the corner which old Meadowfill owned; whereupon there opened before Meadowfill a prospect of excitement and entertainment beside which the mere depredations of a hog would have been as trivial as the trespass of a frog or a passing bird. Because now one of the big oil companies wanted to buy the corner where Meadowfill's lot and the old Compson (now Snopes) place joined—that is, a strip of Meadowfill's orchard, with a contiguous strip of Res Snopes's hog lot—to build a filling station on.

Because old Meadowfill didn't even own thirteen feet of the strip of his land which the oil company wanted. In fact, as the town knew, the title to none of his land vested in him. During the early second Roosevelt days he had naturally been among the first to apply for relief, learning to his outraged and incredulous amazement that a finicking and bureaucratic federal government declined absolutely and categorically to let him be a pauper and a property owner at the same time. So he came to Gavin, choosing him from among the other Jefferson lawyers for the simple reason that he, Meadowfill, knew that in five minutes he would have Stevens so mad that very likely Stevens would refuse to accept any fee at all for drawing the deed transferring all his property to his nine-year-old (this was 1934) daughter. He was wrong only in his estimate of the time, since it required only two minutes for Stevens to reach the boil which carried him into the chancery clerk's vault, where he discovered that the deed which Jason Compson's father had executed to Meadowfill read "South to the road known as the Freedom Springs Road, thence East along said Road . . ." The Freedom Springs road being, by the time Meadowfill bought his corner, an eroded thicket-grown ditch ten feet deep with only a footpath in it: as ponderable and inescapable a geographical condition as the Grand Canyon, since this was before the era when the bulldozer and the dragline would not only alter but efface geography. Which was thirteen feet short of the actual survey-line boundary which Mohataha, the Chickasaw matriarch, had granted to Quentin Compson in 1821, and Charles's uncle said his first impulse was the ethical one to tell old Meadowfill how he actually owned thirteen feet more of the surface of the earth than he thought he did, provided he did something about it before somebody else did. But if he, Stevens, did that, he would be ethically bound to accept Meadowfill's ten dollars for the title search, so he decided to let one ethic cancel the other and allow simple justice to prevail.

That was the situation when the survey line for the new highway was run to follow the old Chickasaw line, and Meadowfill discovered that his property only extended to the ditch which was thirteen feet short of it. But rage was a mild term for his condition when the oil company approached him to buy his part of the corner and he found that his mortal enemy, the hog-raising Snopes, owned the thirteen feet without a clear title to which the oil company would buy none of his, Meadowfill's, ground. There was rage in it too of course, since rage had been Meadowfill's normal condition for a year now. But now it was triumph too. More: it was vindication, revenge. Revenge on the Compsons who had uttered a false deed to him, allowing him to buy in good faith. Revenge on the community which had badgered him for years with small boys and stray dogs, by holding up a new taxpaying industry (if he could, by stopping the new highway itself). Revenge on the man who for a year now had ruined his sleep and his digestion too by the constant threat of that hog lot. Because he simply declined to sell any part of his property, under any conditions, to anyone: which, since his was in front of Snopes's, except for the thirteen-foot strip, would cut the oil company off from its proposed corner station as effectively as a toll gate, as a result of which the oil company declined to buy any part of Snopes's.

Of course, as the town knew, Snopes (Charles meant of course

Res Snopes) had already approached Essie Meadowfill, in whose
name the deed lay, who answered, as the town knew too: "You'll
have to see papa." Because Snopes was under a really impossible
handicap: his hog lot had forever interdicted him from
approaching old Meadowfill in person, of having any sort of
even momentary civilised contact with him. In fact, Snopes was
under two insurmountable handicaps: the second one being the
idea, illusion, dream that mere money could move a man who
for years now had become so accustomed to not having or
wanting one extra dollar, that the notion of a thousand could
not even tempt him. So Snopes misread his man. But he didn't
quit trying. (That's right. A stranger might have wondered
what Flem Snopes was doing all this time, who owned the land
in the first place. But they in the town were not strangers.) He
went to the oil company's purchasing agent and said, "Tell
him if he'll sign his deed, I'll give him ten percent of what you
pay me for them thirteen feet." Then he said, "All right. Fifty
percent then. Half of it." Then he said, "All right. How much
will he take?" Then he said—and according to the oil company
man, bland and affable and accommodating was no description
for his voice: "All right. A good citizen can't stand in the way of
progress, even if it does cost him money. Tell him if he will sign
he can have them thirteen feet."

This time apparently Meadowfill didn't even bother to say
No, sitting in his wheel chair at the window where he could
look out upon the land which he wouldn't sell and the adjoining
land which its owner couldn't sell because of him. So in a way,
Snopes had a certain amount of local sympathy in his next
move, which he made shortly before something happened to
Essie Meadowfill which revealed her to be, underneath anyway,
anything but mousy; and although demure might still be one
word for her, the other wasn't quietness but determination.

One morning when Meadowfill wheeled his chair from the
breakfast table to the window and looked out, he saw what he
had been waiting to see for over a year now: a loose hog rooting
among the worthless peaches beneath his worthless and untended
trees; and even as he sat bellowing for Mrs Meadowfill, Snopes
himself crossed the yard with an ear of corn and a loop of rope
and snared the hog by one foot and half-drove half-led it back

across the yard and out of sight, old Meadowfill leaning from the chair into the open window, bellowing curses at both of them even after they had disappeared.

The next morning he was already seated at the window when he actually saw the hog come at a steady trot up the lane and into his orchard; he was still leaning in the open window bellow-ing and cursing when the drab wife emerged from the house, clutching a shawl about her head, and hurried up the lane to knock at Snopes's locked front door until Meadowfill's bellowing, which had never stopped, drew her back home. By that time most of the neighbours were there watching what followed: the old man still bellowing curses from the wheel chair in the window while his wife tried single-handed to drive the hog out of the unfenced yard, when Snopes himself appeared (from where everybody knew now he had been concealed watching), innocent, apologetic and amazed, with his ear of corn and his looped plowline, and caught the hog and removed it.

Next, Meadowfill had the rifle—an aged, battered single-shot ·22. That is, it looked second-hand simply by being in his possession, though nobody knew when he had left the wheel chair and the window (not to mention the hog) long enough to have hunted down the small boy owner and haggled or browbeat him out of it; the town simply could not imagine him ever having been a boy passionate and proud to own a single-shot ·22 and to have kept it all these long years as a memento of that pure and innocent time. But he had it, cartridges too—not solid bullets but loaded with tiny shot such as naturalists use: incapable of killing the hog at all and even of hurting it much at this distance. In fact, Charles's uncle said Meadowfill didn't even really want to drive the hog away: he simply wanted to shoot it every day as other people play croquet or bingo.

He would rush straight from the breakfast table, to crouch in his wheeled ambush at the window until the hog appeared. Then (he would have to rise from the chair to do this) he would stand up and slowly and quietly raise the window sash and the screen (he kept the grooves of both greased for speed and silence, and had equipped both of them with handles at the bottom so that he could raise either one with a single jerk) and deliver the shot, the hog giving its convulsive start and leap, until, forgetting, it would settle down again and receive the next shot, until at last its dim processes would connect the sting with the report and after the next shot it would go home, to return no more until tomorrow morning. Until finally it even connected the scattered peaches themselves with the general inimicality and for a whole week it didn't return at all; then the neighbourhood legend rose that Meadowfill had contracted with the boy who delivered the Memphis and Jackson papers (he didn't take a paper himself, not being interested in any news which cost a dollar a month) to scavenge the neighbourhood garbage cans and bait his orchard at night.

Now the town wondered more than ever just exactly what Snopes could be up to. That is, Snopes would naturally be expected to keep the hog at home after the first time old Meadowfill shot it. Or even sell it, which was Snopes's profession or trade, though probably no one would give the full market price per pound for a hog containing fourteen or fifteen months of Number Ten lead shot. Until finally Charles's uncle said they divined Snopes's intention: his hope that someday, by either error or mistake or maybe simple rage, swept beyond all check of morality or fear of consequences by his vice like a drunkard or gambler, Meadowfill would put a solid bullet in the gun; whereupon Snopes would not merely sue him for killing the hog, he would invoke the town ordinance against firing guns inside the city limits, and between the two of them somehow blackmail Meadowfill into making his, Snopes's, lot available to the oil company. Then the thing happened to Essie Meadowfill.

It was a Marine corporal. The town never did know how or where Essie managed to meet him. She had never been anywhere except occasionally for the day in Memphis, like everybody in north Mississippi went at least once a year. She had never missed a day from the bank except her summer vacations, which as far as anybody knew, she spent carrying her share of the burden of the wheel chair's occupation. Yet she met him, maybe through a lovelorn correspondence agency. Anyway, still carrying the parcels of the day's marketing, she was waiting at the station when the Memphis bus came in and he got out of it, whom Jefferson had never seen before, he carrying the grocery bag now along the street where Essie was now an hour

late (people used to set their watches by her passing). And the
town realised that "mousy" had been the wrong word for her
for years evidently since obviously no girl deserving the word
"mousy" could have bloomed that much, got that round and
tender and girl-looking just in the brief time since the bus came
up. And "quiet" was going to be the wrong word too; she was
going to need the determination whether her Marine knew it
yet or not, the two of them walking into the house and up to the
wheel chair, into the point-blank range of that rage compared to
which the cursing of small boys and throwing rocks at dogs and
even shooting live ammunition at Snopes's hog was mere reflex
hysteria, since this trespasser threatened the very system of
peonage by which Meadowfill lived, and saying, "Papa, this is
McKinley Smith. We're going to be married." Then walking
back out to the street with him five minutes later and there, in
full view of whoever wanted to look, kissing him—maybe not
the first time she ever kissed him but probably the first time she
ever kissed anyone without bothering (more, caring) whether or
not it was a sin. And evidently McKinley had some determination too: son of an east Texas tenant farmer, who probably had
barely heard of Mississippi until he met Essie wherever and
however that was; who, once he realised that, because of the
wheel chair and the grey mother, Essie was not going to cut
away from her family and marry him regardless, should have
given up and gone back to Texas by the next bus.

Or maybe what they had was a single determination held in
collaboration, like they seemed to own everything else in
common. They were indeed doomed and fated, whether they
were star-crossed too or not. Because they even acted alike. It
was obvious at once that he had cast his lot for keeps in Jefferson.
Since for some time now (this was January 1946, Charles was
home now and saw the rest of it himself) the United States had
been full of ex-G.I.s going to school whether they were fitted
for it or not or even really wanted to go, the obvious thing
would be for him to enter the vocational school which had just
been added to the Jefferson Academy, where at government
expense he could hold her hand at least once every day while
they waited for simple meanness finally to kill off old Meadowfill.
But Essie's Marine dismissed higher education as immediately

and firmly as Essie had, and for the same reason. He explained it: "I was a soldier for two years. The only thing I learned in that time was, the only place you can be safe in is a private hole, preferably with a iron lid you can pull down on top of you. I aim to own me a hole. Only I ain't a soldier now and so I can pick where I want it, and even make it comfortable. I'm going to build a house."

He bought a small lot. In Eula Acres of course. And Essie selected it of course. It was not even very far from where she had lived most of her life; in fact, after the house began to go up, Meadowfill (he had to unless he gave the hog up and went back to bed) could sit right there in his window and watch every plank of its daily advancement: a constant reminder and warning that he dared not make the mistake of dying. Which at least was a valid reason for sitting in the wheel chair at the window, since he no longer had the hog. It anyway had given up—or anyway for the time being. Or Snopes had given up—for the time being. The hog had made its last sortie about the same day that Essie brought her Marine to the house for that first interview, and had not appeared in the orchard since. Snopes still owned it, or plenty of others (by the wind from that direction), or—since that was his business—he could have replaced it whenever he decided the time was right again. But for now at least he had desisted, patched his fence or (as the neighbours believed) simply stopped leaving the gate unfastened on what he considered strategic days. So now all old Meadowfill had to watch was the house.

McKinley built it himself, doing all the rough heavy work, with one professional carpenter to mark off the planks for him to saw, with the seething old man ambushed in the wheel chair behind the window without even the hog any more to vent his rage on. Obviously, as well as from habit, Meadowfill would have to keep the loaded rifle at hand. He could have no way whatever of knowing the hog would not come back; and now the town began to speculate on just how long it would be, how much he would be able to stand, before he fired the rifle at one of them—McKinley or the carpenter. Presently it would have to be the carpenter unless Meadowfill took to jack-lighting, because one day (it was spring now) McKinley had a mule too and the town learned that he had rented a small piece of land two miles from town and was making a cotton crop on it. The house was about finished now, down to the millwork and trim which only the expert carpenter could do, so McKinley would depart on the mule each morning at sunrise, to be gone until nightfall. Which was when old Meadowfill probably touched the absolute of rage and impotence: McKinley might yet have been harried or frightened into selling his unfinished house and lot at any moment, possibly even for a profit. But no man in his senses would buy a cotton crop that hadn't even sprouted yet. Nothing could help him now but death—his own or McKinley's.

Then the hog came back. It simply reappeared; probably one morning Meadowfill wheeled himself from the breakfast table to the window, expecting to face nothing save one more day of static outrage, when there was the hog again, rooting for the ghosts of last year's peaches as though it had never been away. In fact, maybe that's what Meadowfill wanted to believe at that moment: that the hog had never been away at all and so all that had happened since to outrage him had been only a dream, and even the dream to be exorcised away by the next shot he would deliver. Which was immediately; evidently he had kept the loaded rifle at his hand all the time; some of the neighbours said they heard the vicious juvenile spat while they were still in bed.

The sound of it had spread over the rest of town by noon, though Charles's Uncle Gavin was one of the few who actually felt the repercussion. He was just leaving the office to go home to dinner when he heard the feet on the stairs. Then Res Snopes entered, the five-dollar bill already in his hand. He laid it on the desk and said, "Good-morning, Lawyer. I won't keep you long. I jest want a little advice—about five dollars' worth." Stevens didn't touch the bill yet: just looking from it to its owner who had never been known to pay five dollars for anything he didn't already know he could sell for at least twenty-five cents profit: "It's that hawg of mine that old gentleman—Mister Meadowfill—likes to shoot with them little bird shot."

"I heard about it," his uncle said. "Just what do you want for your five dollars?" Charles uncle told it: Snopes standing beyond the desk, not secret: just polite and inscrutable. "For telling you what you already know? that once you sue him for injuring your hog, he will invoke the law against livestock running loose inside the city limits? For telling you what you already knew over a year ago when he fired the first shot at it? Either fix the fence or get rid of the hog."

"It costs a right smart to feed a hawg," Snopes said. "As for getting rid of it, that old gentleman has done shot it so much now, I doubt wouldn't nobody buy it."

"Then eat it," Stevens said.

"A whole hawg, for jest one man? Let alone with going on two years of bird shot in it?"

"Then give it away," Stevens said, and tried to stop himself but it was too late.

"That's your legal lawyer's advice then," Snopes said. "Give the hawg away. Much obliged," he said, already turning.

"Here," Stevens said, "wait;" holding out the bill.

"I come to you for legal lawyer's advice," Snopes said. "You give it to me: give the hawg away. I owe the fee for it. If five dollars ain't enough, say so." Then he was gone. Stevens was thinking fast now, not *Why did he choose me?* because that was obvious: he had drawn Essie Meadowfill's deed to the property under dispute; he was the only person in Jefferson outside Meadowfill's family with whom old Meadowfill had had anything resembling human contact in almost twenty years. Nor even *Why did Snopes need to notify any outsider, lawyer or not, that he intended to give that hog away?* Nor even *Why did he lead me into saying the actual words first myself, technically constituting them paid-for legal advice?* Instead, what Stevens thought was *How, by giving that hog away, is he going to compel old Meadowfill to sell that lot?*

His Uncle Gavin always said he was not really interested in truth nor even justice: that all he wanted was just to know, to find out, whether the answer was any of his business or not; and that all means to that end were valid, provided he left neither hostile witnesses nor incriminating evidence. Charles didn't believe him; some of his methods were not only too hard, they took too long; and there are some things you simply do not do even to find out. But his uncle said that Charles was wrong: that curiosity is another of the mistresses whose slaves decline no sacrifice.

The trouble in this case was, his uncle didn't know what he was looking for. He had two methods—inquiry and observation— and three leads—Snopes, the hog and Meadowfill—to discover what he might not recognise in time even when he found it. He couldn't use inquiry, because the only one who might know the answer—Snopes—had already told all he intended for anyone to know. And he couldn't use observation on the hog because, like Snopes, it could move too. Which left only the one immobile: old Meadowfill. So he picked Charles up the next morning and at daylight they were ambushed also in his uncle's parked car where they could see the Meadowfill house and orchard and the lane leading to Snopes's house and, as the other point of the triangle, the little new house which McKinley Smith had almost finished. They sat there for two hours. They watched McKinley depart on his mule for his cotton patch. Then Snopes himself came out of his yard into the lane and went on toward town, the Square. Presently it was time for even Essie Meadowfill to go to work. Then there remained only old Meadowfill ambushed behind his window. Only the hog was missing.

"If that's what we're waiting for," Charles said.

"I agree," his uncle said.

"I mean, to distract the eyes that have probably been watching us for the last two hours long enough for us to get away."

"I didn't want to come either," his uncle said. "But I had to or give that five dollars back."

And the next morning was the same. By then it was too late to quit; they both had too much invested now, not even counting Snopes's five dollars: two days of getting up before dawn, to sit for two hours in the parked car without even a cup of coffee, waiting for what they were not even sure they would recognise when they saw it. It was the third morning; McKinley and his mule had departed on schedule: so regular and normal that he and his uncle didn't even realise they has not seen Snopes yet until Essie Meadowfill herself came out of the house on her way to work. To Charles it was like one of those shocks, starts such as when you find yourself waking up without knowing until then you were asleep; his uncle was already getting out of the car to begin to run when they saw the hog. That is, it was the hog and it was doing exactly what they expected it to do: moving

toward Meadowfill's orchard at that twinkling purposeful
porcine trot. Only it was not where it should have been when it
first became visible. It was going where they expected it to be
going, but it was not coming from where it should have been
coming from. It was coming not from the direction of Snopes's
house but from that of McKinley Smith's. His uncle was already
running, possibly from what Ratliff called his uncle's simple
instinct or affinity for being where something was going to
happen, even if he wasn't always quite on time, hurrying—
Charles too of course—across the street and the little yard and
into the house before old Meadowfill would see the hog through
the window and make the shot.

His uncle didn't knock; they entered running, his uncle
choosing by simple orientation the door beyond which old
Meadowfill would have to be to use that particular window,
and he was there, leaning forward in the wheel chair at the
window, the glass sash of which was already raised though the
screen was still down, the little rifle already half raised in one
hand, the other hand grasping the handle to the screen to jerk it
up. But he—Meadowfill—was just sitting there yet, looking at
the hog. The town had got used to seeing meanness and vindic-
tiveness and rage in his face; they were normal. But this time
there was nothing in his face but gloating. He didn't even turn
his head when Charles and his uncle entered: he just said,
"Come right in; you got a grandstand seat." Now they could
hear him cursing: not hard honest outdoors swearing but the
quiet murmuring indoors obscenity which, Charles thought,
if he ever had used it, his grey hairs should have forgot it now.

Then he began to stand up from the wheel chair and then
Charles saw it too—a smallish lump a little longer than a brick,
wrapped in a piece of gunny sack, bound in a crotch of the
nearest peach tree about twenty feet from the house so that it
pointed at the window, his uncle saying, "Stop! Stop! Don't
raise it!" and even reaching for the screen, but too late; old
Meadowfill, standing now, leaned the rifle beside the window
and put both hands on the handle and jerked the screen up.
Then the light sharp vicious spat of the ·22 cartridge from the
peach tree; his uncle said he was actually looking at the rising
screen when the wire frayed and vanished before the miniature

blast; Charles himself seemed actually to hear the tiny pellets
hiss across old Meadowfill's belly and chest as the old man
half-leaped half-fell backward into the chair which rushed from
under him, leaving him asprawl on the floor, where he lay for a
moment with on his face an expression of incredulous outrage:
not pain, not anguish, fright: just outrage, already reaching for
the rifle as he sat up.

"Somebody shot me!" he said.

"Certainly," his unce said, taking the rifle away from him.
"That hog did. Can you blame it? Just lie still now until we can
see."

"Hog, hell," old Meadowfill said. "It was that blank blank
blank McKinley Smith!"

He wasn't hurt: just burned, blistered, the tiny shot which had
had to penetrate not only his pants and shirt but his winter
underwear too, barely under his skin. But mad as a hornet,
raging, bellowing and cursing and still trying to take the rifle
away from Charles's uncle (Mrs Meadowfill was in the room now,
the shawl already clutched about her head as if some fatalistic
hopeless telepathy communicated to her the instant the hog
crossed their unfenced boundary, like the electric eye that opens
doors) until at last he exhausted himself into what would pass
with him for rationality. Then he told it: how Snopes had told
Essie two days ago that he had given the hog to McKinley as a
housewarming present or maybe even—Snopes hoped—a
wedding gift some day soon, with Charles's uncle saying, "Hold
on a minute. Did Essie say Mr Snopes gave the hog to McKinley,
or did she say Mr Snopes told her he had?"

"What?" Meadowfill said. "What?" Then he just began to
curse again.

"Lie still," Charles's uncle said. "You've been shooting that
hog for over a year now without hurting it so I reckon you can
stand one shot yourself. But we'll have a doctor on your wife's
account."

His uncle had the gun too: a very neat homemade booby
trap: a cheap single-shot ·22 also, sawed-off barrel and stock
and fastened to a board, the whole thing wrapped in the piece
of feed sack and bound in the crotch of the tree, a black strong
small-gauge length of reel-backing running from the trigger

through a series of screw eyes to the sash of the window screen, the muzzle trained at the centre of the window about a foot above the sill.

"If he hadn't stood up before he raised that screen, the charge would have hit him square in the face," Charles said.

"So what?"' his uncle said. "Do you think who put it there cared? Whether it merely frightened and enraged him into rushing at Smith with that rifle"—it had a solid bullet in it this time, the big one: the long rifle; this time old Meadowfill aimed to hurt what he shot—"and compelling Smith to kill him in self-defence, or whether the shot blinded him or killed him right there in his wheel chair and so solved the whole thing? Her father dead and her sweetheart in jail for murdering him, and only Essie to need to deal with?"

"It was pretty smart," Charles said.

"It was worse. It was bad. Nobody would ever have believed anyone except a Pacific veteran would have invented a booby trap, no matter how much he denied it."

"It was still smart," Charles said. "Even Smith will agree."

"Yes," his uncle said. "That's why I wanted you along. You were a soldier too. I may need an interpreter to talk to him."

"I was just a major," Charles said. "I never had enough rank to tell anything to any sergeant, let alone a Marine one."

"He was just a corporal," his uncle said.

"He was still a Marine," Charles said.

Only they didn't go to Smith first; he would be in his cotton patch now anyway. And, Charles told himself, if Snopes had been him, there wouldn't be anybody in Snopes's house either. But there was. Snopes opened the door himself; he was wearing an apron and carrying a frying pan; there was even a fried egg in it. But there wasn't anything in his face at all. "Gentle-men," he said. "Come in."

"No thanks," Charles's uncle said. "It won't take that long. This is yours, I think." There was a table; his uncle laid the sack-wrapped bundle on it and flipped the edge of the sacking, the mutilated rifle sliding across the table. And still there was nothing whatever in Snopes's face or voice:

"That-ere is what you lawyers call debateable, ain't it?"

"Oh yes," Charles's uncle said. "Everybody knows about fingerprints now, just as they do about booby traps."

"Yes," Snopes said. "Likely you ain't making me a present of it."

"That's right," his uncle said. "I'm selling it to you. For a deed to Essie Meadowfill for that strip of your lot the oil company wants to buy, plus that thirteen feet that Mr Meadowfill thought he owned." And now indeed Snopes didn't move, immobile with the cold egg in the frying pan. "That's right," his uncle said. "In that case, I'll see if McKinley Smith wants to buy it."

Snopes looked at his uncle a moment. He was smart; you would have to give him that, Charles thought. "I reckon you would," he said. "Likely that's what I would do myself."

"That's what I thought," his uncle said.

"I reckon I'll have to go and see Cousin Flem," Snopes said.

"I reckon not," his uncle said. "I just came from the bank."

"I reckon I would have done that myself too," Snopes said. "What time will you be in your office?"

And he and his uncle could have met Smith at his house at sundown too. Instead, it was not even noon when Charles and his uncle stood at the fence and watched McKinley and the mule come up the long black shear of turning earth like the immobilised wake of the plough's mould board. Then he was standing across the fence from them, naked from the waist up in his overalls and combat boots. Charles's uncle handed him the deed. "Here," his uncle said.

Smith read it. "This is Essie's."

"Then marry her," his uncle said. "Then you can sell the lot and buy a farm. Ain't that what you both want? Haven't you got a shirt or a jumper here with you? Get it and you can ride back with me; the major here will bring the mule."

"No," Smith said; he was already shoving, actually ramming the deed into his pocket as he turned back to the mule. "I'll bring him in. I'm going home first. I ain't going to marry nobody without a necktie and a shave."

Then they had to wait for the Baptist minister to wash his hands and put on his coat and necktie; Mrs Meadowfill was already wearing the first hat anybody had ever seen on her;

x

it looked a good deal like the first hat anybody ever made. "But papa," Essie said.

"Oh," Charles's uncle said. "You mean that wheel chair. It belongs to me now. It was a legal fee. I'm going to give it to you and McKinley for a christening present as soon as you earn it."

Then it was two days later, in the office.

"You see?" his uncle said. "It's hopeless. Even when you get rid of one Snopes, there's already another one behind you even before you can turn around."

"That's right," Ratliff said serenely. "As soon as you look, you see right away it ain't nothing but jest another Snopes."

FIFTEEN

LINDA KOHL was already home too when Charles got back.
From her war also: the Pascagoula shipyard where she
finally had her way and became a riveter; his Uncle Gavin told
him, a good one. At least her hands, fingernails, showed it:
not bitten, gnawed down, but worn off. And now she had a fine,
a really splendid dramatic white streak in her hair running along
the top of her skull almost like a plume. A collapsed plume; in
fact, maybe that was what it was, he thought: a collapsed plume
lying flat athwart her skull instead of cresting upward first then
back and over; it was the fall of 1945 now and the knight had run
out of tourneys and dragons, the war itself had slain them, used
them up, made them obsolete.

In fact Charles thought how all the domestic American
knights-errant liberal reformers would be out of work now, with
even the little heretofore lost places like Yoknapatawpha County,
Mississippi, fertilised to overflowing not only with ex-soldiers'
blood money but with the two or three or four dollars per hour
which had been forced on the other ex-riveters and -bricklayers
and -machinists like Linda Kohl Snopes, he meant Linda
Snopes Kohl, so fast that they hadn't had time to spend it. Even
the two Finn communists, even the one that still couldn't speak
English, had got rich during the war and had had to become
capitalists and bull-market investors simply because they had
not yet acquired any private place large enough to put that much
money down while they turned their backs on it. And as for the
Negroes, by now they had a newer and better high school
building in Jefferson than the white folks had. Plus an instalment-
plan automobile and radio and refrigerator full of canned beer
down-paid with the blood money which at least drew no colour
line in every unwired unscreened plumbingless cabin: double-
plus the new social-revolution laws which had abolished not
merely hunger and inequality and injustice, but work too by
substituting for it a new self-compounding vocation or profession
for which you would need no schooling at all: the simple production of children. So there was nothing for Linda to tilt
against now in Jefferson. Come to think of it, there was nothing
for her to tilt against anywhere now, since the Russians had

fixed the Germans and even they didn't need her any more. In fact, come to think of it, there was really nothing for her in Jefferson at all any more, now that his Uncle Gavin was married —if she had ever wanted him for herself. Because maybe Ratliff was right and whatever she had ever wanted of him, it wasn't a husband. So in fact you would almost have to wonder why she stayed in Jefferson at all now, with nothing to do all day long but wait, pass the time somehow until night and sleep came, in that Snopes-colonial mausoleum with that old son of a bitch that needed a daughter or anybody else about as much as he needed a spare bow tie or another hat. So maybe everybody was right this time and she wasn't going to stay in Jefferson much longer, after all.

But she was here now, with her nails, his uncle said, not worn down from smithing but scraped down to get them clean (and whether his uncle added it or not: feminine) again, with no more ships to rivet, and that really dramatic white plume collapsed in gallantry across her skull, with all the dragons dead. Only, even blacksmithing hadn't been enough. What he meant was, she wasn't any older. No, that wasn't what he meant not just older. Something had happened to him during the three-plus years between December '41 and April '45 or at least he hoped it had or at least what had seemed suffering and enduring to him at least met the standards of suffering and enduring enough to enrich his spiritual and moral development whether it did anything for the human race or not, and if it had purified his soul it must show on his outside too or at least he hoped it did. But she hadn't changed at all, least of all the white streak in her hair which it seemed that some women did deliberately to themselves. When he finally —All right, finally. So what if he did spend the better part of his first three days at home at least hoping he didn't look like he was hanging around the Square in case she did cross it or enter it. There were towns bigger than Jefferson that didn't have a girl—woman—in it that the second you saw her eight years ago getting out of an airplane you were already wondering what she would look like with her clothes off except that she was too old for you, the wrong type for you, except that that was exactly backward, you were too young for her, the wrong type for her and so only your uncle that you had even spent some of the ten months in the Nazi stalag wondering if he ever got them off before he got married to Aunt Melisandre or maybe even after and if he didn't, what happened, what was wrong. Because his uncle would never tell him himself whether he ever did or not but maybe after three years and a bit he could tell by looking at her, that maybe a woman really couldn't hide that from another man who was . . . call it *simpatico*. Except that when he finally saw her on the street on the third day there was nothing at all, she had not changed at all, except for the white streak which didn't count anyway—the same one that on that day eight years ago when he and his uncle had driven up to the Memphis airport to get her, was at that first look a little too tall and a little too thin for his type so that in that same second he was saying *Well that's one anyway that won't have to take her clothes off on my account* and then almost before he could get it out, something else was already saying *Okay, buster, who suggested she was going to?* and he had been right: not her for him, but rather not him for her: a lot more might still happen to him in his life yet (he hoped), but removing that particular skirt wouldn't be one even if when you got the clothes off the too tall too thin ones sometimes they surprised you. And just as well; evidently his soul or whatever it was had improved some in the three years and a bit; anyway he knew now that if such had been his fate to get this particular one off, what would happen to him might, probably would, have several names but none of them would be surprise.

With no more ships to rivet now, and what was worse: no need any more for ships to rivet. So not just he, Charles, but all the town in time sooner or later would see her—or be told about it by the ones who had—walking, striding, most of the time dressed in what they presumed was the same army-surplus khaki she had probably riveted the ships in, through the back streets and alleys of the town or the highways and lanes and farm roads and even the fields and woods themselves within two or three miles of town, alone, walking not fast so much as just hard, as if she were walking off insomnia or perhaps even a hangover. "Maybe that's what it is," Charles said. Again his uncle looked up, a little impatiently, from the brief.

"What?" he said.

"You said maybe she has insomnia. Maybe it's hangover she's walking off."

"Oh," his uncle said. "All right." He went back to the brief. Charles watched him.

"Why don't you walk with her?" he said.

This time his uncle didn't look up. "Why don't you? Two ex-soldiers, you could talk about war."

"She couldn't hear me. I wouldn't have time to write on a pad while we were walking."

"That's what I mean," his uncle said. "My experience has been that the last thing two ex-soldiers under fifty years old want to talk about is war. You two even can't."

"Oh," he said. His uncle read the brief. "Maybe you're right," he said. His uncle read the brief. "Is it all right with you if I try to lay her?" His uncle didn't move. Then he closed the brief and sat back in the chair.

"Certainly," he said.

"So you think I can't," Charles said.

"I know you can't," his uncle said. He added quickly: "Don't grieve; it's not you. Just despair if you like. It's not anybody."

"So you know why," Charles said.

"Yes," his uncle said.

"But you're not going to tell me."

"I want you to see for yourself. You will probably never have the chance again. You read and hear and see about it in all the books and pictures and music, in Harvard and Heidelberg both. But you are afraid to believe it until you actually see it face to face, because you might be wrong and you couldn't bear that, and be happy. What you can't bear is to doubt it."

"I never got to Heidelberg," Charles said. "All I had was Harvard and Stalag umpty-nine."

"All right," his uncle said. "The high school and the Jefferson Academy then."

Anyway he, Charles, knew the answer now. He said so. "Oh, that. Even little children know all that nowadays. She's frigid."

"Well, that's as good a Freudian term as another to cover chastity or discretion," his uncle said. "Beat it now. I'm busy. Your mother invited me to dinner so I'll see you at noon."

So it was more than that, and his uncle was not going to tell him. And his uncle had used the word "discretion" also to cover something he had not said. Though Charles at least knew what that was because he knew his uncle well enough to know that the discretion applied not to Linda but to him. If he had never been a soldier himself, he would not have bothered, let alone waited, to ask his uncle's leave: he would probably already have waylaid her at some suitable secluded spot in the woods on one of her walks, on the innocent assumption of those who have never been in a war that she, having come through one, had been wondering for days now what in hell was wrong with Jefferson, why he or any other personable male had wasted all this time. Because he knew now why young people rushed so eagerly to war was their belief that it was one endless presanctioned opportunity for unlicensed rapine and pillage; that the tragedy of war was that you brought nothing away from it but only left something valuable there; that you carried into war things which, except for the war, you could have lived out your life in peace with without ever having to know they were inside you.

So it would not be him. He had been a soldier too even if he had brought back no wound to prove it. So if it would take physical assault on her to learn what his uncle said he didn't know existed, he would never know it; he would just have to make one more in the town who believed she was simply walking off one hangover to be ready for the next one, having evidence to go on, or at least a symptom. Which was that once a week, Wednesday or Thursday afternoon (the town could set its watches and calendars by this too), she would be waiting at the wheel of her father's car outside the bank when it closed and her father came out and they would drive up to what Jakeleg Wattman euphemiously called his fishing camp at Wyott's Crossing, and lay in her next week's supply of bootleg whiskey. Not her car: her father's car. She could have owned a covey of automobiles out of that fund his uncle was trustee of from her grandfather, old Will Varner rich out at Frenchman's Bend, or maybe from Varner and her father together as a part of or maybe a result of that old uproar and scandal twenty years ago when her mother had committed suicide and the mother's presumed lover had abandoned the bank and his ancestral home both to her father, not to mention the sculptor she married being a New York Jew and hence (as the town was convinced) rich. And driven it—them—too, even stone deaf, who could have afforded to hire somebody to sit beside her and do nothing else but listen. Only she didn't. Evidently she preferred walking, sweating out the hard way the insomnia or hangover or whatever the desperate price she paid for celibacy—unless of course Lawyer Gavin Stevens had been a slicker and smoother operator for the last eight years than anybody suspected; though even he had a wife now.

And her supply: not her father's. Because the town, the county, knew that too: Snopes himself never drank, never touched it. Yet he would never let his daughter make the trip alone. Some were satisfied with the simple explanation that Wattman, like everybody else nowadays, was making so much money that he would have to leave some of it somewhere, and Snopes, a banker, figured it might as well be in his bank and so he called on Jakeleg once a week exactly as he would and did look in socially on any other merchant or farmer or cotton ginner of the bank's profitable customers or clients. But there were others, among them his Uncle Gavin and his uncle's special crony, the sewing machine agent and rural bucolic grass-roots philosopher and Cincinnatus, V. K. Ratliff, who went a little further: it was for respectability, the look of things: that on those afternoons Snopes was not just a banker, he was a leading citizen and father; and even though his widowed only daughter was pushing forty and had spent the four years of the war working like a man in a military shipyard where unspinsterish things had a way of happening to women who were not even widows, he still wasn't going to let her drive alone fifteen miles to a bootlegger's joint and buy a bottle of whiskey.

Or a case of it; since it was hangover she walked off, she would need, or anyway need to have handy, a fresh bottle every day. So presently even the town would realise it wasn't just hangover since people who can afford a hangover every day don't want to get rid of it, walk it off, even if they had time to. Which left only jealousy and rage; what she walked four or five miles every day to conquer or anyway contain was the sleepless frustrated rage at his Uncle Gavin for having jilted her while she was away riveting ships to save Democracy, to marry Melisandre Harriss

Backus that was as Thackeray says, thinking (Charles) how he
could be glad it wasn't him that got the clothes off since if what
was under them—provided of course his uncle had got them off
—had driven his uncle to marry a widow with two grown
children, one of them already married too, so that his Uncle
Gavin might already have been a grandfather before he even
became a bridegroom.

Then apparently jealousy and frustrated unforgiving rage were
wrong too. Christmas came and went and the rest of that winter
followed it, into spring. His uncle was not only being but even
acting the squire now. No boots and breeks true enough and
although a squire might have looked like one behind a Phi Beta
Kappa key even in Mississippi, he never could under a shock of
premature white hair like a concert pianist or a Hollywood
Cadillac agent. But at least he behaved like one, once each month
and sometimes oftener, sitting at the head of the table out at
Rosa Hill with Charles's new Aunt Melisandre opposite him and
Linda and Charles across from each other while his uncle
interpreted for Linda from the ivory tablet. Or rather, interpreted
for himself into audible English to Charles and his new Aunt Em.
Because Linda didn't talk now any more than she ever had:
just sitting there with that white streak along the top of her head
like a collapsed plume, eating like a man; Charles didn't mean
eating grossly: just soundly, heartily, and looking . . . yes, by
God, that was exactly the word: happy. Happy, satisfied, like
when you have accomplished something, produced, created,
made something: gone to some—maybe a lot—trouble and
expense, stuck your neck out maybe against your own better
judgment; and sure enough, be damned if it didn't work, exactly
as you thought it would, maybe even better than you had dared
hope it would. Something you had wanted for yourself only
you missed it so you began to think it wasn't so, was impossible,
until you made one yourself, maybe when it was too late for you
to want it any more but at least you had proved it could be.

And in the drawing-room afterward also, with coffee and
brandy for the ladies and port and a cigar for Charles though
his uncle still stuck to the cob pipes which anyway used to cost
only a nickel. Still happy, satisfied; and that other thing which
Charles had sensed, recognised: proprietorial. As if Linda

herself had actually invented the whole business: his Uncle
Gavin, his Aunt Melisandre, Rose Hill—the old, once-small
and -simple frame house which old Mr Backus with his Horace
and Catullus and his weak whiskey-and-water would not
recognise now save by its topographical location, transmogrified
by the New Orleans gangster's money as old Snopes had tried
to do to the De Spain house with his Yoknapatawpha County
gangster's money and failed since here the rich and lavish cash
had been spent with taste so that you didn't really see it at all
but merely felt it, breathed it, like warmth or temperature;
with, surrounding it, enclosing it, the sense of the miles of white
panel fences marking the combed and curried acres and the
electric-lighted and -heated stables and tack rooms and grooms'
quarters and the manager's house all in one choral concord in
the background darkness—and then invented him, Charles, to
be presented to at least look at her creation whether he approved
of what she had made or not.

Then the hour to say Thank you and Good-night and drive
back to town through the April or May darkness and escort
Linda home, back to her father's Frenchman's Bend-dreamed
palace, to draw up at the curb, where she would say each time
in the harsh duck voice (he, Charles, thinking each time too
*Which maybe at least wouldn't sound quite so bad in the dark whispering
after you finally got the clothes off* thinking *If of course it had been you*):
"Come in for a drink." Nor enough light in the car for her to
have read the ivory tablet if she had offered it. Because he would
do this each time too: grin, he would hope loud enough, and
shake his head—sometimes there would be moonlight to help—
Linda already opening the door on her side so that Charles
would have to get out fast on his to get around the car in time.
Though no matter how fast that was, she would be already out,
already turning up the walk toward the portico: who perhaps
had left the South too young too long ago to have formed the
Southern female habit-rite of a cavalier's unflagging constancy,
or maybe the simple riveting of ships had cured the old muscles
of the old expedition. Whichever it was, Charles would have to
overtake, in effect outrun her already halfway to the house;
whereupon she would check, almost pause in fact, to glance
back at him, startled—not alarmed: just startled; merely what

Hollywood called a double-take, still not so far dissevered from her Southern heritage but to recall that he, Charles, dared not risk some casual passerby reporting to his uncle that his nephew permitted the female he was seeing home to walk at least forty feet unaccompanied to her front door.

So they would reach that side by side anyway—the vast dim home-made columned loom of her father's dream, nightmare, monstrous hope or terrified placatement, whichever it was, whatever it had been, the cold mausoleum in which old Snopes had immolated that much of his money at least without grace or warmth, Linda stopping again to say, "Come in and have a drink," exactly as though she hadn't said it forty feet back at the car, Charles still with nothing but the grin and the shake of the head as if he had only that moment discovered his ability to do that too. Then her hand, hard and firm like a man's since after all it was a ship riveter's or at least an ex-ship riveter's. Then he would open the door, she would stand for an instant in it in the midst of motion against a faint light in the hall's depth; the door would close again.

Oh yes, it could have had several names but surprise would not have been one of them, thinking about his uncle, the poor dope, if his uncle really had got the clothes off once maybe. Whereupon he thought now maybe his uncle actually had, that once, and couldn't stand it, bear it, and ran, fled back those eighteen or twenty years to Melisandre Backus (that used to be), where he would be safe. So if the word wouldn't be surprise, maybe it wouldn't really have to be grief either: just relief. A little of terror maybe at how close the escape had been, but mainly relief that it had been escape under any condition, on any terms. Because he, Charles, had been too young at the time. He didn't know whether he actually remembered Linda's mother as his uncle and Ratliff obviously did, or not. But he had had to listen to both of them often enough and long enough to know that he surely did know all that they remembered, Ratliff especially; he could almost hear Ratliff saying again: "We was lucky. We not only had Helen of Argos right here in Jefferson, which most towns don't, we even knowed who she was and then we even had our own Paris to save us Argoses by jest wrecking Troy instead. What you want to do is not to own

Helen, but jest own the right and privilege of looking at her.
The worst thing that can happen to you is for her to notice you
enough to stop and look back."

So, assuming that whatever made Helen was transferable
or anyway inheritable, the word would not be grief at all but
simple and perhaps amazed relief; and maybe his uncle's luck
and fate was simply to be cursed with less of fire and heat than
Paris and Manfred de Spain; to simply have taken simple fear
from that first one time (if his uncle really had got them off that
first one time) and fled while he still had life. You know: the
spider lover wise enough with age or cagey enough with experience or maybe just quick enough to spook from sheer timid
instinct, to sense, anticipate, that initial tender caressing probe
of the proboscis or suction tube or whatever it is his gal uses to
empty him of his blood too while all he thinks he is risking is
his semen; and leap, fling himself free, losing of course the semen
and most of the rest of his insides too in the same what he thought
at first was just peaceful orgasm, but at least keeping his husk,
his sac, his life. Or the grape, say, a mature grape, a little on the
oversunned and juiceless side, but at least still intact enough even
if only in sapless hull after the spurting ejaculation of the nymphic
kiss, to retain at least the flattened semblance of a grape. Except
that about then you would have to remember what Ratliff said
that time: "No, she ain't going to marry him. It's going to be
worse than that," and you would wonder what in the world
Helen or her inheritrix could or would want with that emptied
sac or flattened hull, and so what in the hell could Ratliff have
meant? Or anyway thought he meant? Or at least was afraid he
might have meant or mean?

Until it finally occurred to him to do the reasonable and logical
thing that anybody else would have thought about doing at
first: ask Ratliff himself what he meant or thought he meant
or was afraid he meant. So he did. It was summer now, June;
McKinley Smith's cotton was not only up, Essie was pregnant.
The whole town knew it; she had made a public announcement
in the bank one morning as soon as the doors opened and the
first depositors had lined up at the windows; in less than two
months she and McKinley had won old Meadowfill's wheel chair.

"Because this ain't enough," Ratliff said.

"Enough what?" Charles said.

"Enough to keep her busy and satisfied. No ships to rivet, and now she's done run out of coloured folks too for the time being. This here is peace and plenty—the same peace and plenty us old folks like me and your uncle spent four whole years sacrificing sugar and beefsteak and cigarettes all three to keep the young folks like you happy while you was winning it. So much plenty that even the downtrod communist shoe patchers and tinsmiths and Negro children can afford to not need her now. I mean, maybe if she had asked them first they never actively needed her before neither, only they couldn't afford in simple dollars and cents to say so. Now they can." He blinked at Charles. "She has done run out of injustice."

"I didn't know you could do that," Charles said.

"That's right," Ratliff said. "So she will have to think of something, even if she has to invent it."

"All right," Charles said. "Suppose she does. If she was tough enough to stand what we thought up around here, she can certainly stand anything she can invent herself."

"I ain't worried about her," Ratliff said. "She's all right. She's jest dangerous. I'm thinking about your uncle."

"What about him?" Charles said.

"When she finally thinks of something and tells him, he will likely do it," Ratliff said.

SIXTEEN

THEY met that morning in the post office, as they often did by complete uncalculation at morning mail time, she dressed as usual in the clothes she seemed to spend most of her time walking about the adjacent countryside in—the expensive English brogues scuffed and scarred but always neatly polished each morning, with wool stockings or socks beneath worn flannel trousers or a skirt or sometimes what looked like a khaki boiler-suit under a man's stained burberry; this in the fall and winter and spring; in the summer it would be cotton—dress or skirt or trousers, her head with its single white plume bare even in the worst weather. Afterward they would go to the coffee shop in the Holston House and drink coffee but this time instead Stevens took the gold-cornered ivory tablet he had given her eight years ago and wrote:

An appointment   At the office   To see me

"Shouldn't you make an appointment to see lawyers?" she said.

His next speech of course would be: "So it's as a lawyer you need me now." And if they both could have used speech he would have said that, since at the age of fifty-plus talking is no effort. But writing is still an effort at any age, so even a lawyer pauses at the obvious if he has got to use a pen or pencil. So he wrote *Tonight after supper   At your house*

"No," she said.

He wrote *Why*

"Your wife will be jealous. I don't want to hurt Milly."

His next of course would be: "Melisandre, jealous? Of you and me? After all this, all this time?" Which of course was too long to write on a two-by-three-inch ivory tablet. So he had already begun to write *Nonsense* when he stopped and erased it with his thumb. Because she was looking at him, and now he knew too. He wrote *You want her   To be jealous*

"She's your wife," she said. "She loves you. She would have to be jealous." He hadn't erased the tablet yet; he needed only to hold it up before her face until she looked at it again. "Yes," she said. "Being jealous is part of love too. I want you to have all of it too. I want you to have everything. I want you to be happy."

334

"I am happy," he said. He took one of the unopened envelopes just out of his mailbox and wrote on the back of it *I am happy I was given the privilege of meddling with impunity in other people's affairs without really doing any harm by belonging to that avocation whose acolytes have been absolved in advance for holding justice above truth I have been denied the chance to destroy what I loved by touching it Can you tell me now what it is here or shall I come to your house after supper tonight*

"All right," she said. "After supper then."

At first his wife's money was a problem. In fact, if it hadn't been for the greater hysteria of the war, the lesser hysteria of that much sudden money could have been a serious one. Even four years later Melisandre still tried to make it a problem: on these warm summer evenings the Negro houseman and one of the maids would serve the evening meal on a flagged terrace beneath a wistaria arbor in the back yard, whereupon each time there were guests, even the same guest or guests again, Melisandre would say, "It would be cooler in the dining-room" (in the rebuilt house the dining-room was not quite as large as a basket-ball court) "and no bugs either. But the dining-room makes Gavin nervous." Whereupon he would say, as he always did too, even before the same guest or guests again: "Dammit, Milly, nothing can make me nervous because I was already born that way."

They were sitting there now over the sandwiches and the iced tea. She said, "Why didn't you invite her out here." He merely chewed so she said, "But of course you did." So he merely chewed and she said, "So it must be something serious." Then she said, "But it can't be serious or she couldn't have waited, she would have told you right there in the post office." So then she said, "What do you suppose it is?" and he wiped his mouth and dropped the napkin, rising, and came around the table and leaned and kissed her.

"I love you," he said. "Yes. No. I don't know. Don't wait up."

Melisandre had given him a Cadillac roadster for her wedding present to him; this was during the first year of the war and God only knew where she had got a new Cadillac convertible and what she had paid for it. "Unless you really don't want it," she said.

"I do," he said. "I've always wanted a Cadillac convertible
—provided I can do exactly what I want to with it."

"Of course you can," she said. "It's yours." So he drove the
car back to town and arranged with a garage to store it for ten
dollars a month and removed the battery and radio and the
tires and the spare wheel and sold them and took the keys and
the bill of sale to Snopes's bank and mortgaged the car for the
biggest loan they would make on it. By that time progress,
industrial renascence and rejuvenation had reached even rural
Mississippi banks, so Snopes's bank now had a professional
cashier or working vice-president imported from Memphis six
months back to give it the New Look, that is, to bring rural
banks abreast of the mental condition which accepted, could
accept, the automobile as a definite ineradicable part of not
only the culture but the economy also; where, as Stevens knew,
Snopes alone would not lend God Himself one penny on an
automobile. So Stevens could have got the loan from the imported vice-president on this simple recognisance, not only for
the above reason but because the vice-president was a stranger
and Stevens represented one of the three oldest families in the
county and the vice-president would not have dared to say No to
him. But Stevens didn't do it that way; this was to be, as the
saying had it, Snopes's baby. He waylaid, ambushed, caught
Snopes himself in public, in the lobby of his bank with not only
all the staff but the moment's complement of customers, to
explain in detail how he didn't intend to sell his wife's wedding
gift but simply to convert it into war bonds for the duration of
the war. So the loan was made, the keys surrendered and the
lien recorded, which Stevens naturally had no intention whatever
of ever redeeming, plus the ten dollars a month storage accrued
to whatever moment when Snopes realised that his bank owned a
brand-new though outdated Cadillac automobile complete
except for battery and tires.

Though even with the six-year-old coupé which (as it were)
he had got married from, the houseman still got there first to
hold the door for him to get in and depart, down the long
driveway lined immediately with climbing roses on the white-
panelled fences where the costly pedigreed horses had once
ranged in pampered idleness; gone now since there was no one

on the place to ride them unless somebody paid him for it,
Stevens himself hating horses even more than dogs, rating the
horse an unassailable first in loathing since though both were
parasites, the dog at least had the grace to be a sycophant too;
it at least fawned on you and so kept you healthily ashamed of
the human race. But the real reason was, though neither the
horse nor the dog ever forgot anything, the dog at least forgave
you, which the horse did not; and his, Steven's, thought was that
what the world needed was more forgiving: that if you had a
good sensitive quick-acting capacity for forgiving, it didn't
really matter whether you ever learned or even remembered
anything or not.

Because he had no idea what Linda wanted either; he thought
*Because women are wonderful: it doesn't really matter what they want or if
they themselves even know what it is they think they want.* At least there
was the silence. She would have to organise, correlate, tell him
herself, rather than have whatever it was she wanted him to know
dug out of her by means of the infinitesimal legal mining which
witnesses usually required; he would need only write on the
tablet *At least don't make me have to write out in writing whatever
questions you want me to ask you so whenever you come to one of them
just ask it yourself and go on from there.* Even as he stopped the car he
could already see her, her white dress in the portico, between
two of the columns which were too big for the house, for the
street, for Jefferson itself; it would be dim and probably cooler
and anyway pleasant to sit there. But there was the silence; he
thought how there should be a law for everybody to carry a
flashlight in his car or perhaps he could ask her with the tablet
to get a flashlight from the house so she could read the first
sentence; except that she couldn't read the request for the
flashlight until she was inside the house.

She kissed him, as always unless they met on the street, almost
as tall as he; he thought *Of course it will have to be upstairs, in her
sitting-room with the doors closed too probably; anything urgent enough
to demand a private appointment* following her through the hall at
the end of which was the door to the room where her father (he
believed that out of all Jefferson only he and Ratliff knew better)
sat, local legend had it not reading, not chewing tobacco: just
sitting with his feet propped on the unpainted wooden ledge he

had had his Frenchman's Bend carpenter-kinsman nail at the
proper height across the Adam mantel; on up the stairs and,
sure enough, into her sitting-room whose own mantel had been
designed to the exact height for them to stand before while he
used the foolscap pad and pencil which was its fixture since she
led him here only when there was more than the two-by-three
ivory surface could hold. Though this time he hadn't even
picked up the pencil when she spoke the eight or nine words
which froze him for almost half that many seconds. He repeated
one of them.

"Mink?" he said. "Mink?" He thought rapidly *Oh Hell, not
this* thinking rapidly *Nineteen . . . eight. Twenty years then twenty
more on top of that. He will be out in two more years anyway. We had
forgotten that. Or had we.* He didn't need to write *Tell me* either;
she was already doing that; except for the silence he could, would
have asked her what in the world, what stroke of coincidence
(he had not yet begun to think chance, fate, destiny) had caused
her to think of the man whom she had never seen and whose
name she could have heard only in connection with a cowardly
and savage murder. But that didn't matter now: which was the
instant when he began to think destiny and fate.

With the houseman to do the listening, she had taken her
father's car yesterday and driven out to Frenchman's Bend and
talked with her mother's brother Jody; she stood now facing
him beside the mantel on which the empty pad lay, telling him:
"He had just twenty years at first, which would have been
nineteen twenty-eight; he would have got out then. Only in
nineteen twenty-three he tried to escape. In a woman's what
Uncle Jody called mother hubbard and a sunbonnet. How did
he get hold of a mother hubbard and a sunbonnet in the
penitentiary."

Except for the silence he could have used gentleness. But
all he had now was the yellow pad. Because he knew the answer
himself now, writing *What did Jody tell you*

"That it was my . . . other cousin, Montgomery Ward, that
had the dirty magic-lantern slides until they sent him to Parchman too, in nineteen twenty-three too, you remember?" Oh yes,
he remembered: how he and the then sheriff, old Hub Hampton,
dead now, both knew that it was Flem Snopes himself who

planted the moonshine liquor in his kinsman's studio and got him sentenced to two years in Parchman, yet how it was Flem himself who not only had two private interviews with Montgomery Ward while he lay in jail waiting trial, but put up the money for his bond and surety which permitted Montgomery Ward a two-day absence from the jail and Jefferson too before returning to accept his sentence and be taken to Parchman to serve it, after which Jefferson saw him no more nor heard of him until eight or ten years ago the town learned that Montgomery Ward was now in Los Angeles, engaged in some quite lucrative adjunct or correlative to the motion-picture industry or anyway colony. *So that's why Montgomery Ward had to go to Parchman and nowhere else* he thought *instead of merely Atlanta or Leavenworth where only the dirty post cards would have sent him.* Oh yes, he remembered that one, and the earlier one too: in the courtroom also with the little child-sized gaunt underfed maniacal murderer, when the Court itself leaned down to give him his constitutional right to elect his plea, saying, "Don't bother me now; can't you see I'm busy?" then turning to shout again into the packed room: "Flem! Flem Snopes! Won't anybody here get word to Flem Snopes—" Oh yes, he, Stevens, knew now why Montgomery Ward had had to go to Parchman: Flem Snopes had bought twenty more years of life with that five gallons of planted evidence.

He wrote *You want me to get him out now*

"Yes," she said. "How do you do it?"

He wrote *He will be out in 2 more years why not wait till then* He wrote *He has known nothing else but that cage for 38 years He won't live a month free like an old lion or tiger At least give him 2 more years*

"Two years of life are not important," she said. "Two years of jail are."

He had even moved the pencil again when he stopped and spoke aloud instead; later he told Ratliff why. "I know why," Ratliff said. "You jest wanted to keep your own skirts clean. Maybe by this time she had done learned to read your lips and even if she couldn't you would at least been on your own record anyhow." "No," Stevens said. "It was because I not only believe in and am an advocate of fate and destiny, I admire them; I want to be one of the instruments too, no matter how modest." So he didn't write: he spoke:

"Don't you know what he's going to do the minute he gets back to Jefferson or anywhere else your father is?"

"Say it slow and let me try again," she said.

He wrote *I love you* thinking rapidly *If I say No she will find somebody else, anybody else, maybe some jackleg who will bleed her to get him out then continue to bleed her for what the little rattlesnake is going to do the moment he is free,* and wrote *Yes we can get him out it will take a few weeks a petition I will draw them up for you his blood kin the judge sheriff at the time Judge Long and old Hub Hampton are dead but Little Hub will do even if he won't be sheriff again until next election I will take them to the Governor myself*

Ratliff too he thought. Tomorrow the petition lay on his desk, Ratliff standing over it pen in hand. "Go on," Stevens said. "Sign it. I'm going to take care of that too. What do you think I am—a murderer?"

"Not yet anyway," Ratliff said. "How take care of it?"

"Mrs Kohl is going to," Stevens said.

"I thought you told me you never mentioned out loud where she could hear it what Mink would do as soon as he got back inside the same town limits with Flem," Ratliff said.

"I didn't need to," Stevens said. "Linda and I both agreed that there was no need for him to come back here. After forty years, with his wife dead and his daughters scattered God knows where; that in fact he would be better off if he didn't. So she's putting up the money. She wanted to make it a thousand but I told her that much in a lump would destroy him sure. So I'm going to leave two-fifty with the Warden, to be handed to him the minute before they unlock the gate to let him through it, with the understanding that the moment he accepts the money, he has given his oath to cross the Mississippi state line before sundown, and that another two-fifty will be sent every three months to whatever address he selects, provided he never again crosses the Mississippi line as long as he lives."

"I see," Ratliff said. "He can't tech the money a-tall except on the condition that he don't never lay eyes on Flem Snopes again as long as he lives."

"That's right," Stevens said.

"Suppose jest money ain't enough," Ratliff said. "Suppose he won't take jest two hundred and fifty dollars for Flem Snopes."

"Remember," Stevens said. "He's going to face having to measure thirty-eight years he has got rid of, put behind him, against two more years he has still got to spend inside a cage to get rid of. He's selling Flem Snopes for these next two years, with a thousand dollars a year bonus thrown in free for the rest of his life. Sign it."

"Don't rush me," Ratliff said. "Destiny and fate. They was what you told me about being proud to be a handmaid of, wasn't they?"

"So what?" Stevens said. "Sign it."

"Don't you reckon you ought to maybe include a little luck into them too?"

"Sign it," Stevens said.

"Have you told Flem yet?"

"He hasn't asked me yet," Stevens said.

"When he does ask you?" Ratliff said.

"Sign it," Stevens said.

"I already did," Ratliff said. He laid the pen back on the desk. "You're right. We never had no alternative not to. If you'd a said No, she would jest got another lawyer that wouldn't a said No nor even invented that two-hundred-and-fifty-dollar gamble neither. And then Flem Snopes wouldn't a had no chance a-tall."

None of the other requisite documents presented any difficulty either. The judge who had presided at the trial was dead of course, as was the incumbent sheriff, old Hub Hampton. But his son, known as Little Hub, had inherited not only his father's four-year alternation as sheriff, but also his father's capacity to stay on the best of political terms with his alternating opposite number, Ephriam Bishop. So Stevens had those two names; also the foreman of the grand jury at the time was a hale (hence still quick) eighty-five, even running a small electric-driven corn mill while he wasn't hunting and fishing with Uncle Ike McCaslin, another octogenarian: plus a few other select signatures which Stevens compelled on to his petition as simply and ruthlessly as he did Ratliff's. Though what he considered his strongest card was a Harvard classmate, an amateur in state politics who had never held any office, who for years had been a sort of friend-of-the-court adviser to governors simply because all the state factions knew he was not only a loyal Mississippian but one already too wealthy to want anything.

So Stevens would have—indeed, intended to have—nothing but progress to report to his client after he sent the documents in to the state capital and the rest of the summer passed toward and into fall—September, when Mississippi (including governors and legislatures and pardon boards) would put their neckties and coats back on and assume work again. Indeed, he felt he could almost select the specific day and hour he preferred to have the prisoner freed, choosing late September and explaining why to his client on the pad of yellow office foolscap, specious, voluble, convincing since he himself was convinced. September, the mounting apex of the cotton-picking season when there would be not only work, familiar work, but work which of all the freed man had the strongest emotional ties with, which after thirty-eight years of being compelled to it by loaded shotguns, he would now be paid by the hundredweight for performing it. This, weighed against being freed at once, back in June, with half a summer of idleness plus the gravitational pull back to where he was born; not explaining to Linda his reasons why the little child-size creature who must have been mad to begin with and whom thirty-eight years in a penitentiary could not have improved any, must not come back to Jefferson; hiding that too behind the rational garrulity of the pencil flying along the ruled lines—until suddenly he would look up (she of course had heard nothing) and Ratliff would be standing just inside the office door looking at them, courteous, bland, inscrutable, and only a little grave and thoughtful too now. So little in fact that Linda anyway never noticed it, at least not before Stevens, touching, jostling her arm or elbow as he rose (though this was never necessary; she had felt the new presence by now), saying, "Howdy, V.K. Come in. Is it that time already?"

"Looks like it," Ratliff would say. "Mawnin, Linda."

"Howdy, V.K.," she would answer in her deaf voice but almost exactly with Stevens's inflection: who could not have heard him greet Ratliff since, and even he could not remember when she could have heard him before. Then Stevens would produce the gold lighter monogrammed G L S though L was

not his initial, and light her cigarette, then at the cabinet above
the wash basin he and Ratliff would assemble the three thick
tumblers and the sugar basin and the single spoon and a sliced
lemon and Ratliff would produce from his clothing somewhere
the flask of corn whiskey a little of which old Mr Calvin Bookwright still made and aged each year and shared now and then
with the few people tactful enough to retain his precarious
irascible friendship. Then, Linda with her cigarette and Stevens
with his cob pipe, the three of them would sit and sip the toddies,
Stevens still talking and scribbling now and then on the pad for
her to answer, until she would set down her empty glass and
rise and say good-bye and leave them. Then Ratliff said:

"So you ain't told Flem yet." Stevens smoked. "But then
of course you don't need to, being as it's pretty well over the
county now that Mink Snopes's cousin Linda or niece Linda or
whichever it is, is getting him out." Stevens smoked. Ratliff
picked up one of the toddy glasses. "You want another one?"

"No, much obliged," Stevens said.

"So you ain't lost your voice," Ratliff said. "Except, maybe
back there in that vault in the bank where he would have to be
counting his money, he can't hear what's going on. Except
maybe that one trip he would have to make outside." Stevens
smoked. "To go across to the sheriff's office." Stevens smoked.
"You right sho you don't want another toddy?"

"All right," Stevens said. "Why?"

"That's what I'm asking you. You'd a thought the first thing
Flem would a done would been to go to the sheriff and remind
him of them final words of Mink's before Judge Long invited
him to Parchman. Only he ain't done that. Maybe because at
least Linda told him about them two hundred and fifty dollars
and even Flem Snopes can grab a straw when there ain't nothing
else in sight? Because naturally Flem can't walk right up to her
and write on that tablet, The minute you let that durn little
water moccasin out he's going to come straight back here and
pay you up to date for your maw's grave and all the rest of it
that these Jefferson meddlers have probably already persuaded
you I was to blame for; naturally he won't dare risk putting no
such idea as that in her head and have her grab a-holt of you
and go to Parchman and take him out tonight and have him

back in Jefferson by breakfast tomorrow, when as it is he's still got three more weeks, during which anything might happen: Linda or Mink or the Governor or the pardon board might die or Parchman itself might blow up. When did you say it would be?"

"When what will be?" Stevens said.

"The day they will let him out."

"Oh. Some time after the twentieth. Probably the twenty-sixth."

"The twenty-sixth," Ratliff said. "And you're going down there before?"

"Next week," Stevens said. "To leave the money and talk with the Warden myself. That he is not to touch the money until he promises to leave Mississippi before sundown and never come back."

"In that case," Ratliff said, "everything's all right. Especially if I—" He stopped.

"If you what?" Stevens said.

"Nothing," Ratliff said. "Fate, and destiny, and luck, and hope, and all of us mixed up in it—us and Linda and Flem and that durn little half-starved wildcat down there in Parchman, all mixed up in the same luck and destiny and fate and hope until can't none of us tell where it stops and we begin. Especially the hope. I mind I used to think that hope was about all folks had, only now I'm beginning to believe that that's about all anybody needs—jest hope. The pore son of a bitch over yonder in that bank vault counting his money because that's the one place on earth Mink Snopes can't reach him in, and long as he's got to stay in it he might as well count money to be doing something, have something to do. And I wonder if maybe he wouldn't give Linda back her two hundred and fifty dollars without even charging her no interest on it, for them two years of pardon. And I wonder jest how much of the rest of the money in that vault he would pay to have another twenty years added on to them. Or maybe jest ten more. Or maybe jest one more."

Ten days later Stevens was in the Warden's office at the state penitentiary. He had the money with him—twenty-five ten-dollar notes, quite new. "You don't want to see him yourself?" the Warden said.

"No," Stevens said. "You can do it. Anybody can. Simply offer him his choice: take the pardon and the two hundred and fifty dollars and get out of Mississippi as fast as he can, plus another two hundred and fifty every three months for the rest of his life if he never crosses the state line again; or stay here in Parchman another two years and rot and be damned to him."

"Well, that ought to do it," the Warden said. "It certainly would with me. Why is it whoever owns the two hundred and fifty dollars don't want him to come back home so bad?"

Stevens said rapidly, "Nothing to come back to. Family gone and scattered, wife died twenty-five or thirty years ago and nobody knows what became of his two daughters. Even the tenant house he lived in either collapsed of itself or maybe somebody found it and chopped it up and hauled it away for firewood."

"That's funny," the Warden said. "Almost anybody in Mississippi has got at least one cousin. In fact, it's hard not to have one."

"Oh, distant relations," Stevens said. "Yes, it seems to have been the usual big scattered country clan."

"So one of these big scattered connections don't want him back home enough to pay two hundred and fifty dollars for it."

"He's mad," Stevens said. "Somebody here during the last thirty-eight years must have had that idea occur to them and suggested it to you even if you hadn't noticed it yourself."

"We're all mad here," the Warden said. "Even the prisoners too. Maybe it's the climate. I wouldn't worry, if I were you. They all make these threats at the time—big threats, against the judge or the prosecuting lawyer or a witness that stood right up in public and told something that any decent man would have kept to himself; big threats: I notice there's no place on earth where a man can be as loud and dangerous as handcuffed to a policeman. But even one year is a long time sometimes. And he's had thirty-eight of them. So he don't get the pardon until he agrees to accept the money. Why do you know he won't take the money and doublecross you?"

"I've noticed a few things about people too," Stevens said. "One of them is, how a bad man will work ten times as hard and make ten times the sacrifice to be credited with at least one virtue no matter how Spartan, as the upright man will to avoid the most abject vice provided it's fun. He tried to kill his lawyer right there in the jail during the trial when the lawyer suggested pleading him crazy. He will know that the only sane thing to do is to accept the money and the pardon, since to refuse the pardon because of the money, in two more years he not only wouldn't have the two thousand dollars, he might even be dead. Or, what would be infinitely worse, he would be alive and free at last and poor, and Fle—" and stopped himself.

"Yes?" the Warden said. "Who is Fleh, that might be dead himself in two years more and so out of reach for good? The one that owns the two hundred and fifty dollars? Never mind," he said. "I'll agree with you. Once he accepts the money, everything is jake, as they say. That's what you want?"

"That's right," Stevens said. "If there should be any sort of hitch, you can call me at Jefferson collect."

"I'll call you anyway," the Warden said. "You're trying too hard not to sound serious."

"No," Stevens said. "Only if he refuses the money."

"You mean the pardon, don't you?"

"What's the difference?" Stevens said.

So when about mid-afternoon on the twenty-sixth he answered his telephone and Central said, "Parchman, Mississippi, calling Mr Gavin Stevens. Go ahead, Parchman," and the faint voice said, "Hello. Lawyer?" Stevens thought rapidly *So I am a coward after all. When it happens two years from now, at least none of it will spatter on me. At least I can tell her now because this will prove it* and said into the mouthpiece:

"So he refused to take the money."

"Then you already know," Ratliff's voice said.

". . . What?" Stevens said after less than a second actually. "Hello?"

"It's me," Ratliff said. "V.K. At Parchman. So they already telephoned you."

"Telephoned me what?" Stevens said. "He's still there? He refused to leave?"

"No, he's gone. He left about eight this morning. A truck going north—"

"But you just said he didn't take the money."

"That's what I'm trying to tell you. We finally located the money about fifteen minutes ago. It's still here. He—"

"Hold it," Stevens said. "You said eight this morning. Which direction?"

"A Negro seen him standing by the highway until he caught a ride on a cattle truck going north, toward Tutwiler. At Tutwiler he could have went to Clarksdale and then on to Memphis. Or he could have went from Tutwiler to Batesville and on to Memphis that-a-way. Except that anybody wanting to go from Parchman to Jefferson could go by Batesville too lessen he jest wanted to go by way of Chicago or New Orleans for the trip. Otherwise he could be in Jefferson pretty close to now. I'm leaving right now myself and maybe you better—"

"All right," Stevens said.

"And maybe Flem too," Ratliff said.

"Damn it, I said all right," Stevens said.

"But not her yet," Ratliff said. "Ain't no need to tell her yet that likely she's jest finished killing her maw's husband—"

But he didn't even hear that, the telephone was already down; he didn't even have his hat when he reached the Square, the street below, the bank where Snopes would be in one direction, the courthouse where the Sheriff would be in the other: not that it really mattered which one he saw first, thinking *So I really am a coward after all the talk about destiny and fate that didn't even sell Ratliff.*

"You mean," the Sheriff said, "he had already spent thirty-eight years in Parchman, and the minute somebody gets him out he's going to try to do something that will send him straight back even if it don't hang him first this time? Don't be foolish. Even a fellow like they say he was would learn that much sense in thirty-eight years."

"Ha," Stevens said without mirth. "You expressed it exactly that time. You were probably not even a shirt-tail boy back in 1908. You were not in that courtroom that day and saw his face and heard him. I was."

"All right," the Sheriff said. "What do you want me to do?"

"Arrest him. What do you call them? roadblocks? Don't even let him get into Yoknapatawpha County."

"On what grounds?"

"You just catch him, I'll furnish you with grounds as fast as you need them. If necessary we will hold him for obtaining money under false pretences."

"I thought he didn't take the money."

"I don't know what happened yet about the money. But I'll figure out some way to use it, at least long enough to hold him on for a while."

"Yes," the Sheriff said. "I reckon you would. Let's step over to the bank and see Mr Snopes; maybe all three of us can figure out something. Or maybe Mrs Kohl. You'll have to tell her too, I reckon."

Whereupon Stevens repeated almost verbatim what Ratliff had said into the telephone after he had put it down: "Tell a woman that apparently she just finished murdering her father at eight o'clock this morning?"

"All right, all right," the Sheriff said. "You want me to come to the bank with you?"

"No," Stevens said. "Not yet anyway."

"I still think you have found a booger where there wasn't one," the Sheriff said. "If he comes back here at all, it'll just be out at Frenchman's Bend. Then all we'll have to do is pick him up the first time we notice him in town and have a talk with him."

"Notice, hell," Stevens said. "Ain't that what I'm trying to tell you? that you don't notice him. That was the mistake Jack Houston made thirty-eight years ago: he didn't notice him either until he stepped out from behind that bush that morning with that shotgun—if he even stepped out of the bushes before he shot, which I doubt."

He recrossed the Square rapidly, thinking *Yes, I really am a coward, after all* when that quantity, entity with which he had spent a great deal of his life talking or rather having to listen to (his skeleton perhaps, which would outlast the rest of him by a few months or years—and without doubt would spend that time moralising at him while he would be helpless to answer back) answered immediately *Did anyone ever say you were not?* Then he *But I am not a coward: I am a humanitarian.* Then the other *You are not even an original; that word is customarily used as a euphemism for it.*

The bank would be closed now. But when he crossed the Square to the sheriff's office the car with Linda behind the wheel had not been waiting so this was not the day of the weekly whiskey run. The shades were drawn but after some knob-rattling at the side door one of the bookkeepers peered out and recognised him and let him in; he passed on through the machine-clatter of the day's recapitulation—the machines themselves sounding immune and even inattentive to the astronomical sums they reduced to staccato trivia—and knocked at the door on which Colonel Sartoris had had the word PRIVATE lettered by hand forty years ago, and opened it.

Snopes was sitting not at the desk but with his back to it, facing the cold now empty fireplace, his feet raised and crossed against the same heel scratches whose initial inscribing Colonel Sartoris had begun. He was not reading, he was not doing anything: just sitting there with his black planter's hat on, his lower jaw moving faintly and steadily as though he were chewing something, which as the town knew also he was not; he didn't even lower his feet when Stevens came to the desk (it was a broad flat table littered with papers in a sort of neat, almost orderly way) and said almost in one breath:

"Mink left Parchman at eight o'clock this morning. I don't know whether you know it or not but we—I had some money waiting to be given to him at the gate, under condition that in accepting it he had passed his oath to leave Mississippi without returning to Jefferson and never cross the state line again. He didn't take the money; I don't know yet how since he was not to be given the pardon until he did. He caught a ride in a passin truck and has disappeared. The truck was headed north."

"How much was it?" Snopes said.

"What?" Stevens said.

"The money," Snopes said.

"Two hundred and fifty dollars," Stevens said.

"Much obliged," Snopes said.

"Good God, man," Stevens said. "I tell you a man left Parchman at eight o'clock this morning on his way here to murder you and all you say is Much obliged?"

The other didn't move save for the faint chewing motion; Stevens thought with a kind of composed and seething rage *If he would only spit now and then.* "Then all he had was that ten dollars they give them when they turn them loose," Snopes said.

"Yes," Stevens said. "As far as we—I know. But yes." *Or even just go through the motions of spitting now and then* he thought.

"Say a man thought he had a grudge against you," Snopes said. "A man sixty-three years old now with thirty-eight of that spent in the penitentiary and even before that wasn't much bigger than a twelve-year-old boy—"

That had to use a shotgun from behind a bush even then Stevens thought. *Oh yes, I know exactly what you mean: too small and frail even then, even without thirty-eight years in jail, to have risked a mere knife or bludgeon. And he can't go out to Frenchman's Bend, the only place on earth where someone might remember him enough to lend him one because even though nobody in Frenchman's Bend would knock up the muzzle aimed at you, they wouldn't lend him theirs to aim with. So he will either have to buy a gun for ten dollars, or steal one. In which case, you might even be safe: the ten-dollar one won't shoot and in the other some policeman might save you honestly.* He thought rapidly *Of course. North. He went to Memphis. He would have to. He wouldn't think of anywhere else to go to buy a gun with ten dollars.* And, since Mink had only the ten dollars, he would have to hitchhike all the way, first to Memphis, provided he got there before the pawnshops closed, then back to Jefferson. Which could not be before tomorrow, since anything else would leave simple destiny and fate too topheavy with outrageous hope and coincidence for even Ratliff's sanguine nature to pass. "Yes," he said. "So do I. You have at least until tomorrow night." He thought rapidly *And now for it. How to persuade him not to tell her without letting him know that was what he agreed to, promised, and that it was me who put it into his mind.* So suddenly he heard himself say: "Are you going to tell Linda?"

"Why?" Snopes said.

"Yes," Stevens said. Then heard himself say in his turn: "Much obliged." Then, suddenly indeed this time: "I'm responsible for this, even if I probably couldn't have stopped it. I just talked to Eef Bishop. What else do you want me to do?" *If he would just spit once* he thought.

"Nothing," Snopes said.

"What?" Stevens said.

"Yes," Snopes said. "Much obliged."

At least he knew where to start. Only, he didn't know how. Even if—when—he called the Memphis police, what would—could—he tell them: a city police force a hundred miles away, who had never heard of Mink and Flem Snopes and Jack Houston, dead these forty years now, either. When he, Stevens, had already failed to move very much the local sheriff who at least had inherited the old facts. How to explain what he himself was convinced Mink wanted in Memphis, let alone convince them that Mink was or would be in Memphis. And even if he managed to shake them that much, how to describe whom they were supposed to look for: whose victim forty years ago had got himself murdered mainly for the reason that the murderer was the sort of creature whom nobody, even his victim, noticed enough in time to pay any attention to what he was or might do.

Except Ratliff. Ratliff alone out of Yoknapatawpha County would know Mink on sight. To be unschooled, untravelled, and to an extent unread, Ratliff had a terrifying capacity for knowledge or local information or acquaintanceship to match the need of any local crisis. Stevens admitted to himself now what he was waiting, dallying, really wasting time for: for Ratliff to drive back to his pickup truck from Parchman, to be hurried on to Memphis without even stopping, cutting the engine, to reveal Mink to the Memphis police and so save Mink's cousin, kinsman, whatever Flem was, from that just fate; knowing—Stevens—better all the while: that what he really wanted with Ratliff was to find out how Mink had not only got past the Parchman gate without that absolute contingent money, but had managed it in such a way that apparently only the absolutely unpredicted and unwarranted presence of Ratliff at a place and time that he had no business whatever being, revealed the fact that he hadn't taken it.

It was not three o'clock when Ratliff phoned; it would be almost nine before he reached Jefferson. It was not that the pickup truck wouldn't have covered the distance faster. It was that no vehicle owned by Ratliff (provided he was in it and conscious, let alone driving it) was going to cover it faster. Besides, at some moment not too long after six o'clock he was going to stop to eat at the next dreary repetitive little cotton-gin hamlet, or (nowadays) on the highway itself, drawing neatly in and neatly parking before the repetitive Dixie Cafés or Mac's or Lorraine's, to eat, solitary, neatly and without haste the meat a little too stringy to chew properly and too overcooked to taste at all, the stereotyped fried potatoes and the bread you didn't chew but mumbled, like one of the paper napkins, the machine-chopped prefrozen lettuce and tomatoes like (except for the tense inviolate colour) something exhumed by paleontologists from tundras, the machine-made prefrozen pie and what they would call coffee—the food perfectly pure and perfectly tasteless except for the dousing of machine-made tomato ketchup.

He (Stevens) could, perhaps should, have had plenty of time to drive out to Rose Hill and eat his own decent evening meal. Instead, he telephoned his wife.

"I'll come in and we can eat at the Holston House," she said.

"No, honey. I've got to see Ratliff as soon as he gets back from Parchman."

"All right. I think I'll come in and have supper with Maggie" (Maggie was his sister) "and maybe we'll go to the picture show and I'll see you tomorrow. I can come in to town, can't I, if I promise to stay off the streets?"

"You see, you don't help me. How can I resist togetherness if you won't fight back?"

"I'll see you tomorrow then," she said. "Good night." So they ate at the Holston House; he didn't feel quite up to his sister and brother-in-law and his nephew Charles tonight. The Holston House still clung to the old ways, not desperately nor even gallantly: just with a cold and inflexible indomitability, owned and run by two maiden sisters (that is, one of them, the younger, had been married once but so long ago and so briefly that it no longer counted) who were the last descendants of the Alexander Holston, one of Yoknapatawpha County's three original settlers, who had built the log ordinary which the modern edifice had long since swallowed, who had had his part—been in fact the catalyst—in the naming of Jefferson over a century ago; they still called the dining-room simply the dining-room and (nobody knew how) they still kept Negro men waiters, some of whose seniority still passed from father to son; the guests still ate the table d'hôte meals mainly at two long communal tables at the head of each of which a sister presided; no man came there without a coat and necktie and no woman with her head covered (there was a dressing-room with a maid for that purpose), not even if she had a railroad ticket in her hand.

Though his sister did pick his wife up in time for the picture show. So he was back in the office when a little after eight-thirty he heard Ratliff on the stairs and said, "All right. What happened?" Then he said, "No. Wait. What were you doing at Parchman?"

"I'm a—what do you call it? optimist," Ratliff said. "Like any good optimist, I don't expect the worst to happen. Only, like any optimist worth his salt, I like to go and look as soon as possible afterward jest in case it did. Especially when the difference between the best and the worst is liable to reach all the way back up here to Jefferson. It taken a little doing, too. This was about ten o'clock this morning; he had been gone a good two hours by then, and they was a little impatient with me. They had done done their share, took him and had him for thirty-eight years all fair and regular, like the man said for them to, and they felt they had done earned the right to be shut of him. You know: his new fresh pardon and them new fresh two hundred and fifty dollars all buttoned up neat and safe and secure in his new fresh overhalls and jumper and the gate locked behind him again jest like the man said too and the official Mink Snopes page removed outen the ledger and officially marked Paid in Full and destroyed a good solid two hours back, when here comes this here meddling out-of-town son-of-a-gun that ain't even a lawyer saying Yes yes, that's jest fine, only let's make sho he actively had that money when he left.

"The Warden his-self had tended to the money in person: had Mink in alone, with the table all ready for him, the pardon in one pile and them two hundred and fifty dollars that Mink hadn't never seen that much at one time before in his life, in the other pile; and the Warden his-self explaining how there wasn't no choice about it: to take the pardon he would have to take the money too, and once he teched the money he had done give his sworn word and promise and Bible oath to strike for the quickest place outside the state of Missippi and never cross the line again as long as he lived. 'Is that what I got to do to get out?' Mink

z

says. 'Take the money?' 'That's it,' the Warden says, and Mink reached and taken the money and the Warden his-self helped him button the money and the pardon both inside his jumper and the Warden shaken his hand and the trusty come to take him out to where the turnkey was waiting to unlock the gate into liberty and freedom—"

"Wait," Stevens said. "Trusty."

"Ain't it?" Ratliff said with pleased, almost proud approval. "It was so simple. Likely that's why it never occurred to none of them, especially as even a Parchman deserving any name a-tall for being well conducted, ain't supposed to contain nobody eccentric and antisocial enough to behave like he considered anything like free-will choice to even belong in the same breath with two hundred and fifty active dollars give him free for nothing so he never even had to say Much obliged for them. That's what I said too: 'That trusty. He left here for the gate with them two hundred and fifty dollars. Let's just see if he still had them when he went outen it.' So that's what I said too: 'That trusty.'

" 'A lifer too,' the Warden says. 'Killed his wife with a ballpeen hammer, was converted and received salvation in the jail before he was even tried and has one of the best records here, is even a lay preacher.'

" 'Than which, if Mink had had your whole guest list to pick from and time to pick in, he couldn't a found a better feller for his purpose,' I says. 'So it looks like I'm already fixing to begin to have to feel sorry for this here snatched brand even if he was too impatient to think of a better answer to the enigma of wedlock than a garage hammer. That is, I reckon you still got a few private interrogation methods for reluctant conversationalists around here, ain't you?'

"That's why I was late calling you: it taken a little time too, though I got to admit nothing showed on his outside. Because people are funny. No, they ain't funny: they're jest sad. Here was this feller already in for life and even if they had found out that was a mistake or somebody even left the gate unlocked, he wouldn't a dast to walk outen it because the gal's paw had done already swore he would kill him the first time he crossed the Parchman fence. So what in the world could he a done with two hundred and fifty dollars even if he could ever a dreamed he could get away with this method of getting holt of it."

"But how, dammit?" Stevens said. "How?"

"Why, the only way Mink could a done it, which was likely why never nobody thought to anticipate it. On the way from the Warden's office to the gate he jest told the trusty he needed to step into the gentlemen's room a minute and when they was inside he give the trusty the two hundred and fifty dollars and asked the trusty to hand it back to the Warden the first time the trusty conveniently got around to it, the longer the better after he, Mink, was outside the gate and outen sight, and tell the Warden Much obliged but he had done changed his mind and wouldn't need it. So there the trusty was: give Mink another hour or two and he would be gone, likely forever, nobody would know where or care. Because I don't care where you are: the minute a man can really believe that never again in his life will he have any use for two hundred and fifty dollars, he's done already been dead and has jest this minute found it out. And that's all. I don't—"

"I do," Stevens said. "Flem told me. He's in Memphis. He's too little and frail and old to use a knife or a club so he will have to go to the nearest place he can hope to get a gun with ten dollars."

"So you told Flem. What did he say?"

"He said, Much obliged," Stevens said. After a moment he said, "I said, when I told Flem Mink had left Parchman at eight o'clock this morning on his way up here to kill him, he said Much obliged."

"I heard you," Ratliff said. "What would you a said? You would sholy be as polite as Flem Snopes, wouldn't you? So maybe it's all right, after all. Of course you done already talked to Memphis."

"Tell them what?" Stevens said. "How describe to a Memphis policeman somebody I wouldn't recognise myself, let alone that he's actually in Memphis trying to do what I assume he is trying to do, for the simple reason that I don't know what to do next either?"

"What's wrong with Memphis?" Ratliff said.

"I'll bite," Stevens said. "What is?"

"I thought it would took a heap littler place than Memphis not to have nobody in it you used to go to Harvard with."

"Well I'll be damned," Stevens said. He put in the call at once and presently was talking with him: the classmate, the amateur Cincinnatus at his plantation not far from Jackson, who had already been instrumental in getting the pardon through, so that Stevens needed merely explain the crisis, not the situation.

"You don't actually know he went to Memphis, of course," the friend said.

"That's right," Stevens said. "But since we are forced by emergency to challenge where he might be, at least we should be permitted one assumption in good faith."

"All right," the friend said. "I know the mayor and the commissioner of police both. All you want—all they can do really—is check any places where anyone might have tried to buy a gun or pistol for ten dollars since say noon today. Right?"

"Right," Stevens said. "And ask them please to call me collect here when—if they do."

"I'll call you myself," the friend said. "You might say I also have a small equity in your friend's doom."

"When you call me that to Flem Snopes, smile," Stevens said.

That was Thursday; during Friday Central would run him to earth all right no matter where he happened to be about the Square. However, there was plenty to do in the office if he composed himself to it. Which he managed to do in time and was so engaged when Ratliff came in carrying something neatly folded in a paper bag and said, "Good mawnin," Stevens not looking up, writing on the yellow foolscap pad, steadily, quite composed in fact even with Ratliff standing for a moment looking down at the top of his head. Then Ratliff moved and took one of the chairs beyond the desk, the one against the wall, then half rose and placed the little parcel neatly on the filing case beside him and sat down, Stevens still writing steadily between pauses now and then to read from the open book beneath his left hand; until presently Ratliff reached and took the morning Memphis paper from the desk and opened it and rattled faintly the turn of the page and after a while rattled that one faintly, until Stevens said,

"Dammit, either get out of here or think about something else. You make me nervous."

"I ain't busy this mawnin," Ratliff said. "If you got anything to tend to outside, I can set here and listen for the phone."

"I have plenty I can do here if you'll just stop filling the damned air with—" He flung, slammed the pencil down. "Obviously he hasn't reached Memphis yet or anyway hasn't tried to buy the gun, or we would have heard. Which is all we want: to get word there first. Do you think that any reputable pawnshop or sporting-goods store that cares a damn about its licence will sell him a gun now after the police—"

"If my name was Mink Snopes, I don't believe I would go to no place that had a licence to lose for selling guns or pistols."

"For instance?" Stevens said.

"Out at Frenchman's Bend they said Mink was a considerable hell-raiser when he was young, within his means of course, which wasn't much. But he made two or three of them country-boy Memphis trips with the young bloods of his time—Quicks and Tulls and Turpins and such: enough to probably know where to begin to look for the kind of places that don't keep the kind of licences to have police worrying them ever time a gun or a pistol turns up in the wrong place or don't turn up in the right one."

"Don't you think the Memphis police know as much about Memphis as any damned little murdering maniac, let alone one that's been locked up in a penitentiary for forty years? The Memphis police, that have a damned better record than a dozen, hell, a hundred cities I could name—"

"All right, all right," Ratliff said.

"By God, God Himself is not so busy that a homicidal maniac with only ten dollars in the world can hitchhike a hundred miles and buy a gun for ten dollars then hitchhike another hundred and shoot another man with it."

"Don't that maybe depend on who God wants shot this time?" Ratliff said. "Have you been by the sheriff's this mawnin?"

"No," Stevens said.

"I have. Flem ain't been to him either yet. And he ain't left town neither. I checked on that too. So maybe that's the best sign we want: Flem ain't worried. Do you reckon he told Linda?"

"No," Stevens said.

"How do you know?"

"He told me."

"Flem did? You mean he jest told you, or you asked him?"

"I asked him," Stevens said. "I said, 'Are you going to tell Linda?' "

"And what did he say?"

"He said, 'Why?' " Stevens said.

"Oh," Ratliff said.

Then it was noon. What Ratliff had in the neat parcel was a sandwich, as neatly made. "You go home and eat dinner," he said. "I'll set here and listen for it."

"Didn't you just say that if Flem himself don't seem to worry, why the hell should we?"

"I won't worry then," Ratliff said. "I'll jest set and listen."

Though Stevens was back in the office when the call came in midafternoon. "Nothing," the classmate's voice said. "None of the pawnshops nor any other place a man might go to buy a gun or pistol of any sort, let alone a ten-dollar one. Maybe he hasn't reached Memphis yet, though it's more than twenty-four hours now."

"That's possible," Stevens said.

"Maybe he never intended to reach Memphis."

"All right, all right," Stevens said. "Shall I write the commissioner myself a letter of thanks or—"

"Sure. But let him earn it first. He agreed that it not only won't cost much more, it will even be a good idea to check his list every morning for the next two or three days, just in case. I thanked him for you. I even went further and said that if you ever found yourselves in the same voting district and he decided to run for an office instead of just sitting for it—" as Stevens put the telephone down and turned to Ratliff again without seeing him at all and said,

"Maybe he never will."

"What?" Ratliff said. "What did he say?" Stevens told, repeated, the gist. "I reckon that's all we can do," Ratliff said.

"Yes," Stevens said. He thought *Tomorrow will prove it. But I'll wait still another day. Maybe until Monday.*

But he didn't wait that long. On Saturday his office was always, not busy with the county business he was paid a salary to handle, so much as constant with the social coming and going of the countrymen who had elected him to his office. Ratliff, who knew them all too, as well or even better, was unobtrusive in his chair against the wall where he could reach the telephone without even getting up; he even had another neat home-made sandwich, until at noon Stevens said,

"Go on home and eat a decent meal, or come home with me. It won't ring today."

"You must know why," Ratliff said.

"Yes. I'll tell you Monday. No: tomorrow. Sunday will be appropriate. I'll tell you tomorrow."

"So you know it's all right now. All settled and finished now. Whether Flem knows it yet or not, he can sleep from now on."

"Don't ask me yet," Stevens said. "It's like a thread; it's true only until I—something breaks it."

"You was right all the time then. There wasn't no need to tell her."

"There never has been," Stevens said. "There never will be."

"That's jest what I said," Ratliff said. "There ain't no need now."

"And what I just said was there never was any need to tell her and there never would have been, no matter what happened."

"Not even as a moral question?" Ratliff said.

"Moral hell and question hell," Stevens said. "It ain't any question at all: it's a fact: the fact that not you nor anybody else that wears hair is going to tell her that her act of pity and compassion and simple generosity murdered the man who passes as her father whether he is or not or a son of a bitch or not."

"All right, all right," Ratliff said. "This here thread you jest mentioned. Maybe another good way to keep it from getting broke before time is to keep somebody handy to hear that telephone when it don't ring at three o'clock this afternoon."

So they were both in the office at three o'clock. Then it was four. "I reckon we can go now," Ratliff said.

"Yes," Stevens said.

"But you still won't tell me now," Ratliff said.

"Tomorrow," Stevens said. "The call will have to come by then."

"So this here thread has got a telephone wire inside of it after all."

"So long," Stevens said. "See you tomorrow."

And Central would know where to find him at any time on Sunday too and in fact until almost half-past two that afternoon he still believed he was going to spend the whole day at Rose Hill. His life had known other similar periods of unrest and trouble and uncertainty even if he had spent most of it as a bachelor; he could recall one or two of them when the anguish and unrest were due to the fact that he was a bachelor, that is, circumstances, conditions insisted on his continuing celibacy despite his own efforts to give it up. But back then he had had something to escape into: nepenthe, surcease: the project he had decreed for himself while at Harvard of translating the Old Testament back into the classic Greek of its first translating; after which he would teach himself Hebrew and really attain to purity; he had thought last night *Why yes, I have that for tomorrow; I had forgotten about that.* Then this morning he knew that that would not suffice any more, not ever again now. He meant of course the effort: not just the capacity to concentrate but to believe in it; he was too old now and the real tragedy of age is that no anguish is any longer grievous enough to demand, justify, any sacrifice.

So it was not even two-thirty when with no surprise really he found himself getting into his car and still no surprise when, entering the empty Sunday-afternoon Square, he saw Ratliff waiting at the foot of the office stairs, the two of them, in the office now, making no pretence as the clock crawled on to three. "What happened that we set exactly three o'clock as the magic deadline in this here business?" Ratliff said.

"Does it matter?" Stevens said.

"That's right," Ratliff said. "The main thing is not to jar or otherwise startle that-ere thread." Then the courthouse clock struck its three heavy mellow blows into the Sabbath somnolence and for the first time Stevens realised how absolutely he had not just expected, but known, that his telephone would not ring before that hour. Then in that same second, instant, he knew why it had not rung; the fact that it had not rung was more proof of what it would have conveyed than the message itself would have been.

"All right," he said. "Mink is dead."

"What?" Ratliff said.

"I don't know where, and it doesn't matter. Because we should have known from the first that three hours of being free would kill him, let alone three days of it." He was talking rapidly, not babbling: "Don't you see? a little kinless tieless frail alien animal that never really belonged to the human race to start with, let alone belonged in it, then locked up in a cage for thirty-eight years and now at sixty-three years old suddenly set free, shoved, flung out of safety and security into freedom like a krait or a fer-de-lance that is quick and deadly dangerous as long as it can stay inside the man-made man-tended tropic immunity of its glass box, but wouldn't live even through the first hour set free, flung, hoicked on a pitchfork or a pair of long-handled tongs into a city street?"

"Wait," Ratliff said, "wait."

But Stevens didn't even pause. "Of course we haven't heard yet where he was found or how or by whom identified because nobody cares; maybe nobody has even noticed him yet. Because he's free. He can even die wherever he wants to now. For thirty-eight years until last Thursday morning he couldn't have had a pimple or a hangnail without it being in a record five minutes later. But he's free now. Nobody cares when or where or how he dies provided his carrion doesn't get under somebody's feet. So we can go home now, until somebody does telephone and you and Flem can go and identify him."

"Yes," Ratliff said. "Well—"

"Give it up," Stevens said. "Come on out home with me and have a drink."

"We could go by first and kind of bring Flem up to date," Ratliff said. "Maybe even he might take a dram then."

"I'm not really an evil man," Stevens said. "I wouldn't have loaned Mink a gun to shoot Flem with; I might not even have just turned my head while Mink used his own. But neither am I going to lift my hand to interfere with Flem spending another day or two expecting any moment that Mink will."

He didn't even tell the Sheriff his conviction that Mink was dead. The fact was, the Sheriff told him; he found the Sheriff in his courthouse office and told him his and Ratliff's theory of

Mink's first objective and the reason for it and that the Memphis police would still check daily the places where Mink might try to buy a weapon.

"So evidently he's not in Memphis," the Sheriff said. "That's how many days now?"

"Since Thursday."

"And he's not in Frenchman's Bend."

"How do you know?"

"I drove out yesterday and looked around a little."

"So you did believe me, after all," Stevens said.

"I get per diem on my car," the Sheriff said. "Yesterday was a nice day for a country drive. So he's had four days now, to come a hundred miles. And he don't seem to be in Memphis. And I know he ain't in Frenchman's Bend. And according to you, Mr Snopes knows he ain't in Jefferson here. Maybe he's dead." Whereupon, now that another had stated it, spoke it aloud, Stevens knew that he himself had never believed it, hearing without listening while the Sheriff went on: "A damned little rattlesnake that they say never had any friends to begin with and nobody out at the Bend knows what became of his wife and his two girls or even when they disappeared. To be locked up for thirty-eight years and then suddenly turned out like you do a cat at night, with nowhere to go and nobody really wanting him out. Maybe he couldn't stand being free. Maybe just freedom killed him. I've known it to happen."

"Yes," Stevens said, "you're probably right," thinking quietly *We won't stop him. We can't stop him—not all of us together, Memphis police and all. Maybe even a rattlesnake with destiny on his side don't even need luck, let alone friends.* He said: "Only we don't know yet. We can't count on that."

"I know," the Sheriff said. "I deputised two men at Varner's store yesterday that claim they remember him, would know him again. And I can have Mr Snopes followed, watched back and forth to the bank. But dammit, watch for who, what, when, where? I can't put a man inside his house until he asks for it, can I? His daughter. Mrs Kohl. Maybe she could do something. You still don't want her to know?"

"You must give me your word," Stevens said.

"All right," the Sheriff said. "I suppose your Jackson buddy will let you know the minute the Memphis police get any sort of a line, won't he?"

"Yes," Stevens said. Though the call didn't come until Wednesday. Ratliff had rung him up a little after ten Tuesday night and told him the news, and on his way to the office this morning he passed the bank whose drawn shades would not be raised today, and as he stood at his desk with the telephone in his hand he could see through his front window the sombre black-and-white-and-violet convolutions of tulle and ribbon and waxen asphodels fastened to the locked front door.

"He found a ten-dollar pistol," the classmate's voice said. "Early Monday morning. It wasn't really a properly licensed pawnshop, so they almost missed it. But under a little . . . persuasion the proprietor recalled the sale. But he said not to worry, the pistol was only technically still a pistol and it would require a good deal more nourishment than the three rounds of ammunition they threw in with it to make it function."

"Ha," Stevens said without mirth. "Tell the proprietor from me he doesn't know his own strength. The pistol was here last night. It functioned."

SEVENTEEN

W<small>HEN</small> he reached the Junction a little before eleven o'clock Monday morning, he was in the cab of another cattle truck.

The truck was going on east into Alabama, but even if it had turned south here actually to pass through Jefferson, he would have left it at this point. If it had been a Yoknapatawpha County truck or driven by someone from the county or Jefferson, he would not have been in it at all.

Until he stepped out of the store this morning with the pistol actually in his pocket, it had all seemed simple; he had only one problem: to get the weapon; after that, only geography stood between him and the moment when he would walk up to the man who had seen him sent to the penitentiary without raising a finger, who had not even had the decency and courage to say No to his bloodcry for help from kin to kin, and say, "Look at me, Flem," and kill him.

But now he was going to have to do what he called "figger" a little. It seemed to him that he was confronted by an almost insurmountable diffusion of obstacles. He was in thirty miles of Jefferson now, home, one same mutual north Mississippi hill-country people even if there was still a trivial county line to cross; it seemed to him that from now on anyone, everyone he met or who saw him, without even needing to recognise or remember his specific face and name, would know at once who he was and where he was going and what he intended to do. On second thought—an immediate, flashing, almost simultaneous second thought—he knew this to be a physical impossibility, yet he dared not risk it; that the thirty-eight years of being locked up in Parchman had atrophied, destroyed some quality in him which in people who has not been locked up had very likely got even sharper, and they would recognise, know, divine who he was without his even knowing it had happened. *It's because I done had to been away so long* he thought. *Like now I'm fixing to have to learn to talk all over again.*

He meant not talk, but think. As he walked along the highway (blacktop now, following a graded survey line, on which automobiles sped, which he remembered as winding dirt along which

slow mules and wagons, or at best a saddle horse, followed the
arbitrary and random ridges) it would be impossible to disguise
his appearance—change his face, his expression, alter his
familiar regional clothes or the way he walked; he entertained
for a desperate and bizarre moment then dismissed it the idea
of perhaps walking backward, at least whenever he heard a car or
truck approaching, to give the impression that he was going the
other way. So he would have to change his thinking, as you
change the colour of the bulb inside the lantern even though you
can't change the lantern itself; as he walked he would have to
hold himself unflagging and undeviating to *thinking* like he was
someone who had never heard the name Snopes and the town
Jefferson in his life, wasn't even aware that if he kept on this road
he would have to pass through it; to think instead like someone
whose destination and goal was a hundred and more miles away
and who in spirit was already there and only his carcass, his
progressing legs, walked this particular stretch of road.

Also, he was going to have to find somebody he could talk
with without rousing suspicion, not to get information so much as
to validate it. Until he left Parchman, was free at last, the goal
for which he had bided patiently for thirty-eight years now
practically in his hand, he believed he had got all the knowledge
he would need from the, not day-to-day of course and not
always year-to-year, but at least decade-to-decade trickling
which had penetrated even into Parchman—how and where his
cousin lived, how he spent his days, his habits, what time he came
and went and where to and from; even who lived in or about his
house with him. But now that the moment was almost here, that
might not be enough. It might even be completely false, wrong,
he thought again *It's having to been away so long like I had to been;
having to been in the place I had to been* as though he had spent those
thirty-eight years not merely out of the world but out of life, so
that even facts when they finally reached him had already
ceased to be truth in order to have penetrated there; and, being
inside Parchman walls, were *per se* inimical and betraying and
fatal to him if he attempted to use them, depend on them, trust
them.

Third, there was the pistol. The road was empty now, running
between walls of woods, no sound of traffic and no house or

human in sight and he took the pistol out and looked at it again with something like despair. It had not looked very much like a pistol in the store this morning; here, in the afternoon's sunny rural solitude and silence, it looked like nothing recognisable at all; looking, if anything, more than ever like the fossilised terrapin of his first impression. Yet he would have to test it, spend one of his three cartridges simply to find out if it really would shoot and for a moment, a second something nudged at his memory. *It's got to shoot* he thought. *It's jest got to. There ain't nothing else for hit to do. Old Moster jest punishes; He don't play jokes.*

He was hungry too. He had not eaten since the animal crackers at sunrise. He had a little money left and he had already passed two gasoline station-stores. But he was home now; he dared not stop in one and be seen buying the cheese and crackers which he could still afford. Which reminded him of night also. The sun was now less than three hours high; he could not possibly reach Jefferson until tomorrow so it would have to be tomorrow night so he turned from the highway into a dirt crossroad, by instinct almost since he could not remember when he had begun to notice the wisps of cotton lint snared into the roadside weeds and brambles from the passing gin-bound wagons, since this type of road was familiar out of his long-ago tenant-farmer freedom too: a Negro road, a road marked with many wheels and traced with cotton wisps, yet dirt, not even gravel, since the people who lived on and used it had neither the voting power to compel nor the money to persuade the Beat supervisor to do more than scrape and grade it twice a year.

So what he found was not only what he was hunting for but what he had expected: a weathered paintless dog-trot cabin enclosed and backed by a ramshackle of also-paintless weathered fences and outhouses—barns, cribs, sheds—on a rise of ground above a creek-bottom cotton patch where he could already see the whole Negro family and perhaps a neighbour or so too dragging the long stained sacks more or less abreast up the parallel rows—the father, the mother, five children between five or six and twelve, and four girls and young men who were probably the neighbours swapping the work, he, Mink, waiting at the end of the row until the father, who wold be the boss, reached him.

"Hidy," Mink said. "Looks like you could use another hand in here."

"You want to pick?" the Negro said.

"What you paying?"

"Six bits."

"I'll help you a spell," Mink said. The Negro spoke to the twelve-year-old girl beside him.

"Hand him your sack. You go on to the house and start supper."

He took the sack. There was nothing unfamiliar about it. He had been picking cotton at this time of the year all his life. The only difference was that for the last thirty-eight years there had been a shotgun and a bull whip at the end of the row behind him as a promise for lagging, where here again were the weighing scales and the money they designated as a reward for speed. And, as he had expected, his employer was presently in the row next him.

"You don't stay around here," the Negro said.

"That's right," he said. "I'm jest passing through. On my way down to the Delta where my daughter lives."

"Where?" the Negro said. "I made a Delta crop one year myself."

It wasn't that he should have expected this next question and would have avoided it if he knew how. It was rather that the question would not matter if he only didn't forget to think himself someone else except who he was. He didn't hesitate; he even volunteered: "Doddsville," he said. "Not fur from Parchman." And he knew what the next question would have been too, the one the Negro didn't ask and would not ask, answering that one too: "I been over a year in a hospital up in Memphis. The doctor said walking would be good for me. That's why I'm on the road instead of the train."

"The Vetruns Hospital?" the Negro said.

"What?" he said.

"The Govment Vetruns Hospital?"

"That's right," he said. "The govment had me. Over a year."

Now it was sundown. The wife had gone to the house some time ago. "You want to weigh out now?" the Negro said.

"I ain't in no rush," he said. "I can give you a half a day

tomorrow; jest so I knock off at noon. If your wife can fix me a plate of supper and a pallet somewhere, you can take that out of the weighing."

"I don't charge nobody to eat at my house," the Negro said.

The dining-room was an oilcloth-covered table bearing a coal-oil lamp in the same lean-to room where the wood-burning stove now died slowly. He ate alone, the family had vanished, the house itself might have been empty, the plate of fried side-meat and canned corn and tomatoes stewed together, the pale soft barely cooked biscuits, the cup of coffee already set and waiting for him when the man called him to come and eat. Then he returned to the front room where a few wood embers burned on the hearth against the first cool of autumn night; immediately the wife and the oldest girl rose and went back to the kitchen to set the meal for the family. He turned before the fire, spreading his legs; at his age he would feel the cool tonight. He spoke, casual, conversational, in the amenities, idly; at first, for a little while, you would have thought inattentively:

"I reckon you gin and trade in Jefferson. I used to know a few folks there. The banker. Dee Spain his name was, I remember. A long time back, of course."

"I don't remember him," the Negro said. "The main banker in Jefferson now is Mr Snopes."

"Oh yes, I heard tell about him. Big banker, big rich. Lives in the biggest house in town with a hired cook and a man to wait on the table for jest him and that daughter is it that makes out she's deaf."

"She is deaf. She was in the war. A cannon broke her ear-drums."

"So she claims." The Negro didn't answer. He was sitting in the room's—possibly the house's—one rocking chair, not moving anyway. But now something beyond just stillness had come over him: an immobility, almost like held breath. Mink's back was to the fire, the light, so his face was invisible; his voice anyway had not altered. "A woman in a war. She must have ever body fooled good. I've knowed them like that myself. She jest makes claims and ever body around is too polite to call her a liar. Likely she can hear ever bit as good as you and me."

Now the Negro spoke, quite sternly. "Whoever it was told you she is fooling is the one that's lying. There are folks in more places than right there in Jefferson that know the truth about her whether the word has got up to that Vetrun Hospital where you claim you was at or not. If I was you, I don't believe I would dispute it. Or leastways I would be careful who I disputed it to."

"Sho, sho," Mink said. "You Jefferson folks ought to know. You mean, she can't hear nothing? You could walk right up behind her, say, into the same room even, and she wouldn't know it?"

"Yes," the Negro said. The twelve-year-old girl now stood in the kitchen door. "She's deaf. You don't need to dispute it. The Lord touched her, like He touches a heap of folks better than you, better than me. Don't worry about that."

"Well, well," Mink said. "Sho, now. Your supper's ready." The Negro got up.

"What you going to do tonight?" he said. "I ain't got room for you."

"I don't need none," Mink said. "That doctor said for me to get all the fresh air I can. If you got a extry quilt. I'll sleep in the cotton truck and be ready for a early start back in that patch tomorrow."

The cotton which half-filled the bed of the pickup truck had been covered for the night with a tarpaulin, so he didn't even need the quilt. He was quite comfortable. But mainly he was off the ground. That was the danger, what a man had to watch against: once you laid flat on the ground, right away the earth started in to draw you back down into it. The very moment you were born out of your mother's body, the power and drag of the earth was already at work on you; if there had not been other womenfolks in the family or neighbours or even a hired one to support you, hold you up, keep the earth from touching you, you would not live an hour. And you knew it too. As soon as you could move you would raise your head even though that was all, trying to break the pull, trying to pull erect on chairs and things even when you still couldn't stand, to get away from the earth, save yourself. Then you could stand alone and take a step or two but even then during those first few years you still spent half of them on the ground, the old patient biding ground saying to you, "It's all right, it was just a fall, it don't hurt, don't be afraid." Then you are a man grown, strong, at your peak; now and then you can deliberately risk laying down on it in the woods hunting at night; you are too far from home to get back so you can even risk sleeping the rest of the night on it. Of course you will try to find something, anything—a plank, boards, a log, even brush tops—something, anything to intervene between your unconsciousness, helplessness, and the old patient ground that can afford to wait because it's going to get you someday, except that there ain't any use in giving you a full mile just because you dared an inch. And you know it; being young and strong you will risk one night on it but even you won't risk two nights in a row. Because even, say you take out in the field for noon and set under a tree or a hedgerow and eat your lunch and then lay down and you take a short nap and wake up and for a minute you don't even know where you are, for the good reason that you ain't all there; even in that short time while you wasn't watching, the old patient biding unhurried ground has already taken that first light holt on you, only you managed to wake up in time. So, if he had had to, he would have risked sleeping on the ground this last one night. But he had not had to chance it. It was as if Old Moster Himself had said, "I ain't going to help you none, but I ain't going to downright hinder you neither."

Then it was dawn, daybreak. He ate again, in solitude; when the sun rose they were in the cotton again; during these benisoned harvest days between summer's dew and fall's first frost the cotton was moisture-free for picking as soon as you could see it; until noon. "There," he told the Negro. "That ought to holp you out a little. You got a good bale for that Jefferson gin now so I reckon I'll go on down the road while I can get a ride for a change."

At last he was that close, that near. It had taken thirty-eight years and he had made a long loop down into the Delta and out again, but he was close now. But this road was a new approach to Jefferson, not the old one from Varner's store which he remembered. These new iron numbers along the roads were different too from the hand-lettered mile boards of recollection and though he could read figures all right, some, most of these

were not miles because they never got any smaller. But if they
had, in this case too he would have had to make sure:

"I believe this road goes right through Jefferson, don't it?"

"Yes," the Negro said. "You can branch off there for the
Delta."

"So I can. How far do you call it to town?"

"Eight miles," the Negro said. But he could figger a mile
whether he saw mileposts or not, seven then six then five, the
sun only barely past one o'clock; then four miles, a long hill
with a branch bottom at the foot of it and he said,

"Durn it, let me out at that bridge. I ain't been to the bushes
this morning." The Negro slowed the truck toward the bridge.
"It's all right," Mink said. "I'll walk on from here. In fact I'd
pure hate for that-ere doctor to see me getting out of even a
cotton truck or likely he'd try his durndest to collect another
dollar from me."

"I'll wait for you," the Negro said.

"No no," Mink said. "You want to get ginned and back home
before dark. You ain't got time." He got out of the cab and said,
in the immemorial country formula of thanks: "How much do I
owe you?" And the Negro answered in it:

"It ain't no charge. I was coming anyway."

"Much obliged," Mink said. "Jest don't mention to that
doctor about it if you every run across him. See you in the Delta
someday."

Then the truck was gone. The road was empty when he left it.
Out of sight from the road would be far enough. Only, if possible,
nobody must even hear the sound of the trial shot. He didn't
know why; he could not have said that, having had to do without
privacy for thirty-eight years, he now wanted, intended to
savour, every minuscule of it which freedom entitled him to;
also he still had five or six hours until dark, and probably even
less than that many miles, following the dense brier-cypress-
willow jungle of the creek bottom for perhaps a quarter of a mile,
maybe more, when suddenly he stopped dead with a kind of
amazed excitement, even exhilaration. Before him, spanning the
creek, was a railroad trestle. Now he not only knew how to reach
Jefferson without the constant risk of passing the people who
from that old Yoknapatawpha County affinity would know who

he was and what he intended to do, he would have something to do to pass the time until dark when he could go on.

It was as though he had not seen a railroad in thirty-eight years. One ran along one entire flank of the Parchman wire and he could see trains on it as far as he recalled every day. Also, from time to time gangs of convicts under their shotgun guards did rough construction or repair public works jobs in sight of railroads through the Delta where he could see trains. But even without the intervening wire, he looked at them from prison; the trains themselves were looked at, seen, alien in freedom, fleeing, existing in liberty and hence unreal, chimaeras, apparitions, without past or future, not even going anywhere since their destinations could not exist for him: just in motion a second, an instant, then nowhere; they had not been. But now it would be different. He could watch them, himself in freedom, as they fled past in freedom, the two of them mutual, in a way even interdependent: it to do the fleeing in smoke and noise and motion, he to do the watching; remembering how thirty-eight or forty years ago, just before he went to Parchman in fact—this occasion connected also with some crisis in his affairs which he had forgotten now; but then so were all his moments: connected, involved in some crisis of the constant outrage and injustice he was always having to drop everything to cope with, handle, with no proper tools and equipment for it, not even the time to spare from the unremitting work it took to feed himself and his family; this was one of those moments or maybe it had been simply the desire to see the train which had brought him the twenty-two miles in from Frenchman's Bend. Anyway, he had had to pass the night in town whatever the reason was and had gone down to the depot to see the New Orleans-bound passenger train come in—the hissing engine, the lighted cars each with an uppity impudent nigger porter, one car in which people were eating supper while more niggers waited on them, before going back to the sleeping-cars that had actual beds in them; the train pausing for a moment then gone: a long airtight chunk of another world dragged along the dark earth for the poor folks in overalls like him to gape at free for a moment without the train itself, let alone the folks in it, even knowing he was there.

But as free to stand and watch it as any man even if he did

wear overalls instead of diamonds; and as free now, until he
remembered something else he had learned in Parchman during
the long tedious years while he prepared for freedom—the
information, the trivia he had had to accumulate since when the
time, the freedom came, he might not know until too late when
he lacked: there had not been a passenger train through Jefferson
since 1935, that the railroad which old Colonel Sartoris (not the
banker they called Colonel but his father, the real colonel, that
had commanded all the local boys in the old slavery war) had
built, which according to the old folks whom even he, Mink,
knew and remembered, had been the biggest thing to happen in
Yoknapatawpha County, that was to have linked Jefferson and
and the county all the way from the Gulf of Mexico in one direction to the Great Lakes in the other, was now a fading weed-
grown branch line knowing no wheels any more save two local
freight trains more or less every day.

In which case, more than ever would the track, the right-of-
way be his path into town where the privacy of freedom it had
taken him thirty-eight years to earn would not be violated, so he
turned and retraced his steps perhaps a hundred yards and
stopped; there was nothing: only the dense jungle dappled with
September-afternoon silence. He took out the pistol. *Hit does look
like a cooter* he thought, with what at the moment he believed
was just amusement, humour, until he realised it was despair
because he knew now that the thing would not, could not
possibly fire, so that when he adjusted the cylinder to bring the
first of the three cartridges under the hammer and cocked it and
aimed at the base of a cypress four or five feet away and pulled
the trigger and heard the faint vacant click, his only emotion
was calm vindication, almost of superiority, at having been
right, of being in an unassailable position to say I told you so,
not even remembering cocking the hammer again since this
time he didn't know where the thing was aimed when it jerked
and roared, incredible with muzzle-blast because of the short
barrel; only now, almost too late, springing in one frantic
convulsion to catch his hand back before it cocked and fired the
pistol on the last remaining cartridge by simple reflex. But he
caught himself in time, freeing thumb and finger completely
from the pistol until he could reach across with his left hand and

remove it from the right one which in another second might have left him with an empty and useless weapon after all this distance and care and time. *Maybe the last one won't shoot neither* he thought, but for only a moment, a second, less than a second, thinking *No sir. It will have to. It will jest have to. There ain't nothing else for it to do. I don't need to worry. Old Moster jest punishes; He don't play jokes.*

And now (it was barely two o'clock by the sun, at least four hours till sundown) he could even risk the ground once more, this late, this last time, especially as he had last night in the cotton truck on the credit side. So he moved on again, beneath and beyond the trestle this time, just in case somebody had heard the shot and came to look, and found a smooth place behind a log and lay down. At once he began to feel the slow, secret, tentative palping start as the old biding unimpatient unhurried ground said to itself, "Well, well, be dawg if here ain't one already laying right here on my doorstep so to speak." But it was all right, he could risk it for this short time.

It was almost as though he had an alarm clock; he woke exactly in time to see through a leafed interstice overhead the last of sun drain, fade from the zenith, just enough light left to find his way back through the jungle to the railroad and mount on to it. Though it was better here, enough of day left to see him most of the last mile to town before it faded completely, displaced by darkness random with the sparse lights of the town's purlieus, the beginning, the first quiet edge-of-town back street beneath the rigid semaphore arms of the crossing warning and a single lonely street light where the Negro boy on the bicycle had ample time to see him standing in the centre of the crossing and brake to a stop. "Hidy, son," he said, using the old country-Negroid idiom for "live" too: "Which-a-way from here does Mr Flem Snopes stay?"

By now, since the previous Thursday night in fact, from about nine-thirty or ten each night until daybreak the next morning, Flem Snopes had had a bodyguard, though no white person in Jefferson, including Snopes himself, except the guard's wife, knew it. His name was Luther Biglin, a countryman, a professional dog trainer and market hunter and farmer until the last sheriff's election. Not only was his wife the niece of the husband of Sheriff Ephriam Bishop's wife's sister, Biglin's mother was the

sister of the rural political boss whose iron hand ruled one of the
county divisions (as old Will Varner ruled his at Frenchman's
Bend) which had elected Bishop sheriff. So Biglin was now jailor
under Bishop's tenure. Though with a definite difference from
the standard nepotic run. Where as often as not, the holders of
such lesser hierarchic offices gave nothing to the position they
encumbered, having not really wanted it anyway but accepting
it merely under family pressure to keep some member of the
opposite political faction out of it, Biglin brought to his the sort of
passionate enthusiastic devotion and fidelity to the power and
immaculacy and integrity of his kinsman-by-marriage's position
as say Murat's orderly corporal might have felt toward the
symbology of his master's baton.

He was not only honourable (even in his market hunting of
venison and duck and quail, where he broke only the law: never
his word), he was brave too. After Pearl Harbour, although his
mother's brother might, probably could and would, have found
or invented for him absolution from the draft, Biglin himself
volunteered for the Marine Corps, finding to his amazement
that by military standards he had next to no vision whatever in
his right eye. He had not noticed this himself. He was a radio man,
not a reading man, and in shooting (he was one of the best wing
shots in the county though in an exuberant spendthrift southpaw
fashion—he was left-handed, shooting from his left shoulder;
in the course of two of his three previous vocations he shot up
more shells than anyone in the county; at the age of thirty he
had already shot out two sets of shotgun barrels) the defect had
been an actual service to him since he had never had to train
himself to keep both eyes open and see the end of the gun and
the target at the same instant, or half-close the right one to
eliminate parallax. So when (not by curiosity, but by simple
bureaucratic consanguinity) he learned—even quicker than the
Sheriff did because he, Biglin, immediately believed it—that the
Mink Snopes free at last from the state penitentiary, his old
threats against his cousin, even though forty years old, durst not
be ignored, let alone dismissed as his patron and superior seemed
inclined to do.

So his aim, intent, was still basically to defend and preserve
the immaculacy of his kinsman-by-marriage's office, which was

to preserve the peace and protect human life and well-being, in which he modestly shared. But there was something else too, though only his wife knew it. Even the Sheriff didn't know about his plan, campaign; he only told his wife: "There may be nothing to it, like Cousin Eef says: just another of Lawyer Stevens's nightmares. But suppose Cousin Eef is wrong and Lawyer is right; suppose—" He could visualise it: the last split second, Mr Snopes helpless in bed beneath his doom, one last hopeless cry for the help which he knew was not there, the knife (hatchet, hammer, stick of stovewood, whatever the vengeance-ridden murderer would use) already descending when he, Biglin, would step, crash in, flashlight in one hand and pistol in the other: one single shot, the assassin falling across his victim, the expression of demonic anticipation and triumph fading to astonishment on his face—"Why, Mr Snopes will make us rich! He'll have to! There won't be nothing else he can do!"

Since Mr Snopes mustn't know about it either (the Sheriff had explained to him that in America you can't wet-nurse a free man unless he requests it or at least knowingly accepts it), he could not be inside the bedroom itself, where he should be, but would have to take the best station he could find or contrive outside the nearest window he could enter fastest or at least see to aim through. Which meant of course he would have to sit up all night. He was a good jailor, conscientious, keeping his jail clean and his prisoners properly fed and tended; besides the errands he did for the Sheriff. Thus the only time he would have to sleep in during the twenty-four hours would be between supper and the latest imperative moment when he must be at his station outside Snopes's bedroom window. So each night he would go to bed immediately after he rose from the supper table, and his wife would go to the picture show, on her return from which, usually about nine-thirty, she would wake him. Then, with his flashlight and pistol and a sandwich and a folding chair and a sweater against the chill as the late September nights cooled toward midnight, he would stand motionless and silent against the hedge facing the window where, as all Jefferson knew, Snopes spent all his life outside the bank, until the light went out at last; by which time, the two Negro servants would have long since left. Then he would move quietly across the lawn and open the chair beneath the window and sit down, sitting so immobile that the stray dogs which roamed all Jefferson during the hours of darkness, would be almost upon him before they would sense, smell, however they did it, that he was not asleep, and crouch and whirl in one silent motion and flee; until first light, when he would fold up the chair and make sure the crumpled sandwich wrapping was in his pocket, and depart; though by Sunday night, if Snopes had not been asleep and his daughter not stone deaf, now and then they could have heard him snoring—until, that is, the nocturnal dog crossing the lawn this time would tense, smell—however they did it—that he was asleep and harmless until actually touched by the cold nose.

Mink didn't know this. But even if he had, it probably would have made little difference. He would simply have regarded the whole thing—Biglin, the fact that Snopes was now being guarded —as just one more symptom of the infinite capacity for petty invention of the inimical forces which had always dogged his life. So even if he had known that Biglin was already on station under the window of the room where his cousin now sat (He had not hurried. On the contrary: once the Negro boy on the bicycle had given him directions, he thought *I'm even a little ahead. Let them eat supper first and give them two niggers time to be outen the way.*) he would have behaved no differently: not hiding, not lurking: just unseen unheard and irrevocably alien like a coyote or a small wolf; not crouching, not concealed by the hedge as Biglin himself would do when he arrived, but simply squatting on his hams—as, a countryman, he could do for hours without discomfort—against it while he examined the house whose shape and setting he already knew out of the slow infinitesimal Parchman trickle of facts and information which he had had to garner, assimilate, from strangers yet still conceal from them the import of what he asked; looking in fact at the vast white columned edifice with something like pride that someone named Snopes owned it; a complete and absolute unjealousy: at another time, tomorrow, though he himself would never dream nor really ever want to be received in it, he would have said proudly to a stranger: "My cousin lives there. He own it."

It looked exactly as he had known it would. There were the lighted rear windows of the corner room where his cousin would be sitting (they would surely have finished supper by now; he had given them plenty of time) with his feet propped on the little special ledge he had heard in Parchman how another kinsman Mink had never seen, Wat Snopes having been born too late, had nailed on to the hearth for that purpose. There were lights also in the windows of the room in front of that one, which he had not expected, knowing also about the special room upstairs the deaf daughter had fixed up for herself. But no light showed upstairs at all, so evidently the daughter was still down-stairs too. And although the lights in the kitchen indicated that the two Negro servants had not left either, his impulse was so strong that he had already begun to rise without waiting longer, to cross to the window and see, if necessary begin now; who had had thirty-eight years to practise patience in and should have been perfect. Because if he waited too long, his cousin might be in bed, perhaps even asleep. Which would be intolerable and must not be: there must be that moment, even if it lasted only a second, for him to say, "Look at me, Flem," and his cousin would do so. But he restrained himself, who had had thirty-eight years to learn to wait in, and sank, squatted back again, easing the hard lump of the pistol which he now carried inside the bib front of his overalls; her room would be on the other side of the house where he couldn't see the lighted windows from here, and the lights in the other room meant nothing since if he was big rich like his cousin Flem, with a fine big house like that, he would have all the lights on downstairs too.

Then the lights went off in the kitchen; presently he could hear the Negro man and the woman still talking as they approached and (he didn't even hold his breath) passed within ten feet of him and went through the gate in the hedge, the voices moving slowly up the lane beyond it until they died away. Then he rose, quietly, without haste, not furtive, not slinking: just small, just colourless, perhaps simply too small to be noticed, and crossed the lawn to the window and (he had to stand on tiptoe) looked into it at his cousin sitting in the swivel chair like in a bank or an office, with his feet propped against the chimney and his hat on, as he, Mink, had known he would be sitting, looking not too different even though Mink hadn't seen him in forty years; a little changed of course: the black planter's

hat he had heard about in Parchman but the little bow tie
might have been the same one he had been wearing forty years
ago behind the counter in Varner's store, the shirt a white city
shirt and the pants dark city pants too and the shoes polished
city shoes instead of farmer's brogans. But no different, really:
not reading, just sitting there with his feet propped and his hat
on, his jaw moving faintly and steadily as if he were chewing.

Just to be sure, he would circle the house until he could see
the lighted upper windows on the other side and had already
started around the back when he thought how he might as well
look into the other lighted room also while he was this close to it
and moved, no less quiet than a shadow and with not much more
substance, along the wall until he could stand on tiptoe again
and look in the next window, the next room. He saw her at once
and knew her at once—a room walled almost to the ceiling with
more books than he knew existed, a woman sitting beneath a
lamp in the middle of the room reading one, in horn-rim glasses
and that single white streak through the centre of her black hair
that he had heard about in Parchman too. For a second the old
helpless fury and outrage possessed him again and almost
ruined, destroyed him this time—the rage and fury when,
during the first two or three years after he learned that she was
back home again apparently for good and living right there in
the house with Flem, he would think *Suppose she ain't deaf a-tall;
suppose she's jest simply got ever body fooled for whatever devilment of her
own she's up to* since this—the real truth of whether she was deaf
or just pretending—was one gambit which he would not only
have to depend on somebody else for, but on something as frail
and undependable as second- or third-hand hearsay. Finally he
had lied, tricked his way in to the prison doctor but there he was
again: daring not to ask what he wanted to know, had to know,
find out, learn: only that even the stone-deaf would—could—
feel the concussion of the air if the sound were loud enough or
close enough. "Like a—" Mink said before he could stop himself.
But too late; the doctor finished it for him: "That's right. A
shot. But even if you could make us believe you are, how would
that get you out of here?" "That's right," Mink said. "I wouldn't
need to hear that bull whip: jest feel it."

But that would be all right; there was that room she had fixed

up for herself upstairs, while every word from home that trickled
down to him in Parchman—you had to believe folks sometimes,
you had to, you jest had to—told how his cousin spent all his
time in the one downstairs cattycorner across that house that was
bigger they said than even the jail. Then to look in the window
and find her, not upstairs and across the house where she should
have been, where in a way it had been promised to him she
would be, but right there in the next room. In which case everything else he had believed in and depended on until now was
probably trash and rubble too; there didn't even need to be an
open door between the two rooms so she could be sure to feel
what the prison doctor had called the concussion because she
wasn't even deaf. Everything had lied to him; he thought quietly
*And I ain't even got but one bullet left even if I would have time to use
two before somebody come busting in from the street. I got to find a stick
of stovewood or a piece of ahrn somewhere*—that close, that near to
ruination and destruction before he caught himself back right
on the brink, murmuring, whispering, "Wait now, wait. Ain't I
told you and told you Old Moster don't play jokes; He jest
punishes? Of course she's deaf: ain't all up and down Missippi
been telling you that for ten years now? I don't mean that durn
Parchman doctor nor all the rest of them durn jailbird son of a
bitches that was all I had to try to find out what I had to know
from, but that nigger jest yestiddy evening that got almost
impident, durn nigh called a white man a liar to his face the
least suh-jestion I made that maybe she was fooling folks.
Niggers that don't only know all the undercover about white
folks, let alone one that they already claim is a nigger lover and
even one of them commonists to boot, until all the niggers in
Yoknapatawpha County and likely Memphis and Chicago too
know the truth about whether she is deaf or not or ever thing
else about her or not. Of course she's deaf, setting there with her
back already to the door where you got to pass and they's bound
to be a back door too that all you got to do is jest find it and walk
right on out." and moved on, without haste: not furtive, just
small and light-footed and invisible, on around the house and up
the steps and on between the soaring columns of the portico like
any other guest, visitor, caller, opening the screen door quietly
into the hall and through it, passing the open door beyond

which the woman sat, not even glancing toward it, and went on
to the next one and drew the pistol from his overall bib; and,
thinking hurriedly, a little chaotically, almost like tiny panting
*I ain't got but one bullet so it will have to be in the face, the head; I can't
resk jest the body with jest one bullet* entered the room where his
cousin sat and ran a few more steps toward him.

He didn't need to say, "Look at me, Flem." His cousin was
already doing that, his head turned over his shoulder. Otherwise
he hadn't moved, only the jaws ceased chewing in midmotion.
Then he moved, leaned slightly forward in the chair and he had
just begun to lower his propped feet from the ledge, the chair
beginning to swivel around, when Mink from about five feet
away stopped and raised the toad-shaped iron-rust-coloured
weapon in both hands and cocked and steadied it, thinking
Hit's got to hit his face: not *I've got to* but *It's got to* and pulled the
trigger and rather felt than heard the dull foolish almost inattentive click. Now his cousin, his feet now flat on the floor and
the chair almost swivelled to face him, appeared to sit immobile
and even detached too, watching too Mink's grimed shaking
child-sized hands like the hands of a pet coon as one of them
lifted the hammer enough for the other to roll the cylinder back
one notch so that the shell would come again under the hammer;
again that faint something out of the past nudged, prodded: not
a warning nor even really a repetition: just faint and familiar
and unimportant still since, whatever it had been, even before
it had not been strong enough to alter anything nor even remark-
able enough to be remembered; in the same second he had
dismissed it. *Hit's all right* he thought *Hit'll go this time: Old
Moster don't play jokes* and cocked and steadied the pistol again
in both hands, his cousin not moving at all now though he was
chewing faintly again, as though he too were watching the dull
point of light on the cock of the hammer when it flicked away.

It made a tremendous sound though in the same instant Mink
no longer heard it. His cousin's body was now making a curious
half-stifled convulsive surge which in another moment was
going to carry the whole chair over; it seemed to him, Mink,
that the report of the pistol was nothing but that when the chair
finished falling and crashed to the floor, the sound would wake
all Jefferson. He whirled; there was a moment yet when he tried

to say, cry, "Stop! Stop! You got to make sho he's dead or you will have throwed away ever thing!" but he could not, he didn't remember when he had noticed the other door in the wall beyond the chair but it was there; where it led to didn't matter just so it led on and not back. He ran to it, scrabbling at the knob, still shaking and scrabbling at it even after he realised it was locked, still shaking the knob, quite blind now, even after the voice spoke behind him and he whirled again and saw the woman standing in the hall door; for an instant he thought *So she could hear all the time* before he knew better: she didn't need to hear; it was the same power had brought her here to catch him that by merely pointing her finger at him could blast, annihilate, vaporise him where he stood. And no time to cock and aim the pistol again even if he had had another bullet so even as he whirled he flung, threw the pistol at her, nor even able to follow that because in the same second it seemed to him she already had the pistol in her hand, holding it toward him, saying in that quacking duck's voice that deaf people use:

"Here. Come and take it. That door is a closet. You'll have to come back this way to get out."

EIGHTEEN

"STOP the car," Stevens said. Ratliff did so. He was driving though it was Stevens's car. They had left the highway at the crossroads—Varner's store and gin and blacksmith shop, and the church and the dozen or so dwellings and other edifices, all dark now though it was not yet ten o'clock, which composed the hamlet—and had now traversed and left behind the rest of the broad flat rich valley land on which old Varner—in his eighties now, his hair definitely grey, twelve years a widower until two years ago when he married a young woman of twenty-five or so who at the time was supposed to be engaged to, anyway courted by, his grandson—held liens and mortgages where he didn't own it outright; and now they were approaching the hills: a section of small worn-out farms tilted and precarious among the eroded folds like scraps of paper. The road had ceased some time back to be even gravel and at any moment now it would cease to be passable to anything on wheels; already, in the fixed glare (Ratliff had stopped the car) of the headlights, it resembled just one more eroded ravine twisting up the broken rise crested with shabby and shaggy pine and worthless blackjack. The sun had crossed the equator, in Libra now; and in the cessation of motion and the quiet of the idling engine, there was a sense of autumn after the slow drizzle of Sunday and the bright spurious cool which had lasted through Monday almost; the jagged rampart of pines and scrub oak was a thin dike against the winter and rain and cold, under which the worn-out fields overgrown with sumac and sassafras and persimmon had already turned scarlet, the persimmons heavy with fruit waiting only for frost and the baying of potlicker possum hounds. "What makes you think he will be there even if we can get there ourselves?" Stevens said.

"Where else would he be?" Ratliff said. "Where else has he got to go? Back to Parchman, after all this recent trouble and expense it taken him to get out? What else has he got but home?"

"He hasn't even got that home any more," Stevens said. "When was it—three years ago—that day we drove out here about that boy—what was his name?—"

383

"Turpin," Ratliff said.

"—that didn't answer his draft call and we came out looking for him. There wasn't anything left of the house then but the shell. Part of the roof, and what was left of the walls above the height convenient to pull off for firewood. This road was better then too."

"Yes," Ratliff said. "Folks kept it kind of graded and scraped up dragging out that kindling."

"So there's not even the shell any more."

"There's a cellar under it," Ratliff said.

"A hole in the ground?" Stevens said. "A den like an animal?"

"He's tired," Ratliff said. "Even if he wasn't sixty-three or -four years old. He's been under a strain for thirty-eight years, let alone the last—this is Thursday, ain't it?—seven days. And now he ain't got no more strain to prop him up. Jest suppose you had spent thirty-eight years waiting to do something, and sho enough one day you finally done it. You wouldn't have much left neither. So what he wants now is jest to lay down in the dark and the quiet somewhere for a spell."

"He should have thought of that last Thursday," Stevens said. "It's too late to do that now."

"Ain't that exactly why we're out here?" Ratliff said.

"All right," Stevens said. "Drive on." Instead, Ratliff switched off the engine. Now indeed they could sense, feel the change of the season and the year. Some of the birds remained but the night was no longer full of the dry loud cacophony of summer nocturnal insects. There were only the crickets in the dense hedgerows and stubble of mown hayfields, where at noon the dusty grasshoppers would spurt, frenetic and random, going nowhere. And now Stevens knew what was coming, what Ratliff was going to talk about.

"You reckon she really never knowed what that durn little rattlesnake was going to do the minute they turned him loose?" Ratliff said.

"Certainly not," Stevens said, quickly, too quickly, too late. "Drive on."

But Ratliff didn't move. Stevens noticed that he still held his hand over the switch key so that Stevens himself couldn't have started the engine. "I reckon she'll stop over in Memphis

tonight," Ratliff said. "With ther-ere fancy brand-new automobile and all."

Stevens remembered all that. His trouble was, to forget it.
She had told him herself—or so he believed then—this morning
after she had given him the necessary information to draw the
deed: how she wasn't going to accept her so-called father's
automobile either but instead had ordered a new one from
Memphis, which would be delivered in time for her to leave
directly after the funeral; he could bring the deed to the house
for her signature when they said good-bye, or what they—she
and he—would have of good-bye.

It was a big funeral: a prominent banker and financier who
had not only died in his prime (financial anyway) of a pistol
wound but from the wrong pistol wound, since by ordinary a
banker dying of a pistol in his own bedroom at nine o'clock in
the evening should have just said good-night to a state or federal
(maybe both) bank inspector. He (the deceased) had no auspices
either: fraternal, civic, nor military: only finance; not an economy
—cotton or cattle or anything else which Yoknapatawpha
County and Mississippi were established on and kept running
by, but belonging simply to Money. He had been a member of a
Jefferson church true enough, as the outward and augmented
physical aspect of the edifice showed, but even that had been not
a subservience nor even an aspiration nor even really a
confederation nor even an amnesty, but simply an armistice
temporary between two irreconcilable tongues.

Yet not just the town but the county too came to it. He
(Stevens) sat, a member of the cast itself, by the (sic) daughter's
request, on the front row in fact and next her by her insistence:
himself and Linda and her Uncle Jody, a balding man who had
added another hundred pounds of jowl and belly to his father's
long skeleton; and yes, Wall Street Snopes, Wall Street Panic
Snopes, who not only had never acted like a Snopes, he never
had even looked like one: a tall dark man except for the eyes of
an incredible tender youthful periwinkle blue, who had begun
as the delivery boy in a side-street grocery to carry himself and
his younger brother, Admiral Dewey, through school, and went
from there to create a wholesale grocery supply house in Jefferson
serving all the county; and now, removed with his family to

BB

Memphis, owned a chain of wholesale grocery establishments blanketing half of Mississippi and Tennessee and Arkansas too; all of them facing the discreetly camouflaged excavation beside the other grave over which not her husband (who has merely ordained and paid for it) but Stevens himself had erected the outrageous marble lie which had been the absolution for Linda's freedom nineteen years ago. As it would be he who would erect whatever lie this one would postulate; they—he and Linda—had discussed that too this morning.

"No. Nothing," she said.

Yes he wrote.

"No," she said. He merely raised the tablet and held the word facing her; he could not have written *It's for your sake* Then he didn't need to. "You're right," she said. "You will have to do another one too."

He wrote *We will*

"No," she said. "You always have for me. You always will for me. I know now I've never really had anybody but you. I've never really needed anybody else but you."

Sitting there while the Baptist minister did his glib and rapid office, he (Stevens) looked around at the faces, town faces and country faces, the citizens who represented the town because the town should be represented at this obsequy; the ones who represented simply themselves because some day they would be where Flem Snopes now lay, as friendless and dead and alone too; the diffident anonymous hopeful faces who had owed him or his bank money and, as people will and can, hoped, were even capable of believing that, now that he was dead, the debt might, barely might become lost or forgotten or even simply undemanded, uncollected. Then suddenly he saw something else. There were not many of them: he distinguished only three, country faces also, looking no different from the other country faces diffident, even effacing, in the rear of the crowd; until suddenly they leaped, sprang out, and he knew who they were. They were Snopeses; he had never seen them before but they were incontrovertible: not alien at all: simply identical, not so much in expression as in position, attitude; he thought rapidly, in something like that second of simple panic when you are wakened *They're like wolves come to look at the trap where another*

FLEM 387

bigger wolf, the boss wolf, the head wolf, what Ratliff would call the bull wolf, died; if maybe there was not a shred or scrap of hide still snared in it.

Then that was gone. He could not keep on looking behind him and now the minister had finished and the undertaker signalled for the select, the publicly bereaved, to depart; and when he looked, could look again, the faces were gone. He left Linda there. That is, her uncle would drive her home, where by this time the new automobile she had told him she had telephoned to Memphis for after she decided yesterday afternoon to drive alone to New York as soon as the funeral was over, would be waiting; she would probably be ready to leave, the new car packed and all, by the time he got there with the deed for her to sign.

So he went to the office and picked it up—a deed of gift (with the usual consideration of one dollar) returning the house and its lot to the De Spains. She had done it all herself, she hadn't even informed him in the process, let alone beforehand. She had been unable to locate Manfred, whom Snopes had dispossessed of it along with the bank and the rest of his, Manfred's, name and dignity in Jefferson, but she had found at last what remained of his kin—the only sister of old Major de Spain, Manfred's father, and her only child: a bedridden old woman living in Los Angeles with her spinster daughter of sixty, the retired principal of a suburban Los Angeles grammar school; she, Linda, tracing, running them down herself without even consulting her lawyer: an outrage really, when the Samaritan, the philanthropist, the benefactor, begins not only to find but even to invent his own generosities, not only without recourse to but even ignoring the lawyers and secretaries and public relations counsellors; outrageous, antisocial in fact, taking the very cake out of that many mouths.

The papers wanted only her signature; it had not been fifteen minutes yet when he slowed his car in toward the curb before the house, not even noticing the small group—men, boys, a Negro or so—in front of him except to say, "The local committee validating her new automobile," and parked his own and got out with the briefcase and had even turned, his glance simply passing across the group because it was there, when he said with a quick, faint, not really yet surprise, "It's a

British Jaguar. It's brand new," and was even walking on when suddenly it was as if a staircase you are mounting becomes abruptly a treadmill, you still walking, mounting, expending energy and motion but without progress; so abrupt and sudden in fact that you are only your aura, your very momentum having carried your corporeality one whole step in advance of you; he thought *No place on earth from which a brand-new Jaguar could be delivered to Jefferson, Mississippi, since even noon yesterday, let alone not even telephoned for until last night* thinking, desperately now *No! No! It is possible! They could have had one, found one in Memphis last night or this morning—this ramshackle universe which has nothing to hold it together but coincidence* and walked smartly up and paused beside it, thinking *So she knew she was going to leave after last Thursday; she just didn't know until Tuesday night exactly what day that would be*. It was spanking unblemished new, the youngish quite decent-looking agent or deliverer stood beside it and at that moment the Negro houseman came out the front door carrying some of her luggage.

"Afternoon," Stevens said. "Damned nice car. Brand new, isn't it?"

"That's right," the young man said. "Never even touched the ground until Mrs Kohl telephoned for it yesterday."

"Lucky you had one on hand for her," Stevens said.

"Oh, we've had it since the tenth of this month. When she ordered it last July she just told us to keep it when it came in, until she wanted it. I suppose her father's . . . death changed her plans some."

"Things like that do," Stevens said. "She ordered it in July."

"That's right. They haven't caught the fellow yet, I hear."

"Not yet," Stevens said. "Damned nice car. Would like to afford one myself," and went on, into the open door and up the stairs which knew his feet, into the sitting-room which knew him too. She stood watching him while he approached, dressed for the drive in a freshly laundered suit of the faded khaki coveralls, her face and mouth heavily made up against the wind of motion; on a chair lay the stained burberry and her purse and heavy gloves and a scarf for her head; she said, At least I didn't lie to you. I could have hidden it in the garage until you had come and gone, but I didn't. Though not in words: she said,

"Kiss me, Gavin," taking the last step to him herself and taking him into her arms, firm and without haste and set her mouth to his, firmly and deliberately too, and opened it, he holding her, his hand moving down her back while the dividing incleft outswell of her buttocks rose under the harsh khaki, as had happened before now and then, the hand unchallenged—it had never been challenged, it would never be, the fidelity unthreatened and secure even if there had been nothing at all between the hand and the inswelling incleft woman flesh, he simply touching her, learning and knowing not with despair or grief but just sorrow a little, simply supporting her buttocks as you cup the innocent hipless bottom of a child. But not now, not this time. It was terror now; he thought with terror *How did it go? the man "whose irresistible attraction to women was that simply by being in their presence he gave them to convince themselves that he was capable of any sacrifice for them". Which is backward, completely backward; the poor dope not only didn't know where first base was, he didn't even know he was playing baseball. You don't need to tempt them because they have long since already selected you by that time, choosing you simply because they believe that in the simple act of being selected you have at once become not merely willing and ready but passionately desirous of making a sacrifice for them just as soon as the two of you can think of one good enough, worthy.* He thought *Now she will realise that she cannot trust me but only hoped she could so now the thrust of hips, gripping both shoulders to draw me into the backward-falling even without a bed* and was completely wrong; he thought *Why should she waste her time trusting me when she has known all her life that all she has to do is just depend on me.* She just stood holding him and kissing him until he himself moved first to be free. Then she released him and stood looking at his face out of the dark blue eyes not secret, not tender, perhaps not even gentle.

"Your mouth is a mess," she said. "You'll have to go to the bathroom.—You are right," she said. "You always are right about you and me." They were not secret: intent enough yes, but not secret; someday perhaps he would remember that they never had been really tender even. "I love you," she said. "You haven't had very much, have you. No, that's wrong. You haven't had anything. You have had nothing."

He knew exactly what she meant: her mother first, then her;

that he had offered the devotion twice and got back for it nothing but the privilege of being obsessed, bewitched, besotted if you like; Ratliff certainly would have said besotted. And she knew he knew it; that was (perhaps) their curse: they both knew any and every mutual thing immediately. It was not because of the honesty, nor because she believed she had been in love with him all her life, that she had let him discover the new Jaguar and what it implied in the circumstances of her so-called father's death. It was because she knew she could not have kept concealed from him the fact that she had ordered the car from New York or London or wherever it came from, the moment she knew for sure he could get Mink the pardon.

She had pockets in all her clothes into which the little ivory tablet with its clipped stylus exactly fitted. He knew all of them, the coveralls too, and reached his hand and took it out. He could have written *I have everything. You trusted me. You chose to let me find you murdered your so-called father rather than tell me a lie.* He could, perhaps should have written *I have everything. Haven't I just finished being accessory before a murder.* Instead, he wrote *We have had everything*

"No," she said.

He wrote *Yes*

"No," she said.

He printed *YES* this time in letters large enough to cover the rest of the face of the tablet and erased it clean with the heel of his palm and wrote *Take someone with You to hear you Will be killed*

She barely glanced at it, nowhere near long enough, anyone would have thought, to have read it, then stood looking at him again, the dark blue eyes that whether they were gentle or not or tender or not or really candid or not, it didn't matter. Her mouth was smeared too behind the faint smiling, itself—the smiling— like a soft smear, a drowsing stain. "I love you," she said. "I have never loved anybody but you."

He wrote *No*

"Yes," she said.

He wrote *No* again and even while she said "Yes" again he wrote *No No No No* until he had completely filled the tablet and erased it and wrote *Deed* And, standing side by side at the mantel where they transacted all her business which required communication between them, he spread the document and uncapped his pen for her to sign it and folded the paper and was putting it back into the briefcase when she said, "This too." It was a plain long envelope, he had noticed it on the mantel. When he took it he could feel the thick sheaf of banknotes through the paper, too many of them; a thousand dollars would destroy him in a matter of weeks, perhaps days, as surely as that many bullets. He had been tempted last night to tell her so: "A thousand dollars will kill him too. Will you be satisfied then?" even though he was still ignorant last night how much truth that would be. But he refrained. He would take care of that himself when the time came. "Do you know where you can find him?"

Ratliff does he wrote and erased it and wrote *Go out 2 minutes Bathroom your Mouth too* and stood while she read it and then herself stood a moment longer, not moving, her head bent as if he had written perhaps in cryptogram. "Oh," she said. Then she said: "Yes. It's time," and turned and went to the door and stopped and half-turned and only then looked at him: no faint smile, no nothing: just the eyes which even at this distance were not quite black. Then she was gone.

He already had the briefcase in his hand. His hat was on the table. He put the envelope into his pocket and scrubbed at his mouth with his handkerchief, taking up the hat in passing, and went on, down the stairs, wetting the handkerchief with spittle to scrub his mouth. There would be a mirror in the hall but this would have to do until he reached the office; there would be, was a back door of course but there was the houseman somewhere and maybe even the cook too. Besides, there was no law against crossing the front lawn itself from the front entrance and so through the side gate into the lane, from which he could reach the street without even having to not look at the new car again. Until Ratliff, happening to be standing by chance or coincidence near the foot of the office stairs, said, "Where's your car? Never mind, I'll go pick it up. Meantime you better use some water when you get upstairs."

He did, and locked the stained handkerchief into a drawer and sat in the office. In time he heard Ratliff's feet on the stairs

though Ratliff shook the locked door only; here was another
time when he could have worked at his youthful dream of
restoring the Old Testament to its virgin's pristinity. But he was
too old now. Evidently it takes more than just anguish to be all
that anguishing. In time the telephone rang. "She's gone,"
Ratliff said. "I've got your car. You want to come and eat supper
with me?"

"No," he said.

"You want me to telephone your wife that's what you're
doing?"

"Dammit, I told you No," he said. Then he said, "Much
obliged."

"I'll pick you up at eight o'clock say," Ratliff said.

He was at the curb waiting; the car—his—moved immediately
he was in it. "I'm not safe," he said.

"I reckon so," Ratliff said. "It's all over now, soon that is as
we get used to it."

"I mean, you're not safe. Nobody is, around me. I'm dangerous. Can't you understand I've just committed murder?"

"Oh, that," Ratliff said. "I decided some time back that
maybe the only thing that would make you safe to have around
would be for somebody to marry you. That never worked but
at least you're all right now. As you jest said, you finally committed a murder. What else is there beyond that for anybody to
think up for you to do?" Now they were on the highway, the
town behind them and they could pick up a little speed to face
the twenty miles out to Varner's store. "You know the one in
this business I'm really sorry for? It's Luther Biglin. You ain't
heard about that and likely wouldn't nobody else if it hadn't
kind of come out today in what you might call a private interview or absolvement between Luther and Eef Bishop. It seems
that ever night between last Thursday and the following Tuesday,
Luther has been standing or setting guard as close as he could
get outside that window from as soon as he could get there after
Miz Biglin would get back from the picture show and wake
him up, to daylight. You know: having to spend all day long
taking care of his jail and prisoners in addition to staying close
to the sheriff's office in case Eef might need him, he would have
to get some rest and the only way he could work it would be

after he et supper until Miz Biglin, who acted as his alarm clock, got back from the picture show, which would be from roughly seven o'clock to roughly more or less half-past nine or ten o'clock, depending on how long the picture show was, the balance of the night standing or setting in a folding chair jest outside Flem's window, not for a reward or even glory, since nobody but Miz Biglin knowed it, but simply outen fidelity to Eef Bishop's sworn oath to defend and protect human life in Jefferson even when the human life was Flem Snopes's. Yet outen the whole twenty-four hours Mink could a picked, he had to pick one between roughly seven o'clock and roughly nine-thirty to walk in on Flem with that thing whoever sold it to him told him was a pistol, almost like Mink done it outen pure and simple spite—a thing which, as the feller says, to a dog shouldn't happen."

"Drive on," Stevens said. "Pick it up."

"Yes," Ratliff said. "So this is what it all come down to. All the ramshacking and foreclosing and grabbling and snatching, doing it by gentle underhand when he could but by honest hard trompling when he had to, with a few of us trying to trip him and still dodge outen the way when we could but getting over-trompled too when we couldn't. And now all that's left of it is a bedrode old lady and her retired old-maid schoolteacher daughter that would a lived happily ever after in sunny golden California. But now they got to come all the way back to Missippi and live in that-ere big white elephant of a house where likely Miss Allison will have to go back to work again, maybe might even have to hump and hustle some to keep it up since how can they have mere friends and acquaintances, let alone strangers, saying how a Missippi-born and -bred lady refused to accept a whole house not only gift-free-for-nothing but that was actively theirn anyhow to begin with, without owing even Much obliged to nobody for getting it back. So maybe there's even a moral in it somewhere, if you jest knowed where to look."

"There aren't any morals," Stevens said. "People just do the best they can."

"The pore sons of bitches," Ratliff said.

"The poor sons of bitches," Stevens said. "Drive on. Pick it up."

So somewhere about ten o'clock he sat beside Ratliff in the dark car on a hill road that had already ceased to be a road and soon would cease to be even passable, while Ratliff said, "So you think she really didn't know what he was going to do when he got out?"

"Yes I tell you," Stevens said. "Drive on."

"We got time," Ratliff said. "He ain't going nowhere. Talking about that thing he used for a pistol, that he dropped or throwed it away while he was running through that back yard. Eef Bishop let me look at it. That Memphis feller was right. It didn't even look like a pistol. It looked like a old old mud-crusted cooter. It had two shells in it, the hull and another live one. The cap of the hull was punched all right, only it and the live one both had a little nick jest outside the cap, both of the nicks jest alike and even in the same place, so that when Eef taken the live one out and turned the hull a little and set it back under the hammer and cocked it and snapped it and we opened the cylinder, there was another of them little nicks in the case jest outside the cap, like sometimes that mossback firing pin would hit the cap and sometimes it wouldn't. So it looks like Mink either tried out both of them shells beforehand for practice test and both of them snapped once, yet he still walked in there to kill Flem jest hoping one of them would go off this time, which don't sound reasonable; or that he stood there in front of Flem and snapped both of them at him and then turned the cylinder back to try again since that was all he had left he could do at that moment, and this time one of them went off. In that case, what do you reckon Flem's reason was for setting there in that chair letting Mink snap them two shells at him until one of them went off and killed him?"

"I don't know," Stevens said harshly. "Drive on!"

"Maybe he was jest bored too," Ratliff said. "Like Eula. Maybe there was two of them. The pore son of a bitch."

"He was impotent," Stevens said.

"What?" Ratliff said.

"Impotent. When he got in bed with a woman all he could do was go to sleep.—Yes!" Stevens said. "The poor sons of bitches that have to cause all the grief and anguish they have to cause! Drive on!"

"But suppose it was more than that," Ratliff said. "You was town-raised when you was a boy; likely you never heard of Give-me-lief. It was a game we played. You would pick out another boy about your own size and you would walk up to him with a switch or maybe a light stick or a hard green apple or maybe even a rock, depending on how hard a risk you wanted to take, and say to him, 'Gimme lief,' and if he agreed, he would stand still and you would take one cut or one lick at him with the switch or stick, as hard as you picked out, or back off and throw at him once with the green apple or the rock. Then you would stand still and he would take the same switch or stick or apple or rock or anyways another one jest like it, and take one cut or throw at you. That was the rule. So jest suppose—"

"Drive on!" Stevens said.

"—Flem had had his lief fair and square like the rule said, so there wasn't nothing for him to do but jest set there, since he had likely found out years back when she finally turned up here again even outen a communist war, that he had already lost—"

"Stop it!" Stevens said. "Don't say it!"

"—and now it was her lief and so suppose—"

"No!" Stevens said "No!" But Ratliff was not only nearer the switch, his hand was already on it, covering it.

"—she knowed all the time what was going to happen when he got out, that not only she knowed but Flem did too—"

"I won't believe it!" Stevens said. "I won't! I can't believe it," he said. "Don't you see I cannot?"

"Which brings up something else," Ratliff said. "So she had a decision to make too that once she made it, it would be for good and all and too late to change it. She could a waited two more years and God His-self couldn't a kept Mink in Parchman without He killed him, and saved herself not jest the bother and worry but the moral responsibility too, even if you do say they ain't no morals. Only she didn't. And so you wonder why. If maybe, if there wasn't no folks in heaven, it wouldn't be heaven, and if you couldn't recognise them as folks you knowed, wouldn't nobody want to go there. And that someday her maw would be saying to her, 'Why didn't you revenge me and my love that I finally found it, instead of jest standing back and blind hoping for happen-so? Didn't you never have no love of your own to

learn you what it is?'—Here," he said. He took out the im-
maculately clean, impeccably laundered and ironed handkerchief which the town said he not only laundered himself but
hemstitched himself too, and put it into Stevens's blind hand and
turned the switch and flicked on the headlights. "I reckon we'll
be about right now," he said.

Now the road even ceased to be two ruts. It was a gash now,
choked with brier, still mounting. "I'll go in front," Ratliff said.
"You growed up in town. I never even seen a light bulb until
after I could handle a straight razor." Then he said, "There it is"
—a canted roof line where one end of the gable had collapsed
completely (Stevens did not recognise, he simply agreed it
could once have been a house) above which stood one worn
gnarled cedar. He almost stumbled through, across what had
been a fence, a yard fence, fallen too, choked fiercely with rose
vines long since gone wild again. "Walk behind me," Ratliff
said. "They's a old cistern. I think I know where it is. I ought to
brought a flashlight."

And now, in a crumbling slant downward into, through,
what had been the wall's old foundation, an orifice, a black and
crumbled aperture yawned at their feet as if the ruined house
itself had gaped at them. Ratliff had stopped. He said quietly:
"You never seen that pistol. I did. It didn't look like no one-for-
ten-dollars pistol. It looked like one of a two-for-nine-and-a-half
pistols. Maybe he's still got the other one with him," when
Stevens, without stopping, pushed past him and, fumbling one
foot downward, found what had been a step; and, taking the
gold initialled lighter from his pocket, snapped it on and by the
faint wavered gleam continued to descend, Ratliff, behind now,
saying, "Of course. He's free now. He won't never have to kill
nobody else in all his life," and followed, into the old cellar—
the cave, the den where on a crude platform he had heaped
together, the man they sought half-squatted half-knelt blinking
up at them like a child interrupted at its bedside prayers: not
surprised in prayer: interrupted, kneeling in the new overalls
which were stained and foul now, his hands lying half-curled on
the front of his lap. blinking at the tiny light which Stevens held.

"Hidy," he said.

"You can't stay here," Stevens said. "If we knew where you

were, don't you know the Sheriff will think of this place too by tomorrow morning?"

"I ain't going to stay," he said. "I jest stopped to rest. I'm fixing to go on pretty soon. Who are you fellers?"

"Never mind that," Stevens said. He took out the envelope containing the money. "Here," he said. It was two hundred and fifty dollars again. The amount was indubitable out of the whole thousand it had contained. Stevens had not even troubled to rationalise his decision of the amount. The kneeling man looked at it quietly.

"I left that money in Parchman. I had done already got shut of it before I went out the gate. You mean a son of a bitch stole that too?"

"This is not that money," Stevens said. "They got that back. This is new money she sent you this morning. This is different."

"You mean when I take it I ain't promised nobody nothing?"

"Yes," Stevens said. "Take it."

He did so. "Much obliged," he said. "That other time they said I would get another two hundred and fifty again in three months if I went straight across Missippi without stopping and never come back again. I reckon that's done stopped this time."

"No," Stevens said. "That too. In three months tell me where you are and I'll send it."

"Much obliged," Mink said. "Send it to M. C. Snopes."

"What?" Stevens said.

"To M. C. Snopes. That's my name: M. C."

"Come on," Ratliff said, almost roughly, "let's get out of here," taking him by the arm even as Stevens turned, Ratliff taking the burning lighter from him and holding it up while Stevens found the fading earthen steps again, once more up and out into the air, the night, the moonless dark, the worn-out eroded fields supine beneath the first faint breath of fall, waiting for winter. Overhead, celestial and hierarchate, the constellations wheeled through the zodiacal pastures: Scorpion and Bear and Scales; beyond cold Orion and the Sisters the fallen and homeless angels choired, lamenting. Gentle and tender as a woman, Ratliff opened the car door for Stevens to get in. "You all right now?" he said.

"Yes I tell you, goddammit," Stevens said.

Ratliff closed the door and went around the car and opened his and got in and closed it and turned the switch and snapped on the lights and put the car in gear—two old men themselves, approaching their sixties. "I don't know if she's already got a daughter stashed out somewhere, or if she jest ain't got around to one yet. But when she does I jest hope for Old Lang Zyne's sake she don't never bring it back to Jefferson. You done already been through two Eula Varners and I don't think you can stand another one."

When the two strangers took the light away and were gone, he didn't lie down again. He was rested now, and any moment now the time to go on again would come. So he just continued to kneel on the crude platform of old boards he had gathered together to defend himself from the ground in case he dropped off to sleep. Luckily the man who robbed him of his ten dollars last Thursday night hadn't taken the safety pin too, so he folded the money as small as it would fold into the bib pocket and pinned it. It would be all right this time, it made such a lump that even asleep he couldn't help but feel anybody fooling with it.

Then the time came to go on. He was glad of it in a way; a man can get tired, burnt out on resting like on anything else. Outside it was dark, cool and pleasant for walking, empty except for the old ground. But then a man didn't need to have to keep his mind steadily on the ground after sixty-three years. In fact, the ground itself never let a man forget it was there waiting, pulling gently and without no hurry at him between every step, saying, Come on, lay down; I ain't going to hurt you. Jest lay down. He thought *I'm free now. I can walk any way I want to.* So he would walk west now, since that was the direction people always went: west. Whenever they picked up and moved to a new country, it was always west, like Old Moster Himself had put it into a man's very blood and nature his paw had give him at the very moment he squirted him into his maw's belly.

Because he was free now. A little further along toward dawn, any time the notion struck him to, he could lay down. So when the notion struck him he did so, arranging himself, arms and legs and back, already feeling the first faint gentle tug like the durned old ground itself was trying to make you believe it wasn't really noticing itself doing it. Only he located the right stars at that moment, he was not laying exactly right since a man must face the east to lay down; walk west but when you lay down, face the exact east. So he moved, shifted a little, and now he was exactly right and he was free now, he could afford to risk it; to show how much he dared risk it, he even would close his eyes, give it all the chance it wanted; whereupon as if believing he really was asleep, it gradually went to work a little harder, easy of course, not to really disturb him: just harder, increasing. Because a man had to spend not just all his life but all the time of Man too guarding against it; even back when they said man lived in caves, he would raise up a bank of dirt to at least keep him that far off the ground while he slept, until he invented wood floors to protect him and at last beds too, raising the floors storey by storey until they would be laying a hundred and even a thousand feet up in the air to be safe from the earth.

But he could risk it, he even felt like giving it a fair active chance just to show him, prove what it could do if it wanted to try. And in fact, as soon as he thought that, it seemed to him he could feel the Mink Snopes that had had to spend so much of his life just having unnecessary bother and trouble, beginning to creep, seep, flow easy as sleeping; he could almost watch it, following all the little grass blades and tiny roots, the little holes the worms made, down and down into the ground already full of the folks that had the trouble but were free now, so that it was just the ground and the dirt that had to bother and worry and anguish with the passions and hopes and skeers, the justice and the injustice and the griefs, leaving the folks themselves easy now, all mixed and jumbled up comfortable and easy so wouldn't nobody even know or even care who was which any more, himself among them, equal to any, good as any, brave as any, being inextricable from, anonymous with all of them: the beautiful, the splendid, the proud and the brave, right on up to the very top itself among the shining phantoms and dreams which are the milestones of the long human recording—Helen and the bishops, the kings and the unhomed angels, the scornful and graceless seraphim.

Charlottesville, Virginia
9 March 1959